Games of the Heart

Eva Shaw

CRIMSON ROMANCE

Avon, Massachusetts

This edition published by
Crimson Romance
an imprint of F+W Media, Inc.
10151 Carver Road, Suite 200
Blue Ash, Ohio 45242

www.crimsonromance.com

Chapter 1

Place the blame where it should go: On chocolate.

I opened the front door of my Vegas condo. And nearly slammed it, except the man I faced handed me a golden, foiled-wrapped container with the unmistakable Godiva label. Then he took a step back. He'd baited a hook, and I was caught.

I grabbed the box. If it hadn't been for that lure of dark chocolate, I'd have stayed happily ignorant about sex slaves, black-market babies, cheatin' preachers, and an assortment of lowlifes that intruded on my cluttered, fluttered and frazzled life.

If I'd slammed the door, I'd would never have been rejected, arrested and nearly exterminated. Wait, like always, I'm getting ahead of the story and how it all happened.

You see, at the stroke of another hot summer midnight, I found myself feeling the breeze on my backside and sniffing the corners of a chocolate snare. I ripped open the box, placed a sensually scrumptious chocolate into my mouth, slurped and swirled the wickedly decadent cocoa around on my tongue, and eyed what the devil had dumped on my doorstep. Medical studies have proven it's a bad idea to let woman with PMS eat a pound of Godiva at one time, or some news report said, I think. Trust me. It's an even *worse* idea to try to take chocolate away from a woman, with PMS or not.

The guy didn't know my cycle, but he certainly knew women. So he didn't come closer until I'd gobbled up three more. In a row. Then I handed back the empty box.

Forget what you're thinking. This man was not a hunka hunka burnin' love, but seemed to be my pudgy grandfather. Or a doppelganger dressed collar to cuffs with glitter galore, gold and gosh-awful fake-e-o alligator-esque cowboy boots, with spurs in the shape of skulls. They clanked when he backed up, reverberating like cymbals.

He squinted in the porch light as his chin dragged low. He grumbled, muttered, and withdrew his left hand from behind him, producing yet another box with the chocolatier's signature label. I salivated, snatched it, and stepped back. You see, I'm not addicted to the stuff, I'm chocolate-enriched. I am not officially plump, I'm just short for my body weight.

Okay, that brings you the abbreviated version of why five minutes later my disgruntled relative was huddled on the beige sofa in the sterile Las Vegas condo I got with my current job and why I was stomping in front of him. See, I am usually the one who solves problems, being that I'm a minister and all.

Yes, you heard it right. I might not look like one as I am rounded on all the right edges and with a propensity for wearing clothes showing a smidge of cleavage and it's true if you've heard that I have Victoria's Secret's site as my homepage. Like it or not, that's me, Pastor Jane Angieski. I'm fully licensed, fully educated, and fully confused most of the time.

You're not the first, you know, to wonder how a flashy woman like me got into the ministry business. Most folks do not come straight out and ask if I am a preacher because they're so dumbfounded to find out I know the Good News backward, forward and well done in the middle. My response? "You see, they have quotas. Recall affirmative action? Needed more women who had some curves and padding in the ranks, and that's me," I say. The one who asks gets a glazed look and nods. Honestly? Hold on to something sturdy because here it comes:

During college, I worked in retail (see above Victoria's Secret reference), at a mortuary where I applied make-up to the dearly departed, gave out contraceptives and condoms at a free clinic in Watts, and did time asking, "Want fries with that?" Along the way, I made enough so I could head to UCLA for a master's in psychology because I'm outrageously curious about people. Honestly, a few days before graduation I went to a program on campus, because the A/C in my apartment was broken and I knew there would be cake and coffee. The program was to recruit grad students into the ministry. I signed on the dotted line right then, attended seminary, graduated with honors, accepted an assistant minister gig straight out the door, and got kicked out because I worked with the cops in tracking down hoods in the hood where I was the pastor for this ghetto church. The church council didn't mind that I nabbed the bad guys looking like a lady of the evening who could do it all through the night. What they didn't like was that I appeared on the front of the *L.A. Times* in a hot pink leather miniskirt, strappy sandals that only enhanced the look, and a blouse leaving little to the imagination of your Great Aunt Tillie. The story hit the national news, and wham, bam, thank you, ma'am, little old me was seen and talked about on *60 Minutes*, MSNBC, Twitter, YouTube, and it then went viral. *Time* begged for an interview but better judgment snapped in. I declined—well, only because my denomination's district council put the brakes on that one. Besides, I don't always want to stay second fiddle in church hierarchy. I do have pride. I'd like to be known, someday, as an important minister, but not the television evangelist kind with those flapping eyelashes and hair like Marge Simpson. No offense, Marge, but it's not a good look for either of us.

The happy ending to the above knuckle-rapping was that the jerks who were dealing, drugging, and pimping went to a "helping" place in California, clogging an overstuffed prison system even more, and I got thanked by getting my backside booted to Vegas. I wasn't exactly demoted, but I'm no longer a full pastor. These days, if I should burp without saying, "*Pardonnez-moi*," the council knows. Hence the youth minister I'm filling in for left exact instructions so I wouldn't lead the teens on a slope that has flashing orange signs reading, "Beware: Point of No Return."

Back to the man of the midnight hour—the grumbling continued, and like waiting out a storm, I sat down next to that huddled mass of manhood, Henry J. Angieski, Ph.D., my grandfather. In all my thirty-five years, I'd never seen him defeated.

Quick footnote on my family: He and Gram couldn't have children, and knew it before they married. Gramps always says it like this: "Uncle Sam really needed me and thought a tropical Asian trip might help me to understand humanity better." That meant he was unemployed after grad school, was drafted and sent to Vietnam. About Dad? Gramps says, "I found the son of my heart there, always hanging around the barracks. He had red hair, like your Gram, and the most intense almond-shaped eyes I'd ever seen. When I was accepted into the doctorate program, your Uncle Sam let me come home with the things I found there, from the bullet wound in my knee to a ten-year-old kid." Gramps and Gram made it official—adoption was different then. They couldn't trace Dad's biological parents; the country was in shambles and of course had already been invaded by the French, English and Russians before the US stepped into the mess. Then Gram died, a painful battle with cancer, and a couple months later I came into the picture. When my parents decided that parenthood didn't shake, rattle, or roll on their personal Richter scale, Gramps once more manned up. Story goes that they piled their macrobiotic rice, pine nut smoothies, ceremonial drums, unfiltered carrot juice and love beads inside a rusting, purple VW van dotted with painted daisies, dumped pint-size me on Gramps' doorstep, and went in search of their bliss. I believe they were ten years past the real hippies. Last I heard, when I was sixteen, they were in Sedona, finding and selling therapy rocks to tourists. I'm happy for them, really, but getting a rock in the mail for your birthday stinks. That's enough of me, at least for a minute, as it was the grunting, grumbler grandfather on the ghastly sofa that this is all about.

He sighed from the pointy toes of his red boots. Then grunted. I would have sworn he swore, but I knew better.

"Call me Onesimus." The statement ended in a pheewee.

"What-a-muss?"

"Get a clue, you're a preacher. You should know this stuff, always spouting it off as you do all Bible belting and never letting a man swear without raising those eyebrows. Oh, don't give me that look, girl. Won't do you any good this time. I'm immune. Been looking at myself to long one of your freeze-frame frowns frazzle me. You know I'm talking the truth."

My mouth flapped, "Old or New Testament?" If only someone had videoed my mouth gaping and eyes blinking, I would have been a shoe-in for *America's Funniest Home Videos*. "Onesimus, Pastor." He spoke as if I were a dolt, which I felt like. And a stranger, which I certainly wasn't.

He never calls me Pastor. Never before had he even raised his voice to me. "Who are you and what did you do with my grandfather? My gramps is happily living in Carlsbad, California. That's right along the Pacific and north of San Diego. My gramps is in bed right now, not in Vegas, baby."

We stared at each other, and then a two-watt light bulb my brain flickered. "Do you mean Onesimus, as in the slave the Apostle Paul writes about?"

"Bing-a-ding ding, girl. Listen, Jane, I'm having a crisis, one that's, well, personal, as personal and private as it can get for a man."

From the dancing rhinestones on his denim shirt, past the belt buckle, which was the size of Rhode Island, to the candy-apple red Mustang convertible, which I noticed since it was in the middle of my driveway, the man was either auditioning for a low-budget movie or had lost his senses. Besides, my grandfather never needed help. Never wore cowboy clothes, either, for that matter. He was dependable, taught music at the university, and played with an aging boomer band who'd just found out they were hip. The man had style, grace, out of *GQ*. Okay, there were some fifty- and sixty-something women circling like ravenous seagulls chasing a fishing boat, but he always chose right from wrong when it came to women. Then again, I never had a conversation about the birds and bees with him.

"Ohhhhhhh, personal and private," I muttered, regretting my decision to have the second Lean Cuisine dinner, even if it was diet food because I absolutely, positively didn't want to discuss my grandfather's sexual inadequacies or performance.

Heck-o, I never intended or wanted this talk. But I blurted in more than a squeak than a pastoral voice, "Crisis? Men your age are past that. For Pete's sake, don't tell me you're here in Vegas to marry an eighteen-year-old half-dressed dancer who wears pink feathers that glow in the dark with matching pasties that barely cover her nipples. Or that she's employed in a strip club as a stripper."

A giggle came from me, a grunt came from him.

"Say any of that is true, and I'm kicking your knickers back to Carlsbad." I yanked his sleeve, being careful not to dislodge one of the three million rhinestones on that part of his shirt. He either didn't get my little joke or. . . Wait, this couldn't be.

"She's not some chorus babe, Jane. She has to be, well, I'd say, eighteen or nineteen. But she could be sixteen. I've never asked."

"Whoa, hold the phone. Not a chorus girl? Who is she?" I could no longer hide in the kitchen.

"She's got nothing to do with this. I'm like a package of ham that's been shoved to the back of the refrigerator. The whole world is out to get me, although Switzerland stays neutral. Lately I wake up in the morning and wish my parents hadn't met."

"Get out of here." Mr. Rhinestone started to get up and I grabbed him. "I'm kidding, Gramps. You're better at telling jokes than Jerry Seinfeld."

"Humor is another way to be serious, Miss Pastor Lady. My problem is the damn-blasted stroke."

"The stroke happened, you didn't cause it, Gramps, and the physical therapist said you'd be okay. What changed?" I could feel the corners of my mouth head south. I looked around the room for his Bertha, his ever-present guitar. He was alone, and that troubled me enough, until it finally sunk in that he hadn't reputed that she might be a chorus girl. For once in my life I was speechless, at least for five seconds. "Are you huffy like this to the folks you preach to? Wonder that they let you get in back of a pulpit." He planted his boots in the middle of the "it comes furnished" living room.

I stuck out my arm, because I could sense he was about to bolt. "This isn't about me, Mister. When were you going to tell me about this girl? Have you, um, married an adolescent? If you're sure she's at least eighteen, um, should I be relieved? Wait. What's happening to my orderly world?" I held my head and rocked it back and forth.

"Stop your yammering, Jane, for sanity's sake. It's not like she'd have me," he said and waved a hand in the air, raked it through his abundant steel-gray hair, and frowned. Deeply. He pushed past me and limped to the front window, stretched back the tan drapes. I followed, and we looked at the convertible.

I had to grab the above-mentioned drape for support when it hit me. Ton of bricks to the noggin. He was doing it with a teenager. I slapped my mouth. I tried to take a long, cleansing breath. In and out, yoga style. I sputtered, "Are you, well, cohabitating?"

He didn't even look my way. He wasn't using the cane, so that should have been a good sign until he said, "I'm old, feeble. I'm useless. I'm disabled." He retreated to the sofa, slumped over, blending in with the beige fabric so much that if it weren't for rhinestones I could have convinced myself this was a nightmare and the result of the diet cupcakes I had for dessert.I stared. Was that a yes or a no to my question on lusting after a teenager? His face turned to pea soup with undertones of eggplant and I winced as he slid the knee-high cowboy boots off his feet. He rubbed his toes and then let his head flop back. With his eyes closed, his face was a street map of wrinkles.

When could this all have happened? We talked every other day at least, emailed, and this was the first I'd heard of any setback or a, um, teenage romantic interest. Or his extreme lifestyle makeover to a rhinestone cowboy.

Do you think about ministers as uptight, buttoned down, repressed and sometimes clueless? Heaven help me, I'm not like that and I never get speechless. I like talking, but right then I was without a comeback, snappy or otherwise. As an itinerant pastor, actually, which means I fill in for ministers when they're on sabbatical or away from their flock, I need a stock of flip answers because most of the time I'm cross-examined about my credentials. That was definitely the case in point when I arrived six weeks ago at Mega Church, USA, technically known as Desert Hills Community Church. Don't know what they were expecting. What they got was a slightly less busty version of a young Dolly Parton, just slightly, without the good lookin' makeup. It wasn't what they'd ordered in a new youth pastor. Honestly, that's what I heard when I was quietly taking care of business in the ladies' room as two of the office staff were chatting about me. It wasn't the Dolly comment that hurt, mind you—I love her—it was the dig about my inability to apply cosmetics.

Yes, being a Chatty Cathy helped in most of the scrapes in which I've found myself, but right then, I opened and closed my mouth and still nothing came forth.

With my history of relatives abandoning me (note to self: check the Internet to see if parents have been incarcerated again lately), I was floundering big time with Gramps, who was the color of rotten grapes and breathing unevenly on my sofa. My finger fluttered to my robe's pocket and my cell, ready to punch 911.

You see, he wasn't just my grandfather and a professor, he'd become a heartthrob. With his band, Slam Dunk, he created classic rock hits that you can't stop humming and did it time and again. Sort of a Paul McCartney-esque guy, and maybe I'm a bit partial, but I think he's better looking, in a grandfatherly way, than Sir Paul. He had friends, recording sessions, folks he knew at church and even an on-again, off-again romance with my good friend U.S. Senator Geraldine English.

While looking after Gramps as he recovered from the stroke, I licked my wounds from being sacked along with the serious reprimand from the council and spent quality time nagging him. That kind of stuff. Home was Carlsbad, California, and if you think about golf and tennis at La Costa, locking-block kid heaven of Legoland and a chi-chi beachy town just north of San Diego's city limits, you've got a snapshot of where Gramps calls home, and sometimes me, too. If you're singing a Beach Boys song or something from the Mamas and the Papas, you're a bit younger than Gramps, but you probably know the kind of surf city where I grew up.

So after his stroke, I was Nurse Nancy. I needed a time-out, still store from the above-mentioned butt-kicking. When he refused all coddling, I accepted this temporary position at Desert Hills, which came with a pint-size furnished condo that had no charm or style. Somehow it suited me; I didn't want to care. I was a temp. I would be out of the job in six months, so it would have been nuts to drag anything personal to the desert. I'm to the point when a man asks me out, I tell him to step back and think it over. How was I going to counsel Gramps with this track record? Wait, don't answer that.

"Did you have a setback?" I swallowed fear, and it tasted just like the second boxed chicken Alfredo.

Mumble, mumble. "Yes."

"When?"

"Not another stroke?"

I have no idea why, but I moved to the door and walked out on the porch. Okay, he'd driven here. He could control a car. That had to be a good sign, or had I been hallucinating about the car in the driveway? Even in the streetlamp's meager glow, that Mustang was red. I closed the door. "Gramps, why aren't you driving your Tundra truck?"

"Wanted to breathe new-car smell again before I died."

"So you rented it, good. When did you arrive?" Call it a premonition, but I was glad I was near the sofa when he said, "Three weeks ago."

Now it was my turn to collapse into one of the two nondescript loveseats in my beige and glass living room. "Excuse me?" I clucked. "You've been in Vegas for three entire weeks and you are just now coming over here to see me?"

He tilted forward, lacing his hands, resting his forehand on his fingers and, silly me, I assumed he was praying until he said, "Trying to figure myself out. All I discovered was I am a limp, broken and empty shell. Crumpled. Look at me, really look, Jane. There's no man left. I know I'm not the first to seek refuge in the bright lights of Sin City. Yeah, all I found were bright lights and an old, big city." He studied the cream-colored Berber carpet as if the answer to the meaning of life were in the weave.

I checked it out, too. I didn't find any help so I said, "What you did wasn't that unusual." I was walking a long, thin line, like the one in the middle of a highway, with two semis heading straight at me. "Lots of men find they want a playmate." I added, "Like your very, very, very young one." It was grunted under my breath. It was snide. It felt good. I'm a preacher, but I'm human.

Gramps ignored me, which was just as well, and talked to the carpet, holding his head in his hands. "I'm on the run. From the world, friends, co-workers—heck, even strangers. And especially God. The body you see is as good as it's going to get, but honestly, Jane, I'm hurting. I am angry, angrier than when your grandmother died, a heck of a lot angrier than when your folks decided parenting wasn't their thing. Didn't know I could get so stinking mad. I'm stinking angry at myself for getting old. I'm a worn-out geezer, a windbag, a codger."

I circled him with my arms. He was small. When did he shrink? "Oh, Gramps. I love you. Why did you wait so long? Why didn't you tell me? You're not alone." I squeezed his shoulders, and then it hit me. I pulled my arms back, stiffened my back. "Wait one confounded second. I have called you. I emailed, just today, I sent you a joke. The one about Las Vegas. Remember it? Americans spend three hundred billion dollars every year on gaming in Vegas, and that doesn't even include weddings and elections? You wrote back, 'Ha Ha,' and said everything was fine."

"Cell phones don't care where you are. With the laptop you'll find in the trunk of that car, I was connected with you and the college."

"The college? Classes aren't over. It's not the end of summer session. Did you quit?" It didn't seem that illogical that he'd quit a career spanning three decades since he was driving a hot convertible and living with an underage floozy.

"They let me go."

"The chancellor fired you? The best music professor in the entire University of California system?"

"Might just as well have. Retirement. There, I said it."

I felt the air slide from my lungs. We both knew it would happen sometime, but my grandfather always looked and felt young, at least that's what he said and what I wanted to see. "Retirement." It was the F-word for people who never planned to grow up or slow down. I sounded disgustingly chipper as I said, "This is great. Why, you can create some new music, you can travel, you can have hobbies, you can—"

"Stop your preaching. Jane, look at me. I'm not some coot who lives in the past, who sits around whittling apples and bananas out of wood or solving the world's problems with the other coots at a local watering hole. I'm a musician who had a stroke and now finds even walking a pain in the—well, and a royal pain it is. I can't play because these fingers can't even manage to find the frets." He stared at his hands and balled them into fists. "As for traveling, just getting to Vegas last month was all I could do. This kid, who turned out to be the pilot and was barely shaving, asked me if I wanted a wheelchair to get off the stinking airplane. For Pete's sake, they had me board with the mommies and the babies."

"Gosh, Gramps, I'm coming with you next time."

"Jane. The geezers board first."

"Ah, do you want to tell me what you've done here in Las Vegas?" I asked, and it was a roundabout way to learn if he was doing the horizontal snuggly-buggly with the underage hoochie-coochie strip club dancer.

"Nothing."

"You sure?" Okay, I really didn't ask that because I really didn't want to know. I just nodded.

He loosened the leather and silver braided bolo tie from his neck, slipping it out of a clasp that looked like the great state of Texas. Unbuttoning the shirt's top buttons, he rubbed his throat and said, "Sitting in a hotel room overlooking the Strip, watching the fireworks go off at Treasure Island, that hotel with the pirate theme, ordering room service and watching Nick at Nite, reruns of *Andy Griffith* and old movies. That's what I've been doing. Most of the time, I was having my own, what do you call it, pity party, like you did after Colin's death."

I moved the ten feet to the kitchen and grabbed bottles of water. "But you're here now. We're a pair when it comes to pity parties." I pretended to wipe something off the stove, squeezing my eyes shut. But bringing up Colin's name made an image flash into my mind. For the millionth time I could see me in the stands as Colin's F-15 explode into a fireball right over the airfield. The air show crowd gasped. I remembered falling forward into the crowd with my chin hitting the bleacher in front and then everything in my world went black. Now each day as I brushed my teeth or dried my hair, I saw the scar on my chin from my fall. It was a constant, daily reminder, if I needed one. Pilot error, the final report had said. Not enough left to bury him.

I blinked back tears. "Remember you dragged me back home? I recall you stormed my quarters on the air force base and snapped Ben & Jerry from my quaking fingers. You growled, 'Get that caboose of yours off the sofa and put on some clothes, girly. You're coming home.'"

Gramps laughed. It was hollow with a raspy cough, too, but it was a start.

"Yes, and then you stopped at Denny's, forced me to eat something other than ice cream, and took me to a jam session with Slam Dunk. As I remember it, soda spewed from your nose when I tried to play some of your music."

He laughed a bit more, less shallow.

"Was it root beer or Pepsi?" I asked.

"You were so pathetic."

"Yeah, runs in the family. Look at you. Let's get you an omelet or a peanut butter sandwich. Then you can tell me your plans." And for a second I regretted that word "plans," because a seventy-year-old midnight cowboy driving a brand-new scarlet-colored Mustang might not have the wherewithal to formulate good plans. There was also the matter of the lady with the pasties on her feminine places. She was hanging in the air, at least in the air I was breathing.

"Jane, girl. There's more." By that time, he'd finished the makeshift midnight meal. "The crisis is more than just this failing body, this bundle of bones. God's let me down. I'm not a Christian anymore. Maybe it's me who has let Him down, don't know the answer on that."

"Um, oh." You've probably made notes right now that if you ever need counseling, I'll be the last to be asked. I don't blame you. I wasn't too keen on myself at that second. But you have to understand that this was the man who had taken me to church and introduced me to the congregation three days after I was born. This was the man who had given me away when I married, been there just five months later when the jet exploded, and Gramps arranged Collin's funeral. He had cheered me on when the District Council of my denomination granted my pastoral papers and held my hand when the same District Council threatened to withdraw them.

Jumping from one sure-thing conclusion to the next, exceeding the legal limit, what would I have said to any other man or woman if I heard this? I racked my overly educated counselor's brain and came up with zilch. When the loss of faith comes straight from the mouth of the man you've idolized for your entire life, the earth opens and swallows your most patented advice. Big help I was. I stood there mute.

"I'm a slave to this body. And before you start quoting scripture with all the verses and lines and all that other stuff, which you're good at, it's not like Job and the thorn in his side. There are no earthly reasons why I should continue to live as I have."

Standing at the sink, hot water spewing, I couldn't seem to get my mind to order my fingers to twist the knobs to shut off the flow. When I did find my voice, my hands matched the color of the car in my driveway. "Have you talked with Him?" I picked up the sponge. I scrubbed and scrubbed the plate in my hands, long after the gooey remains of cheese and egg came off. I poured out the last cold cup from the coffeemaker and drank it in one deep swallow. I wiped up imaginary spills on the counter, and I was about to organize the refrigerator and take out the trash, after mopping the floor, when finally Gramps spoke again.

"I've yelled a lot."

"You look pretty calm now." I slammed the refrigerator once I'd placed the maraschino cherries in heavy syrup next to the mayonnaise and close to the Tabasco sauce. I'd alphabetized everything while I was waiting.

"As I was hiding, I realized I was a wretched waste of humanity, actually. You don't need to blink—I saw that—I didn't do anything you'd find disgraceful for a man of my age. Now I think I've worked out a solution, of sorts."

"Men your age still do a lot," I interrupted because I didn't want to putter down the pathway of anything remotely connected with Gramps' young chick, but a gal's got to be tough. "I still don't get it." For the tenth time I washed out the coffee pot that didn't need another rinse.

Gramps stifled a yawn. "Hey, stop grumbling. You're not boring me, but I'm fading fast."

"Cut to the chase, Gramps."

"It's dancing."

"You're going to become a professional dancer, you who refused to dance at my wedding because you have feet of clay or something like that? Positive thinking is groovy, but dancing isn't something you jump into, especially competition dance like those shows on TV. Um, how will this help you?"

"Honey, how can someone with your over-educated brain be so lacking in common sense? I'm old and disgusting, but I've got an ace up my sleeve, and you're going to help me. We're going dancing."

"You've seen me dance, Gramps, and it's almost as disgusting as my playing the rock music you and Slam Dunk perform. Besides, I inherited your left feet."

"How often, Janey, do you miss this point?"

"It's two in the morning. How's that for a reason? If you want to go out dancing tonight, you've got the wrong granddaughter, even if I am your only granddaughter. Besides you've got more explaining to do, especially the part about the little lady who has been making you happy. Wait. Where are you going?"

"Let's settle this tomorrow. This is a wagering town, and my best bet is that the guest room is straight down the hall, and knowing you, Jane, there will be fresh sheets on the bed, a bathrobe in the closet, and plenty of toiletries in the bathroom, still in flowered wrappers. If you want to talk more, you're about to have the bathroom door closed in your pretty little face. The rest can wait until tomorrow, and you can come down a bit off your high preachin' horse." He turned and muttered in a loud voice, "Have you always been this bossy? I'd forgotten."

I was sputtering as he limped out of sight. I really and truly wanted a strong cup of coffee, but at two a.m., that's madness, although I've been nuts before. What I did was to take deep cleansings breaths of the coffee beans, flicked off the light and headed to bed.

I crawled between the sheets, pulled them to my neck and tried to focus on happy thoughts. Where was my happy place? The sandman and I wrestled. Like clockwork, I checked the clock at regular intervals from two to six, when the alarm turned on the radio to those ghastly chipper voices of early morning talk show hosts, announcing another hot, but dry "reallllly fabulous day in Vegas, baby." I slapped the thing to the floor. It bounced, and the sound hurt my head. In my quest to get to my happy place, I'd neglected to shut my blinds before those four hours of tossing and turning not to be thought of as sleep, and now the sizzle had begun to heat the room. It was going to be a scorcher, for sure.

Then from the living room, I heard elevator music. I don't even have an elevator. It was from *West Side Story*. The normal Gramps, before he became a rootin'-tootin' cowboy, would have listened to the Rolling Stones, rap, or hip-hop. This was bad, I thought, as I pulled myself up to sit on the edge of the bed. Now some preachers get on their knees, and trust me, I've got the calluses to prove I do this, but right then God and I needed to look at each other. "I know you never give us more than we can handle, but Lord, I am just not that good. If you want my help, give me a clue." I shrugged into my robe, dove under the bed for my scuffs and headed to the living room as I mumbled, "Help me because I may just do something I regret."

Miracles were real. "Thank you, Jesus," I yelled and waved my hands above my head just like an old-fashion revival meeting.

He was gone. As anyone who knows me will gladly tell you, I have a fertile imagination, so I could nearly believe that he'd left or been Raptured, but the crispy bacon calling my name from the stove told the truth and nothing but it. Plus the table was set for two. At one place were chocolate chip waffles and tall OJ. The coffee smelled strong; the mug was steaming. The newspaper was folded to the comics.

What's a girl to do? I dove in to the feast. If I was wrong and I had been Raptured, I was thrilled to see that the food was yummo.

As I pierced the last forkful, using it to wipe up a puddle of Log Cabin syrup, Gramps limped through the front door with a plastic grocery sack in his hands.

"So, they were edible?"

"I should have waited." My mind raced to the "situation," as I'd named this catastrophe sometime between 3:15 a.m. and 4:30 a.m.

"No way, Janey girl. I figured coffee would get you up. I'm not sleeping well and been up for hours." He poured a mug of coffee, took the carton from the bag, and added enough milk to make this java junkie cringe. "Before you start haranguing an old handicapped geezer about how I don't need milk in coffee because it just takes away the real coffee taste and blah blah blah, you'll want to know the church secretary, Vera, has been calling you every fifteen minutes since the crack of early." He lifted the coffee mug and said, *na zdrowie,* which as everyone of Polish descent knows is the right toast for any drink.

"Forget the 'to your health.' I want to know why you didn't holler for me when I got the calls."

"I've been around a few churches and found that the preachers need their sleep as much as their flock needs to talk with them. Besides, she said it wasn't *that* urgent. Isn't Desert Hills like the rest of them, and if someone stubs their toe they're popped on the prayer chain, or is it more a gossip mill?"

I wasn't going to fuss, although the stubbed toe crack clipped a nick too close to the quick. The prayer chain at Desert Hills did spread the word about illnesses, deaths, and various folks entering rehab. That said, I sometimes thought people didn't pray, but preyed off the info. I'd noticed whispering during the hospitality time and how people quieted when I walked by. Hey, maybe they had me on the prayer chain for God only knew what. A bad hair day? I chalked it up to an ugly part of human nature, and that some folks are uglier than others.

I dialed the church's number and reached Vera. She cracked a "Good morning, honey," and then said, "First off, the District Council is visiting next Friday and requested an appointment with you, but that's not why I've been calling. Pastor Bob says he has a surprise for you and the youth group." I could tell by the tone that her eyes were rolling and her head was making circles. Vera had been the secretary for Desert Hills Community Church for decades, seen other preachers come and go, and little except Pastor Bob's "surprises" fazed her.

There was more to Vera than met the eye, which was plenty considering she looked about as much like a church secretary as sixty-ish Sarah Jessica Parker if she stumbled into Desert Hills, forgot any fashion sense, and plunked her keister behind a computer. The only secretary-like item was cat's eye glasses that perched on her nose. She smelled as if she were marinated in Smuckers jam, which wasn't appealing when mixed with the essence of Marlboro on her breath.

"Any idea what it is?" Did I need a surprise with my beloved grandfather on the lam from God, taken up with an adolescent deviant, and the District Council waiting to slip my neck through a noose? Not.

"You're not going to like it, Pastor Jane. But heck, it's a crapshoot around here. Might be something you can add on to what you're already doing. Hold on, Jane."

I could hear her cooing to someone standing in her office about, "You are so sweet," and then she was on the line with, "Put on your big girl panties and make up your own mind. I gave up mind reading years ago when I quit traveling with the circus."

The line went dead and my appetite with it, which says a lot. Pastor Bob Normal, whom I had begun to secretly and in various muttering times call Ab, apparently was taking over my life in ways that are abnormally annoying even for him.

It took me twenty-five minutes flat to jump into tan slacks and a blazing pink cotton T from the last Victoria's Secret sale and drive to church, just two miles north of the condo. I like to think I'm hip but I'm unhip about mega churches. Give me a steeple and a cross? I'm good. That said, when I drove up to Desert Hills a few weeks ago, I thought I'd stumbled into the Silicon Valley. The building humongous, all windows and sand-colored brick, stretching greenbelts and a flagpole plunked in the middle of it all. The cross? Good question. I asked, too. There isn't one outside, and that, I was told, goes along with the new trend to make the worship center more available to all people. Call me old-fashioned—wait, don't you dare. Yet, it's been my thinking that a church isn't a church without looking like a church. Since I didn't get a vote—and since I was only filling in for the youth pastor, I probably would never get one—on this issue I kept my lips sealed. I know that's a shock.

Faced with a crisis at home and one at church, I gingerly parked my scuffed SUV in the "staff" zone and slapped the sunscreen over the dashboard so that later, when I left for the day, I wouldn't scorch my bountiful backside, and straightened my spine. Like a courteous little soldier, I marched up the marble walk to face my fate. I had barely plastered on a tooth-brightener smile when the pastor met me as I whooshed through the automatic doors into the Foyer of Heavenly Conditioned Air.

"'Bout time you're here. Memo's on your desk. Questions? Vera's got it," said the senior minister, all this with the palm of his hand facing my face.

There was this thing about him that brought out a feeling of grease in me, like the kind that forms on the top of simmering spaghetti sauce when you use cheap hamburger.

He cocked his Elvis-impersonator head. "Yes?"

I was grateful the man wasn't psychic, but I refused to talk to the hand so I waited until he dropped it. "Good morning, Pastor. How are you today? Questions about what?"

"Board decided. Youth group. You. VBS. Great opportunity."

"Excuse me?" I shivered. "Repeat that, please."

"No can do. Off to a fundraiser breakfast. Think again, Pastor Jane, if you have any notions that this place—" He waved a hand around the cavern of the foyer and then swept it toward the marble floor. "—Well, if you think for one second the church is financed by prayer. Money talks, not just here, but everywhere. Vegas is no different. Never kid yourself about that."

Taking yet another cleansing breath, I touched the sleeve of his blue silk suit jacket. "Vacation Bible School starts Monday. And where did you leave that reality check? Today is Friday. You're saying that my youth group will handle it?"

"What don't you get, Pastor Jane?" It came out in a huff as he smoothed the sideburns that went out in the seventies.

Trust me, the man was not into retro. He'd just forgotten we were in the twenty-first century, and possibly women didn't always do what big old strong men ministers said to do.

The gauge on my internal combustion steam-ometer was shouting, "Danger, danger, run for your life." Alas, being low woman on the church totem pole didn't give me any wiggle room. Even if you were on my side, and even if I'd become Old Faithful and blown my cool, I would have been out the door and on the pavement before you could say, "Amen to that, sister."

I bit my tongue, really, clamped it so I didn't shout how he could have found other flunkies to do his bidding, because Ab was in a heated discussion on his cell.

"For golly goodness' sakes, hold it, will you?" he said to the phone. He pulled it away from his ear and turned to me, his eyebrows knit together. We were so close I could see stubble from a unibrow. I might be his flunkie of the month, but the unibrow produced wonderful waves of superiority in a deliciously perverted way.

"Now what is it? Jane, are you or are you not a minister? Then minister. For heaven's sake, do the job you're being paid to do, which if you'll check your business card, madam, it is to be a minister. Organize VBS."

"Yes, of course," I snapped. Flunkie or not, he was the boss, even if the last twelve hours had been rotten.

"Then why *are* we having this conversation? Get on it or get out." His cheeks became blotchy, and I believe I was about to get a royal chewing out when Vera's five-inch platform heels came clopping down the marble hall. We both nodded as she walked by and, not for the first time, I wondered what control the secretary had over the minister. Suddenly he was all milk and honey when he said, "Listen, Jane, you've come highly recommend, can do miracles and walk on water, that kind of stuff. We're excited to have you here at Desert Hills. You know what I'm talking about, even with your very public mishap, shall we call it, and I know you are capable. Besides, these are little children, not something like the hardcore hoodlums you personally arrested while preaching in Los Angeles, in that 'hood. I'll be praying for you. Hey, we'll get the entire prayer chain to jump on this. Works for me," he said. He patted me on the arm and began talking about market gains, and I knew that was the end of our meeting.

Then he topped the icing on the cake with, "We're praying for you." Who the "we" were I had no clue, but he beat all land records as he dashed to the silver Lexus parked next to my dusty SUV.

I've been a happy camper, a cranky one, and also ticked off big time. Right then I skidded to a halt in the third category, with black marks on the pavement of my mind. Let the cookies crumble where they may. Handling sixty puberty-crazed kids in a youth work program, preparing sermons, doing outreach at shelters and missions, keeping tabs on activities, and counseling kids and their parents was making my half-empty cup permanently slosh all over my good intentions. Vacation Bible School? Nietzsche said that which doesn't kill us will make us stronger. And when I get to heaven *if* Mr. N is there, I'm going to give him a tiny little bit of my mind. I give pieces of my mind out so often, you realize, that I can only spare a bit, but Nietzsche is going to get it.

Pastor Bob's comments about, "This place is not financed by prayer. Money talks in this city," irked me and made my breakfast lurch and become a fat belch.

My office is barely big enough for a woman with skinny thighs to move to the desk, but I made it anyhow. I poked *the* memo, moving it with one finger. I read it. I flopped in my typing chair. Then read it again.

I'll cut to the chase. The pastor and the board, with pressure from parents who had decided that they wanted VBS, but never got around to organizing one even though all the advertisements went out to the community over the last month, voted last night that the teens, who didn't work during the day, could run it. Of course, mind you, no teens had volunteered nor heard about this, and their youth minister, moi, didn't know nothing no how, either. Bottom line? Two hundred children would show up at Desert Hills at 9:00 a.m. Monday morning, and I was to give them a week of Godly training. Oh, me and whatever teenagers I could scrounge up in just over forty-eight hours.

You might wonder what happened to the children's ministry leader who should have been in charge of VBS. Me, too. Every workplace has skeletons, yet Desert Hills seems to be over its national average. "Oh, just taking some time off." "Guessing she needs a vacation, baby on the way and things." "Something like a sabbatical." Even Vera looked off into the distance and got a soft look on her drill-sergeant face, which was so nipped and tucked it was hard to tell if she was smiling or grimacing. Only thing she said was, "You'll need to talk to Pastor Bob about this, Jane." So I stopped asking because my first question about the children's ministry leader had to be to good old Ab Normal himself. Clashes happen, even in churches, and the District Council in its wisdom sometimes pulls ministers away from their flocks, such as me being yanked screaming and kicking from that inner-city church. Somebody was bound to spill the beans eventually. See, contrary to the word on the street, I can be patient.

A few minutes later Vera dropped her plentiful posterior in the straight-backed chair across the desk from me, plunked a cup of coffee in front of me, and rolled her big brown eyes. The need to know what happened to the previous children's minister was far, far away in another galaxy.

"Read it? Didn't have the heart to tell you over the phone."

"I know VBS is good for kids and great PR, but honestly, Vera, can I handle this?"

She tipped back the coffee mug, pursed her lips, coated deeply with layers of pink and lined with red, which perfectly matched the Hawaiian print of her form-fitting shirt. Vera wiggled her eyebrows up, squished her nose and said, "Beats the heck out of me."

"Thanks a bundle."

Holding the doorframe to the cubicle Vera said, "Harmony Miller is waiting to see you. She's got a nasty bruise on her arm. Thought you should be the one to ask about it." Then she lifted her eyebrows, and I saw a fleeting bit of grandmotherly emotion cross her eyes. "Want me to stay?" Again, as Vera reached for my now-empty cup, even her face, plasticized by surgery, softened.

"Is she in your office? She wasn't in the foyer when Pastor Bob and I had our chat."

"No, think she went to the kitchen to help prepare the lunch the women's group is taking to the rescue mission. The Daily Bread Team feeds about hundred each day and sometimes more on Fridays. But hey, you know that, since you're there often enough. Either you like what they're doing or you're going for the free lunch—just kidding."

Have you ever noticed when people say, "just kidding," they're really not kidding at all?

*

I saw the bruise before I focused on Harmony. It was fierce and covered much of her forearm, more purple than black. I'd always thought she looked like a very young Meg Ryan, but her vocabulary could have made a sailor squirm, until I reminded her that even this kitchen was part of the church. Lately it would only make a Marine squirm.

"What's on the menu for the Daily Bread today?" I flopped an arm on her shoulder and felt her stiffen before she wiggled out. I dropped the arm. She wouldn't have been the first kid, or adult, to show dislike for a pushy preacher. Second guess? More bruises under her scruffy T-shirt.

"Chicken or cheese sandwiches, pickles, chips, and fruit," she replied and moved out of my reach, rubbing her shoulder. "Always, coffee, water, soda, and milk, too. We'll leave the platters of veggies, hummus, and pita bread for the crowd that comes at night."

"Sounds better than the stuff I have at home. Harmony, you wanted to see me?" I asked in a light, hopefully non-threatening way. I stayed close, but didn't touch.

"No," she snapped in response.

Harmony wasn't like the whiney kids in the youth group. This was the first I'd seen she had a temper and honestly? It made me feel a micron better because all the fight hadn't been kicked out of her like some of the kids that I'd known who had been tossed from one foster home to another.

We both stared at her feet in dusty, ragged, high-top basketball shoes and then, I hope without her knowing, I allowed my gaze to travel to her face, noting she could be the Goth poster girl since black was the only color of her wardrobe. As I looked into her blue eyes, I could see a frightened little girl in there. I continued, "Vera said you asked for me. I have time now. Want to come to my office with me or when you finish?"

She turned away. I wondered if she was willing her eyes in another direction, then she turned quickly, only to turn away again before saying, "I didn't want to talk to you. Vera said I should."

"We're finished here for now," said one of the women, placing the sack lunches in a box. "Thanks, Harmony. See you at the mission? You can get a ride over with me in about an hour if you're going to help serve again today." I waved to the ladies and then whispered to Harmony, "Want to head out of here and get something cold and slushy at Starbucks?"

Harmony looked at me for the briefest second. We walked into the hall and toward my office and then she finally said, "I gotta' find a better place to live."

I would have closed the door, but there wasn't one. Taking a breath, I vowed to respond in my quiet voice, even if I were shocked, which I knew I'd be. "Are you hurt? Were you assaulted? Did someone touch you inappropriately? Molest you?"

Chapter 2

It's the media's fault, you know, that when you think of Vegas, you think of beautiful people having the time of their lives, living large, spending free, and doing stuff that would make their granny's hair turn even bluer. Don't get your knickers in a knot. Las Vegas is fun to visit, and at least eighty-five percent of the area is a fine place to live, work, and raise a family.

The media, advertisers, and who knows who have created an adult playground where the neon lights, four-story-high fountains, and even art museums rub belly buttons with addicted gamblers, hookers, and half-wits who come to drown their troubles in the flash, glitz, and glitter that's Vegas, baby.

Don't believe me? Drive off the Strip just a mile, and the city, like the rattlers found just miles from New York, New York and Paris casinos, will rise up and let its fangs sink into you. Actually, it could pluck out your heart if you have one. It makes you wonder why so much poverty lives like bosom buddies with the likes of lush casinos and high-rise resorts. And mega churches. If you've ever flipped the remote control and stopped at *Cops,* you could have seen what it's like where the Vegas tourists don't frequent.

As Harmony and I sat trying not to look at the bruises on her arm, I thought of this. Harmony lived under the glamour radar, way below it, like a piece of paper that's picked up in the desert wind and tossed around. As with other kids in my pastoral care, her world involved struggles with the courts, little financial support, foster parents who have forgotten why they got into fostering, and the scum that prey on street kids. It took about two minutes when I came on board as the youth minister to figure this out, and I still can't get my heart to mend.

Harmony was one of the lucky ones—then, at least—as she did have a foster home, a clean bed, and food if she stuck around for meals. It was better than when I'd first met her and she was living beneath an I-15 overpass.

"Harmony, look at me. Who hurt you like this? You have legal rights, you know, even if you're not an adult."

"No, ma'am, no one did anything to me like you're thinkin'," she said, and tried ineffectively to pull the sleeve of her shirt over her elbow.

What I had been told about Harmony, I hated. This I got from the gossip grapevine of the kids in youth group, where the haves and the have-nots were divided like the North and South in the Civil War and no Abe Lincoln in sight. Wise up, sure, I listened to gossip. At the core of every good lie is a nugget of truth; the point of being a minister is to tell the difference. While I wasn't a pro, I never hesitated to go to the source and find out what the score was. Last week, I cornered Harmony and asked straight out. It was simple, and she told me in simple sentences. No mom was ever mentioned, and she'd been dragged around with her dad. A few years ago, he was sent to prison for embezzlement and fraud as a result of his gambling addictions. He was serving time in the state prison system.

"I thought you were with a new foster family until your dad gets out of prison? He's about to be released, right? End of summer, isn't it?"

"Yes, ma'am." A flicker of something was in her eyes, definitely not hope. That made me squirm.

Then the flicker fluttered out, and she withdrew into a robotic stare focused somewhere above my head.

She stood planted as if she might decide to run, so I walked to the other side of the desk and sat down, piled papers that didn't need to be straightened, and tried to pretend everything was right in every way. "What happened? Sit down."

Apparently I passed her test because she sat in the straight chair and said, "The foster care people are nice enough."

"Just nice enough wouldn't have caused those bruises. Did they hit you?"

"It was a birthday party for someone, at least that how it started, and what the balloons said that were tied to the trash can near the front door. Lots of people there, motorcycles on the lawn, and I went to the room I share with another girl to hide after some jerk rode a Harley through the kitchen."

"You were part of the party?" It wouldn't have been the first time, and Harmony would not be the last to get mixed up with a mess that even adults shouldn't mess with. "Is that how you got hurt?"

"That was later. The other girl? She left. Told me I should, too. About a half hour later, the fighting started. Dishes and furniture crashing. I got out when these guys, friends of the foster parents I guess, came pounding on my door. Asking me to party." She nibbled at a fingernail that was already too short, slowly looked at me and said, "I got out the window."

"You're on the second story, Harmony, right?" I'd dropped her off after a church dinner one evening. She'd pointed to a room, dimly lighted, at a house with peeling stucco, a car on jacks in the front drive, and graffiti on the wooden fence surrounding the yard.

"Yeah, I jumped then tumbled on the old sofa they pulled outside a few weeks ago, when they had a fire in the living room."

I wondered for the millionth time why some adults bred. Shouldn't there be a Brady Bunch Bill, with a seven-day waiting period or something like that? It'd save kids like Harmony from a miserable childhood that would haunt them forever. I forced myself back to reality and the girl in front of me. Harmony was battered, tattered, and didn't smell too grand either, if you want to know the truth.

Harmony focused on her right index fingernail and worked her way to the pinkie, like someone eating corn on the cob. "I went for a walk. There's a park near us, people hang out nearby. I thought of coming here, too, maybe sleeping in the courtyard, but the buses stop running at eleven through the neighborhood. I walked around a lot, and when I got back to the house at midnight, the place was crawling with cops. Police were everywhere. Didn't want anything to do with that sh—ah, stuff."

"Do you want me to drive you the hospital? Did you get hurt from the fall, or did someone assault you?" I knew she'd told me once, but I asked again. I couldn't bear it if she'd been physically abused, and I promised myself I'd call Child Protective Services the instant we finished talking. There was no way on God's green earth, or even in this city that never sleeps because it thinks it's the best thing since pockets, that this child was going to go back to that foster home that evening or any time.

"I missed the sofa, but this. . ." She glanced at her arm and then stopped talking as a few youth group kids, the "haves," passed near my office. Only as they walked toward the indoor gym, did Harmony say, "This happened when a bag lady who thought my backpack was hers walloped me. She won. I'm just fine. I can take care of myself, but I just need to find another place to sleep."

"We'll get ice for your arm, okay?"

She stood up. She didn't move. "Ya think the pastor would let me sleep on the bench in the foyer? Inside the church? I'm honest. Ask anyone. I won't bother or hurt anything. I never snoop at stuff. Dad will be out of jail in September, so I won't be a bother for long. Once his parole is over, we're going back to California."

"Come on, Harmony, let's get some ice on that bruise. We'll figure it out." In a month of Sundays, I knew Pastor Bob, old Ab Normal, would have a cow before he'd let Harmony camp at church. We'd been through this when I'd suggested the gym might be a good daytime shelter, out of the heat, for street people. Nothing fancy, just water, chairs, and a place to be when it got into the 120s. He nixed that puppy pronto, so talking to him about Harmony wouldn't work, and if she stayed without him knowing, he'd find out from one of the kids and probably have her arrested.

"Or I could put some blankets in the kitchen and sleep there, Pastor Jane. That way I could make the coffee for you first thing in the morning. Unless I'm not welcome." An eyebrow arched, in a challenge I feared, but no smile came to her bowlike mouth.

"Wait." I extended a hand, not trying to touch her. "Harmony, wait a second. Can you help me pull all the craft materials out of the cupboard for VBS? I've got a problem and really need to hire an assistant. I don't have time to put an ad on the church website or the bulletin. Hey, do you know anyone who could help? For money?" This was a big, fat old lie. There was no budget, and if the church with its mega millions couldn't find the money, I'd squeeze my paycheck a little harder. "I can pay ten bucks an hour. It's from nine to mid-afternoon." I saw her eyes widen, calculating a day's pay. "I've got to make a few phone calls, and then we're going to find you a safe place to live. You are never going back to that foster home, unless it's to get your stuff."

Like a feral cat, ready to dart, Harmony backed up and skittered out of my reach. She looked at me as if I were attempting to lure her into a car for some candy, but the ten an hour did the trick. "Yeah, I could use a job, and I got my stuff," she motioned to the grimy, oversized backpack, like a hiker might use. "That bag lady ripped through it. Took my Bible, but I have clothes and things. Just things."

I swear the bag wiggled, but then again, remember, I hadn't exactly come to work rested. I handed her a Bible from the bookshelf in back of me. "This is yours now, honey."

Okay, that was the start of my day, and while odds were not in my favor, the heavens opened and I swear, like in some mediocre movie made in the fifties, a string orchestra let the violins rip. As I went begging for some help about food for VBS, I struck the mother lode. The women who cooked for the Daily Bread were giddy about treats for VBS. Of course, they'd only do it if there were cookies, ice cream, and cupcakes. That actually cinched the deal as three or four gushed, "We never get to make desserts for our families anymore."

As for the veggies and fruit? I'd cross that nutritional chasm later, gator. They'd have plenty of snacks, but their parents could purge the little darlings from those sugar highs when they got home.

Better yet, there were about a dozen teens loitering around the church, some doing maintenance and painting and a few others helping Vera with clerical jobs and others hanging. I used the three B's to get them to help—begging, bartering, and blackmailing. Being new, bluffing would be required on the third B, but it worked.

Vera supplied the number for Harmony's caseworker at Child Protective Services. Overworked and hassled more than even I sounded, the man was appropriately shocked, or so it seemed, about the foster home where Harmony had been staying, and assured me he'd find another for her soon. But for that night? No, not possible, not in any way could he guarantee her a new foster home before the end of the month. "Overcrowding, you know how it is."

I did not know and would not know. She had three choices, the bureaucrat informed me: "Sleep at the foster home, sleep in a juvenile facility, or sleep on the street."

I thought about the Good Book that Gramps had criticized me for always spouting and my "high preachin' horse," as the weary voice at the end of the phone line droned on. I snapped him off with, "None of the above. Make arrangements for Harmony's temporary custody to be transferred to me." I supplied the information to make it happen. "At least until her parent is released from jail," or I left Desert Hills Church, but I didn't add that I was only there temporarily.

Hey, it's Vegas, baby, let's call it a full house. Time I used the local lingo. Anyhow, I had a three-bedroom condo and now two visitors. Not roomies or boarders. Sure as I will fall for the next celebrity diet, Gramps was going to go back to Carlsbad, once he came to his right mind and picked up his guitar and self-esteem. Once he forgot he was forty years past the time of a midlife crisis, I was certain it would happen. Or I could continue telling myself stories of the Easter Bunny, the tooth fairy and how fat girls always have handsome boyfriends. Fool I always am, happily ever after rarely occurs in my world. This is what I was muttering mindlessly as I fished out my cell phone and shoved my purse into the desk drawer. There was a message on it—the phone not the desk drawer.

Nix the idea of it being music to my ears, although I did hear loud music in the background. Gramps listening to salsa or reggae? Visions of some smoky dive or a joint where everyone was smoking joints came to mind. Was he a lost sheep as well as addicted to gambling? The message was: "Listen, Janey girl, Granddaddy here. Meet me at Caesar's Palace at five, near the main entrance. I'll keep my cell on. Call if you can't find me. There's somebody you've got to meet. I *really* need you to meet her. You'll love her as much as I do. Later, gator."

*

I listened to the message again. Okay, this was good. Gramps was happy, unlike the night before when he dragged his slumping body, minus his favorite guitar, into my condo.

He'd said, "You're going to love her as much as I do." Who was the her?

See Jane be stupid. He was bragging about a floozy with bodacious hooters and a tiny brain who had seen a Sugar Daddy in my unsuspecting grandfather, a resident of Lonely Street.

No. Wait, they'd asked me to meet at a casino? Didn't they have chapels and weddings at that hotel and resort as well as gambling? Ohmygoodnesssakesalive, he was getting married. He'd just announced he loved her. He was going to marry someone young enough to be my own child. Okay, at thirty-six I would have been a baby mama, but biologically it could have happened.

That floozy had tricked my grandfather into marrying her at Caesar's Palace. A church wouldn't be necessary for her, or a real pastor, and it wasn't like we didn't, duh, know one. Like, I'm a preacher, and I could marry you both. But I wouldn't do it, and he knew it.

Even though I'd started the day fresh and spanking clean, when the box of colored chalk flew from the top of the arts and craft cabinet and willy-nilly-ed right on my head, face and shirt, I'd given up. Never thought about it until I got the call from He Who Was Marrying at Caesars. Apparently this. . .this *doxy* had already impressed him with her impressive chest and other bodily parts, of which as a minister I tried not to think about, but as a woman I certainly was aware of. And now was coercing my gramps to marry her without any regard for his own family, which consisted of only me.

Well, you've got to do more than that to shut up this minister, this granddaughter, this woman. I am woman, hear me snarl, at least when it comes to protecting my grandfather. I'd tell her a thing or three. Mark my words, I thought, dusting chalk from my bangs, it wouldn't matter how I looked, even if I really truly wished I looked like a million bucks. I was ready to fight fire with a blaze of fury.

What kind of woman was she? Wait, make that a child. The answer could be spelled in four letters: S-C-U-M.

Get this. They had the supreme gall to just leave a message and invite me to be part of the ceremony. Not have me call back and tell me the news, no way, not even that consideration. I flopped back in my chair and thought how about I'd always harbored a secret hope that Gramps and my dear friend, Senator Geraldine English, would marry. What did Geraldine think? Did Gramps' longtime friends from the university even know? Had he called the guys from the band? Would we all end up there to celebrate the nuptials of Gramps and an underage, wannabe *Playboy* centerfold?

Oh, those stupid, calming breaths that a yoga teacher tried to get me to do. I sounded more like the Little Engine that Couldn't, and besides, they never worked, especially when I was jumping to conclusions. There was no doubt in my mind that I could now qualify for the Olympic pole-vaulting event, minus the pole. In and out, I breathed; huff and puff, the train went up and down. Whatever was going to happen at five that night was something I wasn't going to like, that was a sure bet.

*

A Kansas, "Help me, Auntie Em" Tornado Alley tornado had nothing on me for the rest of that day. Dropping Harmony at the condo, she assured me she'd watch TV or sleep. "I didn't get much last night."

"Girls always love bubble baths, so help yourself to the stuff in the bathroom." Nice way to say, "You need to freshen up, girlfriend." I thought so, then added, "Frozen dinners you can microwave and popcorn and stuff like that. You'll find ice cream and yogurt. Oreos and chocolate in the cupboard, too." See, I can share.

These were my favorite cozy comforts, so I thought they'd work for her, maybe. I lead a pretty clean life, but hey, okay, I didn't tell her about the stash of Godiva chocolates with only two pieces left in the second box. A girl has to have something to come home to.

"Not hungry." She was far too skinny, but I had more on the George Foreman grill that was my life than to get a teenager a square meal. She'd have to wait for a future date if there was going to be a lecture on nutrition.

"If that changes, Harmony, help yourself. We'll eat when I come home with my grandfather." And I didn't add, "And his new child bride." She waved. I waved and made a quickie U-turn on the cul-de-sac, sped along the lines of tan stucco, red-roofed condos of the same ilk as mine, and headed toward the Strip.

I may stretch the truth, but the gridlock in Vegas is so bad, the male crap dealers who shave before they head for their shift have stubble when they arrive at the casinos. That sizzling afternoon was no different. Traffic moved like a snail on Tylenol PM. I shunned I-15, where there was even gridlock at the on-ramps, and inched to Caesar's Palace on the surface streets. Tires squealed as I pulled in front, I tossed my keys to a cutie-pattootie valet, took the ticket, and said, "Park it with the Beemers."

I heard him laugh as I blotted my face. Sweat spewed down my back. I dashed into the casino before I was a total sopping mess, rather than half of one.

With the light playing with the sparkles in yet another cowboy shirt, I could not miss Gramps. I wanted to. I longed to snap my fingers and get beamed into a parallel universe where everything was hokey pokey, where chocolate had no calories, size 14 was trim and bathroom scales were forbidden by law.

No luck, but praise the Lord. The bridegroom was alone, sitting on a tall bar stool at the coffee cart, chatting with the blonde little wisp of a barista. He was laughing, and she nodded and spoke to him. Seemed to me that he was pretty chummy with the gal, who he'd probably befriended during his three-week under-the-covers pity party. Maybe he'd come here a lot, and with only our eventful talk the previous evening, I hadn't even thought to ask if he'd gambled away his 401K, the IRAs, and the house in Carlsbad, like that would have instantly come to mind, but it should have because I was thinking it now.

Like it or not, and I did not like it at all, in another few minutes, I'd be making slapdash chitchat with my grandfather's paramour.

"You're a good girl, Jane. Knew you'd come. Would have called you back, but the battery on the cell died." He grabbed my shoulders and gave me a kiss on the cheek. His breath only smelled like coffee. Good sign. At least he wasn't adding alcohol to assault and injury upon the shreds of our relationship in an attempt to find his path down some yellow brick road to ruin.

"Traffic was, well, you know traffic."

"You're here now," he interrupted, and it was just as well because I had no idea what to say next. "Thought you might not want to hang around with this old dude after my confessions."

"Never thought—"

"Baloney. Hey, want you to meet someone special. You're going to love her as much as I do," he said.

"You said that before, Gramps. Let's just get this over with." Okay, I wasn't playing nice, or fair, as I sputtered this and twisted around. Where was his woman? People strolled and dashed, depending on their mood, through the casino, off to dinner, a show, or the Strip. There was a line of ladies of a certain age, none under eighty, making love to a row of slots. Then there were the cool ones, dressed in leather and black silk. Sprinkled here and there were giddy first timers straight from Embarrass, Minnesota. Change girls teetered on high heels that would have given me a nosebleed. Cocktail servers balanced trays of drinks, offering cocktails as twenties stuck out of their Wonderbras. Still, there was nary any eye contact from anyone who might fit the depiction of Gramps' Lady Love.

My head twisted right and left until I spotted her. A few feet away there she stood with bright platinum blonde hair piled to a height that an air traffic controller would admire, wearing six-inch, cherry red stilettos. I could have picked her out a mile away; besides, she made eye contact. I screamed, "Gramps, get your eyes checked. She's forty if she's a day." He didn't hear because a Slot Momma hit the jackpot and started screaming way louder than I did when I found the lizard in my car.

Gramps' bride-to-be was dressed bosom to bloomer in latex leopard fabric, but it was the bosom that got my attention. The knit stretched across breasts the size of watermelons. If she'd toppled, the silicone would've bounced her back up. Diamonds flashed on her wrists, and a studded dog collar dripped with gold hearts. Her earrings dribbled down her husky neck.

Gramps' lady friend switched from one foot to another. Killer shoes had to be the reason. Or maybe she was waiting for me to speak up, or for Gramps to usher us across the three-foot span of carpet that separated the happy couple and my first introduction to my step-grandmother.

I blinked, and suddenly my eyes focused. How could I have missed it? Gramps' ladylove clenched her meaty fists.

She winked at me again and a false eyelash stuck to her lower lid. She had to take her thumb and index finger and separate what looked like a caterpillar. As my eyes became accustomed to the darkness of the casino, I did a triple take. There was stubble on her chin.

Gramps was involved with a man or a woman with severe hormone problems. I couldn't help but see the tufts of inky black hair right above the deep V in her leopard jumpsuit. I've been accused of being as worldly as a pineapple, but I've seen cross-dressers before. Remember, I worked in the inner city, and I've watched a lot of *CSI*.

My eyes rolled and nearly tumbled to the bilious colored carpet. I swayed dangerously. My heart fell to the lower portions of my gut, straight to the end of the lower intestine, if you get my drift.

What does one say to the happy couple when they were about to take the happy leap to become happily husband and husband? Now, trust me, I'm pretty liberal, I just never thought my fuddy duddy Gramps would be gaga for Arnold Schwarzenegger.

I grabbed the coffee cart, missed it and slipped to the floor. Scrambled to my feet, ignoring any shred of dignity. If Arnie made Gramps elated, euphoric, and ecstatic, I'd plaster on a peachy-keen smile. Would the great state of Nevada honor a same-sex union? I didn't want to think about it. The man who would be my relative picked a booger from his nose, wiped it on the back of his dress, and I knew that never in this lifetime would I ever call him "Grandma."

At that second the gal fixing coffee said something, and Gramps caught my shoulder, lifting me up. "Did you get any lunch today, Jane? You don't look good," he said.

Look good? Whatever would it matter how I looked if Gramps was about to walk down the primrose path with a drag queen? I could be jaybird naked and it wouldn't make a hill of jalapeños because I would never be able to top this.

The woman behind the cart spoke again. I could hear sounds, but nothing filtered through. I was about to demand some answers, all righteous and huffy-puffy, when a dapper dude the size of a dime came up and grabbed my grandfather's loving Arnold Schwarzenegger. I gulped as they did that guy thing of knuckle-rapping and trotted off toward the baccarat room.

Someone had just stolen Gramps' beloved and he didn't even squawk. "Did you see that?" I demanded.

"Janey, cool your jets. This is Vegas." The barista handed Gramps a cup of coffee, and a word came out his mouth I'd not heard him say since my buscia, the Polish terms for grandmother, went to be with Jesus. He said, "*Dziekuje*," and then added another sentence in Polish. He was speaking Polish, and I could feel my forehead wrinkling. After a day like it had been, those wrinkles would become permanently etched.

"Jane, are you even listening to me? This is Petra Stanislaw. Petra, I'm pleased to have you finally meet my precious granddaughter, Jane."

She said, "*Czesc, jak sie masz?*"

Then something even weirder happened as I replied, "*Czesc, jak sie masz?*" Where had that come from? I had just replied, "Hello, how are you?" in Polish. Truth be told, I could understand quite a bit more thanks to my grandparents using the language of their parents in order to keep things from me.

"*Czesc*," Petra said, with a far better Polish accent than I could muster and then added a long string of something more, but of course I was still searching the crowd for Miss Hussy of the Year.

My voice caught in my throat, "Can we speak English? Who was—" Yes, I pointed to the young woman "—she and why should I care?"

"Yes, I do," Petra said again with that lilting accent and diminutive smile. She was as pint-sized as I am large, and her hair was real blonde. She looked precious in a coffee bar's apron. I was covered in chalk crumbs that had adhered to my sweaty self.

Why wasn't Gramps worried that his lady, um, love of his life, had exited with a stranger? Why did I need to meet a barista? I hadn't realized these words came from my mouth, until I saw Gramps' eyes squeeze tight, a sure-fire way to know he was steamed.

"Janey girl, let's do this again. Listen up. This is Petra. Jane? Petra."

"Yes? Of course I know this is Petra, the real question was, why will I care that this is Petra?"

"Petra." He said it slowly, as if I were from another planet. "Petra. Remember? This is the woman I wanted you to meet. We're going to be seeing lots of her, and I wanted you to have a chance to meet her before we get down to business."

This time when I attempted to clutch the coffee cart, I made contact, although it rocked like a kayak in a gale. She didn't look eighteen. "Scrape off the makeup and you'll see she's a baby," I screamed. Would I have been more pleased if Gramps was about to marry Arnie? "If you're having Gramps' baby and I'm going to have a step-grandmother who is decades younger than me, you don't know what kind of a scene I can make." The next came out of my mouth in a stifled scream, with a serious dollop of hysteria. "Whatever are you thinking? Are you even thinking?" More screams.

"You're a nutcase, Jane. I don't have to get anyone's approval for this or even have to think much about it," Gramps said through gritted teeth.

I tried to hug him, but he yanked my arms away. I forced a smile at Petra, since I was exhausted and my Polish stinks, especially when I can't even form sentences in English. "Counseling. . .that's what you need."

"Whoa, now you've gone too far. Do you think I've got such a warped sense of reality that I need psychological help for what I'm about to do?" His face was getting burgundy with splotches of blue, unpleasant colors on an older white guy, and while I'm far from white, the color was probably close to mine at that second.

"Yes, I do. It doesn't have to be a real counseling session, just a friendly chat before you get in over your head, before you take the next step. I always recommend some counseling, some time to talk with others who can help you avoid pitfalls. There are plenty of counselors if you don't want to talk to your pastor. Why, I bet even here in Las Vegas, and even at Desert Hills Church, why, I bet Pastor Bob could squeeze in a session for you. You really don't want to jump too quickly, really, this is a huge step. . ." Would that next step be marriage or birth announcements? Was that apron hiding Petra's pregnancy? I am very proud to say that by this time my squawks and hysteria had leveled out to something of a squeal. What hadn't were my arms, which were still flailing around, and my head was shaking of its own volition.

I couldn't seem to stop the arms or the head until Gramps carefully put his right palm over my mouth and said, "Jane, you're taking this awfully hard. Petra understands."

"Well, goody-goody-gobble-'em-up gumdrops for Petra," I said. "This is a life-changing decision, Grandfather. Are you unclear about that? How many fingers am I holding up?" Yes, I did do this and added, "If you don't see the pickle, peanut butter, and tuna sandwich you're about to bite into, I will take control. You haven't even thought this through, have you? And stop glaring at me like that. You're not the first man your age to go through a time when cognition becomes less than crystal. You've just had some shocks with the stroke." I took his arm, but his feet were cemented to the floor because no matter how I pulled, he didn't budge. I used my quiet voice. "We'll just take you home now, maybe have some cocoa and talk about this quietly."

He cocked his head, and his steely blue eyes burnt into me. "I am not going home. You're not going home. I certainly hope I know what I'm doing. I could use some life changes in my rusty old body, but what bad could come of this?"

I sputtered, I stumbled, with spittle flying like the fountains at the Bellagio. It wasn't one of my proudest moments so I'll spare you more graphics. Okay, given five more seconds, I could have listed about two million reasons as to why it was wrong to romance, marry, and father a child at his age, with a woman who could have been my own daughter. Maybe not my own daughter, but something like a much younger sister. Heck, a daughter, who was I kidding?

Most of my reasons, I had a sinking and stinking feeling, should not be spouting from the mouth of a minister. But it was all true.

For a man who was no spring or summer chicken, the guy was strong. He snatched my arm and nearly pulled me up and that should have gotten my attention. Yet I was in scold mode so the words kept spewing forth, of which, thank heaven, I have no memory. Mind you, at this time I simultaneously reached for the coffee on the counter and attempted to balance. I slipped and blinked as coffee rained on my parade, I mean shirt. And I didn't feel a thing. I tossed back a sizzling sip that hadn't gotten over me as Gramps manhandled my arm and the rest of me past a row of gray-hairs making whoopee to slot machines. Not one head turned, even as I hollered, "Stop it. Take your bloomin' fingers off me." Yeah, the ads are right, whatever happens here stays here.

"What has gotten into you?" His eyes were mere slits now as he grumbled, "How dare you get on your old high and mighty Biblical horse with me, madam."

"Madam? Are you blind? I'm the one who's about to be ten years older than my new step-grandmother."

"Your what?"

"That's what she'll be. Or don't you actually plan to make it legal? Just going to live in sin?"

"What planet are you from? I've never seen you like this, even when you've over-consumed coffee or chocolate. Petra is a fine young lady. A hard-working young woman who has had a tough life, and I don't even know the half of it yet. There's a terrible trouble in her, in her gut. I thought better of you and now that I'm thinking of it, how dare you treat her like that? You, Jane, of all people, and a minister, too."

It felt as if my face had been slapped, but of course he didn't touch me. His words sunk in with the speed of cold butter on colder toast, that is, slowly. I gulped and said, "Do you have to get married? Do you, um, know her as in the Biblical sense of the word? Oh, Gramps, Petra seems like a darling little girl, but don't you see? She's a child. I thought better of you, too."

Ever heard the expression, "Bust a gut"? Okay, then you've got the picture of my grandfather as I blurted out the above. He weaved back and forth and roared, holding his middle, rocking with laughter. Not just a little tinkling kind of laugh, but the kind that makes you think you're going to have to fall on the floor or run to the restroom. I thought he was going to do the former. When he caught his breath, he looked at me and burst out laughing again. I stood mute.

"Marry? Janey, you're a piece of work. Petra and I are friends—at least I hope so—but marrying her is about as far from my mind as running around this casino jaybird naked. And that certainly won't happen."

"But you said I would love her."

"Yeah? I hope you will."

"You brought me here because you said she's special."

"She is." The laughter slowed and he scratched his bristly chin.

Gramps had given up shaving, too, along with God, other acts of personal hygiene, and a normal style of clothing.

"Gramps, before you say anything else, please tell me yes or no. Is she your girlfriend? Are you romantic at all?" I could not, would not, absolutely ever get the word "intimate" out of my mouth regarding this woman and Gramps. Although I probably had in the previous bursts.

Those familiar blue eyes smiled. He put a hand over his mouth in a futile attempt to stop more laughter. "Oh, Jane, switch to decaf."

"What is this about?"

"Petra is my ballroom dance instructor." He did a little bow and wiggled his hips, with only a slight frown when his hip headed to the left side, the side of his stroke.

I tossed the overly curvy crone clutching a walker her huge purse that was plopped on an adjoining stool and balanced on it as the words finally penetrated my muddled brain. "Dance instructor?"

"Let's clear this all up. You got a clue how tragic this could have been, how mortifying for Petra?" He said the words with nearly a straight face and then shook all over like a wet dog. "Oh, boy, how I will enjoy sharing this with the band, but, then again—" He looked down at the sequined shirt and the silver tips of his cowboy boots. "—if either of us ever decides to grow up properly, I have a feeling we should keep this to ourselves."

Call the *Guinness Book of World Records* or Channel 10 News. I was speechless two days in a row. Not only that, but I'd been dead-in-the-water wrong. I had egg all over me, mixed with coffee and colored chalk. "I don't know what to say."

"Start with an apology, young lady." He wrinkled his forehead. "Maybe to me and, without a doubt, unless I'm very mistaken, to Petra."

"I am sorry, Gramps. But you still don't understand."

"Spit it out, girl."

I inhaled as if I'd just finished a marathon and said, "In the last twenty-four hours you've given me more than enough shocks to make this, my naturally fabulous hair, streaked with gray."

"Given a few minutes, I know I could recall every one of your stunts that produced gray. You were a trial, child. Turnabout should be fair play." He pulled me into his arms, and I was ten years old. "Now, let's get this straight. I told you this yesterday. I am going to get my body back in shape." He held me at arm's length. "Petra is a dance instructor for the program that's held at the Las Vegas Senior Center. She works here a few hours a week. This is where I met her, actually. Then I signed up for the class."

As we walked back to the coffee cart, he said, "And where you come in, Jane, is that you're going to be my partner. Everyone else has partners. I need one."

"We went over this last night." Okay, there was an edge, if voices can have edges, because I can't dance.

He wiggled a finger in front of my face, but his eyes were serious. "I don't have Alzheimer's. Time you learned. Besides, if you don't, I'll limp around your condo all summer and pretend I'm suffering from dementia. I promise to make your life wretched and depressing. Either help me get this rickety body back in working order or else." His eyes got the size of a spaniel's and twice as pathetic.

He was right. However, two things were stopping me from agreeing, and they were my feet. I'd never been comfortable dancing, never had any desire to get on the dance floor, other than fantasizing with *Dancing with the Stars*. "Are you sure?"

"Come on, Janey. Class is in an hour. We don't have much time to get to the center."

Within an hour, I was being instructed to hold my arms in a certain way, wiggle my hips to loosen them up, and bend a bit at my knobby knees. Imagine this vision of grace and poise. Don't even bother. There I was at the senior center, shaking my booty and, surprisingly for those who know me and have seen me in jeans, even with my bountiful backside, booty shaking doesn't come naturally for yours truly.

"Please, Madam, Miss Pastor Jane, relax." This was Petra. "Feel the music. In your bones. Don't look at your feet. Your muscles will work better if you count."

At break time, when everyone else was getting coffee or a soft drink, Gramps pulled me aside. "Talk with Petra, will you? She needs some girl talk, honey. Something's troubling her."

"I just met the woman, Gramps. As you may recall, especially when you stare at the coffee all over this shirt, my actions spoke louder than my words. Forget the sterling first impression, because she knows I'm a screwball. And I have principles. I usually wait at least two hours before I meddle in someone's business."

That wasn't entirely honest. I have been nosey quicker than that and he knew it, so after getting a grandfatherly shove I trotted over toward the woman I'd recently insulted.

I smiled, stayed a few feet away in case she hadn't forgiven me and said, "Hey, Petra. Thank you for getting Gramps to come here. This is good for him."

"Dancing is good for us all." She nodded, like a delicate bobble head, and slipped the paper she'd been reading into the pocket of her electric blue crinkly peasant skirt, which would have made me look as big as Texas.

I replied, "I'm a good listener if you ever want to talk. Gramps thinks you might have something weighing on your heart."

"It is a big thing, Pastor. Too big for you." She inhaled sharply and then straightened her shoulders. "It's too big for me."

"It's not too big for our God, Petra. Call me Jane. Our God is a specialist in really big problems. I don't have any more of a direct connection with Him than you do, but I've solved some huge problems in my day, in and out of the ministry, and maybe I can help you find some answers." I didn't tell her that I'd created colossal quandaries single-handedly; no need right then for full disclosure.

She looked down her feet, which by the way were in the sweetest, softest taupe pumps, beyond adorable with a tiny strap across the top. It was enough to make me sick since I lusted for the shoes, and feet that size. We both looked up at the same time. "With permission, may I call you later?" she said.

"That works for me." I patted her hand. In 120 minutes or less, I'd gone from making horrid, spoken accusations that Petra was a gold digger to attempting to console her.

To add a bit more drama to whatever had stirred her up she wiped a tear from her eye and patted her pocket where she'd hidden the paper I'd seen her reading. She flicked a switch on the portable CD player, and we went back to attempt the foxtrot with "You Make Me Feel So Young" crooned by Frank Sinatra pouring over the crowd.

Gramps didn't wince more than twenty times as I crushed his toes, amazing through those alligator-skin boots he was sporting. Everything was rosy, until Petra called out, "Now everyone, it's time to twinkle."

That did it. I stopped dead. "Tinkle? Gramps I never have and never will tinkle in public."

"A twinkle. It's a twisting side step, a running in motion dance move," he said and called across the room. "Petra, I can't handle this."

As if they had a secret code, she rushed over and replaced Gramps in the man's position. The music got louder.

I'm a preacher and in the miracle business, which is a preachy line I use, but this had to be an honest-to-goodness one.

You see, as Petra took my partner's position, I was transformed into a swirling, gazelle-like ballroom dancing professional. Twirling, twisting, and twinkling, it didn't matter one whit that I was dancing with a girl, who happened to be a trained dancer. In all my born days, I never ever thought I'd feel light as a feather, feel the music to my marrow. It coursed in my veins. I was as free as a butterfly, free as falling leaves in an autumn breeze, light as Cool Whip on Jell-O and nary a toe came between my size eight feet and the dance floor. It was heaven. It was sublime. It was what my body was made for. I was going to throw off the preacher's garb to scoot straight for Broadway. Look out chorus girls, look out Rockettes, and look out for Jane Angieski. I spun, smiled, and wiggled in all the right places, since I do have an abundance of those "places" to wiggle. The music turned to a polka, and my Polish blood surged. I let go of Petra's hands. I was born to dance and dance I would, with nothing to stop me.

For a good ten seconds.

What happened next was not my fault. As I shouted, "I'm twinkling." I took to the air. I flew straight at, not into the arms of, one of the handsomest hunks of manhood I'd seen in a good long while.

Chapter 3

Carl Lipca. That name seemed to erupt from every other mouth in Las Vegas. I heard about him first in a gushingly, girlish, dishy kind of conversation between Vera and one of the teens. I swear Vera had to wipe drool from her mouth as she ogled Carl's photo, which appeared next to his editorial in the newspaper. Vera has a crush on Carl, I wanted to taunt, but I was too mature for that, even though I sang it in my mind. He was young enough to be her grandson. Oh, yuck.

I shoved that ick-o piece of too-much-information to the back of my mind.

Carl was this straight-arrow journalist for the local paper who seemed to be one step ahead of every issue, a homegrown celebrity and the city's most eligible bachelor. Talk around Vera's desk had been that he might run for mayor, might try out to anchor CBS News, and had been seen at the Academy Awards on the arm of a starlet. As to whether they were an item, Vera said, "Not at all, but he has been taking acting lessons," certain as all get out.

For about two seconds at the most, I wondered what a card carrying AARP-age church secretary and cuddly, most definitely hunky journalist would have in common. I tossed that tantalizing thought through the window with some of my more obscure romantic fantasies and realized it was probably pubescent infatuation on Vera's nipped and tucked face.

Yes, these life-in-front-of-me flashings were circling my brain whilst I was airborne.

So picture this: Me, Little Miss Twinkle Toes, making an impression on the suave Carl Lipca. Boy, did I do it. Imagine if you will, while pondering my look-away embarrassment, a pleasingly plump pastor parading in a precarious polka as I became a potent projectile zeroing in on this picture of pulchritude and perfection. Yep, I made a donkey's south end of myself.

"You okay, lady?" he said between puffs of ragged inhalations.

Love at first sight? My heart was racing, my pulse pulsating. His luscious lips were close to mine, and all I had to do was scream straight at him, "Um, yeah, my, um, foot slipped." My foot may have slipped, but the bottom line was that my backside was now squarely straddling him in a variation of the missionary position. If we were alone and hadn't had clothes on. . . Oh, dream on. Yes, I planned to do just that, at length, when I was thoroughly alone.

When I write my book on ways to get guys to notice a woman, this will not be in the manual. "Stay still. Are you hurt?" I asked as I lifted my buttocks off his lower-than-the-waist midsection, if you get my drift, and tried to balance with my hand on the floor. Unfortunately my palm was sweaty. Unfortunately the floor was slick, and I flopped down in his face with an, "Ohhhh." And for your information, our mouths touched, and he'd probably have a fat lip since my teeth collided with the aforementioned lip. I tasted blood. It wasn't mine.

Hands grabbed me around the waist. I think it was Petra, and I rolled off his body. "Oh, I'm so sorry."

Carl dashed to his feet, terrified that I'd heave myself at him again, and pulled Petra between us. Her tiny size wouldn't help much, but I guess it made the guy feel safer because I'm certain he considered me a Looney Toon. Make that a dangerous Looney Toon.

"Jane, oh, my, please let me help you to a chair." Petra wrapped an arm around me. "You'll be fine, you slipped. It can happen," she said, cooing as if she were talking to a baby.

I would have gobbled it up; I'm a sucker for sympathy, but I saw Carl retreat, placing a tissue over his mouth. He pulled it back, saw the blood, and clasped it to his lip again. Gramps dashed over to me. No sad and worried look on his face; my grandfather was quaking with laughter. He'd had two belly laughs in two hours. That was beyond his legal limit, especially since they were both at my expense.

He motioned for the journalist. I swear the guy cowed. Heck, would you blame him? Yet Carl obeyed and came within ten feet of me while every other bystander in that entire room took ten giant steps back. Who knew who I'd throw myself at next? They feared for their lives and reproductive organs.

"Carl, my friend, I'd like you to meet my granddaughter, Pastor Jane Angieski. You two certainly hit it off." Whatever else he was going to say dissolved into laughter, and now the entire class, middle-aged and older, was joining in, suddenly less fearful of Rocket Girl, Jane the deadly projectile of the dance floor. I guess because I was sitting.

Carl was the genuine article, all arm candy and even better looking when I wasn't piercing his lips with my front teeth. His eyes were not too bad, either, sultry brown like bitter chocolate, the kind that melts on your tongue. He might have a Polish last name, but he was one hundred percent American male in my book.

He nodded and looked at me—not too close, mind you. He dabbed his lip and said, "Wait. I know you."

Words to make a girl's heart turn to jelly? Yeah, until he said, "You're the fighting minister, aren't you? Love to get an interview while you're in Vegas. Make a great feature piece. You pack a wallop."

I dusted my hands. "I'm a lethal weapon," I said, and then it hit me. "You know me?"

Carl's smile was sly. "Blame everything I know on Henry. He and I found our families lived in the same area in Poland and we talked about you, too. I'd like to hear some time about your efforts in Los Angeles since I saw you on the Internet. You've got a story, Pastor."

"Really?" I cooed much like some cooing I'd overheard Vera doing in the telephone one day. The thought momentarily made me queasy.

"You're some minister always digging up dirt. I want to be kept in the loop, okay? So if you hear anything, just call me."

What *had* Gramps told him? In a highly caffeinated moment I might have forgotten the slip from grace straight at his lower-than-middle and grabbed the hunk's arm for a spin around the dance floor, minus the deadly twinkles. Then I happened to look at Petra, who was looking at Carl, who was looking at Petra. It was goo-goo, ga-ga all around. My fears that Petra was about to whisk Gramps off to the honeymoon delights of Aruba seemed as non-reality-based as my unexpected talent for dancing.

I rubbed my knees and dusted off my backside. "I've hung up my Super Minister cape and mask. I'm going to become a professional dancer." Heads spun in circles as the entire class looked in horror.

I always say why make a fool of yourself unless there's a really good crowd? I tried that giggling, joie de vivre sounds you hear actresses do on *Access Hollywood*. "Just kidding, Carl. Nice meeting you. Let's hope we bump into each other again." I wiggled my hips and heard him gasp. Then added, "In different circumstances? Gramps, isn't dance time over?" Like the parting of the Red Sea, a path cleared between me and the exit and I boogied. Can't blame them. When I dance, people are harmed.

We waved our good-byes, and I attempted to leave with whatever dignity I had still intact. Attempted is the operative word because I assumed I was stepping toward an automatic door. My nose will tell you that wasn't the case.

I was still rubbing my forehead as I walked into the condo, with Gramps limping behind me. He was still laughing—not all the time, only when he looked at me. There was no sign of Harmony. I called her name and then the place exploded. It was filled with a yapping dust mop hitting my shins at four hundred miles an hour. Wait, make that a shag carpet on steroids.

"Tuffy." Harmony screamed, dashing from the kitchen. "Oh,

Pastor, you're not supposed to see him yet, not until I could tell you about him." She chased it in circles around my feet, in a futile attempt to capture the wiggling creature. "Stop, Tuffy, stop. He just rushed out when he heard the key in the door." The faster she ran, the faster the shag carpet dashed. If it had been happening to someone else, I would have squealed with laughter.

"I promise you he won't be a bother," she yelled as *it* leaped over the sofa and then continued making laps around the living room, yapping as it ran.

"What *is* it?" I bent to snag it and bam, just like that the thing bounded and flung itself into my arms.

"Jane, you must've hit your head when you attacked Carl. It's a dog." Gramps ruffled the dog's head, and he nearly kissed it. I think we both picked up the smell in the same second. Make that a wet shag carpet on steroids. Wait, make that a wet rug on steroids who'd been Dumpster diving.

"Harmony, is it yours?" I was using my righteous "high preachin' horse" voice again. I'm cringing as I admit that it grated on me. I smashed my lips. Might this be why I was boyfriendless and childless with the big four-oh ever looming? Was I that bossy? That quick to criticize? I might ponder my self-righteously wrong mindset at some future time, but at that second, I had a filthy dog nesting in my embrace. He seemed to love me, even if I wasn't keen on myself.

I looked at the girl and gone was Harmony's armor, replaced by tears, like sprinklers, great lines down her face. "I've been taking care of him. Tuffy's his name. He's been with me, secretly, since Dad went to jail. The woman at that last foster home went into convulsions when she saw him, sent him to the pound, but I bailed him out. I've been hiding him. She said she'd make sure I never found another foster home if I brought in another dog."

With lips pushed forcibly into a smile, I managed, "Well, you're here now. Along with your little dog, too." And yes, I did think

I sounded like the Wicked Witch. That dog needed fumigation.

Gramps stuck out his hand to Harmony. "Hello, I'm Henry, Pastor Jane's grandfather." I thought for sure he was going to try to hug Harmony. I had a feeling she'd let him, this girl who constantly shied away from me. He took the dog from my arms, wrinkled his nose, and handed it to Harmony. "I bet Jane has some really fine shampoo in her bathroom. She usually does. Let's give this little dog a bath. Been a while since I've bathed a dog." He reached out and took Harmony's hand, like it was the most natural thing in the world, and said, "Some like it, some don't. We'll close the door so we can find out what kind his royal dogness is." He was jubilant, bouncing as the threesome headed down the hall. To wash a dog. Men. Who can understand them?

God brought us all together for some reason other than to bust the seams of this pint-sized condo. At least that's what I thought before it sunk in that they were going to use my extravagant twenty-nine-dollar-a-bottle shampoo, which my hairdresser swore would keep my hair color as shiny as gold dust. I dashed down the hall as the door slammed shut. I yelled at the closed door. "His fur better not look nicer than mine when he's finished."

It was three hours past my bedtime when I finally got to sleep. Takes time to blow dry a pooch. I swear, they even tried to use my curling iron on him. Okay, I'll admit it, the mutt was cute, especially after I trimmed his face and we could see his little brown, almond-shaped eyes. We all worked together with Gramps and Harmony cooing and coddling his chinny-chin-chin.

Then, everything slowed. Harmony went to one guest bedroom, Gramps tramped to the other. The dog? Sleeping, finally, after making 651 mad dashes around the house. He was glued to my hip and in my bed. It won't shock you to know I'd hoped for a male, even a snoring one, but a male pooch wasn't not what I'd had in mind.

*

In less than two days' time, I had gone from being miserably, pitifully lonesome to cohabitating with two of the sloppiest humans on the face of God's green earth, plus a canine, in a condo that had shrunk to the size of a peanut. Speaking of Tuffy, he never walked anywhere, but sped like Satan himself was about to pull that little stub of a tail.

The place was a pigpen. It might even stink. And the funny part? I could not remember being happier, most of all because my grandfather was smiling. As my Polish grandmother used to say, "Have fun now, Jane. Those dirty dishes aren't going anywhere." She was right. It had been too long since I'd had family that I didn't recognize the emotion of joy when it landed on me like I'd landed on the newspaper reporter.

Around me, of course, Harmony was still the kid who clammed up. Yeah, it was me, because with Gramps? She was Miss Motor Mouth, a real Chatty Cathy. They seemed to have their funny bones in the same location, joking like buds. Standing at the breakfast bar the next morning, I swallowed more coffee, not wanting to think that a few years ago, I was his only pal. I was now a grown-up minister, I told myself, and only half listening to Gramps sketch their plans for that day.

"Janey, we're goin' to the doggie park. I just Googled them, and we've got a choice of four." He pointed to the patio where Harmony and Tuffy were romping in the early morning heat.

"How did Harmony think she'd be able to hide him from me? Didn't matter. The dog was out of the closet so to speak. He's shampooed, fluffed and. . ." I finished the coffee. "Don't you think he's some kind of ratty terrier in that squirming body?"

Gramps fished his keys off the counter and Harmony and the dog joined us. "After the park, we're going to the super pet store for some super pet food for this super dog, maybe get him a new leash. Yeah, a new leash on life, that's what this pooch needs, right, Miss Harmony? I understand, because he's a lot like me, Jane.

We'd probably better buy a comb. Unless it's okay that he keeps using yours?" He turned to me, and I stuck my tongue out in reply. "Didn't think so. Get his old leash, Harmony, will you? Oh, yeah, Harmony and I decided the dog needs a real name. Yep, it's going to be Tough E. Angieski," Gramps rattled on, spilling breakfast dishes in the sink, splashing water on the oatmeal that would turn to mortar. He high-fived Harmony before she dashed down the hall.

"Our last name?" I did a double take from the mess in the sink to my grandfather's face. While I was still sighing over the fact that I wasn't going to have a new step-grandmother, giving a dog with our last name was creepy.

"Lighten up, Jane baby," he growled in a whisper and I snapped to, just like when I was Harmony's age. "That's what she wanted. She said you'd go postal, but I argued you'd be okay. She worries what think of her, you know."

"She likes me. . ." I trailed off, thinking that she didn't hardly say anything to me, didn't initiate conversations. On the plus side, her dog's fur was fabulous. My hairdresser would love this.

I'd just finished the above lie to myself when Harmony walked back into the room. Gramps turned to her. "Ready for the park and the store, Miss Harmony?" And she nodded as Gramps said, "We're off, and eventually will head to the market. We need snacks. Thought we might stop at the Senior Center to see if Petra's there." Gramps gave me a quick kiss on the cheek.

"Harmony." I smiled as brightly as a toothpaste commercial. "I think your dog's new-name is perfect." And with that I won a flicker of a smile. My day was made, at least for another twenty minutes.

Tough E. Angieski yapped, making victory laps, then dashed to Gramps' Mustang. I stood on the porch, waving until the car turned out of the neighborhood, feeling empty and lonely and, okay, weird. I wanted to go with them, like a family, and have fun. "Get outta here, girl," I said to myself, and the grown up took charge because in ten minutes I was on my way to church.

A church on Saturday is bliss, quiet and people-less. There was a boatload of work to be done for Vacation Bible School, and like it or not, it'd barrel into the station marked "Jane's Responsibility" on Monday. Moving into the left lane to enter the church, what I saw nearly made me swerve, make a U-turn, and run away.

Pastor Bob's spanking new Lexus was hogging two handicapped parking spots near the entrance. Odd? Not the hogging, but that he was there on a Saturday. Why did I have such an aversion to him? Paranoia? Always over-caffeinated?

I slowed the SUV to five miles an hour, but eventually, even at that speed, I'd have to park among the BMWs, Hummers, classic Corvettes, and five Mercedes so new they still with temporary plates. Through the huge, glass front doors I spied a crowd with Pastor Bob in the middle. I swear they were doing a cheer, like, well, cheerleaders.

My first, second, and third choices would have been to totally avoid the perky pastor and his precocious surprises. Gosh, I hate being a adult at times, I thought as I headed into the foyer where Pastor Bob was holding court, encircled by adoring fans, huddled with their arms circling each other.

They yelled, slapped each other, and the laughter rang in the cavernous foyer. I inched around the crowd, but I'm rather tough to miss because of my pleasing plumpness.

"Look who's here, everybody. Pastor Jane, perfect timing. As usual. These are my personal prayer partner, Ms. Delta Cheney. Yes, my goodness, it's our new youth minister. We are getting really huge things done around here with Pastor Jane on board." Pastor Bob's face shined, moist with sweat. He started patting me on the shoulder. "You should hear this woman talk to those teenagers. And now the news. God has great plans for our VBS, especially with Jane in charge. Real PR move getting neighborhood kids here, lots of new faces, to um, bring to the Lord, and to help beef up the coffers so we can launch new programs. Right, Jane?"

They clapped and cheered, like a high school pep rally, jumping for joy at whatever Pastor Bob said. It was spooky. There I stood in my Saturday "ensemble" of baggy jeans, hot-pink scoop-neck T-shirt, down to my flip flops, pumping hands with the movers and shakers of Las Vegas.

The weirdest thing happened after that. Maybe not as spine-chilling stuff as from the last forty-eight hours, including nearly having Carl Lipca in a position where in some states we'd have to marry, but with these bashful baby-brown eyes, it looked a heckava lot like Ms. Cheney and the good pastor were in cahoots, cookin' and plannin'. They were chummy. Like that Supreme Court judge said about pornography, you know it when you see it.

My niggling whisper preceptor was on red alert because something weird and creepy was going on, which was perceptible in a body-language, Patrick Jane on the *Mentalist* sort of thing. It was disturbing and perturbing. I tried to smile like I didn't have a care in the world but the thought occurred to me that I could be slightly psychotic. Or is that like being slightly pregnant? Hopefully it was just the heat. Or perhaps it was from being in close proximity to the ever-surprising, always-something-up-the-sleeve Pastor Bob Normal.

Ms. Cheney was, as Jerry Seinfeld says, "a close talker," in breathing distance and in my face although I knew she was ignoring me. She smelled of cigarette breath, which spilled on me like a douse of Taboo perfume. She was tall, muscular, and athletic as if she'd been in sports, like a forward for the Chicago Bulls.

I started a string of small talk, weather, my move, the price of peanuts in Peoria. She wasn't really listening or looking at me. Her eyes were only on Bob, for whom she'd seductively licked her lips. He turned briefly and she caught his eye. I had front row seats to it all, and I swear, before Bob smiled, there was a hint of something other than adoration for Delta Cheney crossing his face. Now, I've been all wet about relationships but you know about looks. Pastor Bob may have been gushing good gravy about Delta Cheney, but his eyes didn't reciprocate. Just FYI, Bob is married, which of course, didn't stop some men—didn't bother a few preachers, either.

Suddenly something I had said got her attention. "What? What did you say?"

Apparently even though she was inches from me and discounted that I was there, she had heard me say that I'd been raised by the Amish on a turnip farm in Toledo. We both knew she wasn't listening so I asked, "Which teen in the youth group is yours?"

With a coquettish, toothy smile, Delta fingered the bracelets cascading up and down her arms, like someone might an abacus. I was hypnotized by the fat sapphires that sparkled on her ears, the ring of diamonds and rubies around her neck, and the opal as big as Rhode Island on her thumb.

"Jane. Delta. Glad you're getting on like a house on fire." Pastor Bob broke the trance just as I was pondering why the woman didn't have that pushed up, prefab boob look, like some with her style. Plastic enhancement is big business in Vegas, or so I'd been told by a telemarketer who had called the evening before last.

We certainly hadn't been talking about fires or houses, but Pastor Bob sounded like an on-the-take politician running for reelection. He pulled our elbows, gathering Delta close to me, and spouted about building for God in a way that would have made God blush. Talking louder, he touched Delta on the shoulder, and the woman glowed. Bob? Again, I could have been wrong—I often am—but a tiny corner of his upper lip slipped south.

"Our Delta is the CEO of the Philemon Society of America, locally known as PSA. For five years, right? Know you've heard of it. Just had a feature in a parenting magazine. Got a call from our local newspaper guy, the *Las Vegas Review Journal*, about it, too. Why, don't you know, rumor has it *People* magazine is going to run an article. A few weeks back, *60 Minutes* even sent a scout out here to get some background information. All hush-hush, mind you, Pastor, top secret, I suppose, since the producers wouldn't say why they wanted to know. Gosh, those television people frown a lot."

He rambled, then took a deep breath, and I thought he'd stop. Wrong again. "We're certain it is because they've touched hearts and placed children in God-loving homes. Oh, yes, hallelujah and oh, boy, here we have real live angels working in this sinful city of Las Vegas. The angels sent by God have created one of the best faith-based adoption organizations in the world, right here, I say, right here. Right in this little old dusty city, yes, I say, right here. These are great times, say hallelujah, brothers and sisters, great times for forgotten orphans, I tell you, great times, and for our city, too. I am proud to be a small part of your work and the work of our Lord who is directing you, Delta."

Two waved their hands skyward, another shouted, "Amen." With the fervor he'd created, it's surprising they didn't start rolling on the floor and speaking in tongues. I'd seen the good pastor at the pulpit. The guy had been called charismatic; I called it overly dramatic for my traditional tastes, but he was certainly spirited with this group. Looking at the glowing glances of his adoring fans, I had a feeling Pastor Bob was about to jump with both feet right onto the sermon box.

Delta Cheney yelled, "Oh, yes, Bob, yes, oh, yes," in a way I didn't even want to connect with anything outside of his preaching. It creeped me out, big time. Or so I thought until she reached one manicured index finger, touched his chest, and the man became mute. That was creepier by far.

"Oh, Bob, don't go filling this little pastor with such stuff. We're just a-doing what we can." The southern accent poured out, like gravy over biscuits with a Denny's breakfast. "You're doing God's real work in here." Then she looked down at her perfectly polished fingernails and twisted the bracelets. Fluttering mascara-laden eyelashes, she dipped her chin and whispered something to Bob. It was too much for me to stare this time. I turned and gagged.

Bob glanced at his Rolex. "Off you go now. Know you have to all get going. Hallelujah. Brothers and sisters, I say hallelujah. Good to have you here. We'll do it again soon."

As the crowd filed out, I stood like a bump on a log, although my eyes were glued to the cozy chat between the pastor and Delta Cheney as they walked to her cream-colored Mercedes. He bent close. He cocked his head. I wanted to dash to the restroom and scrub my hands, face, and entire body with antibacterial soap.

Even in the short time I'd been in Vegas, I knew that Delta and this crowd weren't that unusual. A few of the people, I had come to learn, seemed to think that living here automatically turned them into missionaries serving in a foreign land. A few residents I had met in this church family seemed to wear their citizenship like a bright medal.

As a newcomer, I didn't want to upset the applecart to tell them every city and town has a dark side. I wondered what the crap dealers, pit bosses, cocktail servers, and the thousands of other workers at the gambling palaces thought about their lives. Mind you, it is the service industry, but did some of them need more in life? I had no answers. Besides, what did I know, being a new preacher on the block? These ideas zipped through my caffeine-addled brain as I smiled brightly. Hey, I'm not a hypocrite. Smiles are part of the job because, I'll have you know, preachin' is like sales. Yeah, think it over.

However, as soon as possible, I'd dive into Google to get the scoop on Delta and PSA. Maybe God in His wisdom had plopped Delta in my life because I'd thought of adoption. If it hadn't been for adoption of my father into Gramps' family, well, there wouldn't have been me. Delta seemed to be doing a heavenly job.

As Pastor Bob returned, he snagged my elbow and said. "Coffee, Jane? Oh, see you've already got some. What I wanted to do was some strategic brainstorming on an idea Delta, um, well, the others had. You're going to love it. It's got everything we need, including raising much-needed funds. Wait until you hear."

He ushered my unwilling body into his office and said, "All the hubbub of ballroom dancing, and everyone nowadays is fanatical about it. Banking on that and the fact we need to raise money, if we want to construct a youth building, we must do something. Mind you, we have seed money, but this shouldn't just depend on sponsors. Don't you agree, Pastor Jane? Of course you do. Why, we must take action. Right now, hallelujah." He was waving his arms and speaking as if there were a roomful of converts rather than just little old me.

Taking the guest chair, I placed my Starbucks iced coffee drink cup on the creamy colored carpet, careful to put it in a safe spot so I wouldn't knock it over. I relaxed and sipped occasionally from my cup, listening to the rest of his spiel, including occasional hallelujahs, and the air conditioner was lulling me into agreement until Delta Cheney's name came up in one of his outpourings.

I waved my hand like an excited first-grader and yes, I was amazed when he allowed me to ask, "Ms. Cheney comes here to church? I haven't seen her before."

"Hardly." But that didn't seem to bother the man as he continued, "Our Delta talks about attending church, says she does when she's in New York. Says our little dusty church right here is as good as it gets. Oh, what a help she is. You understand that she's on call 24/7, busy with the PSA." He looked at his steepled fingers and added, "I pray one of these days Delta's heart will change. Jesus is speaking to her. I can tell these things, Jane. I'm praying hard. Hallelujah."

Could he tell? Could anyone tell what was going on in another person's spiritual walk? When would the hallelujahs stop?

Pastor Bob bounced in his overstuffed chair, which quivered but stood fast to its task of holding up the pastor. He leaned forward in the leather chair the color of butter, re-folded his hands in a steeple on the broad desk's polished mahogany surface, and seemed to inhale something that smelled bad. He looked down his nose and became pious. Not a good look for him.

I sniffed the air—politely, mind you. But all was well in my air pocket.

Then he turned over the papers scattered on his desk so that prying eyes, such as mine, couldn't see what he was working on. His sermon? Perhaps he wanted it to be a surprise for Sunday? Perhaps he was working on his stock portfolio? I didn't care, until he looked at me, swallowed, and shoved the papers into the top of his desk drawer. My limited interest flipped into overdrive. It revved again as he locked the desk. "Now, back to dancing."

I wanted to ask, "What are you hiding?" but managed, "Ms. Cheney is going to teach ballroom dancing for the VBA or youth group?" Visions of a statuesque chorus girl complete with humongous purple feathers cha-cha-ing in the church multipurpose hall tangoed around my brain.

Pastor Bob clasped his hands in front of him with a slap. "Why, hallelujah, Jane, you are a team player. I knew it. This has to do with our precious teens. It was just dreamed into reality by those folks you've met. We're going to raise money by auctioning off dance partners from the elite of our little desert community. Brilliant or what?" He rubbed his hands together and grinned like he'd just had a visit from Publisher's Clearing House.

Oh, my goodness, and could it be that his plans included me? Is the pope Catholic? What I thought really didn't make any difference. First of all, I knew a steamroller when one hit me. I'd been squashed. Second, my service as youth pastor at Desert Hills would be for just six more months and then I'd be off to another location. The previous youth pastor would be back after maternity leave, and she would deal with Pastor Bob's ever-enthusiastic ideas. "You're going to host a dance?" Logic screamed, "Head for the hills. Get out while you can."

Good manners, a regular paycheck, and the A/C kept me glued to the chair. Besides, it was about the kids. They needed that center, and if I could help raise the money so they'd have a place to congregate, rather than the mall or worse, then I wanted to be counted in.

"Not just any old dance with crepe paper roses and strings of lights or disco balls. Get with the program. Delta has clout. Why, we have real stars—yes, celebrities—in this old town out here in the wilds. Don't need the mayor or the stuffed-shirt governor when we can get the hot ticket names. You know Gladys Knight? Yep, Delta's pals with her, but she's peanuts compared to Madonna, Cecile, or Rosie." He was standing now, flailing his arms, preaching to some unseen congregation and me. "Bundles of celebrities come and go, playing the huge shows here. Why, Pastor Jane, go on, really, name anyone, and I bet Delta knows them. Jennifer Lopez? Yes, she knows her. Matt Somebody. Brad? How about that little blonde gal that the teenagers are so wickedly wild about, what's her name? Whatever. Yes, yes, yes. Why, think of the Blue Man Group, or would that be Two Blue Men, which doesn't sound grammatically correct, but that's show biz. She knows them. Knows them all. How about Carrot Top? We went out to dinner, Delta and I, with the guy, and what a scream. And what about some circus acts from Circus Circus? Lions and tigers. Why not.? Imagine—just imagine—the bundles of bucks generated in just one event. Why, my good Pastor Jane, we would have enough funds to build that youth center in the next six months—well, maybe next year—and you can put down money on that."

Now, our denomination isn't against blue men or circus acts, but the idea of them performing in a dance-athon would get no agreement from me, lowly, sub-sub stand-in pastor that I was.

Then, jumping up and down like the winner on *Wheel of Fortune*, he exploded with the kicker. "Tom Jones. That's who we need to MC."

"*The* Tom Jones?" I sucked in air and there was a wheezing sound.

"One and the same. Delta'll get him. You can bet on this. The program will be gargantuan." He rubbed his hands together and flopped back into the desk chair, which squeaked under his pastoral weight.

When I could breathe, I gulped out, "The same man who made 'What's New Pussycat' a hit decades ago? Nothing against Mr. Jones, but just bringing up visions of him swiveling his middle-aged hips and making suggestive faces on the stage in the church multipurpose hall for a fundraiser so that we can build strong moral character among our teens seems a tad inappropriate, at least in the circles I've been preaching in before coming here."

Pastor Bob jumped, figuratively, at me. "Deal with it. This is Vegas."

"Are you going to bring this up to the church board, sir?"

"They have no say," he snapped. "Why even bring that up, Pastor Jane?"

Hold the phone, I wanted to shout, but asked, "The church board doesn't have a say?"

"You can bet on that, Missy. Wouldn't know a good deal if it was tied around their necks with balloons. Concentrate on this. The whole enchilada will be up to us. We want sophistication, big-timers. Nothing else. My um, well, friend Delta can make all that happen. She's connected like ugly on an ape to everyone here in Vegas, New York, and in D.C., too. I've been to the PSA offices and seen pictures she's taken with all the last three presidents and a bundle of other VIPs. Now, back to our little church in the desert." He chuckled again, repeating one of his favorite phrases because there was nothing little about the humongous Desert Hills Church. "Why, we have a responsibility to our families. And perhaps there's good from this, we'll never know. We'll never know why Delta has come into our fold, or close to it, so to speak."

The idea of dancing lions jumping through fire hoops flashed in my mind as Tom Jones swiveled, leering and winking at our youth, would be forever engraved on my eyelids. He stood and smoothed a hand over his spare tire, a Dunlap, as the kids say, as his belly "dun lapped" over his belt. "Wonder if my Armani tux still fits well enough? Do you think I should get a new one?" He patted his bulging midsection. I diverted my eyes. "Yes, we want it formal. Frilly dresses for the ladies. Better hold it on the Strip, mind you, not here. At church. Churches won't bring in the money, I mean, folks. Ah." He leaned back. "Can't you just imagine that?"

"Excuse me? You're suggesting this will be held at a casino?" I was speaking but at the same time going through a mental list of the board members and those I knew well enough to announce that their pastor was crackers. The few I'd met would probably rubber-stamp his ideas. Was it power? Charisma? They just gobbled him up like I did with chocolate. Which was odd, because I typically fall for anything that sounds reasonably sensible, like the grapefruit diet and candy bars as health food.

"We've got them all over this little town. Casinos with grand ballrooms. Nothing cheesy."

"Then our teenagers would not be involved?"

"Oh. Um." The runaway train huffed and puffed.

"Because of the part about the kids in the casinos?"

His eyes widened. "Yeah, well, you're right, Pastor Jane. We'll need to noodle that."

"We just might, Pastor Bob," I said, wondering if he had a noodle in that noodle, but I nodded. "If, that is, you're planning an appropriate function for our youth."

He slowed, sputtered and stopped. He took a breath and plopped in his chair. He inhaled, refocused his glassy eyes, and bam, started again. "Good, good." He rubbed his palms together as if he were about to gobble a five-star meal. "Glad we're on the same page, Pastor. Now let's put our brains cooking. Better yet, why don't you start without me?" He glanced at his Rolex. "I want you to put all your energy into this because I want a class act, and I know you've been well recommended. This is ambitious, big, big, big, Jane, and I'm only asking because I'm certain you're perfect for it. I was going to wait until Monday to tell you. But you're right here right now so I'll pop the news. We want you to captain the challenge. You'd be our point man. The top banana. Head honcho. Guardian angel. All that, I tell you. Why, I am positive God is asking for you to say 'Yes.' and amen. I tell you the truth, I'm absolutely certain of it. Just think of the legacy you'll leave and the report I will forward to the District Council. Pastor Jane, my friend, you'll be known as the pastor who single-handedly helped fund our youth building. You'll go down in our church history. Oh, yes, ma'am, I'll be able to write to the District Council that Pastor Jane Angieski is ready for a senior position, oh, yes, I certainly will."

Okay, my attention was officially grabbed, even if I back pedaled a bit. "I have no experience organizing dances, Pastor. Mind you, I don't even dance well." Fresh in my mind was being in an unflattering, flattening position over the top of a local journalist. It still made my cheeks burn down to my toes.

"Listen, Jane, you started a church in one of the roughest districts in L.A., and it's still got a chance to survive. I was chatting to one of the directors with the District Council about you the other day, and they were telling me how that strip mall church has changed that entire community." He stood up and walked around to my chair.

I could feel the nastiness ooze from that remark and knew I was being used. He knew about all me and knew my fears. The smile on his lips told me I could not say no if I wanted to stay in the ministry. He was a bully. His way or the highway, and I'd been recruited to captain the *Good Ship Lollipop* with the fate of the youth center steering its course. God willing, we'd dock safely, but I had a boatload of doubt. Shaking off the cruising metaphors, I gathered my purse and exited his office before agreeing to anything else.

My intentions were good, God knew. Yet would what had happened at Grace Valley and the drug enforcement unit always hang over my pretty little head like a noose? I had done the right thing. Okay, posing for snapshots in my hooker ensemble for the *L.A. Times* and letting my YouTube interview go viral might not have been swift. Can't dwell on hindsight, can you?

Then I complained to the High and Mighty: "Sure, along with *Dancing with the Stars*, there was VBS starting Monday, my grandfather's midlife crisis complete with cowboy boots and a red muscle-car convertible and then, oh, yes, Harmony and her little dog, too, camped at my condo. I don't need anything more."

God didn't answer, if you're wondering.

Multi-worrying had become my way of life. Not a problem for a woman like me? Give me a break.

*

Like Linda Blair in *The Exorcist*, I made it to my cubbyhole. I flipped through the gold-trimmed budget info folders Pastor Bob had handed me at the door. It was a dizzy array of cost-analysis schedules, spreadsheets, diagrams, pie charts, flowcharts, and mission statements. What if I'd been five minutes later, or what if I'd sipped my Starbucks at the shop rather than bringing it here to the church offices when he was finishing up with the pep rally? What if I wasn't around to hear that big fat idea? Would he have found some other flunky who had the District Council breathing down her neck?

I could go along with Ab Normal's idea to turn a teen event into *Casino Royale*, or I could squeal to the District Council. Guess who'd they side with? Yeah, that was a no-brainer after my last encounter with the DC.

"Ah, shucks," I muttered. I'd left my iced coffee in the pastor's office. His door was ajar. His voice boomed, whined, and crackled.

I could see his back, turned away from the door, and the phone at his ear. He stood up and I listened. I wanted to hear what I was headed for. That's my excuse and I'm sticking with it.

"Listen, man, you'll have it. You can bet on that. Yeah, you've heard that before. Give me a chance, will you? Can't you trust me on this? Just once more, I'm good for it."

Then he turned. Our eyes met, but his were bulging. His mouth stopped mid-word. I've never seen a human with that color red on his face as he spurted into the phone, "Yes, yes, why, of course. Amen and good talking with you. Of course, I'll get back to you on that matter. Yes, within the hour. You'll have to excuse me, as one of my pastoral staff is here." He slapped the phone in the cradle and ground out between his teeth. "What is it now, Jane?"

"Sorry, my coffee. On the floor. Next to your desk." I hustled in, grabbed the cup, and stubbed my toe on the chair and kept the "ouch" to myself. Closing his door firmly, I skedaddled.

Now, rather than look at the folder for Dancing with Vegas Stars that I was about to hurdle myself into, my brain zoomed back to another conversation. What had caused Pastor Bob to change from Bombastic Bob to Benevolent Bob from just my presence at the door?

The desk phone was ringing when I entered the cubicle laughingly called an office. "Jane Angieski here."

"Madam Pastor Jane?"

"Petra, how are you? Did Carl survive my attack to his manliness? Not that I'm saying you've personally inspected it or anything, but not that there's anything wrong with that if, well, um, did you rush him to the ER?"

Long silence. "Madam Pastor, I do not understand."

"Oh, nothing. Call me Jane. Everyone does and especially my friends. I certainly hope after our first introduction and embarrassing myself with the situation between you and my grandfather and flinging my petite self out of your arms and into those of your squeeze that we can be friends."

"I am sorry, ah, Jane. What does squeeze mean?"

"Carl. Um, it's slang." Speak first and reason second is a way of life for me, a burden most of the time, but it does make life with my mouth stimulating.

"Carl squeezes nicely, yes. But you said I could call you. Henry said you can listen well. He said you went to special school to learn listening. I cannot imagine someone kind like you to need teaching to listen, but he says so. I believe Henry. He is a good man."

"That he is, Petra. I did go to school and have become a good listener. Come here by the church and talk, or meet someplace?"

"I am Catholic," she whispered.

"Everyone is welcome here, Petra, and that includes Catholics. Would you be more comfortable, my dear, at Starbucks near the recreation department? Say about eleven?" I geared up for another icy iced coffee, with relish, mind you.

"It is just blocks for me but you must drive here. Thank you for your kindness. It is a big trouble that is troubling my heart, Madam Jane. Yes, Jane. No one can solve this, I am thinking, but Henry said you are a good solver."

As we started our positively polite good-byes, an itsy bitsy, and absolutely brilliant idea came to mind. It was scrumptious, and smacking my lips I tried to think it through. Once I listened to Petra's troubles, doing my best to help fix them, it would be a natural segue to get her to help with the fundraising extravaganza, wouldn't it? Besides, she could dance and help our teens to learn some of the finer points of grace and poise.

I tossed the now painfully depleted cup in the trash, grabbed my purse and keys, and headed to the car. The A/C would probably just be making the seat possible to sit on by the time I met Petra, but if whatever was troubling her had forced her to call me, a stranger and a lethal weapon on the dance floor, it was significant. I buckled up, settled my scorched buttocks on the burning seat and headed to the coffee house.

Pulling into the Starbucks near the rec center, it all dawned on me why she'd called. It was as if God had opened the heavens and an angel was speaking, or sort of. I didn't truly think that, but it could have happened that way.

Suddenly, I understood that Petra was a slave. She was addicted to something. Drugs, diet pills, something. "As skinny as she is, it's taking a toll," I said out loud. Why hadn't I brought the resource directory from my office? Vegas had scores of self-help programs because, well, many need help and are smart enough to ask. This was not a town where folks hid from excesses or weaknesses, I considered as I trotted inside. I breathed in the fragrance of fresh-ground beans, stirred not shaken, with a hint of whipped cream. I'd arrived first, vowing I would help the woman, get her into a program, and rid her body and spirit of the demon controlling her. The Prophet Moses and I shared spiritual beliefs and a love for flowing robes. He brought the chosen people into the desert. I thought perhaps I had been brought to the Nevada desert for just this reason. I didn't think this through enough but that didn't stop me from moving with absolute surety. Being personally convinced of anything, when that belief is based on hunches, can be treacherous, and I lead a hazardous life.

B-I-G time. I was so far off the mark the mark was in another solar system. Mind you, that didn't stop me from putting my foot, once again, in my mouth but I'm getting ahead of the story again.

Chapter 4

Starbucks snacks nestled, snuggled, and called me from the display case, like some siren's song. Hypnotic. I fought hard. Muffin or cookie? Cookie or muffin? Is one better for the buns? The cookies were the size of dinner platters, the muffins replicated soup pots. They haunted me, consuming my soul, and I coveted the crunch I'd feel in one tiny munch.

I tore napkins into shreds, counted backward from a hundred, repeated the mantras I'd learned in a weight-loss program. "A minute on the lips, a month on the hips." "Hippy today, skinnier tomorrow." "A donut in the hand should stay in the hand." "Fat is an F-word." "Cookie crumbs count."

Yes, I do have those all memorized. As I got to the last, the desserts stopped whispering and started using a sugary bull horn. "Jane, come and get us, you want us, come take us out of the case. We love you." I was a zombie. They controlled me with their menacing powers. I used the shreds of the napkins to blot drool from my chin, and I was just getting up from the café table when Petra came in.

I hugged her skinny little shoulders with all my might. I think she thought I was relieved to see her. I was really relieved that I hadn't eaten my way through the Starbucks biscotti, cookie, and muffin selection. I didn't tell her that. "Can I get you a chocolate-covered macadamia nut cookie?" Yeah, I'd buy one for her and four for me.

"No thank you, nothing, or perhaps something to drink." She looked like a blast of desert air would knock her on her knickers, so I made a decision to sacrifice my own caloric intake and get us both something sugary. I've always thought of others first.

With my iced coffee and her iced tea, and two huge cookies between us, I began with a bite and small talk. Okay, it was the weather again. Some delicate conversations work best in privacy. Others need crowds, or a dark room. I had no clue which this would be. I knew one thing. The sooner I got her into a twelve-step program for her addiction, the sooner I could organize VBS and figure out how to put on a rootin'-tootin' "Dancing with the Vegas Stars" event that would generate about two million dollars for the new youth center.

I had all the time in the world as long as it was done by Monday. Then, to put icing on this can of worms, I remembered stuffy official from the District Council was coming to visit me on Friday, maybe even to hand me new walking papers.

Could the future get rosier? That's a foolish question.

I stared at the cookies, willing my hand to not hover over hers. If it was food she was avoiding, then maybe the cookie would bring that topic up more quickly. If not, well, I could always squeeze in another one.

"Thanks for seeing me, Jane. I have sadness, I mean, much sadness, and my heart is heavy."

"Would you like to pray about it?" I placed my icy plastic cup down and reached over to take her hand, straight over the cookies, mind you, without hesitation. She snapped her hand back as if I were a maniac preacher waving and shouting, "The End is Here."

"No, I mean, yes, prayer is good. But I need advice from someone who knows America."

"Wait. You need a travel guide? Or about Americans? Americans are loud, pushy, and do awkward things such as heave ourselves on top of each other during a dance class. If you want travel information, there's a Barnes and Noble around the corner; we can get a book. I have my favorite apps, too."

Petra shoved a long strand of hair behind her ear, looking like Reese Witherspoon, pointy chin and all. I wanted to hate her, and

I would have, if she weren't so stinkin' sweet.

"I love America." She sighed.

"Good, that's very good, but what does loving America have to do with your addiction? Wait, it's gambling, isn't it? There's so much around nowadays, and let's not even talk about who has seen what or whom doing what to whom on the Internet, or so I've been told." Okay, I blurted this but it didn't stop my mouth. "It's so easy to lose everything, including self respect. Is that what America has done to you?" Now I did grab her hand and began to pat it.

She was staring at me. Did I see horror? Oh, how could I be such a dolt? It wasn't gambling. She shook her head, and golden curls swung from side to side as I leaped straight in. "It's sex? Or is it porn? You are not the first to be addicted to having sex with many people, men and women, and in various locations." Although, trust me, leading this celibate life, I haven't gotten in any primary research in that area since Collin died. I watch TV and hey, I'm a preacher. I know stuff.

"Sex? Pornography? Oh, I do not know what to say."

"You can tell me. I can be trusted," I whispered, and her cheeks got the color of cotton candy. So, hey, I plunged on. "Have you seen a counselor? Are you, um, in any situations that others can see, such as in movies, on YouTube, or the Internet?"

She jumped up so quickly the café chair tipped back and slammed to the floor. "I do not know what you're talking about, but people in Poland warned me that perversion was everywhere. You perverts would try to take advantage of me."

I grabbed her arm, and I believe it was only because Starbucks was suddenly jam-packed that she didn't get away. "Wait, please. This is all wrong, stop." I had a tighter hold on her than I thought, or maybe it was the linebacker from UNLV who blocked her escape, but I quickly went on. "This isn't about any addiction, is it?" My head ached. I grabbed a cookie for strength. I ate it in two bites. Sugar has medicinal effects, or so some society somewhere must believe.

"No. It certainly is not."

I patted the linebacker on a biceps as big as my leg because he was still hovering over Petra, paralyzed by her beauty and petite form. Or maybe it was that he thought he'd seen her in a magazine, with staples in her middle. I talked fast, to Petra. "I don't know what got into me. Forgive me, Petra. You came to talk with me. Can we start over?" I attempted to withdraw my feet from my mouth as she sighed and sat down on the chair offered by her hulking admirer.

I looked up at the football player, handed him a five-dollar bill, and said, "Get something lip-smacking at the counter, pal. She's not available."

"But, lady, you said she was a porn star." His eyes glassed over and his nostrils flared. "Can I have her autograph?"

"Mistake, my friend. Just kidding. We always tease so much. You know how women are. Oh ho ho ho," I tried and then pulled Petra back to the table.

"No, Jane, it's me. I am hard to understand, I know. But you speak no Polish, is that correct?"

"Yes, that is correct, honey. I can understand a lot of it. My grandparents spoke the language fluently, but I've never learned the mechanics."

"Mechanics? You want to talk about cars?"

"Mechanics, like grammar and syntax."

"Yes, I see, yes, we will speak English, but forgive me if I am awkward." She nibbled the cookie; the bite was the size an ant would have taken. "I studied English in Warsaw."

I took a bite of the cookie let saliva melt the chocolate sweetness. The rush of cocoa and sugar streamed into my veins, so when Petra said, "I am an orphan," I was ready with: "Oh, I am sorry. Did you ever know your parents? Do your birth parents, your biological ones, the ones who created you, live in the States?"

Her perfect forehead crinkled. "No, they gave me up for adoption when I was born. I have a letter." She produced it from her purse. The edges were soft and the color was like almonds. Slowly, Petra unfolded it on the tabletop, smoothed it, and caressed it with her hand. I couldn't read a word of it. It was in Polish. We looked at each other. "It says that they loved me but wanted the nuns at the orphanage to give me to parents who could take care of me. They had no jobs. They barely had food for themselves or their other babies. They could not feed me and could not raise me."

"So the nuns found a good home for you?" I made my voice bright and chipper. It was disgusting.

Her teeth were straight. Her complexion was like a dewy morn, all softy and creamy. Please don't make me go on. You get the picture, don't you? Since she worked in the casino, even at the coffee cart, she had to be in her twenties.

"A happy home? No." The words were spoken in a huff. We were in a bubble of our own, created by the words she'd said.

The din of Starbucks customers and the grinding of the coffee machines continued. "They did not care for me. I was bad."

"You? I can't imagine anything you could do, especially as a child, to be bad." She looked rather like an angel on a Christmas tree, but then again, some angels have dark sides.

She placed the cookie in the center of the paper napkin, taking each corner, folding it toward the cookie. "I am, what is the word, retarded. That is it. I couldn't move or sit up like the other babies. No one wanted to adopt a baby who was not healthy."

Unless there was something terribly amiss under that postage-stamp-white T-shirt that exposed her middle, or the hip-hugging Capri pants, with a neon green and navy sash tied around itty-bitty hips, I couldn't imagine this woman to be disabled. I'd seen her dance like a feather, too.

"You look normal to me."

"I have a terrible secret." She inhaled deeply.

Oh, now, Lord, here it comes. What could be worse than pornography or gambling? Murder. *She's killed someone and is asking for forgiveness. No wonder she's pale, no wonder she was crying last evening.* I held the edge of the table.

"The nuns sent me, when I was a baby, to a special place for stupid and sick little ones. I was not good enough for Polish couples to adopt. Everyone wants fat and healthy babies. They want rosy cheeks and plump arms. I was undersized and I cried much."

"You were filled with hate from so much sadness. I see. You were hurt and sick and you retaliated? Did you murder a nun?" I gulped, but someone had to say it.

"Killed a nun? No, Jane. I've killed no one. May I continue?" Her blue eyes widened but she didn't stop.

Have you ever wanted to pick up your hand, make a fist, and hit yourself in the nose? No, I hadn't, either, until that very second. Lord knows why she tolerated my false accusations, but the only reason had to be the blessed language barrier. I sighed and swore to keep my lips zipped until she finished her story.

Since Petra didn't have to interrupt me again, she continued, "I know now that the institution kept me in a crib, and it was from there that I was sold to another organization."

"Sold. You were sold?" She had to mean something else. Her English, she'd said, wasn't good. "I'm confused. Didn't you just get transferred, perhaps to a special school?"

"I know what that means. I was sold. Like a car or a dog. Please, I do not want to be disrespectful to Americans, Jane. If you do not want me to say this, if you feel I am wicked, please stop me."

A vein pulsated in her swanish neck, her lips trembled, and it was clear from the pain in her eyes that whatever she was thinking, it broke her heart. I'd been with troubled people but she was a poster girl for desperation. Besides, whatever she was about to say could not be that bad. Come on. This was America.

I'd been a preacher for six years and before that taught at a university. If there was anything appalling or ghastly bad in life that I had not heard, it would have been news to me. "Go on," I said, because if I went on, the Lord only knew where the conversation would head, most likely to a place called Dead Wrong.

"I think you know these people, awful organization they come from but look good. Las Vegas thinks they're a good company."

"Who are they? What does this have to do with you? Tell me why you said you were sold."

Once more, she squished her lips into a thin line. Her cookie sat there untouched until she unfolded the corners of the napkin and nibbled one tiny chocolate chip in the time I would have gobbled the entire thing plus a half dozen more. "When the government doctor said I would always be sick, and the orphanage closed, I went to another institution. In English, it is called Child's Play Baby Home. I do not know why I lived. Now is the bad part. I have some bad things to say about Americans."

I can only claim that the coffee and sugar finally kicked in because my vow of not jumping to any more conclusions worked. "What does this have to do with Las Vegas?"

"In America, everything can be bought for a price."

"Yes?"

"Here in America, here in Las Vegas, is the company that buys and sells babies and children."

"Buying and selling children?" I pushed my backside against the back of the chair, lest I fall off with whatever the explanation was to be.

"Yes, they buy children and sell them. It is not adoption. This is a business. Like selling cattle. Or here in America, like fancy show dog or even furniture. You see, Child's Play Baby Home does not have doctors or nurses to care for infants. The company buys the babies and brings them to the United States of America. This is good, right? No, this is not good. It is bad." When she said "bad," it looked like she was going to spit, and I ducked to the side.

Okay, I was lost. It was sorrowful that the Child's Play Baby Home didn't have care for special-needs children, but around the world in developing nations and those with limited medical care, these things happened. From what I'd just heard, the Child's Play Baby Home creating adoption arrangements with couples here in the United States seemed to be a good thing. "How can this be bad if there are shortages of qualified medical people?"

"Child's Play Baby Home sells babies to a company. These are sick babies. Hopeless babies, some without arms and legs, too. This company sells them to mothers and fathers who think they are paying for perfect, fat babies with fat cheeks and blond hair."

"It's unfair, Petra, but it's true. Most adoptive parents want perfect babies." I thought of how Gramps had told me that when he found my father, an emaciated ten-year-old, he grilled everyone connected with the Army barracks, but no one would take claim to the child. Until the US soldiers came to Vietnam, bi-racial kids like Dad survived by feeding with the neighborhood dogs, running drugs, or prostitution.

"That I do understand, but from Child's Play Baby Home they pay for perfect and get sick ones. Most babies cannot sit up, or move, or crawl, or speak. They break the hearts of mommies and daddies and those of the babies, too."

"What happens? Surely something can be done about this company?" I felt a bitter taste in my mouth now, and my stomach squeezed a queasy feeling into my throat. It definitely was not from the coffee; I don't have any problem with multiple cups of Starbucks.

"You have not heard the whole bad story. This buyer and seller of babies is smart, Jane. They tell people that God is on their side. They say God is directing them to give special babies to the people who pay money. All lies. When the parents don't want a child who will only live shortly, they pay to have the company take the baby back. All the time the company knows this will happen since the babies are severely handicapped."

"It's a conditional adoption?" I wouldn't have left my chair for anything. How in the world could this company do that with human lives, knowing the babies were unsuitable for adoption?

"Then they sell the same baby again. Sometimes again and again, all the time the baby is getting sicker. Some die." She looked down into her lap and as if on cue, a solitary tear dropped from her eye and straight into the middle of the cookie.

Petra Stanislaw had been one of these babies, sold time and again.

"What happens if the baby, who may now be a toddler or young child, never finds adoptive parents willing to take on a special needs child?"

"Deserted. The frail die. Some starve on the streets. Others do terrible things to survive. Most learn quickly to steal food."

I didn't expect her to cry. I knew the Polish determination well, and from my endearing buscia, who was soft on the outside and solid steel inside. I had an inkling of what Petra was made of, so when she did, I blubbered myself. She even made crying look like fine art.

She dabbed the single tear spot, dotted her eyes, touched her nose with a tissue, and said, "I was left alone when I couldn't be sold again, watching the car drive off. I sat on a park bench. I was too frightened to cry. I was returned five times. Each time, the adoptive parents would take me on a conditional lease, but the new parents always thought I was too difficult to handle. The company dumped me one summer evening. I got a new pair of shoes and a few American dollars. It was on Ellis Island. So you know the place? Many Polish immigrants know it. I was eight. No adoptive parents would ever want me. That I was told."

We sat in silence. My perfect plan to have Petra lend a hand and her feet with the dance and fundraiser, once I got her into a twelve-step recovery program, evaporated. I've been accused more than once of finding silver linings where none exist, but this time, I couldn't even see where a silver-plated one might be.

"A police officer came toward me. I cowered. I thought he'd hit me. I must have said something in my language because he spoke to me in Polish." She exhaled and continued, "They sent me to a children's jail at first, then a home for runaways. Finally Immigration and Naturalization sent me back to Poland, to an orphanage."

Years ago, I'd been on a mission to Warsaw. It was one of those college trips; a group of us were going to help rebuild a church. On the off days, two others and I went to visit orphanages. Think of a scene from a Dickens novel. Orphans were warehoused, huddled around bowls of oatmeal. That's what we saw. That's what still haunted me. That's why I couldn't let this lie. Here was Petra, alive and educated, somehow having managed to survive the dismal terrors that still troubled my heart.

She dusted a nonexistent crumb from her lip. "I was lucky. The orphanage where I grew up was sponsored by a foreign lady. She made sure I learned and had physical therapy. She gave money for many of to get university degrees. I never found my birth family; records were destroyed. I believe the company wanted to hide all the evidence. I am learning international law at UNLV. But I cannot forget." She straightened her spine. "I will not."

"You shouldn't, Petra. This is abominable, um, awful. Tell me this company was brought to justice. This makes my skin crawl. Drat, if I don't stop the slang, those worry lines on your forehead will need Botox. Skin doesn't crawl, like babies crawl—oh, never mind. We must do something." Um, notice the 'we'?

"I am doing things and I am not afraid. I will revenge the evil that has been done."

The knuckles on her fists were white. I was certain she was up to whatever retribution would stop the horror. While I'm not big on taking over God's duty when he said, "Revenge is mine," I could see her point. Payoff is so bloomin' tempting, even for pastors. "Have you contacted the authorities? The police or the Center for Missing and Exploited Children? The Polish Consulate?"

I thought she'd found a rotten chocolate chip in the nibble of cookie her mouth was so pinched. "They do nothing." She placed her delicate fingers in her lap and locked her jaw.

"Tell me. Who are these criminals?"

"They work for the Philemon Society of America, and the worst is Mrs. Cheney."

"*The* Philemon Society of America? PSA? As in Delta Cheney?"

"They are wicked, Jane. You are shocked because I say cruel things about Americans. These are bad Americans. They hurt children. I will stop them from hurting more."

The ability to delude one's self might be a survival tool, but the view from my mind's eye pointed to something very rotten with the PSA.

*

The morning coffee crowd was replaced by the lunch bunch and then replaced by the after-lunch-grabba-club clan. Near one o'clock we hugged good-bye, and yes, I'd given my word to help. I'm horrified to tell you that I don't remember the drive back to church, but I got there. I didn't realize how shaken I was until I went to the refrigerator in the church kitchen, pulled out a bottle of water and stood there with the door wide open. I thought of Petra's words as she revealed even more details, the starvation, the deprivation and, oh, non-existent sanitation. It was done in a whisper, and the truths poured out of illegal adoptions and human trafficking.

Here's the *Reader's Digest* version of what I learned between my first struggle-for-breath revelation that I'd been small taking with the ring leader all the way to the Eastern European kiss on each cheek when Petra and I parted.

Petra was a sickly child. The reason for her delayed growth was never identified but she did have dyslexia. She graduated with honors from *Uniwersytet Warszawski*, the University of Warsaw. She attempted to stop the PSA in Poland, and when that became impossible, she applied for a master's program in Las Vegas.

"I am here to crumple PSA," she whispered in my ear, and there was no doubt that meant hunting down and stopping Delta Cheney in whatever way it took. If you'd seen her eyes, you'd know it didn't matter whether this was within or outside of the law.

What could I do? Two hours later, in front of an open refrigerator, which was constantly running and no longer cooling, I was clueless. Petra needed a champion. I couldn't even muster closing that heavy white refrigerator door.

So what if the Philemon Society of America was behind immoral orphanages and adoption? But if PSA disposed of kids who weren't adoptable like last year's must-have jeans, that was wrong. A few survived, I had to believe that, but the others? What happened to the ones left to fend for themselves and forced into things I couldn't even mouth the words for? Were the children brought here by PSA and tossed out any better off than those scuttled from the system in Poland when they reached sixteen and no longer thought necessary to protect? Any way I looked at this, it was illegal and immoral. Throw in sinful, too. Visions of starving, half-frozen urchins limped through my mind, pleading for a morsel of food. This stayed in my brain for a nanosecond, and then I imagined the PSA discards found dead with no ID, buried in an unmarked grave, in a city where they'd been deserted.

If the authorities wouldn't listen to Petra, I could ask some questions and maybe get attention for the orphans who were here in the States. I had a contact with the local press, in the cute body of one Carl Lipca, who I'd been in firm and cozy contact with as I'd sat squarely on his middle just hours earlier.

Agreed, I am no stranger to stirring things up, some of them things that hit the front page of the newspaper. But the big pothole of this solution was just down the hall from me, in the senior pastor's office, sitting at the walnut desk, and drinking out of the coffee mug with *I'm the Man's man* emblazoned on it. He and Delta had been chummy and clingy. Now, I'm not one to jump to overly nasty conclusions, just regular ones, but there was *that* look in her eyes telling me to keep my mitts off Pastor Bob if I knew what was good for me. She never had to worry about that. Talk about ick.

Now the ick was about Ab Normal and the implication of human trafficking, even through association.

What was I to do about Pastor Bob's adoration for the leader of PSA, Delta Cheney, if in fact Cheney was as evil as I was led to believe? Wasn't the Cheney woman Pastor Bob's goose that laid the golden egg, his high hope to make money to build our much-needed youth center? If I went to the newspaper, that goose would be cooked, even if Petra's allegations weren't true.

I wouldn't turn my back on Petra and those unspoken cries of help for babies and children I might never know. Would Pastor Bob even give me the time of day if I presented what I'd learned to him confidentially? From what I'd seen of him these last weeks, Pastor Bob wouldn't even listen to Petra's version of the PSA when he had his "cheerleader" Delta Cheney puffing up his ego. He was already counting on the sizable cash donation from PSA.

I spent the next few minutes chilling. I couldn't move from the open refrigerator. I stared at the oversized mayonnaise, gallons of orange juice, refrigerator cookies to bake for VBS the next day, and the bright white interior.

What if I took what I had learned to the police or the district attorney? They'd bust a gut. It was hearsay. I had nothing to back it up but the eyes of a young woman and a letter in Polish, which could have been a grocery list for all I knew. I would have called Cowboy Henry, aka my grandfather, but he was out of touch with reality and probably doing the tango with the kitchen mop. I could call Vera, but a tiny voice inside asked what her loyalties were. Sometimes people who seem to be great listeners are the biggest gossipmongers, and she seemed to know a lot of tidbits about the congregation. Could I call the District Council with a half-baked crime saga? They'd say Pastor Jane Angieski was being the certified buttinski they already knew I was. Would it add fuel to the fire come Friday and my special appointment with their representative?

I prayed. Do you ever have those times when you're praying when you suddenly realize that perhaps God has even more important things on His plate than what you're dishing, like keeping the solar system in place and making sure gravity keeps things stuck? When I got no immediate response from my Boss, I tossed back a cola and jumped when my cell rang. Since He doesn't ever call, I knew He'd put one of His servants on the line for me.

The big, squawky laugh that greeted me was none other than my pal Geraldine. The woman never did small talk, but jumped straight in as if we were in the middle of the conversation.

"You been fried yet? That heat's bad for the skin, girl. Can't you get the District Council to transfer you to Washington, D.C., so we could pal around together? Or have you ruffled so many feathers that you've been exiled like some ol' Bible prophet? You getting punished? There's nothing wrong in the world with Las Vegas—some of my favorite quarters have stayed there in their slot machines—but it's hot as you-know-what. Maybe that's the District Council's way of telling you to shape up or you'll have even more heat from them?"

"Do you ever just breathe? Did you call to talk at me or with me?"

"You, girl, you. Just had a feeling I needed to call you."

I'd never ever been so happy to hear the blasting, foghorn voice of the senior senator from California in my entire life. I loved Gerry, even though when she gushed about Gramps it got a bit too personal. She was gaga for him and he hardly knew she existed, or so it seemed.

"What's up? But first, how's that rascal of a grandfather, my dearest snuggle face?"

I am not a pint-sized person, which I know you know. But compared to Gerry, I'm petite. She was a plus-size model in the days when it wasn't acceptable to be a woman of size. She made it okay to be big and beautiful with a line of clothing for generous women, a company where she'd been the CEO. Now she used her ample measurements to influence fellow lawmakers in D.C.—at least that's what she'd told me time and again.

"I'm between a stone wall and San Quentin." I sighed.

"You're going to prison?"

"Might as well. And don't you dare put me on hold, even if the president is calling."

"I'm sitting on my balcony, overlooking Georgetown, sipping some bubbly water with a slice of lime. I'm not alone. Come on, guess who's here."

I'm not keen on games, unless it's something like kiss and not tell. Wait, that's another story. I bit. "Donald Trump? Brad Pitt?"

"How did you know? This is frightening," she shrieked. Okay, it was more than a shriek. A shriek is when you see a mouse charging at you with twenty of its chums. It was a scream like you might heard or make when you're sipping a cola and munching peanuts as your plane plunges a thousand feet and the oxygen bag bounces off your forehead.

Chapter 5

I screeched back.

Gerry was glued to the inner circles of Manhattan, Boston, D.C., and the West Coast with the high, mighty, and well-connected, but was she entertaining *the* Brad Pitt or Mr. Trump of "You're Fired" fame?

"Got ya." She gagged with laughter. I could imagine the drama queen's head was thrown back and big brown eyes were watering. "I got you, I got you. I have my new best friend with me. Meet Miss Louella Antoinette English." The phone went quiet, and I swear there was a sniffing sound. "Louella, I'd like you to meet Jane. Say arf arf, or do they say bark? Hers sounds like buff, buff, buff. Besides, I never know with Yorkies. Except when they growl."

"I do not believe this. You bought a canine accessory? You're the normal one in our friendship. What's happened to you?" I was nauseated thinking of how she'd drag a pooch of minimal poundage around with her, probably on a rhinestone leash and wearing matching outfits. I shivered.

"Yeah, it's that bad. I am bone weary of being alone." She was whispering, which to regular people would be an "outside" voice. "I needed something alive when I got home, something to snuggle. Adoption was the answer. I'm not going to tell Lulu, that's her nickname, until she's older that she's adopted. I'll figure out the right time. When she's old enough to handle it." She made some kind of clucking sound. Then said in a normal voice, which meant booming, "Besides, Jane, your grandfather left me high and dry. Probably out with some woman half his age."

"Try a quarter of his age." I didn't mean to make her scream.

"That hurt, Jane. You are not funny. He isn't returning my

phone calls and the e-mail isn't accepted; it keeps bouncing back when I put a return receipt request on it. I sent a certified letter to him a week ago, and he still hasn't retrieved it from the post office. I even had the local Carlsbad city police stop by his house. He refused to answer the door. I know he's alive and kicking someplace, Jane, because you would let me know if he wasn't. Would you?"

"I would."

"So I found a replacement."

"A replacement? Are we talking about a barking trinket?"

"She is challenged in the size, okay, but that doesn't mean she's not a full blooded D-O-G."

Did she actually think that midget ragamuffin could spell or be offended? "Can we talk about my problem now?"

"Still *my* turn." She took a deep breath and said, "I was going to get a male dog, call him Henry. Didn't want to have to find a doggie psychiatrist after I'd had him neutered. So Lulu is now my entire life, and your grandfather can take a flying leap and stick his head where. . ."

I didn't give her the opportunity to continue what he could do after he took a flying leap or any head sticking, but yelled into the receiver. "Stop. It's my turn." Then I told her about Gramps' crises, the emotional, physical, and spiritual ones. I told her exactly where he was and what he was doing.

The weirdest thing happened next. If I hadn't been part of the conversation, I wouldn't have believed it. Gerry was blubbering. I felt like dirt. "Oh, sweetie, shouldn't have told you everything straight out like that."

"Jane, I figured you knew." Snorting and nose blowing followed. "I love your gramps even if I'm wrong for him. Your little grandmother, who had a disquieting resemblance to June Cleaver, was his world. Not to take her place, but I thought maybe I could become his wife anyway. I'm too loud, I'm too aggressive, and I'm fat. Boy, am I fat. And keep getting fatter."

"Put a sock in it, you are perfect." I meant that.

"Yeah, then why doesn't the man know it?"

"Just shut up for a second and let me tell you why I need you to put on your super-sleuth tights and cape and scrounge information." I spilled my tales of woe, including Harmony, the dog Tuffy, and Pastor Bob's admiration for a woman who was selling "guarantees" and policies to return illegal and immoral adoptions from inhumane orphanages in Poland.

"I thought serving on the energy commission was vexing." She blew her nose, and then made some goo-goo sounds. "I don't know anyone, at least I don't think I know anyone, in the World Health Organization or Mental Disability Rights International, but my name isn't Senator Geraldine English, commonly called 'That Big Ol' Trouble Maker on Capitol Hill' for nothing. Give me a few days, honey, and I'll see what I can dig up. You know this gal likes nothin' better than a good shake-up, especially when too many fat-cat bureaucrats are up for reelection. We're talking fun on Capitol Hill. It sounds like Cheney is in the baby business for the wrong reasons. I'm adopted, you know."

"No, you are?"

"Mom told me when I was about three how I'd been chosen. I liked that, because she'd chosen Dad. Never knew what happened to the birth parents. To me the chosen ones were the real thing. All twelve of us were chosen kids; being adopted was the norm at home. My story can't come close to some hoochie-coochie beauty from Poland, who is probably as big as a dime, in today's money."

"Cool your jets."

"You don't know Henry's real feelings, girl, or you wouldn't be in such a tizzy."

Was my grandfather ever going to return to himself, or would he be lost in cowboy heaven forever? "What should I do, Gerry?"

"You're asking me? Is this about your senior pastor's adoration for a crook that is managing to swindle unsuspecting women and men and hurt babies? Possibly being an accomplice to child endangerment and manslaughter? And human trafficking? Or about the child who is living with you, and her little dog, too, who is probably anorexic or maybe was abused in the foster home? Or a little matter of the Dancing with the Vegas Stars gala event you're suddenly heading up? Wait, what about the District Council's visit?"

"Friday. They're coming to meet with me privately." The sentence came out with a squeak at the end. "I love you, Gerry, but you we need action, not tears."

"Put a lid on it. That was Lulu. She doesn't like whiners. I told you'd I'd do some checking on the crook, the Cheney woman. Gotta go. Lulu just did go and I have to get paper towels."

I sat with the phone cradled in my hand for long enough to numb my bum, then waddled to my cubbyhole office, where I sat for the longest time, maybe ten minutes, without thinking of chocolate or coffee. I snapped my laptop shut, slipped it in my briefcase and headed for Starbucks.

Once more that day, I stood in line, drooling over which chocolate chip muffins behind the glass showcase would come to Mama. I heard my name, and Carl Lipca touched my forearm. Like in some stupid commercial, his eyes sparkled as brightly as his professionally whitened teeth.

He didn't jump back or throw the little couple in front of him to save his manliness from a Pastor Jane Angieski attack. Could I have been mistaken, and he didn't really have a look of lusty longing for one Petra Stanislaw? He winked and I inhaled, then he rubbed that same eye. Whatever was I thinking? Was I thinking? That doesn't require a response, thank you very much.

"Small world." He chuckled. Our eyes met because we were the same height. "Been meaning to call you."

"Me?" Did that really come out as desperate as it sounded?

There's never a way to make sure, especially after the fact.

"Yeah, you know I'm with the *Journal*, the Vegas paper." I saw his mouth move, but I wasn't listening. I was with a futile attempt to get grown-up and professional thoughts back in their upright and locked position, rather than thinking arm candy and lustful fantasies.

He spoke straight over the tiny twosome between us. They didn't even pretend they weren't listening; the woman actually craned her neck forward as Carl said, "Let me be frank."

"Carl's a really nice name," I responded, still in my fantasy world of a drive-through wedding chapel with Carl the Cutie, since I'd instantly moved past arm candy to "I take thee for my lawful husband." Caffeine deprivation was the only thing I could blame. I shrugged, returning to earth.

"No, I want to be frank about why I wanted to talk with you."

"Oh." Nix the wedding. Glad I wasn't mentally picking out what to include in my bridal registry.

He smiled at the husband and wife. Then said, "I'm doing an article on Cheney, and I heard from a viable source your church and Pastor Bob Normal were darned cozy with her. What's the story on that?"

I ordered a jumbo-sized coffee and a jumbo-sized chocolate chip chocolate muffin. I needed fuel if I was going to get VBS going and solve eight or ten other problems that had entered my sheltered little world. Now I was going to be asked about Cheney.

"Ask Pastor Bob. You know I've only been on staff a few weeks, taking over for the other youth pastor while she's on maternity leave."

"I did a Google search on you because something was whispering to me when you were introduced. I mentioned it when we met, I think, but then I did some more digging." He slipped a twenty on the counter and paid for my stuff and the coffees for the couple between us, too. Then he grabbed an espresso and motioned me to a table.

A smart, normal woman might have skedaddled at that, but I wondered what he knew about the Cheney woman and PSA. Okay, I'll tell the whole truth and nothing but it. Carl was a nice accessory with my coffee, and a girl can pretend.

I took a mega bite of muffin and mumbled, "You know Delta?"

"Not well." He slugged back a good measure of scalding java without a flinch.

"But you want to get to know her better?" Cat and mouse had begun.

"Yes, I do. How about you? What do you know of her?"

I sipped the Brazilian brew of the day. "I'm just filling in, you know." I took another sip and added, "She's respected here in Vegas, right?"

"Depends who you ask." He took out a notebook and jotted something I couldn't see, then held it in a way that concealed the writing. "Who should I ask?" He frowned. "Your minister seems to know her well."

"My minister? Pastor Bob? Why?" I knew my foot was jiggling beneath the table at the same beat as my pulse, which was far too fast. "Lots of people like her and yes, Pastor Bob seems to be part of her fan club." Better jiggling the foot on the floor than in my mouth.

"Jane," he said and again touched my forearm. The fingers were cold. This wasn't a sensual caress, but a way of telling me he was concerned. Or I could have been way off base, or I was being played as a fool. The votes came in that it was the last on the list. "Yes?" I pulled my arm away. I could feel his fingers on me and while I didn't hate it, I was not naïve. People in all walks of life, especially journalists, use whatever talents they have to get information or to get something. Maybe this was the beginning of flirting with little old me to get whatever real facts and assorted info I had on Cheney, which was nil, in order to do whatever journalists and writers did with tidbits that could be turned into innuendos. Even rumors make good stories. Hey, look at TMZ.

"Can we talk off the record?"

"I'm a minister, Carl. I'm sworn to keep all my conversations that do not do any bodily or emotional harm to anyone off the record. So shoot."

"I'm curious about this."

"What is 'this'?" Was "this" something that involved my senior pastor? He might have too many irons in the fire, which meant that he delegated a lot, even stuff that shouldn't be, especially since I was to "captain" the dance and had only one day, excluding the weekend, to put together Vacation Bible School. But basically, everyone seemed to think Pastor Bob was an okay guy.

"You already know." He looked at me and then down at the table.

If I were older I would have attributed the heat on my cheeks to a hot flash, or if I were younger, to girly mortification. Now I just squirmed and felt warm. "I do?" Then it dawned on me as I remember the lustful longing look Petra had given him at that dance class. She had feelings for him. Serious ones. Was she somehow using him, with her womanly charms, to find out about the PSA's work or even to muddy the PSA's reputation if a respected journalist did a story on the organization? Had she told Carl what she'd told me? How naïve to think I'd been her only confidant. Could he know about the scandal, pondering if breaking this story would get him a Pulitzer for scooping the crime story of the decade? Or snuggled in the arms of his ladylove?

"So you know why Petra is here in Vegas and her link with PSA? How she's vowed to ruin the organization?" I said, watching his eyes become squinty slits, then get bigger. And bigger. Then his mouth opened. There should have been recognition in his mannerisms, rather than shock just hanging there. I stopped breathing. I don't know how you feel about the Rapture, but at that second I wanted it. Then. Right then.

"Actually," he said, and I could almost see him willing his hands to be steady as he brought out his notebook again and inched his chair closer to mine. "What I wanted to talk to you about can wait now."

"What?" My fingers covered my lips, covering the trembling. "Tell me what you wanted to talk about," I managed, with a demand that came in a whisper.

"It's. . .well, it doesn't matter now. Okay, I heard that you were heading up the 'Dancing with Vegas Stars' and I was assigned to do some goody-two-shoes feature on charities." His knuckles were white, the only giveaway to any person with eyes that I'd just stepped too deep into you-know-what.

"Oh." I was attempting to think fast. Never my forte.

He took a slug of the muck at the bottom of his cup. "Sure, I heard the rumors that the faith-based service might be involved in money-back guaranteed adoptions. What does the Cheney woman have to do with this? It's the national level PSA, isn't it?" Now he was whispering, but the words hurt my ears.

"Wasn't it in the paper today?" I looked around; we were nearly alone. The baristas were busy flirting, and the few other customers were on their cells.

"Nothing on this. Tell me why Petra is involved." His hand was on my bare forearm, clamped on. We both looked at it and then at each other.

"Then it has to be the TV news? Terrible things going on in our world." My voice came out in a squeaking flutter.

"Not on the news." Then he released my arm, exhaled, and put his face in his hands. I saw him sigh, a ragged one.

I couldn't even reach for the coffee. Everything stopped. The secrets Petra had confided in me had now been blurted to a newspaper reporter, albeit the man with whom she was smitten.

"I thought there was more. Thought there was a real reason," he said in a whisper, as if he were talking to himself. He seemed to be trying to smile, but the corners of his mouth pulled down.

"What real reason?"

"Petra doesn't trust me. She's involved. She's kept this whole thing from me because she does not have faith me." He looked straight ahead. "I know she's stunning, smart, and worldly. I'm the guy who thinks a good time is a six-pack of beer, pretzels, and onion dip along with a football game. When I'm wild I get pizza delivered. She likes the opera and ballet. She knows about books and goes to lectures. For me, camping is a vacation. I worked three jobs to get through college, a state college, on a low-income loan, and only made it because, oh, man, I've tried to live this down. I'm a halfway decent bowler. Imagine going to college on a bowling scholarship. That's below any geek status. She didn't have to come right out and shout that she doesn't trust me. She asked for your help, didn't she? What's the Bible say about actions speaking louder than words? Or is that Bruce Springsteen?"

"I offered to help Petra."

He grabbed my arm again. I'd have to make a mental engraving to keep it away from him, and why, oh, why didn't eligible men want to grab my arm or all of me, instead of those who were distraught.

"Listen, Pastor Jane. Tell me the truth. You're a minister, you don't lie, right? You wouldn't lie to cover stuff up, would you?"

I wanted to plead temporary insanity, be dragged away muttering the ingredients to banana nut bread, because I'd just spilled the beans and the goo was so thick, it oozed into my lap. I blinked and I was still in Starbucks. "What do you need to know?"

"She's using me, isn't she? Digging for info on the PSA? Getting me to snoop? Hey, don't get me wrong, Jane, I'd do it if I thought that there was dirt to dig on Cheney or the adoptions weren't legit. But there's nothing I have seen. Oh, you don't need to say it. Petra's just using me. It's true, I can see it in your eyes. What an easy con I've been."

"Carl, don't be a brainless twit."

"Could I be more of a jerk than I already am?" He slapped a hand on the table. "Petra was the first woman to ever look at me like she does. I'm a dork. I fall over myself when I'm with women unless I've got this dumb reporter's notebook in my hands. You want to know what's ironic? The first time I felt like this in my whole stinking life, and I had to do it with someone who saw me as a big fat sucker. I'm usually the one who uses women, but forget that. Petra flirted and I gobbled it up. Just so I'd look into the PSA."

He started to get up, but no way was I going to let him go.

"Stop it. Drop it. Listen up." I pulled his arm this time. Good and hard, too. He wasn't leaving Starbucks until we straightened this out. "I've seen her looking at you when you were not looking at her. You can't fake that gooey glow in her eyes. The girl likes you. So stop being a jerk on this, will you?"

"You think she does?" A glint? Anticipation to know? I had to fuel it.

"I know that look, my friend. I don't know everything that happened to Petra or what the entire situation is—I just learned about it—but let me tell you something. I know love. I've been in love. I've seen it on the faces of couples I've married, seen it on the faces of those who are afraid to take that step. You cannot pretend to be in love, or the beginnings of it, as Petra is with you."

"Why didn't she tell me? Why did she tell *you*?" He stood, looked me up and down and not in a good way, and you know what I mean. I thought he was going to try to leave, but then he shook his head. "Get you more coffee? Anything? You ate that muffin pretty quick."

I shook my head. Of course I ate it in three bites. Which made sense at the time since with a muffin in my mouth there was less chance of me saying more stupid things. "I'm a minister. People trust me. Here's a news flash, Mr. Reporter. Why don't you see if she'll tell you her whole story, everything she told me? Don't blurt it out over the cell phone or in a public place, but just the two of you alone. Talking. Ask her why she's really here in Las Vegas."

"Will this work?"

"Carl, were you raised by male wolves? Women talk, in case you were, about everything, including feelings, and if she's to be special, you need to understand what she's feeling right now. If that's fear, okay. If it's hatred, okay, too. Ask her to trust you more, or enough to share her burdens." I sighed. "You're a big guy. You don't need to solve her problems, but you do have to listen."

"Can I find out about the mission to destroy Cheney? And why she's seeing me?"

"Try a less direct route."

"What if she tells me it's because I am a reporter?"

"Then you'll know. You'll understand her situation, and make the decision to help her or let her help herself. The truth will set you free, you know?"

"What if the truth hurts?" He put on the sunglasses.

I handed him my card with my cell number scribbled on the bottom. "If you need to talk, or if I can help, let me know."

He nodded. Petra's goo-goo eyes for him might just be a ploy. It had happened before. So I added one more worry to my kettle of colicky crocodiles as I headed home. I mumbled something like, "God doesn't give us more than we can deal with," and tried to pretend life did have happy endings. So when I turned the corner to see a half dozen squad cars in front of my condo, I felt certain I could handle it. Yeah, right.

*

I tried to convince myself those cop cars were not in my driveway, that they were after the neighbors with the garage band that played past midnight. Or came to visit the parents of the skateboarders who had erected a ramp in my cul-de-sac. Or that Mrs. Bates, ancient and so nasty the skateboarders feared her, had gotten locked out again.

But it's tough to kid yourself when your front door is wide open and a uniformed officer is talking with your grandfather. Harmony sat on the curb, her arms circling her knees, which were touching her chin.

I parked across the street, since Las Vegas's finest were hogging the drive, the middle of the street, and the curb. I was an adult, and I had to do grown-up things so I got out of the car. Besides, Gramps saw me.

I waved to him, walked to the curb, and sat next to Harmony. I opened my arms. If Harmony was bent on rejection, it'd be okay, but I wanted her to know I cared, whatever had happened.

"It's Tuffy," she sobbed, folding her skinny frame into my well-padded embrace.

"He's not. . ." I couldn't get the word "dead" out. "What's happened?"

"He's, he's, he's okay," she wailed in a slobbery stutter.

Good, the mangy mix was fine, but why were cops at my homestead? And why was Harmony, under my current protection as her temporary foster parent for the great State of Nevada, sobbing her heart out. "You'd better explain, honey." I reached into my tote bag for a pack of tissues.

"They're taking me to jail. They told me to sit here until a female officer comes. Oh, Pastor Jane, it's all a big lie."

Gee, that wasn't a new line, as in fact I'd used it before. "I'm sure this can be straightened out," I started to say just as a limo parked in the middle of the street, blocking the road even more. The driver, whom I knew from a Chippendale's billboard I passed each day on the way to church, opened the door for a woman who was dressed for New York City's Fifth Avenue instead of Calle del Rancho in Las Vegas, Nevada.

I watched as one manicured part of her body after another glided toward the two of us. I have no idea about designer labels, but the coral suit looked like silk, and her scarf fluttered in the sweltering breeze. Her hair was long and taffy colored, and diamonds the size of my thumbnails studded her ears. I'm never good at guessing ages, although that doesn't stop me, but she had at least ten years and Botox on me.

"You are a common thief." Was she pointing at Harmony or me? It really didn't matter. "You are the one who stole Over the

Silver Moon's Playful Platinum and Gold. Good, the police are here. Park the car, Oscar then get the dog."

If she was trying to be Cruella DeVille, of *101 Dalmatians* infamy, it was letter perfect, minus the Brit accent. She pointed at us. "Arrest her. I order it," she added, shaking that finger toward the cloudless sky.

Harmony's body was pulsating with sobs, and yet she pulled me close to whisper, speaking more words in a row, than in all the time I'd know her.

"I didn't steal Tuffy. He's mine. I love him, but I didn't take him from anyone. I never lie, Pastor. Ever, even when the police came for my father. I told them where they could find him. I hated that, but I don't lie. I found Tuffy drinking from a puddle near the homeless shelter where we serve lunch, where the church ladies go every day and I help out."

I got up. I'd heard plenty. No one would take away that mutt, the only thing Harmony could count on in her tenuous existence. "Listen up and listen good, madam. Let's talk with the authorities before we start shouting about arrests." I grabbed Harmony's hand, and we trotted toward the house. I could feel Cruella's self-righteous breath on my back.

"Janey." The cowboy formerly known as Gramps, greeted me with a one-armed hug, "Good you're here."

"Care to tell me what's happening?"

"Been a mix up of some sort, and Tuffy is the ringleader."

"Pastor Angieski? I'm Captain Tom Morales, LVPD. Dogs aren't my usual beat, but the mayor asked me to check on this." Add thirty or more pounds to Antonio Banderas, and you'll get the full, delicious picture. The captain filled out his tan uniform well—broad shoulders, great smile and best yet, no wedding ring.

I looked from his left hand back to his smile. "Does the dog really belong to her?" I asked, turning slightly before Cruella could throw more verbal daggers.

"Apparently." He pulled some papers off the clipboard he held. "The lady is a prominent person in our city. And Mrs. Wainwright-Dobson breeds Welsh terriers." He nodded in her direction. The woman was stinking mad. She was stomping a foot—a tiny one, but it was still a stomp—and yelling at a detective.

"When your grandfather and his granddaughter? Harmony? When they had the dog groomed, the owner of the shop remembered something about the missing dog and called the owner."

Cruella squawked, "He is not just a dog, I'll have you know. Why, he's a Westminster champion and now. . .oh, my word. No." The driver rushed to her side when she swayed toward the pavement. "He's ruined. Look at the cut. From a pet shop. Why didn't they call me before taking clippers to him? My personal groomer will never correct his coat in time for the next dog show. He's ruined, I tell you, ruined. Wait." This came out as a shriek. "His ear is torn, oh, I didn't see that before." She looked like she was going to faint, but I had a feeling she was made of much stronger stuff than facing a dog that had been homeless and apparently in a tussle or two when he was on the street. "He's worthless. Throw him away."

Harmony straightened her spine. "He was living on the street, near the shelter, for about a month before he would even come to me." Her voice was tiny voice, but we all heard her, especially the captain. "I fed him some scraps, and when some kids were throwing him around like a football, I grabbed him, punched a few, and we ran."

"Oh, my, no." The woman let out a scream that could have curdled fresh milk.

It wasn't because of what Harmony had said, because she was looking through her bifocals at something on the little dog's, um, well the opposite end of his anatomy from that sweet button nose. The good and handsome police captain and taken her arm as she swayed. "He's been neutered."

Of course, we all looked at the dog, you know where, and nodded. Yes, it was true, but one didn't normally have a heart attack about that.

"One foster home made me take him to the shelter. The shelter fixed him, said it was the law. Then I ran away from that home, earned enough money to bail him out. Now he's my dog. I have a receipt to prove it." Harmony sniffed back tears. "I got proof and it's in my backpack."

"You might need that, Harmony, but the dog shouldn't have been placed with you. Ma'am." Captain Morales turned with a solemn nod. "Do you want me to have the sergeant put the dog in your, ah, limo?"

"In my car? You have got to be kidding." Cruella squirmed. She brushed something off the sleeve of her linen suit and stepped away from the captain and her dog.

"Don't worry. He's clean," Gramps said. "He got cut, washed and manicured. Got checked by a vet this morning—got shots, rabies and the works. Saw to it myself. The vet said that everything, ah, down under, ah, was healed, and the rip on the ear was nothing for a dog that had been Dumpster diving for food." Gramps ruffled the dog's head.

"Are you all idiots? He was my best show animal, a champion ready to take the Kennel Club title at Crufts in London. I cannot let anyone know about this. What would people say?" she said, but it was more like gargled because the words choked her. "He's useless. You must all promise not to tell the press. Or the American Kennel Club."

"He's useless?" I asked, as an itsy-bitsy idea bloomed into a bloomin' bouquet. "What is the price for a dog that has no show value? That you don't want anyone to know about? A dog that is useless?" Everyone looked at me. "Just wondering."

"Nothing. I could never show him again, and breeding is out," she snapped.

I held my breath and watched as her face suddenly became the color of overripe strawberries.

"What a waste of time. You police people called me here for nothing. Don't you realize I'm a busy person?" She examined her ponderously pink and pointed fingernails and picked another speck off her suit. "Get rid of the dog any way you want to, Captain. Give it to your kids, the Humane Society, or even put that thing to sleep for all I care." If she had long hair, she'd have thrown it behind her shoulder. What she did do was once again stomp her foot. "I hereby release this animal. I'll sign whatever's necessary. Just get rid of that dog."

Chapter 6

In unison, Harmony, Gramps and I yelled, "No." Everyone within a five-mile radius got the idea that Tuffy was not going to be forced to climb over that dreaded Rainbow Bridge toward the big doggie play park in the sky. Even the rock band next door exited their garage, finally realizing the police were after their neighbor, the preacher, and not them.

I was the first to speak. "You heard her, Captain. She doesn't want the dog, and he needs a good home. She said you can have him."

"I don't have kids," he said. I swear those eyes were sparkling at me when he added, "And no wife. Did have one a few years ago—a wife, that is—but the lady found my unpredictable hours and being a rookie cop's wife didn't mesh with her socialite upbringing. Don't have time for a wife or a dog." Then he smiled at Harmony. "But I know someone who does." He took the now well-groomed terrier, which was barking for the fun of it, from the officer who was cuddling the freeloading pooch, and placed the mutt in Harmony's arms. "You'll want to get a license, and microchip him so that if he does start running with the wrong crowds you can find him quicker than Mrs. Wainwright-Dobson did."

Harmony ran her chin over Tuffy's fluffy forehead, sobbed like a banshee, and ran into the house as Tuffy barked at a volume that'd guarantee a return of LVPD. Mrs. Wainwright-Dobson, bringing to mind the Big Bad Wolf, huffed and puffed her way to the limo. Odds were it wasn't the loss of the dog but the sheer inconvenience, not to mention mingling with the unclean hoi polloi. "Case dismissed," I said.

Gramps was suddenly engulfed by the teenage boys from the garage band next door, who had realized they were living next door to Slam Dunk's lead guitarist.

Captain Morales and I stood in the minimal shade of the entryway. He looked at me. I sized him up, too. He smiled. I returned it.

"This isn't my typical MO, Pastor, not by any means. I feel like one of those kids talking to your grandfather. But might you, well, sometime, could you want to have a cup of coffee with me?" he asked, smoothing back the blackest hair—a full, fat headful of it—and the kind I momentarily was lost in.

"Sure." I was proud of myself for not drooling and not reading anything into this. Lots of police officers need someone to talk with. I was all business, at least in my voice. "Why don't you come to church with me tomorrow, and we can talk about it?" I figured if he balked at the idea, then I'd know we had a major chasm between us even if it was that he needed a spiritual ear. I didn't feel any breath coming or going from my lungs. I waited.

He lifted his generous eyebrows, which were as chocolate as his eyes. I got ready to hear, "No thanks." But then he asked, "Service starts at what time?"

"Ten. Youth Bible study is at nine, and then we go into the sanctuary for the service."

"I'm pulling the night shift again. We're short on staff right now. If everything's quiet, which means the usual chaos of Vegas, I'll take you up on that offer." He handed me his business card, but not before he scribbled his cell phone number on the back, nodded curtly, and left the scene of the crime.

You know you know stuff, right? Well, I was certain hat the captain knew I was watching his bum-ski all the way to the patrol car. What I didn't know was that he was going to turn to see me looking. What I hadn't expected, too, was that he would lift one side of his mouth, like a secret laugh. And wave. Man, the man was good.

*

The rest of that day passed in quiet contemplation of the Psalms and a devout study of Proverbs with a tad of the New Testament thrown in for good measure.

Not.

I scrubbed two toilets, ran the vacuum, dusted a layer of grime off the furniture, and tried to figure out how to immediately get in touch with Clinton Kelly to tell me what not to wear, because I needed help. I had nothing in my closet that would knock that officer's socks right off.

I was Goldilocks, with one outfit too tight, the next saggy. Another two were frump-o-rama, and the rest I wore when presiding at funerals. Only so much cleavage cuts it then.

By three, I'd worked up a royal sweat pulling clothes on and off, and headed to the Fashion Show mall. The heaven-to-my-fingers blouses at Neiman Marcus made my credit card hyperventilate. Old, dependable Macy's was an exercise in extensive frustration because it was buzzing with tiny women asking, "Don't you have this in a size 2?" By the time I got to Victoria's Secret, the idea of pleasing any man while having my clothes on had caused me to buy a sampler box of Godiva chocolates. Which I ate on the spot.

I trudged home with ten pairs of new panties. Hey, Victoria was having a sale. I resigned myself to a red linen jacket, a creamy colored skirt with a slit that stopped six or seven inches above the knee, and a cross-my-heart white silk blouse. Outfit du jour. I'd have to win the guy with my intellect, I thought, swilling more iced coffee on the way home.

My insta-family was lounging on the shady patio, tossing a tennis ball for the pooch. I brought out water and a bag of oatmeal cookies and plopped down next to Harmony and Gramps. I peeked her way and wondered what was going to come of Harmony when her dad was released? She pushed her chair closer to Gramps. Maybe I should have been thinking about our relationships. It'd work out. Or not. I'm a realist with relationships as long as they're not with handsome men.

As for Gramps, I knew we'd turned a corner. He was strumming Bertha, and that was good. The guitar sang and so did he. When Harmony got up to refill the pooch's water bowl, I whispered, "What's your two cents on Harmony?"

He snorted. "You're asking me? You're the overly educated expert in psychology." He played "She'll be Coming 'Round the Mountain," as if that would mean something to me.

Sunday came, church was church, just don't ask me what was said because I spent the morning with my head bouncing like a bobble head as each shadow crossed my peripheral vision. No sign of the smooth Antonio Banderas-looking police captain, who had been told to arrest my foster child of less than twenty-four hours.

I grunted, "No show," sometime between the service and the hospitality time that followed. I went back to my office and stacked supplies for Monday and VBS, then I cleaned the shelf above my desk. I organized my top desk drawer and took out the trash. I'd been jilted even before I could form a deeper, absolutely unrealistic crush on the man.

I shrugged, shaking off the sting of rejection even before acceptance. See, I knew it would never work. Heck, I was way too busy with Harmony and her problems. I had other kids in the ministry with shattered teenage hearts, messed-up home lives, parents addicted to crack and meth, and a few juveniles with police records thrown in for good measure. Besides, there was a little concern about the spiritual leader of Desert Hills Church and the head of what could be the killing machine of black-market babies, the bangled Delta Cheney. I couldn't forget that Petra and the delicious Carl were in this, too. Plus there was, looming larger than life, my appointment with the District Council's representative on Friday. And let's not ignore the entire Dancing with Vegas Stars fundraiser balanced on my trusty shoulders.

Okay, I was bummed. Tom had discarded me. If you think you have problems catching a man's eye and keeping it, try being a preacher. My chances of sexual attraction are about zippo to nil. Heck, I can't even get male clerks in Home Depot to wait on me. That's not what I hoped to achieve with Tom, although I hadn't gone as far as naming our children or writing Mrs. Jane Morales in a notebook. I might be sophomoric, but I'm not a total idiot, only a part-time one.

I wallowed the rest of the evening. It's asinine to admit to others that one is wallowing over something that wasn't, so I stiffened my upper lip and put on a good show. I even fooled myself. For about two seconds.

*

Monday came, as it often does. Here in Vegas it was hot and bright. Spreadsheets, budgets, and reports littering my desk screamed for attention, so when Vera's voice on the intercom sounded tighter than typical, I jumped. She said, "There's a police officer here asking for you." Then added, in a creepy, lowered, sexy voice, "Quick, he's a fox. You've got to see him." Then in a louder voice, "Thank you, Pastor, yes, I told him I'd get some coffee and we could wait in the hospitality room. But he said he'd see you in the lobby."

"I'll be right up." I sighed and wondered which of my kids was to be handcuffed this time. Harmony was in the recreation room talking to the four-year-olds about pet kindness, with Tuffy yapping his two cents. There were dozen or so others who were more in trouble than out, which worried me, but at least the kid who held up the liquor store a few months ago had checked in with her parole officer and with me fifteen minutes before. Another with arrests for shoplifting was doing community service at the hospital. The kids who had counterfeited tickets to a rock concert had real jobs to pay off the scam. The boy who'd decided to blackmail the mayor by videotaping him with a vivacious blonde in a romantic lip-lock and, unbeknownst to the boy the hot mama was the mayor's wife. The kid had been invited to a film school at the University of Southern California. Apparently the video flashed on YouTube and a professor at the film school saw the kid's work so the teen blackmailer won some kind of prize for it. Isn't life a hoot in the patootie?

I rounded the corner to the foyer at about eighty-five miles per hour and skidded to a stop. "Tom? Tom. And bearing gifts?" His hands were filled with Starbucks cups and with the instinct of someone whose caffeine levels had dipped to zero, or maybe that was my common sense, I reached for one and would have reached for him, but for the ladies' auxiliary that was in the foyer, getting ready to take food to the mission.

"Good time for a break? I'm just getting off duty."

"You look terrible," I blurted. It was a lie. He was gorgeous, and I forgave myself for lying in order to protect me from being even more dazzled than I appeared.

"A little honesty goes a long way, you know." The stubble on his face could have sanded paint off a wall, and sweat had circled beneath the arms of his tan uniform.

As I said, he was yummy. "Of course, this isn't any of my business, but do you wear a bulletproof vest beneath that poly-blend shirt?"

"Yeah, why? Only in the field. Concerned for me?"

"Do bureaucratic sadists work for the city? Have they no idea that polyester doesn't breathe?"

He bent over and sniffed his armpits, wiggled his eyebrows and said, "No Police Fashion Award?"

"If I ran the city, you'd be wearing cotton. But you're not here to discuss polyester, are you?"

He took my hand for the merest of seconds, and we sat on the bench in the foyer. Honest to Pete, his eyes drew me in worse than the Godiva chocolate shop in the mall. "You deserved to know."

Oh, boy, here it comes, I mumbled, I hoped to myself. "You're allergic to preachers." I'd heard it before and didn't need it again. I started to stand, and he grabbed my arm.

"Allergic? Huh? Where are you going? I wanted to tell you I didn't come yesterday because I worked a second shift. A detective had twins. I filled in. It was a busy night. Then had paperwork. Those fake cops on TV never do the paperwork. Heck, they arrest a felon, read him his rights, stick him in the slammer, and are lifting a cold one by commercial break. In reality? There are reports, and even if most of it is computerized, it's careful work. If a cop doesn't dot an I or cross a T, the dirt bag that maimed or murdered or molested walks out of the station. Drives me batty."

"That's what I thought," I fibbed. There was no way on God's green earth I was going to admit I thought he'd jilted me. "Hey, what happened? Your knuckles are bruised. They were okay on Saturday."

"Don't change the subject." But he did look at his hands. "This is nothing. Well, just an intoxicated and belligerent citizen said no when I asked that he drop the knife. But Jane, you have a right to tell me to take a hike. I should have called. Give me a second chance?"

"You don't have to report to me, Captain. But honestly—" Oh, it gets sick here—I fluttered my eyelashes. It was a knee-jerk reaction, and I was a jerk. "—I'm an advocate for the three strikes law. You're only down by one." I laughed. He did, too, at my lame joke. This was good. I figured he had to be in his mid-forties, and this time I looked closer at his left hand, which was about two and one-quarter inches from my right thigh. Still no ring and no ghostly mark where he had taken it off. I giggled just as two dozen six-year-olds crossed the foyer and began singing, "Pastor Jane's got a boyfriend."

"Want to come for dinner? How about tonight?" I said, talking first and thinking second. As usual.

The guy gulped. "Ah, Preacher, I thought maybe coffee to start."

"We have coffee. And stop whatever you're thinking, Mr. Police Officer, Captain Sir. This is not a date. My grandfather, whom you met, and Harmony, the foster child who could have been arrested Saturday, and that dog are all living with me. It'll be take-out pizza, and we will be watching ESPN, if you like sports, because that's the only choice in town when my grandfather's in charge of the set."

Like locusts, more kids swarmed into the foyer, and their teenage Bible school teachers leaned to listen. Suddenly they were crawling over the top of Tom.

"Can I touch your gun, sir?"

"I want to be a policeman."

"Can I try on your boots?"

"Let me hold your badge."

"You killed any people today?"

Tom tried to move but the kids inched closer until there was a deer-in-the-headlights look in the policeman's eyes.

"Did you arrest Pastor Jane like she got arrested before?"

Tom stood up, towering about the kids. "You were arrested?"

"Misunderstanding," I gulped as the kids swarmed in an even tighter mass around us grabbing for his badge, his radio and the gun on his hip, and then, in a flash, Tom ran for his life.

Yeah, big, brave police officer. "Hey, mister, welcome to my world," I yelled to his back, patted some pint-sized heads, and returned to my office, knowing full well I couldn't go through with having him come to dinner. Cold feet? How about frozen ones? I'd talked to Tom twice, and I'm mortified to admit this to you, but I was mentally flipping through *Bride*. My fingers fished in my purse for his business card. It'd be simple: I'd call and cancel. He'd understand. I found my cell and began popping in the numbers when there was a knock on the partition that was my cubbyhole. I froze. It was Delta Cheney with Vegas's own Cruella

DeVille so close on her heels that when Delta stopped, Cruella bumped into her shoulder.

"Pastor Jane?" Delta said, maybe twice, since my eyes were transfixed on the twosome. Mrs. Wainwright-Dobson dressed from Talbots, and Delta from Fredericks of Hollywood.

Apparently Cruella, impeccable once more, hadn't made my life miscrable enough, so she'd come back for the one-two punch. Mrs. Wainwright-Dobson smiled, but that could have been just to get my guard down.

"May I introduce. . ." started Delta.

"We met Saturday," said the lady who had demanded Harmony's arrest and who was now all smiles and white teeth. "Did the dog find a home?"

Delta looked from one side of the desk to the other.

"Call me Monica," and then Mrs. Wainwright-Dobson gave Delta an abbreviated version of our acquaintance, minus her attack on my foster kid.

I smiled. Yeah, but it was because I remembered the horror on her overly nipped and plenty-tucked face when she checked out what wasn't underneath Tuffy's little tail. "I'm the girl's foster mom."

Delta's forehead wrinkled, like we were speaking Greek, apparently unable to fathom that her glamour-gal chum and I might move in the same galaxy.

"Forgive me. I'm not usually that rude," the lady formerly called Cruella DeVille replied. "It was a horrendous day."

I motioned them to sit. "I've had my share that belong in the toilet."

She took the only chair and Delta hovered. Cruella smiled, seemed to relax and said, "I must explain. My father passed away three weeks ago, and I'd spent all afternoon getting some of his business dealings settled, including his debts, then came home to a message that a medical test I'd just had done had to be repeated. It's positive. In this case, positive is not good. Then I heard my prize dog had been found. Your family got my wrath."

"There's no need to explain." But I was glad she had.

Delta huffed and puffed. "Darned straight. She doesn't have to explain anything. To the likes of you." The final snort from her wide nose nearly knocked me over. Not an attractive sound for anyone, especially a woman of Delta's size and loudness. "Can we get to business now? We're busy people, you know, Pastor." Delta's bracelets punctuated the end of the sentence. She turned to her friend. "Monica, do you want me to share the fabulous news with her, the, um, pastor?"

She said fabulous like "fab-u-loose," and with the "um," I knew she'd nearly called me an underling or lackey. Both were close to the truth.

"I'll handle this," said the society matron. While Monica still wore too much blusher, but at least her face wasn't scarlet like before. "You see, I have a home."

"Monica. Don't make your mansion sound like one of those butt-ugly cookie-cutter red-roofed suburban houses." This time "suburban" sounded like a swear word. "It's a jewel, over ten thousand square feet. The previous owners were featured in *Architectural Digest* or on the Fine Living Channel," Delta gushed.

I got the point. It surpassed my cookie-cutter townhouse and my beige, unimportant life. Beyond that, every time Monica talked, Delta interrupted, but as Monica raised one finger, Delta stopped dead cold. I had to remember that.

"Delta, would you be kind enough to get my briefcase from the car. The driver will show you where it is," Monica said. Like a devoted Pekingese, Delta Cheney jumped, bracelets clanging and clinking, and she was out of the office doing someone else's bidding.

Monica chuckled. "Delta tends to get excited."

Wasn't that the pot calling the fish barrel full? My mouth stayed shut, for once.

Monica cleared her throat, but whispered, "Listen, we don't have much time. Would you like to have Wayne Newton at the fundraiser?"

"Who wouldn't?" I might be twenty years or more too young to have heard his music, but everyone in Vegas knew him. The guy loved people, dishing wealth like I added extra scoops to my bowl of Ben & Jerry's. "There's no budget for celebrities. I thought we'd get some local support, a discount coupon from restaurants. That kind of stuff."

"I spoke with his people, and if you can keep this a secret, Pastor, because Wayne doesn't want to get mobbed when he visits here at the church, I will make it happen. I don't know if I can get him to dance, but we'll try." The woman chuckled and her eyes crinkled at the sides.

I was looking a gift horse in the mouth, but asked, "Why are you doing this?"

She squinted like people do who wear contacts and turned toward the hall. So she didn't want Delta to hear? That was interesting. "Before I became Mrs. Wainwright-Dobson, I was someone else, very different than what you see today. I was also a foster kid. Through the kindness of strangers, I escaped from what was happening at my biological father's home, which was everything bad about families and. . ." She looked around again. "I inquired about that girl, Harmony, and know her story. There are other kids who have needs. A new youth center isn't much, but it can be a place to hang out when hanging elsewhere is dangerous."

"You do understand, ma'am." I relaxed. The woman didn't once mention Tom Jones, strobe lights or Britney Spears, although I'm sure Ms. Spears is a delightful young woman. I do like how she dresses, actually.

"You'd better call me Monica since we're going to work together," she said as Delta returned and handed her a sleek brown leather case, which Monica placed on top of my desk and didn't open. Instead she stood, extended her hand and said, "Can we meet sometime soon, say, a few days from now? Would Wednesday work? Why not come to my home, and I can show you some options if you want to have the fundraiser there."

We three walked toward the lobby. I kept my cool. When Monica's limo headed out of the church parking lot, I let it loose. I did the moves Petra had attempted to teach me in dance class before Carl's near-death experience. I twinkled and boogied and twinkled in circles. Around the foyer I tangoed, pretending I was dancing with Wayne Newton. I tapped out a tap dance. I shook my bountiful booty. I belted whatever I could from "Danke Schoen" to "Red Roses for a Blue Lady," uncaring that I couldn't carry a tune in a tub. I shrugged my shoulders, threw my buttski and bosom into it, danced as if I could hip-hop and finished three twinkles in a row. I took a breath and wondered if I could still do a cartwheel, like when I was a kid. Heck, no one was around and my world was bloomin' beautiful and bright. The fundraiser would not be my swan song as an itinerant preacher. The world was my oyster, ostrich, or oboe, it didn't matter. Monica would make the right event happen. No circus act, but a class act. If Monica and Delta were involved, Pastor Bob would toe the line. Hallelujah and amen, praise it all.

What happened next can totally be blamed on too much coffee, so if you've ever thought you've had too much, you have. Just a word to the wise on the issue of caffeine.

I backed up to do a cartwheel, put my arms out, ran three steps, and did it. I was amazed that, after all these years, I could still do 'em. Then I bumped straight into legs and plunked on my backside. They were male legs. Strong, male legs, in tan slacks. My eyes went from the polished shoes to the sharp crease in the slacks, up quickly to the belt, and over a broad chest and into the face of Captain Tom Morales.

"Hey, Preacher." He smiled.

"Hey, Policeman." I steadied my breathing, but I felt as if I'd just run the Boston Marathon, looking like a moron in preacher's clothing to the one man who, for some unknown reason, I wanted to impress. We both pretended all was right in my fruit-loop world even after I said, "Did you forget something, Tom?"

He stared down at me. He blinked a few times. "Um, well. Thought you'd want to know that Harmony's dad is getting out of jail tonight. There's overcrowding, and he's only in there for passing bum checks. We in the law enforcement game gotta make room for the more impressive criminals."

"Oh, well, thanks." I smoothed my skirt with my hands—yes, I was wearing a crinkly peasant skirt. No comments, please. I had enough horrification to avoid, considering he'd just seen the whole enchilada or maybe more than anyone who isn't romantically connected should.

He looked around. His face was still straight. If I'd been in his police officer boots, you would've seen skid marks on the carpet for how quickly I'd darted out of that foyer. Tom just smiled like I was sane. "Yeah, well, he's not going straight out on the street because of a probation issue, but to a house for those who are part of a new program. The terms, as I understand them from the district attorney, are that Albert Miller must work in an industry not at all related to gaming for at least six months, or he's certain to get an all-expenses paid trip to state prison. I'd bet against him if a wager's involved. It's a sickness."

I crossed my arms in front of my chest after I pulled up the neck of my gathered blouse that had crept astonishingly down toward my navel, which does not have a stud in it, thank you very much for asking. That aside, the weird thing was that we were having an adult conversation right after my circus act. Had to be that Tom often worked with lunatics. I took a couple of deep breaths, hoping the blaze in my cheeks would pale to a mild magenta. "What else is there around here? Everything is connected with gaming."

He held out a hand, pulled me up as if I were weightless and said, "Yeah, that's a problem. The place has more folks addicted to gambling than any city around, or so I believe. I doubt he'd get back into the roofers' union, though he was one. Heck, Jane, around here even restaurants have slot machines. Can't see him working at the public library, but then again, I'm sure he's a good enough guy. Just made some stupid choices and got caught. The real criminal act, as I see it, is that he's a dad to that girl who's living with you. A rotten father, for my money. But I'm not a parent, so this is only hypothetical."

We looked at each other and I swear just the slightest, teeny part of his upper lip curled. "You always do this?" He swept a hand around the room where I'd just performed my happy dance.

"Fitness. See, a girl's gotta stay in shape."

"Listen, I'll ask around for non-gaming jobs for Miller. But, hey, what about something at this big old church of yours? Just curious, mind you."

"It's only my temporary big ol' church, but you're right, there has to be some work. You definitely won't find any gaming here, unless it's competitive hopscotch or a heated game of Monopoly. Let me ask."

"About tonight, Jane. Hate to leave you in the lurch like this, but there are some Feds in town sniffing around. I don't know why, and I don't like it. I'll call you in a while."

"Not a problem." He turned, and I watched again as the beautiful backside of Tom Morales exited the building. The vacillation had nothing to do with Feds sniffing—it was the Looney-Toon minister who scared the big strong policeman away. You couldn't blame him, right? Yeah, I thought that, too.

I was still watching, standing outside the entry, hoping some hot, dry air would evaporate the sweat I'd accumulated during my gymnastics performance and moments of abject embarrassment. Then he turned, saw I was still watching, and walked back. Will the humiliation ever slow?

"Preacher? Can I tell you something? Well, something about me?"

"Yes?" I'd met the man two days ago. I didn't care about the man, didn't care about him coming over or not coming over, and didn't usually lie like this, either. Truth was, my heart fluttered when he looked my way, it nearly did a handstand when he showed a whisper of a smile, and my tummy felt as if I were riding a roller coaster after eating hefty portions of cotton candy, French fries, saltwater taffy, a strawberry soda, and nachos, with an extra serving of nachos. It was unlike anything I'd ever felt for my husband, and a bit of me wanted to scream, *Stop it, you stupid fool.* The other part of me was picking out china patterns. Luckily my brain overpowered my heart, clamping my jaws together, lest something disturbing sneak in, like my foot.

Chapter 7

Tom looked around. Checking for public offenders, I thought. I did see a few folks who should have been cited by the fashion police. Tom sighed, so it seemed to be a felon-free zone.

"It was my total inability to be counted on that ended my marriage. Sure, you've heard that cops are womanizers, hockey puck like that, but basically, we're working stiffs. Doing a job. Ex-wife got ticked that I wasn't where she wanted me to be. Alone too often, I know, then, well, she found someone who could be there for her."

"You don't have to tell me this, Tom." Okay, you know it. I devoured every word.

"I want to." After a buzz buzzed, Tom touched his belt. "Oops, sorry." He looked at his phone. "It's a page, the chief, and just maybe with some answers as to why the FBI is visiting our fair city. They usually only come during the months when it's freezing in D.C. When you can cook eggs on the sidewalk, even in the shade, they're in Maui. Or so it seems. Don't know what's up, but the mystery will be solved soon. Count on me for pizza. I'll be there." He saluted, and stopped. "I'm an open book, Jane, a sandwich guy, who likes football, tinkering with my old Chevy truck, and country music. You've seen the world, your grandfather's more famous than McCartney, and I've lived in Nevada my whole life. Just want you to know."

"I like sandwiches," I replied, but he was already at the police cruiser. I blasted a golden oldies station all the way home. It didn't help.

I was screaming, "Fool, fool, fool," at myself when, seconds after I walked into the condo, Gramps and Harmony blasted through the front door. The Tuffster yapped at their heels, Vegas heat pulsating off all their bodies. I'd known him two entire days, been together less than two full hours, and I was acting like some stupid movie starlet on a reality show, which was going to challenge even me when I talked with Harmony.

"Harmony, honey, can we talk a minute?" I asked. Gramps flopped next to me on the beige sofa. Tuffy bounced from one sofa to the other, and Harmony sighed. I couldn't tell if it was boredom or teenage angst.

She stopped, yanking down the sleeve of the black T-shirt. The bruise was still purple and still as big as if she'd been hit with a baseball. "I knew it. You don't want me to help at VBS any more, do you?" Her bottom lip quivered, and I swear this was the first emotion visible on her face, except when it came to the pooch.

"No way. You've got the job. It's your dad. Your father is being released from jail tonight." No flicker flicked, no glimmer glimmed, and her eyes stared at me. It was as if she were dead to him, or he to her.

"Oh." She pulled a comb from her pocket, and Tuffy rushed to her side to be groomed, yapping and with his tiny pink tongue dancing as he jumped around.

"Hey, that's great, Harmony. You'll have to let me get to know your dad," Gramps said, patting her on the shoulder and heading for the kitchen.

"Yeah, great," she muttered but her mouth looked like she'd just bit into a lemon.

"He's not coming here, honey, if that's a worry," I explained.

"You mean I don't have to leave?"

I sat down next to her on the carpet. "Leave? Oh, no, you just moved in. You're my foster kid for a while."

"Oh." Still no emotion, but I'd seen through her façade. She did care.

I touched her arm and she didn't withdraw. "I need a promise. No running away from this house. I know you've done that before, and I know it happened because of the situations, but you're with me now. For better or worse. I promise to be the best foster mom I can, which I've never done before so I have no clue how to do it, but you've got to promise to stick it out with me. If you can't promise, I can't promise."

"Promise," she said and shoved out her hand to shake.

Tuffy slathered my sweaty face with doggy kisses, which was pleasant in an icky way.

I flopped onto the sofa with my doggy friend pouncing on my chest just as the doorbell rang.

Since no one except Tuffy rushed to answer it, I heaved myself up and opened it a crack, then flung it wide. "Oh, no, Pastor Bob." I screamed. Not at him. The mutt was attacking my boss's ankle with a vengeance, growling like a Doberman trained for police work. Tuffy snapped hold on the cuff of Pastor Bob black slacks. No joyful tug-of-war—it was all-out war. The pastor's arms flailed, he screamed words I was surprised he'd repeat, and then plunk, Pastor Bob was on his butt in my brick entryway. With a thump. And a crunch. Mind you, the dog was still growling and pulling and shredding.

Even as the growling mutt turned his pants into confetti, the minister barked orders up to me. "I need your attention, madam, and I need it at once. Where's your study?"

I could have been faster. I could have probably yanked the nutso muttso off. God forgive me, I let the dog continue the assault for a minute more.

"Pastor Jane, madam, call off your dog this instant. We must talk." Pastor Bob's voice was abrasive, but he'd just been by the mutt. Pastor Bob teetered, grabbed for me. I backed off, grabbed Tuffy as Bob regained his balance.

"My what? Study?" As the irony turned into a laugh, the mutt wiggled from my hands, danced on his back legs, and yapped as if he were proud of himself to saving me from the intruder, who of course was my boss.

Pastor Bob smoothed his hands down the jacket of a gray silk suit, impeccable except for the shredded trouser cuff, and said, "We can speak privately in your study."

I retied the knot at the waist of my T-shirt and juggled the diet cola as the dog ran circles and yapped. "Pastor, this is my home, which is full with family. And we're certainly not meeting in my bedroom. It'll have to be the living room." I stepped aside to let him in, but the guy didn't budge. The dog finally stopped the circles and now sat directly in front of me. I was getting to like the mutt.

"Won't do. No. Not at all. All hush-hush. Confidential." He didn't move from the front porch, just kept rubbing that ankle.

I snagged Tuffy and said, "How about your car?" I saw the sleek auto parked next to Gramps' muscle car.

"Since it a car about which I wish to dialogue, Pastor, I suppose in an ironic way it is appropriate." He limped away.

I ruffled Tuffy's tufted beard, shoved him inside, closed the door, and high-tailed it over the hot cement. My feet were crispy critters.

"This goes no further." His lips were pinched, and he rubbed his nose with the back of his hand as he got behind the steering wheel. "Understood?"

"Your confidences are always safe with me, Pastor." I climbed in the passenger seat.

"Better darned well be, madam." He snorted and blew his nose, stuffing the tissue into the car's ashtray before cranking up the A/C. "You are going to help me. The church board cannot know any of this, do you understand? Not ever."

Ah, the sweet taste of blackmail. Whatever he was about to spill would be deliciously on my mind for less than lily-white purposes. Yeah, that's how it starts, and yeah, evil and I duke it out often. Heck, I'm human. Curiosity won and I asked, "What is it?" It had to be immense, or he would have demanded that I do his bidding in his plush church office, rather than seeking me out at my lowly condo. Perverted? Okay, I'm guilty, but it was delicious seeing the man so thoroughly riled.

He lifted his puffy chin. He checked his bouffant hair in the rearview mirror. He smoothed his eyebrows with a lick of a finger, which nearly made me gag, and blurted, "I have lost my driver's license."

"Just clear your mind. Did you retrace your steps? Where do you think you left it? I lose stuff all the time. It's not a biggy."

"I am not stupid. You are not paying attention again. I have had it taken away by the police."

"Uh, you drove here."

He didn't say "Well, duh," but the look came through. The glare added drama. "You have forced my hand. I may as well tell you everything," he began. "I have asked God for forgiveness, and He's forgiven me. After all, I am a man of the cloth."

I mumbled about a forgiving spirit, clueless as to why we were sitting in his car and he was the mushy color of a peach gone bad.

"I was coming home late from. . .um, well, just late. God knows where I was, so you need not have to burden yourself with those details. More so, as I have previously said, He's forgiven me. Briefly, Pastor Jane, I had my thoughts on something more important than driving."

"You were exceeding the speed limit?"

"Well, um, it was not the first time I've been ticketed. I've been forgiven, you understand. God understands. I, um, didn't stop because, well, I was distracted by something that had happened."

"So?"

"Why are you making this so confounded problematical?"

"Why? Because I'm a clueless dolt. Why else would I ask straightforward questions that require simple answers?" I snapped.

He seemed to miss my biting wit and nodded that yes, I was a clueless dolt, then jumped back into issuing orders. "So that's it. Good. You'll be driving me to all my appointments for the rest of your tenure as youth pastor." He clicked the key, and the engine purred to life. He checked his hair once more, puffing the poufy part in front, put the car in reverse, and started to pull out of the drive.

I grabbed his hand on the steering wheel, which made his foot hit the brake. The disconnect came when that jolt threw me against the dash with the subsequent thunk bringing him back to this reality. Yes, I hadn't evaporated, even if he had desired that to be true.

"Hold the car where it is and keep your bloomin' bloomers on. I am stretched like a worn-out rubber band. I have no time or inclination to chauffer you all over Vegas." I was sticking to that seat like Super Glue until this was settled. Smooth-talking Pastor Bob Normal was not going to get me to take on more. The end. Period.

"I see no options. Your dog has injured me. My ankle is twisted, perhaps broken. It is your fault." His mouth formed a microscopic line, his nostrils flared, and his beady eyes got beadier.

We stared at each other, the old dagger to the eyes look. Then *plunk*, brain cells connected. "You need a full-time driver." The driver would be Albert Miller, God had whispered, and I'm pleased to report I was listening.

"Impossible." He again wiped his nose on his knuckles, which are hairy if you want to get the full picture.

"Not at all. Match made in heaven."

"I think not. Be realistic. What would people think? I can't interview and hire someone, Jane, because how would that look?"

"What's your position on sinners?"

He straightened his posture, and the pudgy chin jutted out. "We're all sinners. If you don't know that, there's not a minute to spare. Why we'll pray for your forgiveness right here and now." He tried to grab my hand—mind you with the same one recently wiping his nose.

I yanked free of his clammy fingers.

"There's someone who is, well, nearly a part of the congregation and could be a chauffeur. No, you don't know him yet, but he needs a job. He'd be just the ticket as your driver."

Speaking of brain cells, I could practically see Pastor Bob's forming thoughts. Or maybe he was grimacing because of the ache in his ankle, which by looking at it from across the space of the front seat needed medical attention if the swelling was a sign of a sprain. Or worse.

"You can thank the Lord that this is solved, madam. I can see how this was supposed to be. Yes, Lordy me, he wanted me to help a sinner and shine a light in a horrible world of sin, and that's the reason I lost my license. God works in mysterious ways, Pastor Jane. Just say hallelujah with me and then amen." He sat up straighter, if that was possible. "I hope you've learned a valuable lesson here. We must focus not on things of the world, but on forgiveness and understanding the mystery of prayerful life, Jane. And if you want to have me counsel you on this, because it certainly seems you could use some help in this area, why, just make an appointment with Vera. You understand I can't promise to see you this week, but we'll make it very soon."

See Jane steam. See Jane with scowl. See Jane wonder how many days until the regular youth minister returned. Or would that be unnecessary to count since the District Council would be bringing in a replacement? Had Pastor Bob, old Ab Normal, called for them to come since he wasn't man enough to give me the boot? I simply couldn't ask.

I sighed and he yammered on. "Yes, I suggest you pray about this. I have a forgiving heart. Jesus knows that," he prattled on until a scream rose in my throat, which I thought I could contain.

No luck. Yet the high-pitched blast didn't change Pastor Bob's once more droopy face. I took a few hundred deep breaths, counted backward from 25,000 and managed, once the scream subsided, to say, "Your new driver is Arthur Miller, Harmony's father, one of the teenagers in our youth group who is currently my foster child. Want him to pick you up tomorrow morning? What time would be good? Or should I call a taxi to take you to the hospital straight away to get that ankle attended to?" Okay, the medical bill would come out of my salary, of that I was certain.

Pastor Bob cleared his throat, and a sermon was approaching, like a thunderstorm.

I pulled the door lever and swung my legs from the car, about to slam the door when he said, "I want him at my home, you know the address, no later than 7:00 a.m. tomorrow. I have a breakfast meeting with Ms. Cheney. It wouldn't do to be late." He started backing up before I let go of the door handle.

Luckily, from that coffee, my reactions were razor sharp, or I wouldn't have fingers today. I shut the door and jumped back. I even did the courteous thing and waved. He never looked my way again and took the first corner at a speed unbecoming a minister. Then his Lexus fishtailed, brake lights flashing, which made sense because a police cruiser was coming down my street, with the oh-so-delicious Captain Tom Morales in the driver's seat.

*

Only in my fantasies is pizza delivered by a fine-looking man in a snug police uniform. As Tom commented, getting out of the car, "I get quicker service than you could, and now the pizza is hot. You shouldn't have to cook tonight, and you're dressed just like a woman should be."

I swear, if he thinks I'm hot in a T-shirt and shorts, this guy is a keeper. I fanned myself and grabbed the pizza.

While Gramps and Tom bonded over ESPN, I went through the motions, while having an out-of-body blast from the past. Throughout dinner, I had emotional flashbacks. Not combat. About Collin, which at times in our short, stormy marriage could have been called the same thing. We were oil and water, pink and neon green, vinegar and baking soda. I don't dwell on it, but that's the whole truth.

After he was killed and I moved home to be with my grandfather, returned to school and then seminary, life was orderly, quiet, and dull. Gramps' place felt like a hotel, and our housekeeper even folded the end of the toilet paper into a triangle just like she did when she worked in a Hilton. I grieved for Collin, but more than that I grieved for what I had perceived a perfect future might include, with those 2.5 little rug rats and a bungalow in the suburbs.

Now we sat around the empty boxes and paper plates, water bottles and soda cans piled on top, watching the Dodgers and the Mets slug it out. The weird thing? It felt as natural as my bare feet. I sighed and returned to Planet Earth, Las Vegas style.

"Walk me to the cruiser, Jane?" Tom said, dusting pizza crumbs off his chest at the seventh inning stretch.

"Sure. Don't want cookies or sorbet? Hey, thanks for dinner," I said, having sense enough to put on sandals. I followed him, closing the front door after me.

Tom started to speak, looked at his boots, stopped and, finally moving back to the shade of the entryway, said, "I heard something. No need to comment. Code of clerical secrecy stuff. But do you know anything about a young woman named Petra Stanislaw?"

"Why?" I looked away, and apparently he got the answer. Then I huffed, which was like admitting it, "Why would you even think to ask me?"

"Hunch, actually, you being a buttinski and all." He grinned, and I felt my harebrained heart flip. "You know why she's here in Vegas?"

"Why?" I bent down to the flowerbed, snapping off faded buds on the few coral-and-white striped impatiens that weren't fried.

"What's with the PSA?" Tom stuck his hands in his pockets, which emphasized his broad chest and a stubborn streak that matched it.

"Why?" I tried to make it sound noncommittal.

"You clamming up, or you don't know anything?"

"Tell me why you're asking." Would he? *Ask and you shall be given*, says the instruction book I live by, so I did. "Are you going to tell me?"

"Your pastor is involved with the PSA and those folks who offer adoptions from Poland. Petra is Polish. Remember how I filled in for another detective the other night? Looking through some paperwork, I saw that she has a restraining order out against her to stay away from Cheney's office and home. Did you know that? Petra is the name of the dance teacher that Henry's raved about all during the fifth inning. Coincidence?"

"Ah, no." Didn't know the little gal was dangerous, because heck, even in my checkered past, I never had one of those against me.

"Listen, Jane, this is bad business."

"I know what Petra told me, know she's grandfather's ballroom dancing instructor and his friend, maybe my friend too, but it's too soon to tell."

"But she's confided in you?" he asked, one eyebrow raised.

"Is this official, Tom? Because if it is, you'll have to take me into the station. I'm not at liberty to discuss spiritual matters I've learned or discussed with others unless someone is breaking the law or in harm's way." I stood taller, or hoped I did, pulling my shoulders back. I wouldn't be bullied by a cop, especially this one.

"When you were doing your gymnastics workout earlier today, remember I got a page from the Chief? She wanted to see me because I've gotten a promotion."

"Hey, Tom, congratulations." I patted his arm, okay, and let my fingers linger longer than patting required. He didn't smile. "Is this a bad promotion?"

"Yeah, well, it's a special unit, newly organized to uncover exploitation of children and aliens in Vegas."

"Children I understand, but aliens? We're not talking about Area 51, are we? We're not too far from there, I hear." Could this actually have anything to do with the story Petra had told me about the much-bespangled Cheney woman?

"Wish it could be. No, these are undocumented folks, and this is a human trafficking division. Your Petra has a Polish passport, on a study and work visa. It's legit. The stuff I've been assigned to check out could have ramifications, big ones. Guess only you can decide if this trouble is worth the trouble."

"You expecting an amen? Or are you warning me off? Or are you being my big, strong protector?"

"Never would attempt that." He touched me, his fingers now lingering on my bare shoulder, or it could have been lustful thinking—even though I was still ticked for being told what to do, other parts of me quickly ignored it.

"If you hear anything that needs to be brought to the authorities, can I depend on you to call me? Day or night?"

"That's a big promise, Tom, knowing I'm a minister."

"Just say you'll consider it."

We locked eyes, of course, I had to look up to do it. But do it, I did. Almost as if I were waiting for him to flinch, and he may have, but Gramps' voice bellowed from the open door. "Jane, baby, Wayne Newton is on the phone."

"Gramps, just tell the caller to wait," I screamed in a melodic voice and turned to Tom, "If you hear anything that could negatively affect Harmony or my church, will you tell me?"

"We got a deal." He took my hand; I held my breath. "Thanks for the family time. Back to finish some reports."

It was Wayne Newton. Honestly and truly and it was because Monica, she I had formerly called Cruella, had asked him to call me. The woman was a treasure, a jewel, a joy. Wayne—yes, he asked me to call him Wayne—came straight to the point.

"I can't sing—not that I *can't*, but I'm under contract to only perform at the casino," he said in that golden voice and then explained that he'd show up, even dance. "I'm not much of a ballroom dancer," said the legend, "but I'll try if you're gentle with me, and if you'll give me a few pointers."

I blubbered and sputtered and spittle sprayed as I tried to sound somewhat intelligent. I also forgot to get his phone number or how to contact him. Gramps is a legend, too, in the world of rock and roll and with Baby Boomers, so I've met my fair share of celebrities, but somehow *the* Wayne Newton, as much of a legend as Elvis, turned the sensible side of me into mush.

I threw my precious, petite head back for a good, old-fashioned, honking laugh, then picked up the phone again to pop in Petra's number. Life was good and would be a whole bundle better once I cleared up a few loose ends, such as if Petra would teach Mr. Newton to dance and why she had a restraining order against her. I was so tickled pink that at that second I didn't even think about Pastor Bob and his issues with forgiveness, or what he'd done to need that kind of forgiveness.

I sure as shootin' should have.

*

I left a message on Petra's voice mail and paced the condo watching Gramps teach Harmony to play a few chords on Bertha, his guitar, as the little dog cooled his belly on the kitchen's marble floor. I might never be totally a dog person, gaga over the ball of fuzz, but there was no doubt in my mind that the pooch was doing good for Harmony, even though heaven only knew what the landlord would charge me for having a mutt in the family. *Jeopardy* was on. I hollered, "I'll take Polish Black-Market Babies for a thousand, Alex." Alex didn't answer, didn't even look smug.

I called to my household, "There's a report I have to finish at church. See you later," but only his Royal Tuffster looked my way as I headed out the door.

The church parking lot was packed with cars. The Community College of Southern Nevada held senior fitness in the rec room, and I dodged a gaggle of grandmothers practicing their kickboxing grunts as I blitzed around a corner, colliding smack dab into Delta Cheney. We jumped apart, cooties coming too close. Apparently even though Monica and I were bosom buds, Delta and I were not. Fine by me.

Bracelets clanged. "What are you doing here?"

"Good evening to you, too. I work here. Remember?"

"Shouldn't you be home with your husband or boyfriend or something like that?"

My dateless, unmarried state of living was none of her darned beeswax. Besides, she reminded me of those girls in high school who always ridiculed us social outcasts. I held my sharp little tongue and let just a little bit of venom out. "How nice of you to remind me." Then, out of the blue, I leaned closer to her, smelling White Diamond perfume, and whispered, "Delta, do you have a few minutes? I'd like to ask something. Didn't want to say anything in front of Monica or Pastor Bob. It's personal."

One thing girls knew growing up—if there was anything snobby high school social types loved it was getting the dish on us creepy geeks. Even though it had been nearly a quarter century since I'd been in high school, my inner nerd was alive and well. For once, it was useful. Delta slipped a hand in the crook of my arm, all girlfriend like. Apparently cooties were a thing of the past as she said, "I have a few minutes."

We got to my cubbyhole. "Please. Sit down. Well, you see, I'm not married."

"Better sometimes, honey, don't kid yourself," she said, pushing ten of the forty bracelets back up toward an elbow.

"My husband Collin died about five years ago. We wanted children, but. . ." I waved my hand. This was cutting close to my heart, and while I wanted truth from her, there was just so much this girl was willing to share. "I understand PSA arranges adoptions."

She placed her palms on each side of her face, and her mouth turned into a red heart shape that smacked a kiss. Disgusting. "You want to adopt one of our precious bundles of joy?"

"You understand I'm not married, nor are there any prospects on the horizon."

"Jane, you're educated, you are financially secure, and as a person of the cloth, you're a pillar of the community."

One out of three wasn't bad. I wasn't currently penniless. I didn't owe anyone anything much if you disregard the recent charges at the plus size sections of Victoria's Secret, Macy's, and J. Jill on my Visa. A summer sale cannot be missed—it's the code of a true shopper. As for a pillar of the community, well, don't ask the police in Los Angeles or San Diego, because they'd tell you my nose has a way of getting into trouble. And after my meeting with the representative from the District Council come Friday, I might be unemployed, but gee, as for educated, I'm good.

"So there are babies?" I squinted, hoping this added a gooey dollop of glimmer to my eyes and a goofy smile.

She extended a bebangled arm and patted my hand. "PSA is the largest and most respected faith-based, not-for-profit-adoption service in the country. We're proud of our work placing Polish babies and children with families who are not blessed with offspring or are doing God's work by bringing more children into their homes."

She pushed a yellow diamond, something like I'd just seen on *Antiques Roadshow* that bagged bundles of bucks, around her index finger, straightening in a way that if the sun were shinning directly on it, it would have blind me. She could have inherited money, some folks do, although I've personally never known any. I've continued to harbor a grudge against my great-grandparents because they weren't filthy rich, but that aside, she smiled. I did, too.

"I've just been hearing a lot about the PSA, Delta."

"Because we're connected with orphanages, babies are ready for adoption without American parents flying all the way over to Europe for pickup. Our mommies and daddies simply don't have that much extra time. And time is money, isn't it?"

"I'm beginning to see," I agreed. And I felt creepy.

"We ensure that the right parents are placed with each of our precious little ones."

"Oh, my goodness, that would be essential," I replied, wondering if this was the "insure," as in their insurance policy, or ensure? Where did the disposable kids come in?

"I'd just get all cozy inside if I could show you some photos of our orphanages and the biological parents who have placed their precious bundles of joy with our American friends. Ohhh, you'll just melt."

"Delta, what if the baby doesn't like me or I don't like her? I'd feel just terrible if that bundle of joy didn't like me." I made my voice sound tiny, good trick for a gal my size, but I've perfected it for lethal use over the years.

"Silly girl. We have that all arranged."

Out spilled the details of the insurance plan to avoid this awkwardness, with a monthly service fee before parents paid for the final adoption and which continued for five full years. "The service fee can even be continued after five years in case," she whispered, "the children become willful as teens and too difficult to handle."

"Parents can return them like an appliance they don't like?" Rumor had it that the most loving parents of teenagers sometimes wanted to return their own offspring, yet my stomach lurched. Where were those trashed by PSA? Did Petra know? Did I dare tell her or Tom?

Delta must have noticed the grimace even though she had pulled out a compact to add yet another a coat of powder and lipstick. "Let's be honest, Jane. There are times when adopted children do not bond. This happen. We give choices," she said, adding lip-gloss, and smacked her lips together. "We simply arrange for another child or darling baby to be exchanged for the one previously in that home. Or adoptive parents can opt out—" She continued to smile, once she checked her teeth for lipstick and removed the inky pink flecks from her incisors. "—when the return fee is paid."

I felt my eyes bug out. "So I pay a fee and return the child?"

"Exactly. It's privately arranged and not part of our bungling, red-tape-filled silly old government or even part of the bureaucratic programs in Poland. Makes it ever so much easier. You can be sure of a smooth delivery of your child, unlike the natural type." She chuckled, in what I thought was meant to be a woman-to-woman joke on labor pains. She rubbed a finger across her teeth, then checked the compact again. "I haven't been blessed with babies. It's because He knows I help mommies and daddies to be parents." She sighed and half closed her eyes, before they flicked open then shut, just to see if I'd taken the bait.

"This is exactly what I wanted to know, Delta." Not that she didn't have children, but about PSA. "What do I do next? Some background checking?"

"Oh, I'm sure working with Bobby, I mean Pastor Bob, you've got a perfect record. Come to the office and see some of the photos of the babies and the Child's Play Baby Home in Poland, where most of our infants and children reside for just a few days before they come here to the United States."

My cell rang. I didn't recognize the number. "Jane Angieski here."

"Jane, Tom. Can't talk much. You asked about the PSA?"

"I'm in a meeting. Can I call you back?"

"No, actually, I wanted to know something. This sounds odd, but any chance your grandfather speaks Polish? I thought he said something to that mutt who brought us together."

"Yes, but it's not unusual."

"How fluent is he?"

"The dog?"

"Yeah, the dog. The guys at the station are going on *Letterman* and need a dog that barks in Polish. Jeeze Louise, are you even listening?"

"He's good. Gramps."

"I've called your condo, just got the machine. I can't leave right now. Could I have a favor? Get him to come down here, like pronto?"

"Good talking with you. You bet." I closed the phone. Tom didn't need to know I was chumming it up with Delta, but whatever it was, I could get Gramps to return Tom's call. "I need to head home now and speak with my grandfather. May I see you tomorrow, Delta?"

We shook hands, and she held mine a tad too long, rubbing a circle on the back of my hand with her index finger. "Do you, um, have a special, um, life partner?" She smiled again.

"Are you asking me out, Delta?" I know the gulp was audible, even to me, but it didn't stop her next question.

"You're attractive, Jane, in a wholesome, well-padded way some women like. So do you?"

Okay, I'd go so far to help orphans, but dating Delta Cheney wasn't my cup of cocoa. "I hope to see more of one special man." She'd been flirting with me and, duh, I didn't even know it and it dawned on me that this was the reason that Pastor Bob seemed to be conflicted with her attentions.

"Never hurts a girl to ask." She shrugged and sashayed out of my office, stilettos echoing as Delta left the building.

I breathed. "That went well," I said out loud, then closed my desk and ran to the SUV. Fifteen hot minutes later, I was pulling into the driveway as Gramps and Harmony were pulling out, with the top down on the car. "Off to see Tom?" I asked.

"Who? Oh, your cop friend. No, Harmony and I are going to meet her father for a short visit. Got a call from Child Protective Services and if she's supervised, we can visit with him tonight at the program home. I tried to call you, but your phone was busy."

I watched Harmony's face sitting next to Gramps, and it looked like she'd rather have seconds of succotash and liver than visit with her father. The girl at least could talk to her dad.

Then I saw something missing. "Where's the pooch?"

"Had to leave him in the house. You might want to check. Got a bad feeling about it." Then he looked at his watch. "We've got to go. See you later."

I let the engine run, cranked up the A/C to higher than high, and thought about the dog. I knew some Polish, could read a bit, and if I could help Tom with something about the PSA, maybe I'd get some information, too. As I opened the door a crack, I had a queer feeling that Tuffy had been listening. He was statue still next to his leash near the door; only the stub of a tail wagged.

I didn't want to, but I peeked down the hall. Toilet paper. Tiny bits of the stuff. Then I saw shreds of leftover pizza boxes on the kitchen floor. "Executive decision. Let's go for a ride, my little menacing friend." I picked up his leash and car harness and slipped the end into the buckle of his collar.

Fifteen minutes later Tuffy and I arrived at LVPD, central station, and he walked in like he owned the joint. "Captain Tom Morales?" I said Tom's name and felt a hand on my shoulder.

"Nicer to see you than Henry." If possible, Tom was more rumpled, and now I could see the bristle on his face had flecks of gray.

My hormones took over and I leaned in to smell him, then blinked out of that fantasy and stepped back.

But he moved into the spot I'd retreated from. "You go everywhere with that fur ball?"

"He's safer here and so is my living room furniture. Gramps and Harmony are off for a parental visit with her father. You get me instead." I caught a glimpse of myself in what I decided was a one-way mirror in the reception area and didn't like what I saw: frazzled, hassled and yet oddly attractive to Delta Cheney. You can cringe if you want to. I did.

"You speak the language, too?" He took my arm and Tuffy's

leash, escorting us down the neon-lighted hall.

"My vocabulary stinks, to be honest. Could never conjugate the verbs."

As the door opened, I saw her. There was a Miss Nevada look-alike in sensible tan slacks and a pale blue lawn cotton shirt I'd recently coveted at J. Jill, with a bright badge on her tan leather belt. Her red hair had gloriously almond highlights. I coveted that hair, too.

"Officer Christina Nelson, community service rep. Officer Christy, Pastor Jane." He looked at her and me. "Don't let the girly looks fool you. Christy's a tough cop, and we're working together on this case."

I pulled my eyes from her perfect complexion and there was a child standing, no hiding, right behind her. He was no more than five, sunken cheeks, puffy lips and eyes that would have been perfect in a Dickens play.

Tom looked from me to Officer Christy. They didn't speak; they didn't smile. Who was the boy? Tuffy wasn't waiting for humans to make a move. He snapped the leash from Tom's fingers and snuggled up to the child, rubbing his body against the boy's thin legs. The boy's blue eyes froze on Tom, waiting for the nod before he touched the dog. Then the kid was on the floor, hugging Tuffy and scratching his chin. Then the belly.

"A Polish orphan." I felt as if someone had kicked me in the gut. It was one thing to hear about the horrors and another to face them in the flesh.

"This time of day, there was no one around to tell if the kid speaks Polish. I thought maybe. . ."

"*Czesc. Nazywam si, e* Jane." I sat on the floor next to the child. He looked at me and nodded. Did that mean he understood my, "Hello. My name is Jane"? He didn't freak out, so I tried another question, this time, "*Jak si, e pani nazywa?*" or "What is your name?"

"Mikel."

"So, it is Polish. Okay, now we're getting someplace," Christy said, and ruffled the boy's head. He nearly melted into her touch.

I lifted the leash and tried to piece together the Polish words for, "Do you want to take my dog for a walk?" At least, that's what I hoped I said.

"*Prosze.*" The "please" he'd responded meant that I hadn't mangled the question. Last time I tried out my questionable language skills in a Polish restaurant, I ordered poached shoelaces over borscht with a side dish of camera lenses. And that was just the appetizer.

Mikel stood only to my waist, and his hand was heaven in my own. We didn't speak as I led the way down the corridors and outside to the grassy areas surrounding the police station. Christy and Tom walked a distance behind us.

"Do you like dogs, Mikel?" I asked in Polish. This time he wrinkled his forehead. I tried again with something like: "Dogs? You like?"

"*Tak. Tak.*" He nodded yes, in case I didn't know that, which I did, but not much more.

He took Tuffy's tennis ball that I'd shoved in my pocket before we left the house, and the two raced down and back on the grass. Mikel's limp didn't keep him from running. I walked over to Tom. "Where was he found?"

"Wandering around downtown. Near the homeless shelter, close to city hall. Got a call about the boy and just glad I was here when it came in. Gotta be a disposable kid out of the PSA refund system."

"Thought they dumped them in New York or Chicago?"

"Yep, but maybe the law is getting close. Kid tumbled out from behind an alley, probably smelled the food since a lot of the churches are serving meals. No ID, natch, labels cut out of his clothes. Some bills in his pocket. He looked scruffy. This really ticks me." He slammed a fist into his other palm and Mikel jumped.

Tom waved and smiled, waved again before the child relaxed. "Nothing to trace. I think the women serving at the shelter thought he was with the regulars. Or the kid had run away and wasn't talking. Somebody called the police, and it got into the Amber Alert system. Got a call from their unit today, and Christy here brought him back to stay in a group home until we can get him in a foster home. Then get this nasty stuff straightened out."

"Will he tell you anything?"

"What *do* you know about the kids that PSA supposedly turns out? Is it more than hearsay from Petra Stanislaw?" Tom waved to the boy as Officer Christy walked down the path to keep an eye him.

"I believe Petra, Tom. She thinks what she's trying to do is moral. She believes she must avenge the harm caused by PSA. Remember that case about Hollywood Presbyterian Medical Center in L.A. a few years back where the HMO was heaving paraplegics out on Skid Row as the poor souls dragged colostomy bags along after them because they had no coverage? Why not with children who can't be sold? Why not dump them, too? It's not that far-fetched."

I was rocking and rolling, and about to go postal.

"I don't know if you'll consider this, Jane. Wait, before you scream that I'm using you. Think it over. I asked around about you, nothing official, didn't check for a criminal record. Hey, I'm a cop. I do this."

"Smacking that cop was necessary. How else could I make it look real? Besides, how did I know he didn't get the memo that I was only pretending to be a prostitute? Plus nobody told me he'd just had dental surgery, either. He fainted, for goodness' sake. Then a rookie rushed in and wrestled me to the ground, like one bad dream after another."

Tom didn't blink, but his sensual lips held the promise of a smile. "So would you consider, in your position as a minister, asking some questions that could help answer why Polish children are turning up in cities all over the country? Why the PSA stays lily white even after the clients who adopt and then rejected the children are found? Why in God's name doesn't anyone bring charges? Are they that shallow? Stupid? Or cruel?"

"Maybe they're embarrassed?"

"Oh, my left foot. You take in a baby, don't like it, return it, and *you're* embarrassed?"

"I'm not defending anyone, Tom. I'm asking questions, like you. So want my response to your proposition now?"

"Let's get out of this confounded heat." He turned and waved to the other officer. "Hey, Christy? We're going to get some water. When the kid's tired, or you are, come on in and get him some juice. Better bring the mutt, too."

The station cafeteria suddenly emptied when Tom walked in after me and pulled a bottle of water from the fridge. I rolled the icy bottle on my cheek and said, "If I'm concerned about someone's spiritual survival that will take precedence over telling you anything."

"These people are nasty sewer rats, Jane. They have no souls. Human trafficking is one of the sickest crimes around. We're dealing with felons who use babies and little kids to make money."

"Some of the kids must go to okay homes."

"Yeah, sure. Most, as far as we've been able to investigate. But, Jane, that's not the point and you know it. Even one thrown on the streets is too many."

His voice was raspy. He looked away, but not before I saw his jaw tighten in barely concealed anger. When he looked back it was gone, and he was the logical cop again, fully in control of his emotions.

"It's the ones who are rejected that end up as drug runners or hookers. If they live," he added. The guy was a marshmallow inside, and I consider that a fine quality in a man.

Christy stuck her head around the corner. "Boss? I'm going to take Mikel and the dog into the lounge. The strangest thing happened. The boy said something to the dog, which I suppose was 'sit,' and the dog did it. Then he said something which probably was 'stay,' and the dog did that, too. The kid's got the dog doing tricks."

"What's this about, Jane?" Tom asked, as if I knew anything more about Tuffy than he did.

"I can find out. I'm meeting the woman soon who happened to be his former owner. You remember her from that afternoon we met? Yeah, figured. She's not all that evil apparently, since she's arranged to have a star-studded event to benefit my youth group. We need about two million dollars for a new youth center at church, and she's offered to help raise it. Along with Delta Cheney."

With the mention of the PSA's executive, Tom's smile flat lined.

"My bet's that the dog had a Polish trainer," I said.

"What's your answer?" came the grumble.

"Sure, I'll ask about the trainer. Oh, about working with the department. Would I be with you?" I tried, actually prayed, that I didn't sound too eager, no drooling allowed.

"Us. The team."

"Oh, absolutely." I chug-a-lugged the bottle of water. "I have an appointment with Delta Cheney to adopt a child."

He blinked five times, and yes, I counted. "You're serious? Or snooping?"

I held up my hand. "Wait, I'm a minister. I want to see what's there for myself."

"After all you know? After seeing that skinny little guy playing with the Polish therapy dog? Oh, I get it. You're kidding me. Okay. Right. So if I'd planned to put an undercover cop in their reach, I couldn't have done better, Jane, but only if you're ready to roll on this. Deal?" He stuck out a hand, and I grabbed it. It was more to touch him than agree. He tossed his empty bottle in the recycling bin and said, "When you see the Cheney woman tomorrow, Jane, ask about 'pre-birth' adoption possibilities."

"What? I don't know what pre-birth adoption is, but it stinks like gray-market babies, infants produced the traditional or even new-fashioned way on order for a customer."

He was watching my eyes, apparently, because he filled in the blank stare. "Yeah, hmm, you didn't hear that one? Rumor has it, from something the Feds slipped, that the PSA has a community of women in some Eastern European nation, Albania they think, who continue to produce babies on demand. The sick part? The Feds seem to think the women are there without their consent."

"Sex slaves. Baby machines." I breathed the bitter words.

He frowned so deeply he could frighten small children, dogs, criminals, and possibly preachers. "You realize this has international implications. That's why the Feds are involved, but they're allowing us regular cops on the beat to snoop around, too. So, Jane, can you ask about that? You're a preacher. It's your moral duty."

Could I actually ask Delta Cheney how babies were made? Could I sleep at night if I didn't?

Chapter 8

Tuffy and I got back before Gramps and Harmony. The pooch hit his designer-style water bowl, lapping like he'd crossed the Sahara rather than just East Sahara Boulevard on our way back to the condo, then did three twists and belly flopped on the kitchen floor. I knelt down and petted his well-cut doggie trim, scratching him around the ears. "So you understand Polish, my mutty pal? What if Mikel could talk to you? Would he tell you what happened? Could what he knows stop the black-market adoptions and those gray-market babies? Would he ever tell anyone?" Tuffy licked my fingers, sighed deeply, and closed his eyes in dog bliss.

I headed to the refrigerator. A girl has to eat when she's befuddled, and I was befuddled. Sex slaves. Baby machines. Faith-based swindlers breaking the very golden rule I held dear while the PSA stayed lily white.

Where were the disenchanted customers? There had to be some, someplace. And why no legal charges? Did the PSA somehow blackmail those who returned handicapped kids?

Why wouldn't anyone come forward? What power could Delta Cheney hold? Were they embarrassed or made ashamed, like rape victims of years past?

I wanted to commit gastronomical suicide. But everywhere I looked, from the freezer to see if there was any Ben & Jerry's left (there wasn't), to the vegetable drawer (for carrots, but I passed on them), I saw Mikel's sapphire-colored eyes, saw the tentative smile when he was hugging Harmony's dog, and cringed with his limp as he ran with Tuffy to get the ball.

What heartless scumbag could have dropped the child off in the middle of a sweltering city like this, most likely thousands of miles from anyone who spoke his language?

Pastor Bob Normal, good and faithful pastor to Desert Hills Community Church, boasted of his connection with PSA. He had created a mega church out of a tiny group of believers, built a campus that was getting bigger by the year. Was the church built with funds from PSA? How was Ab Normal connected?

I snapped up a bag of Oreos and headed to the living room. Using at least two hundred calories to open the confounded plastic sleeve, I licked the frosting out of five, then systematically crunched the cookies. It helped, for a second or three.

Then there was that tasty and sweet Carl Lipca. Could he be working with the Feds? Or for a story? I'd seen some journalists wave their First Amendment rights like banners, and some were tossed in jail because they wouldn't reveal their sources, yet Carl didn't seem the type. Was it all an act with Carl just to impress Petra? Guys have been known to do more for full-body contact. Or did he want to be there when the Feds cracked this open like a watermelon being tossed from the top of the MGM Grand Hotel?

Maybe Monica Wainwright-Dobson, my brand-new BFF, would know something. I wondered, too, if my senator pal Geraldine had sniffed stuff on the PSA in Washington D.C. If anyone could get some dirt on them, it would be Gerry.

WWJD? In case you missed this, it's "What would Jesus do," the hip Christian saying of the 90s, but bam. It really meant "What would Jane do?" Not in any lifetime would I keep my nose out of this. Listen, if I could do something about women being sold as sex slaves and children produced and sold much like trendy shoes from Jimmy Choo, you betcha I would.

I was in bed when Gramps and Harmony returned and pretended to be asleep. I didn't want to talk about what I'd learned, not yet.

So for a five hours I flipped from one position to another blaming it on the cookies, pizza, a handful or three of chips, and that carrot. Darned vegetables. You just cannot mix junk food with produce without problems. I woke with a smashing headache and a raspy cough. As I sat on the edge of the bed, snot poured from my pink little nose, and I knew the germs came straight from those kids at VBS.

But buck up I did, because there were no substitutes for the weary. At about eleven I was standing in Vera's office as a volley of sneezes knocked me on my knickers.

Vera scooted her typing chair away from me at warp speed. "Your fault, you know." She rubbed on hand sanitizer, reapplied lipstick, and brushed more blusher on her apple-colored cheeks. "You get close to those rug rats, those kids, and they'll gladly share their germs."

I mumbled, "Ah be fine."

"Yeah, like fun you'll be fine. Hey, here's the deal." Vera stood and patted my head as if I were a child, then withdrew and used hand sanitizer. "Got to take the offerings to the bank. Pastor limped off to a city council planning meeting today. So could you fill in for me, and I'll cover for you this afternoon so you and that bulbous nose can sniffle out of here?"

I mumbled it was allergies and added, "I'll be okay. Why don't you get lunch, too?"

"Might," she said, jumping back after another round of sneezes, and grabbed her purse. "There's some of that non-drowsy allergy stuff in the middle of my desk drawer or in the storeroom, upper shelf. Take two. You're disgusting."

I slumped at her desk, answered the phone a few times, swallowed pills, and was holding my head when Carl Lipca came in around the corner with a mission in mind or a bug in his boxers. He squealed to a stop when he saw me at Vera's desk.

"Carl. Morning." I shoved snot away, flipped a tissue, my last, in the trash.

"Vera here?" He had the look of a deer in the headlights.

"Da bank." Which meant "at the bank," and because mucus

waterfalled over my top lip at that second, I covered my nose and mouth with my hand as I dug into Vera's desk drawers for tissues.

"Ah, oh, I'll come back."

"What do you need? Are you here to see Pastor Bob?" Still no tissues. I was now heading into the storage room, filled with paper, copies of Sunday bulletins, stacks of church manuals, heck, even a secreted away Hershey's dark chocolate bar, but no stinking tissues. A roll of paper towels or a sheet of sandpaper would have done the job. Heck, a sleeve would have been good, but I was wearing a sleeveless shirt with a ruffled collar that buttoned in a V at my cleavage, and that ruffle was looking mighty handy. I sat down again at the desk, exhausted as the germs began to take over my entire body.

He pulled a chair up close to the desk and lowered his voice. "Vera and I have coffee and chat sometimes. What do you know about that Polish social club?"

"With Petra? You're still a couple? Did you talk about the issues of trust?" I sniffed and once more tried to yank open the small cabinet next to Vera's desk. But of course, they were still locked. The situation was speeding from simply disgusting to a downright downpour.

"I never tried. I know in the club there are these women, grannies that I interviewed for an article I'm doing on second careers. They're a wild bunch, and my mom is one of the ringleaders. At first I thought they were pulling my leg, you know how older ladies can be."

Not one stinkin' tissue in the place. I pinched my nostrils, which was as helpful as that Dutch kid and the dike. Snot spilled over my fingers. "Wait, Carl. Hold that thought."

Pastor Bob's office door was open. "Tissues," I muttered. "So much for those stupid allergy pills." I flopped in the pastor's overstuffed chair and swung around to the credenza, opening and slamming the cupboards. Okay, this was an invasion of privacy, but frenzied situations require frenetic measures. With great buckets of snot cascading down my chin, or so it felt, common sense wasn't cutting it.

Then I spied them. Tissues. Straight back in a nook to the left was pay dirt, a jumbo box, and as I pulled it out, along with it came a stack of papers. I honked until geese flew overhead looking for mates, and scuttled down to snatch the scattering of papers.

"Jane, are you okay in there? Did you find the tissues?"

I choked, gasped, and wheezed, not from snot, but from the words on the papers. "Achoo. Be right there," I managed.

These weren't everyday, ordinary scraps of paper. They were promissory notes from low-end casinos. No degree in rocket science needed to see that. One Horse Club, Hearts and Clubs, Pete's Gulch and the Last Chance Saloon. Bob Normal was a dude in debt.

He owed way more than I could make in the next thirty years, with IOUs ranging from a few hundred, to wait, $25,000 at Harrah's in Laughlin, a hundred miles south of Las Vegas. I skittered under his desk, snatched the last promissory note, swallowed hard, snagged more tissues, and then tried to stack the notes and the tissues back as they had been.

And just in time. Carl filled the doorway. He was chunkier than I remembered, and his eyes scanned the room. Could he know what was on the shelf? Was he here as a friend of Vera's or a snoopy journalist? "You better?" Carl asked as I walked to Vera's desk and plopped down.

"No, worse," I said, but at least I had a wad of tissues, even if I'd gathered up a wad of troubles. Big time.

Carl was talking. His mouth moved, I heard noise, but my brain could only focus on all those zeros on the promissory notes.

"Back to the grannies. Could you focus, Pastor? The Buscia Brigade, that's what these grannies call themselves. They had all sorts of questions for me. Mind you, I thought I was going to get to interview them."

"Oh?" I said. "Frankly, Carl, I don't get what that has to do with me."

"Yeah, they know a lot about the PSA and your Ms. Cheney. More than they told me. There's some bucks going in and out of that organization. Makes me wonder who's doing the laundry there."

"She's not 'my' Ms. Cheney, Carl." But the guy had gotten my attention. Was my good pastor gambling to somehow support the PSA? The only way to double your money, I had heard, was to fold it over, but there was plenty more going on here than my folksy ideas.

"You don't look so good," he said, reaching into his L. L. Bean briefcase to hand me two mini tissue packets. In the next move, he withdrew a notebook from his pocket and dropped a bomb. "You heard how they're killing unsuspecting children by leaving them penniless in cities around the country when they can no longer place the kids up for adoption?"

I faked a sneeze to cover the gasp. He knew. "Sounds like a plot for a movie." I willed my mouth to stop moving.

"You're smart, Jane. Think that Delta Cheney could be involved in this sort of unsavory business? She's socially connected in the community, and she's known around here as one of the biggest philanthropists Vegas has, right?" A pen hovered over his tablet but he wrote nothing. "Petra clams up when I want to know, even though we're. . .well, um, getting romantic." He winked.

I wanted to retch. Way TMI. I snorted snot and asked, "Have you talked with the right people, Carl?" And most likely those "right people" were me because unless I shut up, I was certain my direct quotes would be in the *Journal.*

"Even my mom won't let this go. I'm a no-account journalist, not one of the talking heads on FOX or CNN."

That might be true, I didn't know, but I did know that he squinted and a crooked smile came on his lips when he asked questions, a smile only a fool would trust. He winked. "Can you talk to Cheney? And tell me what she says. You could be all girlfriend like. It's your moral duty."

Girlfriends with Delta? I think not. "My moral duty?" The same words Tom Morales threw at me last evening. What is it about men in Vegas? Who are they to tell me to join their moral squad?

"Will you?" He bent over his briefcase and pulled out a red folder. "Here's a file of what I know about Cheney. Everything looks aboveboard. That's the scary part. Everyone has something concealed, skeletons in the cupboard and phobias and stuff, right?" He looked at me and smiled. "Everyone, including preachers."

"Including preachers." Did he know about Bob's dirty little gambling secrets? What else did he know? Had he intended to bribe Vera with the two-pound box of Sees Candy, from the shop on Sahara, and I know the place, that was sticking out of his briefcase? Then again, what did Vera and Carl have going? I grossed myself out on that one, but stranger things happened in real life. I accepted the folder and wondered if this was one of the stupider moves in my life. What would I owe Carl? Would Tom expect me to share this information? How many women had been sold into slavery to produce unwanted babies while I was standing there bewildered, muddled, and in deeper excrement than any preacher should be?

*

By the time Vera came back, VBS was over, the kids had gone home, and the teens were heading for pizza or the mall or their afternoon jobs on the church campus. The allergy pills made my head swim, but I wasn't so dizzy that I left the scarlet-colored folder that Carl had given me anywhere that Vera might question it, because I'd shoved it under my T-shirt and crossed my arms to keep it snug near my bosom. I asked if she'd had a good time, and she modeled neon green stilettos. With glitter inside the plastic heels.

"Get out of here, Jane." She reapplied lavender lipstick, tucked her curly gray hair behind her ears, and took off her shoes to rub her heels, which already showed blisters.

"About Pastor Bob, Vera. Is he distracted? I don't know him well." The folder slipped; I held my bountiful chest tighter.

"Yeah, distracted. Nice word for it. Freaky might be better. If you want my two cents, the guy's always been a sandwich short of a picnic basket. You met his missus? Prudence Normal is the poster girl for a church lady, buttoned up and pinched lips." Vera proceeded to reach inside her blouse to adjust the cleavage, plumping the girls up. Then added, "She's gone to the East; their daughter's having twins. Course, it's none of my business, but if they wanted privacy for a blowout fight, they should have had it at home."

"Here in the office?"

She settled back to spill the beans, with relish and joy. "Throwing stuff. Thought she was going to kill him. Told him what he could do with himself in anatomic detail and that she was heading home to pack her bags."

I sat on the corner of her desk. The cold pills must have suddenly kicked in, because I could think. "So you heard their, um, conversation?"

"The root of all evil. Money. Me and the hubby? Not close to being suited for each other. The man sells cleaning supplies. But I stay amused, even if he isn't exactly Mr. Romantic, if you get my drift." She wiggled her shoulders, and the cleavage looked like jiggling Jell-O.

I did not want to get her drift. Step away. Too much information. I didn't want to know any of the intimate tidbits of Vera's sex life, thank you very much. "The Normal's have separated?" Everyone under the sun seemed to think it was my moral duty to ask nosey questions, so I'd do it, steering clear of the above-mentioned drift into Vera's sexual encounters.

"Didn't know Prudence had it in her, always working on teas and missionary stuff. She makes my skin crawl."

If she was crawly with church stuff, why did she stay at Desert Hills? I didn't ask, as my thoughts were off in another direction. "How is Pastor Bob handling it?"

"It?" Vera crossed her legs, inspected the calves for the need of a shave. "He's hardly here anyhow, but do you mean has he changed?"

I nodded. Anyone who owes casinos roughly a quarter of a million might be an itsy bit distracted. I certainly am when I don't return a grocery cart to the store or if a library book is late.

"Changed? No more than I would expect for a man leading a double life." Satisfied about her legs, Vera swiveled and flicked on her computer.

"Say again?"

"Yeah, he does counseling for couples who are scheduled to adopt through PSA."

Pastor Bob Normal might seem idiotic, comical, and a bit slick, but he definitely did not seem a fool. There had to be more.

Vera gave me a squinty look. I didn't know if she had more to tell or if what she'd told me was only half truth. The money part made sense since I'd seen with my little eyes the end result of Unlucky Bob Normal.

"I have a few personal calls to make so, hey, Jane, get out of here for a while, will ya?"

"Okay, now off to the PSA."

She squinted through the rhinestone cat's eye glasses, if possible looking more suspicious than usual. "Getting some extra money with counseling work?" Her well-lined eyebrows went skyward.

"I'm looking into their adoption process." Which was the Lord's truth. And I was thinking about illegal and immoral adoptions, moral duties, and asking Delta some questions, one of which was not for a date this Friday night. I pulled the folder from under my shirt, tucked it beneath my arm, blotted a gob of snot teetering on the brink of my left nostril, and headed to my office.

Vera hummed as she punched in numbers and then whispered into the phone. I knew the world didn't revolve around me, but I had the feeling she was telling someone I was going to adopt through PSA. Whoever gossips to you will gossip about you, and Vera knew secrets to share.

*

I drool over babies like some women get mushy over appliances or shoes; wait, I do that with shoes. I'd considered adopting, but it'd never happen with PSA. Delta Cheney might be innocent as vanilla ice cream with white chocolate sprinkles, but the buck stopped with the CEO. Looking to point a finger? In my book, it'll be directly directed to Delta Cheney. Hence, I prayed she'd go down with that ship when the truth surfaced on deserting children, abuse issues, and the baby mills. As sure as I was burning my backside getting into the SUV, I'd get to the bottom of what was happening. I might end up looking like an idiot, and Pastor Bob and Delta might be pure as the driven snow; however, the odds as they were stacked were not in their favor.

I put the car in reverse, only to slam on the brakes. I'd nearly flattened Vera. She didn't seem to notice and handed me a green leather purse. "Jane, one of the women, Judith, who takes lunch to the mission, forgot this. Told her you'd drop it."

Best plans of preachers and mice go astray, so rather than off for a shower before my appointment with Delta, I headed downtown to the Daily Bread Mission. Cars jammed the street, and construction crowded it more, so I parked where I could and hiked the blocks to the mission, a big empty store with chairs, folding tables, and a soda machine. As I walked in, the "lunch ladies" were cleaning up, and I returned the purse to Judith and grabbed a leftover chocolate chip cookie.

Inside the mission, kids played Twister and board games, like the affluent ones at VBS. Four women huddled around a scarred coffee table, flipping through tattered magazines. A man yelled orders to himself, jumping up and sitting down, saluting to no one in particular. A clerk, eyes glued to a computer monitor, mutely moving a mouse while playing Solitaire. I bought a diet iced tea from the vending machine, finished the cookie, and sat with the women. While I was hot, sweaty, and germ-ridden, I was immediately pegged for just another do-gooder. They knew it; I knew it.

"I'm Jane." I sipped the drink, held the can next to my cheek. "Are some of those your children?" I nodded to the group of girls, toddlers to early teens.

One tossed down *Real Simple* and picked up *Vanity Fair*. "Yeah, their kids," said one woman, the tank top showing more muscle in her arms than I had in my entire body. Her face said, "Don't you give us trouble."

Another smiled, a child herself. "Too hot outside for 'em to play."

"Good place here," I agreed.

"You looking to convert the unfortunates? The homeless? You're a preacher, right? I seen you here before. You come to tell us about how we's all sinning?" asked another.

"Always drumming up business for God," I said and smiled. It wasn't returned by anyone but the child/mother. "But I wondered if any of you might know anything about a little boy, a blond little boy who limped? Here yesterday."

She with the muscles shrugged, snorted, and walked toward the restroom.

Another said, "My girls made friends with him. He didn't look good. Wouldn't talk to them."

She looked worried, and I replied, "He'll be in a foster home soon. Did you see where he came from?" It was a long shot.

"Not me," said one and another shook her head.

"Nope, me neither."

"I saw them," said the child/mama.

Muscle Lady was at my elbow. She smelled ripe, but so did I. She turned on the group. "Don't need to tell that woman anything."

The young mother's face softened as she looked my way. "Yes, them."

I walked away from Miss Massive Muscle Ratio and sat next to the other young woman. "Who did you see?"

"The boy and two people."

"When?"

Muscle Plenty skidded a plastic chair next to us. She growled, "It works this way. You pay us, we tell you."

I kept my eyes squarely on the mom who had spoken up. "Are any of those kids yours?"

"Why?" Her eyes blinked.

"What if I told you that child had been sold into slavery after being taken from his mama in Poland and/or he was brought here to be sold to people who could afford to adopt a blond and blue-eyed boy? But he wasn't good enough so they threw him out on the street?"

"How do you know that?" Child/mama closed *Martha Stewart Living* and looked at me, brown eyes wide. Maybe she'd been abused or deserted.

I could see it in her gentle face and said, "He was dropped off in the city, and the people who left him didn't care if he lived or died on the street."

The child/mama twisted a corner of *Martha* and said, "Ignore her." She pointed to Muscle Madam. "I don't want money. The men dropped the boy about three blocks from here. There's a park, and I was sitting there on Thursday evening, watching my girls on the playground. We's sleep here at the shelter, but we gotta be out after dinner while they's set up. I gave the little guy a juice box, and he did the darnedest thing."

I waited and watched. The saluting man now marched up and down the sidewalk shouting commands we could hear, but chose not to. Muscle Woman grimaced as if she'd just taken a big bite of rotten cheese; I didn't give her the opportunity to speak. "What? What happened?"

"He cuddled close to me, right under my arm, and fell asleep. I just brought him along when we came to the shelter that night."

"Did you see the people who left him? Could you tell what they looked like?"

"The car was gray, nice car, but they's lots of nice cars in Vegas. They opened the door and pushed him out. He tumbled on the pavement. Then one man said something like 'do widen'. But didn't know what had to be widened. Crazy thing, yelling at a boy who was lying on the road."

I sat back. "Could it have been *do widzenia*?" Could the man have said, "good-bye" to Mikel in Polish?

"Yeah, that was it. That's what he said."

I dug into my purse and came up with a twenty. We both looked at the bill, and I swear I could feel She With the Muscles inch closer. I moved my hand toward the mom.

"Nah, I have all I need here. My girls are happy and healthy. We have food, and I'm going to college in the mornings to get a degree so I can work in a daycare center. Not easy but it's good. You see, we had a home until the baby, Yolanda, in the blue T-shirt there, she got sick. My husband left cuz he didn't want to be a nursemaid, he said. The landlord kicked us out of the trailer. My car gave up the ghost, as my mother would've said. We had no other place to live. But then I heard about this shelter. They helped me to get in a program. We've got all we need. So you keep your money. You need it, too. I know about the preaching business. My grandpap was a preacher in Alabama. He and Mama are gone now ten years, God rest their souls."

"Thank you for your generous spirit," I replied and started to get up, but the Muscle Maiden had my arm. I sat down. She sat down. And let go.

The woman cracked her knuckles one slow knuckle at a time. When number ten was complete, she pushed away a greasy lock of hair that fell over her shoulder and said, "Okay, church lady, let me ask you some questions. This religious stuff, the free food, like that is good. Lots of us be hungry if not for that. What you doing to help these kids? Do you have a God only for the folks who live in those nice houses with bank accounts and jobs? What about us who lives here? Yeah, us, right here and on the streets?" A muscle rippled in her jaw. It was not attractive. She put a hand, like a vise, on my shoulder.

Chapter 9

My friend of just a moment before disappeared, as did the man issuing orders to an unseen battalion and the clerk who'd been clicking long fingernails on the computer's keys.

There was no doubt that Muscle Mama understood life on the streets. I had a few clues after serving in South Central L.A., but I'd never huddled in an alley or begged for spare change.

Our eyes met and I stared. "You're waiting for me to fail, to be some church-talking charlatan. I can see it on your face. I might be a lot of things, and there might be a lot of me, but I am no stinkin' hypocrite," I said and straightened my spine.

She stared. Still, her words echoed in the empty building. "When I was little in South Carolina, my mother yanked us kids to Vacation Bible School. You make one here." Her hand swept around the mission. It was an order.

My mind raced. The materials were organized, the teens could help, the place would work. "How about next week? That be okay?"

She of Many Muscles didn't get a chance to respond, so I had no clue if it would meet her expectations. What did happen is that out of the woodwork a crowd formed around me. One danced. Another raised her hands crying, "Thank you, Jesus. We've been praying for months. He led you in here."

Another corrected, "It weren't Him, but that boy. He musta been some angel." Tears streamed down faces.

I turned to the weight lifter, who seemed to be in charge, or just the pushy sort. "Will you be my assistant? Can I count on your help?"

"What's your name again?" The edge in her voice was directed at me like a dagger, but suddenly it was drowned out by others making plans and laughing They turned and listened. She'd lost whatever war she was waging. She knew it and forced a half smile on her puffy lips.

"Jane. Pastor Jane."

She flexed her fingers. The room got quiet again as she spoke. "I'm Eddie." She once more cracked each knuckle, each one bursting in a slow, hypnotic rhythm which made the tattoo of the America flag gracing her forearm tremble as if it were touched by a breeze. "We can get twenty kids, but don't be surprised if more come."

Another shouted, "We'll have this place jumping for Jesus, bringing all to the Lord. Maybe some men and women, too." And the child/mama simply hugged my neck.

I was walking to the SUV on air, making lists, calculating cookies for snack time, when I caught a fleeting glimpse of perfectly coiffed hair. What in Vegas was Monica Wainwright-Dobson going to do at the shelter? Rude of me to think that, but some stuff is just wacky, right? I couldn't see how the pedigree dog-raising socialite could even find her way to this neighborhood. As nice as Monica seemed to be, her world was at the other end of the solar system from the homeless.

I blotted my face with the ruffle on my blouse. "Gotta be the heat," I muttered and cranked up the A/C and headed to the U.S. headquarters of PSA.

The office had a chandelier, sofas that would fit in a Victorian palace, and what looked like museum-quality masterpieces on the walls, in gold frames. A receptionist sporting a sleek black bob haircut and skinny black clothing that I was certain had Anne Klein along with a size 0 on the labels, whispered for me to fill out a questionnaire about my profession, race, religion, health, and economic level. There were five couples in the cushy waiting room, and we were all on the edge of our seats. The difference between them and me? I wanted information, and I'd stumbled in at just the right time since Delta was hosting an "Everything You

Need to Know to Adopt a Child" meeting.

We were surrounded with live orchids (no silk ones for the PSA), paintings of children playing (no prints for PSA), and upbeat music (classical for the PSA), as the couples and I finished the forms and returned the clipboards to the receptionist.

Upper crust, white, and well fed would have been how I would have described them if they'd just robbed a bank and I needed to give descriptions. One twosome giggled like high school sweethearts, although they were dressed like Wall Street. Another twosome in Dockers and matching crisp, blue Lands' End shirts whispered. The third couple both smiled at me in the same instant and nudged each other. Then I heard the whisper, "She's probably one of those who doesn't want a husband," to which the husband pulled *Golf* magazine up in front of his eyes as his wife, the whisperer, played with the heavy gold cross around her neck. The wife of Couple #5, right next to me, held a Bible and quietly read from the Gospel of Matthew to her husband as he balanced a white cane against his knee. Mrs. Couple #5 finished a passage and turned to me shyly and said, "We're all a bit nervous, aren't we?"

"That's for certain. Is this your first time at PSA?" I asked.

In a butter-on-a-hot-scone British accent, Mr. #5 purred, "We heard about the organization from people with whom I work. We have prayed for a child. One must be careful to listen to the Lord in these matters, don't you agree, madam?"

Mrs. #5 purred again, "It matters little if he or she is big or a baby. We want to give a foreign child a godly home." She could have been an announcer on BBC radio, that type of accent. But her touch made his face glow, almost as if he could see her, and my heart skipped.

What did it feel like to have that kind of love? I popped the last blue M&M in my mouth from the package I kept in my purse for medicinal purposes and smiled back. I believe on the eighth day, God created chocolate, so I savored the last morsels, calming my nerves, and tried to move on from the idea that men and women were made to be couples.

I focused on my happy place of chocolate's lingering memory until the receptionist cleared her throat. Then my senses jingled like the bracelets on Delta Cheney's arm as she parted double walnut doors with a sweep, smiled at the crowd, and winked at me.

"Good afternoon, everyone," the bespangled one belted as I slipped the empty M&M bag in my purse. "Isn't it marvelous how God makes special times for us to meet and bond? Now that you all know each other well, you can support one another through this miraculous journey—the adoption of a precious baby so desperately in need of love and a home in your hearts." Then she focused on me and winked. Again. With the other eye. "Jane. I've been thinking of you."

I nodded and followed the group into a room with overstuffed chairs circling a round table. She wasn't my type, i.e., she was a woman; however, I wasn't here to discuss gender roles or same-sex dating. I was at PSA for answers on black-market babies and child endangerment.

In front of each place was a folder. They were embossed PSA's logo of a baby encircled with the image of a man and a woman and all done in gold.

Delta was babbling on bonding, lit up with excitement like the candles on my next birthday cake. But since I was deficient in both those categories at that second—cake and excitement—I only thought of Mikel, Petra, and Tom.

For the next two hours, with only one potty break, we heard about the slums and the scum that preyed on the parentless children in Eastern European countries. We saw the plights of the Polish babies. And then we saw, joy in the morning, praise it all, amen to that, when PSA took charge of the formerly half-naked and underfed waifs with runny noses and unkempt hair as they were safely snapped up to safety. Suddenly Delta's voice, which was as dour as the conditions that would face these orphans, rose two octaves, and up came films of the Child's Play Baby Home in Poland. Chunky tykes and babies, fat cheeks, blond hair. Little sailor-style uniforms. Hopscotch and games. Children in circles sang "God Bless America." Oh, there was more. Like propaganda, there were upper-crust Americans cradling babies as women dressed in old-fashioned nursing uniforms, straight from a movie set during World War I, placed infants in their arms. The people in the video spoke and moved like actors. Everyone spoke at the perfect time, unlike real conversations where everyone tries to butt in while someone else is yammering. Plus? Yeah, there wasn't a squalling baby in the bunch. Had to be actors. Babies were never that squawkless, always smiling, nor pristine.

I noticed that with the exception of Couple #5, the group sighed, ohhed, laughed, and clapped at the right times. Mrs. Couple #5 and her hubby, for whom she'd given a whispering play-by-play of the video, raised her hand. "Ms. Cheney, the babies are fine-looking, but Drexel and I want a special needs child. We understand PSA can accommodate this request."

Just looking at Delta's face, I swear she wanted to scream, "Liar, liar, pants on fire."

I wouldn't have moved from my chair for all the chocolate in Hershey, PA.

I saw her smile. If the program was legit, that wouldn't have been such a strange question, would it?

"What a dear and precious pair you are. All our babies and little ones have special needs." She straightened the papers in front of her. "Let's take a few minutes' break right now."

"Wait," said Mr. #5, with force that was strong for a man who hadn't seen Delta ready to flee. "Tell us about the guarantee. Where do the children go who cannot be placed?"

Delta's face went from cherry blossom pink to pasty orange and then she gulped, "So glad you have brought this up. Shortly we'll go over our unique program that guarantees that you'll have the right children in your loving arms. Should you find, after you pray and consider the child, you'd prefer another, or if adoption doesn't fit your lifestyle, we have created a provision that solves that. Without guilt."

Four couples smiled and sighed. Not Couple #5. Delta's ramble turned to a high-speed, well-practiced speech. "At this time in our lives, why settle for a child you must work to love when you can pick the best one, with God's approval of course, for you? This is such an exciting opportunity to complete your family, just like you've always dreamed."

She clicked the remote, and on the screen we saw a toddler in the arms of yet another a blond couple, dressed straight from Bloomingdale's, with the baby in pink ruffles. The three were standing in front of a McMansion, a limo complete with driver in the background. "Here's a happy family. James, Bernadette, and baby Elizabeth Ann. This can be your family in just four weeks. Or less."

The more Delta looked at Couple #5, and their challenging faces and pointed questions, the quicker she sped through the PowerPoint presentation seeming to have forgotten it was break time but suddenly she stopped as the door opened. Then it really was break time, and even with the fresh-baked chocolate chip cookies on the credenza and the steaming coffee in a porcelain pot that the receptionist had brought in, I wasn't budging until I talked to Couple #5. Bonding was in order.

"You want a child with disabilities?"

Mr. #5 replied, "May I be honest?"

"Weren't you before? Sure, shoot. See, I'm a novice at this, and it's overwhelming."

He smiled, keeping his voice lower until I leaned in to hear. "Contrary to what the videos show and what the organization says, most PSA children are handicapped and placed with unsuspecting couples. Did you know? Ms. Cheney is avoiding my questions. We'll have to make a private appointment."

What did they know? Were they in cahoots with Petra? I

said, "Special children have been on my heart, too," just as Delta returned with a stack of forms for us to take home and fill out. In minutes we were dismissed and the rest filed out. Three of us didn't budge.

I spoke first, "Delta, what about disabled babies and children? How does PSA place those?"

"I thought we'd covered this." She shoved two dozen silver bracelets up her arm and check the time on her watch again.

The wife of Couple #5 looked at me as her husband's brow wrinkled. She said, "Some friends of ours adopted through PSA. When the child arrived, she had club feet. They're good Christians and knew they had the right child. Now, after surgeries, she's running and playing. My husband and I have fallen in love with the child."

"Highly unusual for a child of ours. I'll check into this." She fussed with papers, restacking and making sure the corners matched. "We do not accept any children with disabilities into our program at the Child's Play Baby Home. Perhaps it was the other PSA, the Polish Social Association, who you're talking about."

Delta's eyes squinted. She looked like a caged animal as I asked, "Special needs children aren't available, Delta?" I tried to sound curious and perky.

"Oh, how like you, Pastor Jane. Would you, and you—" She indicated Couple #5 with a sweep of a bangled arm. "—like me to make some inquiries? Of course. What a generous group of Christians you are. Highly unusual, you realize, but perhaps we can find some babies who need extra loving care."

"Actually," Mr. #5 whom the wife referred to as Drexel, said, tapping the edge of the table with his white cane as he stood. "We've known two couples here in this area and a few more in California who have adopted through PSA, and they've all been blessed with special needs children." He looked toward where Delta had been, but she'd moved to stand by the big doors, hoping, it seemed, that we'd vamoose. "Can't you help us, since there seem to be so many?"

Delta's uncomfortable giggle was surprisingly deep. "What a misunderstanding. I hope you'll be able to give me the names of these people. Didn't they just adore their little ones?"

"Yes, they did," said Greta. Nodding to her husband, she said, "Drexel and I want our family to include children who are disabled."

Delta began waving her hands, indicating we should vacate pronto, but Couple #5 didn't budge.

"We'll stay and fill out the forms now," said Drexel. "Greta and I want to start the process today. We've heard that all we need to get the adoption going is to finish these forms and give you cash." He nodded at Greta and, from her canvas bag, she pulled out wads of bills, the size of a toaster oven.

"There must be a misunderstanding, sir." Delta dashed to the front door, swinging it open. "If you're looking for children with handicaps, go to the county adoption service. All of our children are perfect, darling bundles of joy. I wish our regular counselors or even one of our special ones, a man of God, our dear Pastor Bob Normal, were here for you. You see, I don't normally do the orientations, but with all the colds going around. . ." Her excuses faded faster than my resolves to stay on a diet.

Pastor Bob *was* on the PSA payroll. Oh, Lordy, the plot was thick. I got up. "I'll fill out the forms, Delta, and have them back to you tomorrow," I said, shaking her clammy hand.

"Yes, we will be in touch. You can be sure of that," said Greta. She slipped a hand in the crook of her husband's arm, guiding him carefully through the maze of cars that was the parking lot.

I'd been given the bum's rush too, even without a final wink from Delta, but I was glad it had happened, because my bladder was getting all my attention. However, I stopped so quickly at the sight in the parking lot, bathroom and bladder were forgotten.

Out in the parking lot, I spied a miracle of Biblical proportions. My eyes bugged like a goldfish as Drexel walked quickly to a Honda, folded up the white cane, and slid behind the wheel of the car. Greta crawled in on the passenger side.

"He was blind and now he can see," I shouted, waving my hands like a Pentecostal who'd just received a directive from on high and hallelujah.

A smart woman would have taken down the license number and made some quiet inquiries. A smarter woman would have called a certain teddy bear police officer and asked him to check on the couple. And the smartest woman of all would have minded her own darned business and left the mystery to professionals. If they recast *Dumb and Dumber X* count me in for an audition. I did the only really normal-for-me thing and sprinted across the parking lot.

If you're squeamish, then now's the time to look away or skip the next part. Why? It probably wasn't pretty when I heaved my less-than-petite body straight on top of the hood of their car. Yes, and trust me, they stopped the car. I hadn't worked out what might happen if they didn't.

Greta and Drexel's car lunged as the formerly blind man hit the brakes. The jolt tossed yours truly backwards where I ended buttski down, facing the ever-present sizzling sun of Vegas. And baby, what a ride. I certainly got this couple's attention, yes, sir.

My guardian angel, I'm certain, is swapping stories around the angelic water cooler with the others definitely thanking their stars Jane Angieski wasn't under their angelic care.

How I ended up without a concussion can only be attributed to the above-mentioned GA because after the flip, I flopped on a parking strip that had grass the softness of down. I shook my head, and nothing rattled. While my cold pills had stopped my nose from running while I was inside the PSA office, the crash switched it like a faucet at full blast.

Among plenty of screaming, including my own, Drexel hopped from the car and Greta leaped to my rescue. Greta screamed and screamed at me and at him. Then she shouted to Drexel, "What is the number for 911?"

*

Greta grabbed the car door, nearly swooned, and dropped her cell before her finger could find any numbers. I wasn't road kill, I quickly realized, so I checked for blood, of which I found none, and questioned my sanity. Okay, I didn't do the third thing, nor did I move my backside from the grass. What I did was say, "Listen, you two, see here, since you actually can see, Drexel, tell me what you really know about PSA and their handicapped kids. What's the skinny?"

He was in my face and spittle flung as he yelled, "Why in the hell did you throw yourself on my car, madam?" Even yelling, Drexel's voice sounded like a news announcer.

"You tell me first and then I'll explain." Okay, it was a bluff because I had just been nearly killed by a moving car driven, I might add, by a man who had been blind.

"You are a lunatic. You could have been killed. And it is none of your business why we're at PSA. We will do whatever is necessary to get answers." Drexel ground out the words.

"So you'd murder Delta Cheney to stop this?" Now where did that come from, I wondered? "If you'd do anything, why not just drive over me?" A girl doesn't get to ask that kind of question often, especially when this same girl was the one to accost the car.

"Yes, I would." He kicked the curb. "No. I don't know."

Greta, seemingly fully recovered, yanked at the sleeve of his shirt. "Tell her, Drexel. Tell the woman why we're here in Las Vegas."

I looked at Drexel. He squinted, giving me the feeling that he trusted me about as far as he could throw me with his moving vehicle. So I jumped in where words failed him. "You're here to stop the PSA from their black-market baby agreements, their return policies, or their sex-slave pregnancy homes?"

"See, Drexel, she knows." Greta was crying, pulling her jacket around her chest, tighter and tighter. "Everyone knows. We are the fools. How can we find out any more?"

"Oh, my dear Greta," he said. He plunked on the grass next to me and sat there, as if he were too tired to move. Finally he said, "We need to find out what happened to my nephew. What is your name?"

"I know we introduced ourselves, but you were blind then so maybe you didn't hear? It's Jane, Jane Angieski."

He grabbed me and suddenly all the extra air that I'd managed to recapture after my tumbling act was squished out of my lungs. "Another Pole? You are an answer from heaven."

Drexel kissed me on both cheeks as Greta, on her knees, brushed grass from my hair, grabbed my body, and rocked me like a baby. Me? In a rather icky way, it was nice. Then reality set in. "Wait a minute, you two." I pushed them aside and got to my feet, feeling that my ankles, knees and thighs were still where they previously had been. "You aren't Feds?"

"Feds? Police? We are dance instructors." The couple said in unison. Like peas in a pod, they struck a waltz pose straight from the end of *Dancing with the Stars*.

"Give me a freakin' break. Dancers. You know Petra, don't you? Are you in cahoots with her?" If that were true, then this wasn't just one woman's vendetta against a shady adoption agency. Like, duh.

Greta pulled a tissue from her pocket. Guess she couldn't stomach me wiping snot off my face. Heck, if a girl creates a collision with her body, fluids leaking from the nose are hardly worth a second thought. But I accepted the tissue as Drexel said, "Petra, Greta and I, and many others must stop the killing. In Poland, orphaned young women are sold into slavery, underfed and without medical care, and forced to have sex to produce babies. The babies, most in bad health, are sold and resold and then resold again by the PSA and in the name of God, for God's sake." Drexel's hoity-toity Brit accent had turned into a guttural Polish one. He might be a ballroom dancer, but he was frightening at that second.

"But you'll do it legally. Right?" I asked. It was like a ping-pong match, with the looks the couple exchanged. "We're in the United States. We of course have fine legal systems. But were you handicapped and adopted?" Other than the evil-tinged scowl on Drexel's face and the tears on Greta's, they looked as normal as a couple could be who had just crashed, bammed, and slammed into a preacher.

Drexel scowled. "First tell us what your interest is in PSA? Who are you really? Are you one of those fat bureaucrats or some overpaid federal office that doesn't seem to care about anything except asking inane questions, gathering information never to do anything with it?" He spat into the roadway.

Point taken, but it didn't stop me. "I take exception to that well-padded remark, mister. I'm a pleasingly plump, pushy, and prodding preacher, I'll grant you, but I'm here because I want answers. Hey, can we head into this McDonald's and stop standing in the blistering sun?" I'd been verbally manhandled before by better stuff than this guy. I turned around and walked into the fast-food joint and plopped into the first booth, my legs suddenly feeling a bit like mush.

"So you're from the Center for Missing and Exploited Children. I thought so, from your look. And it's about time you finally made it here after so many of our calls," Drexel said, glowering over me.

"Wrong again, Drexel. And sit down. I simply care." Now it was my turn to growl.

He folded his frame into the booth and looked down, smoothing manicured hands on the table and flicking away crumbs from the previous customer's lunch. "Unlike Petra, I am not afraid. My sister was impregnated by a man she hated, had a baby she had to give up for adoption, in Warsaw, five years ago. It's a sad story, and now she regrets it, as do I. The baby was sold to PSA from the Child's Play Baby Home." He spewed out the name.

Greta came to the table balancing three large cold drinks. I grabbed one. Diet or not, I needed liquids.

She said, "We know Drexel's nephew had physical problems. We do not know the extent. Through a private investigator in

Warsaw, we found that he was transported to the United States, to New York with one family, and then to a fancy Beverly Hills city near Los Angeles to another family. These were very rich people who wanted to have a playmate for their biological son."

Drexel swore in Polish and looked like he wanted to spit, turning to see where the projectile should go, then swallowed. "Such stupid rich people."

Greta interrupted, "The Polish people we know here in Las Vegas, who are only a social club, think the boy was rejected and returned to PSA. They lost contact with him when he was sent to the PSA home in New York, an unlicensed orphanage where they keep the disposable children. Then a family in the Las Vegas area put in an order and got him. We have lost track since then."

I didn't know much about blood types, DNA, or anything medical, but I knew who to ask: Captain Tom Morales. What were the odds that Mikel was the child they were search for? In my world weirder things happened.

Drexel took the plastic straw and twisted it violently. "We have politely—yes, politely—asked your government and the Polish Consulate and so many others for help, for our cause, for the children's sakes. Deaf ears. What happens to babies who aren't desirable? The PSA tosses them for the street wolves to devour. The survivors end up in prostitution, drug running, begging on the corners, and living in the subways. Some die. Now our people who are part of the Polish American Club are asking to look at the PSA's records. Still, nothing comes of it. We have no voice. I've been in the States for a year, and we are this close." He held his index fingers about ten inches apart.

I asked, "What came of your effort today?"

"We learned that they're hiding the fact that the children are disabled." Drexel stood, smoothing the creases in his perfectly unwrinkled slacks.

"What will you do with the information?"

"In order for the adoption of children into the United States, the Polish government has to approve the papers. They believe, I am certain because I love my country and always try to believe the best, that the PSA is helping special babies and children find loving parents. Everyone knows that you people are too rich and have too much money and eat too much. Everyone knows that you buy whatever you want. Including babies."

Greta linked her arm in Drexel's, attempting to smile, patting his hand. "Americans will help correct deformities that Polish families, especially unwed parents, may not be able to."

"We're not all rich, you know," I replied, thinking of the people I'd met at the Daily Bread Mission that afternoon. Some of those were thankful to get a meal, a bed, and a shower.

"Now we know this, but in Poland, we did not," he replied. "Our country is only just coming out of the economic depression caused by your Wall Street. There is so much corruption and abuse of power. It's happier now than when my parents were alive and when the Soviets held us by the throats, but life is never easy. Now I have told you too much." He stuck out his hand. "I'm Drexel Bendyk and Greta is my bride. We married a few weeks ago. She's also an actress; she teaches dance and does the early morning traffic and weather report on KTNV, Channel 13."

"I thought I knew your face, Greta. I'm happy to officially meet you." I stuck out my hand.

"You will help us? Help us find my baby nephew, my *siostrzeniec*? That is the word for 'sister's boy' in the Polish language. Yes, together we end the tyranny." He raised a fist in the air.

"Wait one darned second, m'friend. You're not looking at a miracle worker."

"I saw you with Ms. Cheney. She likes you. She smiles and winks at you. That's right, isn't it, Greta?"

Should I burst their bubble and tell them Delta was putting the moves on me? Greta, thankfully, interrupted. "Her face changed with our questions. But you, Jane Angieski, you can continue to go through the adoption process and find out all you can about the babies, where they come from, and who knows where they end up? This is perfect. It's the answer to our prayers." They hugged each other and attempted to reach across to make me part of the group.

"Hold the phone, folks." I pulled away and held up my hand. This had to stop. I could not single-handedly stop the human trafficking or the abuse. "Are all the babies imported by PSA deformed or handicapped?"

"Most. Some just have, how do you say this. . ." He stuttered as the Polish accent shone through. "Some handicaps don't show up until the child is older. Like autism and dyslexia. You Americans think it's the luck of the straw."

"Draw? Straw? It doesn't matter," I said, and Drexel wrinkled his perfectly youthful and perfectly perfect forehead, looking ten years younger than the face that had recently been yelling at me when we came eye to eye, nose to nose, with only his car's windshield between us.

Greta whispered for our ears only, "Some believe it's God's will that they receive a special child; others do not want anything but perfect. They demand flawless babies. So they send back the baby, and PSA sells the infant again. That's what happened with Petra, you know. She was one of the first to be rejected. This has been happening for fifteen years. Now, as foreign adoptions have become popular, Cheney, that heartless witch, has become more merciless. More babies have died. Slaughtered."

The images of babies being neglected and deserted would haunt me unless I did something about it. The mental picture of slaughtered babies had already haunted my heart. I knew I had to do something, but did I want these two to know? I hedged. "Greta, Drexel, let me mull this over, and I'll let you know."

No three ways about it. It was time to call Tom or Officer Christy to find out about Mikel's limp and what exactly was wrong with the child.

"Come to Petra's class tonight, Pastor Jane. Please, and tell us your decision," Greta whispered.

WWJD? Even with Jane as the J, it came out the same. It'd be impossible to look myself in any old mirror if I looked away. Hopefully I wouldn't find myself out of a job, in a jail cell, or forced to date Delta Cheney to get the goods on PSA.

We said our good-byes, and I rifled in my purse for Tom's business card. After popping in the numbers into my cell, he picked it up on the first ring. "Morales, here."

"Tom? Jane Angieski. I need advice. About PSA." I wasn't that surprised when Tom huffed straight into my ear. "Are they breaking laws when the kids offered for adoption are supposed to be in good health, with sturdy little bodies, and they're not?"

Tom exhaled, and I swear I could feel it through the cell phone. "Holy moly, Preacher, who have you been talking to?"

Did he need to know? Rather, I said, "Is the noose getting tighter on the PSA? I went to an adoption introductory meeting, and the photos were of babies and kids who looked normal, nary a crutch or wheelchair in sight. But Delta Cheney nearly went into coronary arrest when one of the couples at the meeting demanded to adopt a kid who has special needs."

He inhaled for what seemed forever, exhaled as if he had all the time in the world. "There's probably some frickin' fine print in the 'kid rental and return agreement' that doesn't hold them liable if the baby or child is disabled. It'd make my day to get my hands on some of those forms, but it's too soon in the investigation to subpoena them."

"You're day's made. I have the forms."

"What? Are you at church?"

"I'm about a half block from PSA and near. . .wait, let me see." I looked out the window. "Do you know the McDonald's across from the One Horse Club on Tropicana, about a block east of the Strip? Wait, that sounded like I'm in the club but I'm sitting at McDonald's across the parking lot from it."

"Hold on a minute, Jane, I've got to get this other call."

So I did and continued to look out a window, which had just been cleaned by a sweating kid dressed in a uniform that needed to be washed. The young man cleaned off the foam, ran the squeegee down the glass, circled it all with a grubby paper towel, and went on to the next window. That's when I saw it. Pastor Bob's Lexus, minus the good pastor or Albert Miller, his driver, an arrangement that had come into being with Tom's help.

Yes, that was the same Albert Miller who wasn't to come close to any gambling unless he wanted to go back to prison for an exceptionally long time. The car was smack dab in front of the club's door, in the zone marked "Handicapped Only."

"Jane? You there? Sorry."

"I'm here, Tom." Physically, at least. "Darn it, you jerk, Albert Miller." I put my hand in front of the phone and grumbled.

"It's cutting out. Can you hear me? Stay put. I'll be there in twenty-minutes, twenty-five at the max, even without sirens."

I tossed the soft drink into the trash. Phewy. No man of God gambles. Period. And you'd better put that in italics and underline it, especially when I realized he was doing it in broad daylight, taking along someone who had to steer clear of casinos like I steer clear of more than one trip into the Godiva's Chocolate Store per mall visit. You probably won't see the One Horse Saloon and Game Club on any AAA must-visit list, and forget about getting a glimpse of it on the Travel Channel. Dives like that club stay well below the radar so they won't be cited for patron endangerment by just breathing the air inside. The grubby gaming hall was sandwiched between two low-end day spas, which in Vegas-ese means houses of prostitution, with a tattoo parlor and a cell phone store finishing the block. There was a fake Western boardwalk and hitching post in front of the casino with a railing that was broken on one side.

I was across that parking lot before sanity reined me in. It was one thing if Ab Normal wanted to ruin his entire life and make

Desert Hills Community Church the focus of suspicion and gossip for believers and non-believing folks in a hundred-mile radius, but dragging Harmony's dad in on his gambling was a shoe of a rotten color.

A stench like bad meat meets sauerkraut throttled my senses as I pulled at the heavy door. I held my breath. But a girl can only do that for so long; I gulped some air before entering the lair of sweat and sorrow.

In a Danielle Steele novel this would be a "despicable den of sin," with the hero there to convert sinners, and he'd probably have a halo around his head. Sure, there'd be sunlight glimmering down, enshrining him in a Godly glow. But this was Vegas, and inside it was even more icky, sticky, and grimy than I thought it could be. If I were doing a docudrama about out-of-luck gamblers and wasted alcoholics, I'd have filmed it at the One Horse Saloon. The varnished wood bar ran the length of the room. Ten or twelve tables sat in the middle. I blinked from the fumes and darkness.

Oh, yeah, I had one trifling glitch. I hadn't the foggiest notion of what Arthur Miller looked like other than Harmony's complaint to Gramps that her dad was, "Gross with that bald head." Picture this—I was feeling my way into a blackened casino, looking for a bald guy who I didn't know from Adam. Adam would have been easier to find, fig leaf and all.

With celebrities, football stars, and everyday guys shaving their heads more often that I shave my legs, you'd think this search for a bald man would have turned up lots of possibilities. Not so. I leaned on the bar and my forearms stuck tight. A layer of arm skin ripped off as I stepped back, and the bartender got closer to my chest than my Wonderbra when I said, "I'm looking for a man."

He drooled, wiped spittle from the corner of his puffy mouth, and said, "Yeah, well, I can certainly help you with that, honey. But if you're working, looking for a john, you're on your own. This is a poker club. You know, you are a first-rate-lookin' specimen of a woman. I like 'em plump, mores to hold on to and squeeze, and I gets off at six. That is, unless you're working, and in that case, I'm not buying."

"Thanks. I am employed, but not working in that way. Besides, I'm looking for a specific man, a friend."

"That's what they all say. How about a drink while you're waiting?" He leaned even closer, but I was hip this time, and me and my Wonderbra moved back.

"The guy I'm looking for a guy with a shaved head and he'd be with another man, a short, chunky man with hair that reminds you of Elvis."

He took a long drag on a cigarette. "Don't know about the bald dude. But look that way and you'll see that Elvis hasn't left the building." He pointed and, sure as shootin', Pastor Bob was chatting it up with three of Vegas's scruffiest.

"Bingo." Albert had to be nearby, probably in the toilet, although there were no chips at the empty stop next to my good pastor. Probably because Albert had lost his shirt already, I mumbled to myself.

I ached to lash out. Have a hissy fit to beat all hissy fits, both at Albert and Pastor Bob and maybe the creepy bartender too, just for good measure. I wanted to do them serious bodily harm. What would it accomplish to catch Bob in the act of gambling? What would it do for our church? What would it mean for Harmony's dad, other than a one-way ticket back to prison?

I had been batty to come in, and the dim-witted act swept over me like Gatorade on a football coach. Nearly blinded, I now saw a shadow behind the steering wheel of Ab Normal's car. The head was clean-shaven, and I dashed to the driver's side and said, "You're Albert Miller?"

"Who wants to know?" he grumbled, opening the car door and unfolding his body one part at a time. With each movement, the frown grew deeper. He wasn't just tall, he was *tall*, basketball player tall.

I bluffed and stepped closer to him. He stepped back. I liked that in a man, that he could read that I meant business. "I'm not threat to you. Besides, I'm Jane Angieski." Nothing registered, a gal can tell. "You know, like Pastor Jane, the woman who is Harmony's foster parent and her pastor at church?"

The man grabbed me. Squeezed the breath straight out of my lungs in a crush that would have garnered applause on *Wrestlemania.* "Thank you, ma'am, I cannot thank you enough for taking in my little girl. You are an answer to all of my prayers. Having you and Harmony together is a Godsend."

The squeezing stopped but then he twirled me, which isn't an easy task. "Ah, Albert, put me down now." I gulped in what air I could and pushed on his chest.

"Oops, sorry. Let's talk in the shade. Thank you and bless you. All those months in jail, I prayed that sweet Harmony would be protected. She shouldn't suffer for my sins. I don't understand why you just walked out of that dive. You don't gamble, too?" He shoved his meaty hands into his jeans and nodded toward the door.

"I thought I'd find you in there. I saw Bob playing cards."

"Losing at cards," Albert huffed the correction, and smoothed a hand over his bare head, as if he were used to a full head of hair.

"You've been working with him, driving him around for only two days. How can you be sure he's losing?"

"You're kidding, right? Believe me, he's losing, or you can pretend the Easter Bunny is dancing with the tooth fairy on top of the poker table as your pastor is saving lost souls. Give me a break. A guy who spends a lot of time in the cheap casinos, Pastor Jane, and comes out steamed and not plastered or being ushered out by the bouncer as he's hollering stuff I can't say to you, my bet is that he's a loser. I'm no saint. I know what he's doing, and it's ruining his life." He backed off and shrugged. "Yeah, okay, I'm not paid to think. I'm a driver, happy as a hog in new mud to get this gig. But yesterday and into the night, we were doing a version of this. Except it's hotter today."

"He's been gambling for two days straight? You just wait here, Albert. I'll be back." Okay, maybe this wasn't one of my most impressive career decisions, but there was a decent guy sizzling in the sun while a certain unscrupulous Las Vegas minister was inside with air conditioning and losing heaven only knew how much. And, might I add the question: Whose money was he gambling? What would you have done?

I marched right back inside and over to Bob and put a Vulcan Death Grip, straight from *Star Trek*, on his shoulder. "May I have a word with you?"

Bob flinched, and the cards flew across the table. Another guy at the table spilled his beer. One swore. The dealer grunted, "That's it. Table closed."

Guess they figured I was the wife. Probably looked like it, too.

Pastor Bob's eyes got twice the size of the chip on the table. "Jane. Oh, my. You don't understand."

"Oh, I am certain I do."

"No, Pastor Jane, you don't. Let's get out of here. This is so easy to explain." He laughed, high and unmanly. "I'll explain everything, everything you need to know. And only what you need to know."

He took my arm, I yanked away, but took off ahead out of him and out of the casino, squinting in the light, tripping over the railing of the One Horse Saloon. I caught myself, regaining my balance as Albert looked the other way.

I glared at Pastor Bob. "I don't have time to listen right now, Pastor. Get help, please. If not for yourself, then for our congregation, your flock."

"Wait. I order you to wait," he hollered in my direction, but I was moving toward the tan cruiser with the LVPD insignia on the side as it pulled into the McDonald's across the parking lot.

Ab Normal could concoct whatever story he wanted; I'd seen the truth with the IOUs and him in action. What did he think

I planned to do with these tidbits of incriminating evidence? Phewy, what did I plan to do?

I was boiling, and it had nothing to do with Las Vegas in July. Should I go to the church board? Best to write or email the District Council? Bob needed help, but Lord help me, I didn't want to be his counselor.

As I stormed into McDonald's at the same second grabbing the PSA adoption application papers from my big ol' purse. Tom was just inside the doors and I, shoved the papers into his extended hand, and flipped around. I'd had enough of human nature for one afternoon.

"Whoa. Hold it." Tom held fast to my elbow, and quickly, for a guy his size, he was in front of me. Think brick wall. There was a lot of him. "What's the rush?" His chocolate eyes squinted.

"You would not believe who I just saw in that place over there." I pointed. My finger quivered.

Tom's eyes followed my finger. "The devil himself? Hey, just joking. You too ticked to laugh? You can't drive anywhere in this condition. Take some breaths. And sit with me for a few minutes. I need a break. My, you are a fine-looking woman when you're steamed."

"Put a sock in it. I have decisions to make." But my feet didn't scamper away, and my elbow felt all tingly in a delicious way. Okay, my body was easily nudged into a booth.

"Can you wait until we have iced tea? I won't make any more 'gosh, you're beautiful when you're angry' remarks, either. Promise. That was daft of me, but gosh, I haven't had much practice being with a woman in a long while."

"What about your Officer Christy?" How that "your" got into the question, I have no clue. I regretted it the second the cop's eyes sparkled.

"She's a co-worker, Jane, a co-worker who happens to be married. To a fullback with the San Diego Chargers." His eyebrows, which were lush, went up and down. "You care." He made a fist like he'd just gotten the winning touchdown, which I felt was cute and weird at the same time. Then he said, "I don't have much experience with dating a smart kind of woman like you. Sit still, will you? Don't move. I'll be right back."

"I'm making myself nervous, Tom." I shrugged, attempting to shake off the stench of Pastor Bob as I watched Tom head to the counter. I said to his back, "Just a few minutes and then I'm off to dance class."

"Need a partner?" He handed me one of the iced teas he had carried to a booth.

"No. Um, Gramps is expecting me to dance with him." I didn't want Tom with me. Okay, my brain didn't, but my body seemed to have other longings. But brain won when I realized that having Tom there when I just might do something not fully appreciated by the law, like serious snooping without a license, could be bad for our budding relationship.

"I've been dumped plenty of times, Preacher, but I've never heard that line." He sipped the tea like it was the most important thing in life.

Was he kidding me or did he feel bad about being shot down? "Handsome guy like you never gets dumped. It's in the Code Book of Cute Men, isn't it?" I flipped out the line, and then wanted to slap my mouth. I was flirting, in public and in less than ten minutes after my senior pastor was found gambling, by me, no less. "Wow, I'm out of practice, if I ever had any practice at making suggestive repartee, that is in the last decade. As for being dumped, seriously, I find it hard to believe that you'd have any trouble with women."

"Soon as they find out I'm a cop, they smile politely. Some look guilty and comment about parking tickets. Then I'm history."

"Try being a minister. Guys run. Every time it seems I've met Mr. Right, his first name turns out to be Always. He's not reserved about that, either. Seems I'm meant to be a widow for the rest of my life, which is okay."

"Widow?" He frowned. Like that meant something to him.

"Yeah, long story. Heck, it's tough to counsel couples on marital problems when I'm single and childless, but when they find out my pilot husband died just months after we were married they know I have no on-the-job experience. Oh, way TMI—too much information. My mouth doesn't stop, especially in awkward situations. That sets off a silent alarm in men."

"I look like I heard any alarms?"

"You're a cop. You're not supposed to be scared." I laughed again. So much for not telling too much too soon.

He studied his hands, rubbed the bruised knuckles, and said, "Don't let anyone tell you it's easy out there. If a cop stops being scared, he or she is usually dead. Will ya knock off staring across the street? Okay, and now, answer this: Have you seen anything in me that would be frightened by a woman of conviction? A woman who was confident and smart?" He put down the iced tea.

A bear-like hand stretched out. It moved toward mine. It was either going to touch my fingers or I'd have to take my hand off the table. Quickly.

The world and my breath stopped.

Have you heard of deciding moments? Have you ever felt your next actions might, just might, change your life? No, me either, but as if it had a mind or heart of its own, my left hand stayed put, with the palm up. Decision made.

If it's true that there's a season for every purpose under heaven, was this where my heart would be restored? Or smashed to smithereens?

Chapter 10

Tom's palm was calloused, his fingers muscular, and his grasp felt just right, rather like settling into an overstuffed chair. Not that Tom really looked all that much like furniture, although he had a few to lose. Heck, if I were equally honest, so did I, but we're not talking about me here.

One touch, and I was ready to flip through *Brides* magazine. Just what does a nicely padded preacher wear to her own wedding? When that question settled into my pea-sized brain, I pulled my fingers out of his grasp with the same speed used when you touch a boiling pot.

He jumped too. Electricity between us? Sheer fear, my guess. "Tom, we've known each other for, what, four days? I'm an adult, a solid citizen, a woman with a doctorate in religion and so much on my plate right now that it's all spilling over onto the floor and getting splattered on my shoes."

He pulled his hand back, empty as it was. He took a long drag on the straw connected to the iced tea. "Forget it. I've always moved too fast for my brain to catch up. Four days? Yeah, I'm the fool, but it felt as if I've wanted to know you all my life." He gulped, clenched and unclenched his jaw. "My folks were married fifty years. They married after knowing each other two days. Thought it might run in the family. If you laugh, Jane, I swear, I'll be emasculated for life."

For the first time, I heard the Spanish lilt, and I gulped. I was Silly Putty in the guy's hands. I reached across the bright yellow table and grabbed his hand. "I'd never laugh at you, Tom. Besides, we have lots in common." But luckily, I didn't say, "And someday maybe I'll tell you about my revelation about *Brides*."

We both looked at our hands, and he asked, "Think we might go on a regular date sometime, Preacher? Movies or dinner?"

"Will you issue me a citation for a rain check, Policeman?"

"No."

I swear tears sprouted to my eyes. "What? Just like that?"

He looked about a zillion percent more comfortable and laughed. It sounded as smooth as Ben & Jerry's Brownie Batter ice cream. I've done plenty of research on that variety so I know smooth. "It's going to be your turn to ask me. That's the rule, from now on. Ball's in your court."

Was it that easy to fall in love? Pshaw, not me. I was too old, too tough, too religious, and I lied to myself too often.

Tom checked his watch. "Break time's over, got a mountain of paperwork to go through." He took the pile of adoption forms with PSA's pretty logo and said, "I've got to make some sense of these. You need them back?"

"Yes, I want to proceed. But before you go, how's Mikel? I met the woman who found him when I was at the Daily Bread Mission."

"Did you meet the gal, Eddie, who could be a professional wrestler? Seems she runs the place. There's always one. Yeah, we talked to them all. Mikel is okay. We're still trying to find a Polish psychologist to talk with him, but the three we know of happen to all be on vacation or down with this flu stuff. All at once. Ought to be a law against that."

We walked toward the doors. "My grandfather is a kind person, Tom," I said, "and speaks fluent Polish, but he's not a psychologist. Hey, there's a Polish Social Club meeting tonight after dance class. Would you like me to ask if there are any psychologists in the group?"

"You'd do that? You liked that kid, didn't you?"

"Call me Saran Wrap, see right through me. Will you tell me if there's anything odd in the forms? Can you have somebody drop them at the church tomorrow? I'll be there all day."

Driving back toward church and sitting in my office, I tried to think about VBS, tried to focus on the report that waited for my attention—tried, but heck, trying didn't cut it. By a quarter to six, I was back in the SUV and heading to my six o'clock dance class date at the East Las Vegas Senior Center. As I pulled into the lot, Gramps called me, double-checking my arrival time. He was giddy. Some redhead he'd been dancing with had invited him to the coffee klatch afterward. I couldn't tell if he was starving for female attention or the kolaches or honey cakes they served.

*

I found a spot in the shade of a spindly tree as Petra pulled in next to me. She locked her battered gray Toyota then waved calling to me, "Jane, I heard news in the berry vine."

"Grape?"

"No not about grapes. About a young boy, just five years old walking around in the bad section of town. Limping. You must understand. This could be important. My friend Drexel's nephew had a limp, and he is about five or six. The records from the Child's Play Home said that the boy had a severe knee ailment. He was born with only one kneecap." Her delicate lips formed a pained straight line and her forehead, the color of vanilla ice cream, actually wrinkled. She put a hand up, shielding the sun so she could see me.

"Why didn't you tell me about Drexel and Greta sooner?"

"They wanted everything to keep as secret. I know Drexel and Greta talked with you today, but this berry vine talk came from the *buscias*, the grandmothers. They talk a lot—too much sometimes. They think it's bad for me to be here to fight the PSA all alone. They're going to help, but what can a group of little old ladies do to fight these criminals?" On cue, one headed straight toward me. Petra scooted, at full speed, in the opposite direction. The girl was no fool.

"I am a buscia. Do you know what that means?" said the one who charged at me first. She was fierce, and I knew better than to try to grab back my arm.

"Yes, Grandmother," I responded in Polish.

"Good, then you know I am serious. Stop the PSA or we will." She extended an arm, motioning toward the door.

I turned back to see. Five endearing grandmothers were standing there. "Look over there. That's the Buscia Brigade. There are more of us, too, more around the country."

"I will do my best." She let go of my arm and I rubbed it. That'd leave a bruise, I thought. "A phone call I have to make might even help. May I go now?" I sounded about five years old, but this lady looked like my own buscia. Dangerous.

"You'll come back after." It wasn't a question. "We're having social time and there are nice men for you to meet. You are not married, says your sweet *dziadek*—ah, grandfather. He's not married, either, is he? Oh, this is good. You will help us, and we will find you a good, strong husband to give you many babies," she said and slapped me on the backside. "You are a good fat woman. Good to have babies."

"Let's see if I can help you first, shall we?" I jumped away before she could slap me again. "Get the guys to line up, and I'll check them out to see if they're worth marrying me." I tried to laugh, but the buscia pulled me down to her level and smacked a kiss on both cheeks, whispering, "I am glad you're here, *dziewczynk*. That means baby girl in Polish. Help us stop the PSA, and we'll find the right *maz,* that is, a husband for you."

The buscias kept circling me like sharks, but I managed to move through their lines. What would they do to me if I didn't help them stop PSA? Violence would be the answer, I had no doubt. You've heard about mama bears being separated from their young? They're regular pussycats compared to Polish grandmothers. It would not have shocked me if they'd decided to storm the PSA office and tar and feather Delta Cheney if she refused to stop the black market baby business.

I opened my cell and pushed the numbers for Tom's office only to get his voice mail. I pushed the numbers for his cell phone and got another one. I was standing there wondering how in the world to find him when my phone rang. "Jane here."

"Jane, it's Tom. Are we okay?"

"Are we a 'we'?" I was way too confused about our relationship or what it might be or even morph into to encourage this line of talking or thinking so I snapped, "Tom, what exactly is wrong with that little Polish boy Mikel?"

I could hear sirens in the background. Again. Tom responded, "His foot, a malformation in his ankle and knee. The docs seem to think it can be surgically repaired, but I have got the Feds breathing down my neck and I can't worry about that kid right now. Sorry."

Chapter 11

"You sure?" I trembled then I asked, "Not a hip or an ankle? Or a kneecap?"

"Awfully curious about that kid's bone structure. Yeah, why?" The sirens were getting louder. "Hey, Jane, looks like I have to take off. In my business, there are interruptions."

I swear I heard a crash and what sounded like, "Put your hands against the car," but then I have been known to have a fertile imagination. "Is everything okay?" Those sounds were beginning to grate on my under-caffeinated nerves.

"Part of the job. Why?"

The siren ended it for me and fantasies of snuggling with Tom. I'd buried one lover who thrived on adrenaline, and each time an F-15 flew overhead out of Nellis Air Force Base, I saw Collin's jet burst into flames and heard the sirens on the airfield. Period. No more "we." I mumbled, "Yes, yes, it was the noise."

"You've got to loosen up, Jane, especially if we're going to see more of each other. Do you? Can we?"

Changing the subject was safer than heading down that dead-end highway. "Which knee? Which foot?"

"I'll have to check. Something from trauma to his mother before his birth. Probably beat when she was pregnant. But the doctors only checked him out to make sure he hadn't been physically abused."

"And, was he?" I held my breath.

"Physically, other than the limp, he's good. Breaks me up. He loves playing catch. The kid's pretty good. Maybe we can take him to the park. Or something?"

I didn't answer his question about getting to know me better or the park, but ended the conversation by closing my phone as I walked out. I felt queasy. Could the doctors be wrong? Could Mikel be Drexel's long-lost nephew? There were a million reasons why this wasn't possible and about a million more why it could be. Sweat popped out on my top lip, bottom lip, armpits, and in the crevice between my breasts. Some from the heat, but most because coincidences do happen. Could I make this come true by holding my breath, keeping my fingers crossed, or sprinkling salt over my shoulder?

I was a-wishin' and a-hopin' and a-prayin' as Carl Lipca touched my arm, circling his fingers around my elbow. "Jane, have a second? There's something I wanted to ask." He looked down at his soft-soled dancing shoes, then up at me with gooey eyes, the bedroom kind he'd flashed at Petra just before I had wrestled him to the dance floor.

"Is Drexel still around? I have some news," I said.

He looked hopeful and stepped six inches closer. "Tell me something I can print that's going to throw mud on the Philemon Society."

"There was a Polish boy found walking the streets this past weekend. Drexel said he was looking for his nephew, and I thought it could be the same boy. But there's no real way of telling."

Carl continued to look at me, as if I should be saying something more, then he said, "You mean Mikel?"

"How do you know? Of course, you're a reporter. You know everything, right? Probably more than I do." He laughed, and again, I felt uncomfortable with the guy. "What else do you know about the PSA?"

"Nothing you'd be interested in. Just stuff. Petra probably told you, too," he said.

I was certain, or my favorite chocolate isn't chocolate, that the man was not being honest with me because once again, I got an irritating, itchy feeling about Carl, like wearing a wool scarf on an August afternoon. My brain instant messaged my mouth, and my woman's intuition screamed for me to listen. I obeyed.

I could see Gramps whooping it up with one buscia after another; he waved, but I turned around, away from Carl. "I forgot something in the car," I muttered. I needed air, needed to not feel obligated to hang out with Carl and possibly say something about Drexel and Greta and especially how I'd met them.

"Get your dancing shoes and come back. We can talk more about the PSA," he said.

I was on information overload, but still, as I walked from the center, I saw a shadow. Have you ever turned and felt someone there? It was that creepy feeling, but then again my entire day had been creepy to the core. Nonetheless, I slipped my keys between my fingers to protect myself, just as I'd read in some safety article in *Cosmo.* I'd never tried it. Yet, when that grip landed on my shoulder and I flipped around to maul my assailant, I knew I could. The assailant, however, was none other than Pastor Normal.

My hand stopped nanoseconds from perforating his face and I said, "Are you stalking me?" My hand dropped to my side. "You tracked me down here? I thought your ankle was damaged, and I know your driver's license has been revoked. What did you do with Albert Miller?"

"He thinks I'm at the meeting at the senior center. Those old people are always yammering about something. I went out the back door."

"The local press, a journalist, is inside, Bob." Why did I care? Was I protecting him? Was I totally nuts? Wasn't this contributing to his sins? Wasn't it time I stopped second-guessing myself and gave a lot more thought to the man who was attempting to remove the keys from my fingers? I pulled my hand out of his reach; he tried to grab them back. There was no wrestling because I would have won, but the death grip on my hand had hurt.

I squeaked, "What do you want?" Maybe if I hadn't seen him at the casino, totaled the IOUs in his office, or gotten an earful of his pseudo self-righteousness, I would have been a little more understanding. Alas, I was not.

"Let's talk in your car. Drive someplace quiet and private. We must talk alone. I'm your senior pastor, remember? This is an order."

Thank you, I do have a brain inside this head, and the man gave me the willies. "No, Bob. We won't just drive someplace quiet. We can talk here."

"Have it your way, Youth Pastor Angieski. Which is your title for now," he ground out the words, waiting for me to unlock the passenger side.

I did, then rolled down the windows, although there was not a breath of breeze. "What do you want to say?"

"Earlier today. The casino where you walked in on me. It was just a friendly game, a diversion from the stress of my job. Nothing more."

"There were lots of chips on that table, Bob. I don't know much about gambling, mind you, but chips are money. Right?" Where was this going? What could I do to counsel him? My addictions tended toward chocolate, spas, and expensive hairdressers. I could afford two out of three, and I often dreamed of spas.

Now it was officially dark in the parking lot, yet I could feel him looking at me. I tried my death stare, but his buggy eyes were locked on mine.

"How could you, a woman, understand what it's like to be a man of responsibility?" His body started to straighten as if a sermon was forming and his jaw worked up like he was chewing a wad of bubble gum. Then he said, "I was there doing God's work." He snapped his fingers. "Yes, God's work is mysterious and hallelujah."

I guffawed, which included snorting, a la Sandra Bullock in *Miss Congeniality*. "That's rich, Bob. Give me a break."

"I am not surprised that this is beyond your limited feminine thinking. I was there, like Jesus who went to talk with the sinners, the ladies of the night, the tax collectors. Do you see that? Don't you know my job, um, *our* job is to be with sinners and not saints?" His voice boomed as if from a pulpit before an admiring audience of thousands.

"Bob, cut the malarkey."

"Pastor Jane, Pastor Jane, Pastor Jane," came the voice, with a singsong quality. "There are sinners everywhere, the fields are ripe. The sinners all need our Lord Jesus Christ. Just say 'hallelujah' to that, woman, say it with me." He was waving his arms. He turned.

I wasn't hallelujah-ing a nut job and watched his arms fall to his lap.

Even in the twilight, Bob's eyes were spooky, best seen in a Stephen King movie and not in my SUV in a deserted parking lot. My mouth could have used an order to shut up, but it didn't. "You weren't in that poker game to save souls. You were there—"

"I wasn't going to bring it up to them until the game was over," he snapped. "Wanted to show 'em that the Lord can work wonders with money, winning at poker if they'll just believe."

"But you were losing."

"Never, you're looking at a winner. I am a winner, woman. Frankly, women cannot understand such matters." His chest puffed out, but the eyes blinked like he was off his meds or on a sugar buzz.

I tried to remember I was attempting to communicate with a sociopath but couldn't stop trying to use logic. "Bob, if you're gambling as much as you do, you're a loser in life. Besides—"

"Hold it right there, Miss Virgin Purity, you are so wrong. And you call yourself a pastor. How dare you preach to me? Look at you, a woman who cannot even hold on to her own church. You travel around the country as an itinerant minister, hoping some poor schmuck of a preacher will die, and you'll sneak in and fill a real man's shoes. You're the loser, big time, no doubt. Even the District Council knows it. Oh, don't look so shocked. Why in the world do you think you were sent here? It was so you could learn how to preach from a real man. From me."

Perhaps there was truth coming from the mouth of a maniac, but I'd had enough. "Get out of the car, Bob." My hand was on my cell phone. "Get out of the car right now or calm down. I will not have you insult me as you've been doing."

"I'm not a loser," he said. His voice had switched to that of a recalcitrant child.

"What of those promissory notes in your office, in the credenza? You've lost nearly a half million dollars. Whose money is it?" Accusing him was not part of any plan. It jumped out when I wasn't thinking.

"How dare you pilfer through my desk? Have you no shame?" He opened the door but didn't budge. "I'll report you to the District Council. I'll do it tonight." He pulled his phone from his belt.

"Please. Call now, if you'd like. I'll chat with them, too." Maybe I should play poker, because he seemed to believe me, as he didn't touch the phone.

"Everything is legitimate with our financial statements at the church. You're not going to get dramatic now, are you? I can do without all that whining and whimpering."

"Have you heard me raise my voice? Have you seen me become hysterical?" I do, but hadn't yet in his presence, which was a miracle in my book.

He cleared his voice, and an arm went up as if he were in back of the pulpit. The booming voice was there again. "I've been a minister for twenty-two years, twenty-two good years, I say. I've been an excellent steward of our church money, including our building fund."

"I didn't say anything about the building fund, Bob. Is that where the money is coming from?"

"Money that is left in the bank earns squat, but this has nothing to do with you or your frilly goody-goody female notions."

"Who else knows?"

"Forget this conversation, darn it all, if you know what's good for you. You will forget it." He inhaled the words. Then suddenly the anger turned 180 degrees, and he was sobbing.

I let him blubber. "When you're ready to talk, I'm here." Trust me, at that second I would have rather jumped on a scale with my weight digitally displayed on a scoreboard as big as a football field in a stadium filled with supermodels then talk to Bob.

We sat in the darkened lot for too long. I listened to my breathing and then Bob's. Finally he spoke. "You know, I could stop you from ever telling anyone we had this conversation." He looked straight ahead. "I could. I'm strong, you know." His voice was once again filled with pouting sounds, whiney, craziness that now sounded frighteningly rational. "Here's the plan. We'll drive out to that truck stop in Barstow, but you won't ever get that far because I'll dump you out. I'll wipe my prints from the car—yeah, I do watch crime shows—and tell everyone how you confided that you were going off with some truckers for a good ol' time.

"I'll just leave your car there and hitchhike back here to Vegas. Hitch a ride with someone who doesn't know me. I've already had questions about your abilities from the congregation. No one will really be shocked, especially after I put your name on the prayer chain saying you need spiritual counseling. There have been numerous complaints about your style of dress. You don't look like a minister, madam. It's rumored you're living in sin. Why, even Delta asked about your sexual orientation. I'll tell them you were having one-night stands with truckers. You just went off with one. That's it."

He was talking about doing away with me like I might wonder if I should supersize my Taco Bell order. I couldn't speak; it felt as if I were in a bad dream or reading an Anne Rice chiller starring yours truly.

He turned and stared at me. "Worst case? The District Council wouldn't argue that you're unpredictable to put it kindly since we've all seen your permanent record with its scores of infractions and complaints. As for the money, if they ever find it, well, I didn't get a degree in accounting to mess up something this little. But now, Pastor Jane, it's all messed up. Because of you." His voice went from a whisper to a shout that rocked the car.

The man was certifiable and to quote him, "that was putting it kindly." Me? I was in deep water with no life preserver in sight. "Get out of my car or I'm screaming bloody murder." Just then the life preservers came into sight as I looked in the rearview mirror. I turned and pointed, and he followed the point. "Get out now, Bob. See those little ladies in back of the car?" I'd never in my life been so tickled to see the buscias. In full force. I waved with both arms out the car window. I shouted, "Yoo-woo." It saved my bacon.

Bob's faced changed to look like a frozen pizza, blotchy and brittle as I opened the car door. "Buscias? Over here. I've changed my mind. I want to meet your handsome young men, men who need wives." I looked back at Bob and sneered. "You'd best vamoose. These ladies won't leave me alone for quite some time."

The gaggle of buscias swarmed closer, the intensity of the chatter directly attributed to the amount they'd consumed of the three C's: cookies, cakes and coffee. They were in rare form for matchmaking, and I was in their crosshairs.

Bob winced, swore, and opened the car door. He put a foot on the pavement and turned to me. "You win, Jane. I will be praying for you that you forget this entire conversation. I will pray for you, but remember, I have the power of the District Council right here." He put out his hand, palm side up, and ground his thumb into the spot where a heart line might have been. "Yes, I'm leaving but, madam, watch what you say. I'll be watching you. Never doubt, I can and will make your measly little life even more revolting than it is. And do it any time I choose to."

With that, he left, crouching so the women didn't see him leave as the buscias descended on me. I knew I'd be trapped with their version of *The Bachelorette in Vegas* as they mentally had me marrying Smiley, Dopey, Mopey, Donder, or Blitzen, or whatever my prospective grooms were named. Bob was gone, and I was about to hug the breath out of the ladies for saving me from my untimely demise at the hands of Pastor Bob Normal. I'm not enough of a Pollyanna to ignore that Bob wasn't down for the count, but a girl can catch her breath between rounds. That was all I needed.

*

The next morning at VBS, not one child ate crayons. No one puked or had a little accident. We didn't even need to call the paramedics. I was in the kitchen helping to organize lunch bags to take to the mission when Tom called. I ignored his message.

Later a courier delivered the adoption papers from PSA, which I would fill out that afternoon, then drop off. The PSA had to be stopped before another kid like Mikel was dumped on the street to die. How would my filling out the papers help? Call me clueless. It seemed in this spot any action was good.

I purposely avoided getting near Bob's office but met Vera in the kitchen, where she was sipping coffee. "Pastor's ticked today and stormed out with some kinda' business on the Strip," she shrugged.

Poker tables on the Strip was closer to the truth, but I kept my trap shut, and thank you, I can do that once in a while. If I could get proof that he'd threatened to murder me, he'd be dealing poker in the slammer. Honestly, who would believe me, a new minister with a criminal record, against a pillar of the religious community?

The day was hot and dry and it dragged. With the adoption forms completed, I drove to the PSA offices to find the doors locked. Had the police arrested the scoundrels?

This good and happy thought crumbled as Delta's cream-colored Mercedes pulled into lot. She trotted the short way toward me. "Well, Jane, so good to see you," she purred, smoothing her hands over the hips of a pearl-colored linen suit, teetering up the sidewalk in pink stilettos. "Did we have an appointment, Pastor Jane? Not a problem, unless it matters to you." She giggled and jingled her bracelets. "Oh, what a week. One benefit event after another. PSA is in heaven's hands with all the publicity we've been getting."

"I could have a few minutes?" I asked, still marveling at her balance in those shoes.

"I really wanted to spend time alone with you, um, telling you about how we're bringing so many dads and moms together with babies. From the money that's pouring in day after blessed day, why, we can help more babies." She kept fumbling for something in her hot pink, snakeskin-motif leather bag the size of Rhode Island. "Oh, you know the money isn't the reason why we are doing this. Of course, you do, since you know Bob. You are so lucky to be working closely with him." She sighed. "Although he's not really my type."

I swear there was longing in her eyes, and I knew what type she preferred. After last evening, I also knew Bob too well for what he was: a maniac. When I finally got to bed, I'd tossed plenty, thinking of what could have happened if. Thanks to the buscias, it never came to "if."

Still fishing in the bag, she said, "Now, don't get me wrong, the babies and their adoptive parents are the stars of this. Did you see me on KTNV this morning? I had a half-hour interview, little old me, on the news. It was fantastic." Bracelets banged and bobbled as she dug more deeply into her purse. "Where are those naughty little office keys?"

"Delta, could we talk about the children?" It was now or never. "I have concerns regarding the handicapped kids."

The fumbling stopped and then started again as her pancake makeup seemed to get brittle. "All of our children are guaranteed to be perfect, flawless, right as rain. Unblemished in every way."

We stood at the locked door. She fumbling. Me waiting. Even

though we were in the shade, the heat had melted her multi-layered foundation, and midnight blue eye shadow was crinkled at her crow's feet. The mascara looked like she was becoming a raccoon, and her blush now matched the color of her purse.

The color on her face intensified, and not in a flattering way. "Stupid, crummy, idiotic keys. Where are they?" Sweat dripped down the side of Delta's face. A droplet plopped on the walkway in front of her office. We both watched it evaporate.

"Let me help," I offered. I reached out to grab her bag as she was excavating the deepest regions of it, and our purses collided, as did our bodies. Girl stuff scattered, sprinkled, and shattered on the walkway.

"You've helped now." Delta screamed. Anger welled, at the purse I'm happy to say, and she flipped it upside down to shake, rattle, and roll all the contents on the cement. "May as well throw it all on the pavement."

With the last, violent jiggle, the keys flew out, preceded by a compact, sunglasses, notebooks, aspirin, a gold-colored pen, a hair clip and lots of bobby pins, breath candy, credit cards, hairbrush, hair spray, hair gel, a CD, loose tissues, lip gloss, gum wrappers, glasses, Mars bar wrapper, toothpaste, a silver bracelet, coins, a plastic bag with a very brown banana, a nail file, a pair of pantyhose, and a plastic fork. As if she was possessed, she gave the jumbo purse one last shake, and we both watched as an inch-thick stack of promissory notes clearly showing Bob Normal's name flew from the jetsam of her purse. As the bundle tumbled, the rubber band snapped, and the desert wind picked up the papers like confetti.

She could move fast for a tall, broad woman. She giggled, made gargling sounds, and grabbed the papers with Bob's scribbled signature, dashing after one that was swept away. Straightening up, she dried her fingers on the hips of her skirt and said, "Just look at what little old me has done now. Oh, Jane, what silly stuff we girls put in our purses."

She knew.

I'd seen the promissory notes. Bending over, we sorted the innards from our purses—some for her, some for me.

I gathered the CD Gramps had recorded of the neighborhood garage band's music, a grocery list, a pencil, a calendar from Staples, tampons, a chick lit novel, and a wad of slightly used tissues and thought: Were these the same ones I'd seen in Bob's office or yet more debts? I'd never know because she had them all again. But why was she carrying them around now?

I tried to hand her the adoption papers but she was backing up away from me. "Can't we talk, Delta?"

She nabbed the brown banana and the plastic fork. Without looking at her watch she said, "Oh, the time. I simply cannot spare a second." She reached down once more to stuff the Visa card and a gum wrapper into the bag and ran to her car, waving. "I'm late right now."

"Wait, Delta. You've got my lipstick."

She screeched to a stop, reached in her bag and tossed me one, a gold-colored tube that definitely wasn't a color I'd ever buy. Pink. No one wears bright pink, right? Made me wonder why she did. To prove she was girly?

I called to her, "Can't you spare a few minutes? We need to talk about this, um, business. And the adoptions? About the families? Me being a mom?"

"Come back again, Pastor. Real soon, you hear?" The tires squealed as she pulled out of the parking lot.

I looked down and found a pencil that had tumbled away and then saw a gold-handled hairbrush. Delta's. I felt beneath the bushes near the office door for anything that had rolled there, and my fingers touched a paper. Not a scrap of litter. It was a debit form from one of the big casinos on the Strip and in the amount of $5,000. Bob Normal's signature was on the bottom. The due date was today.

What really happens when gambling debts go unpaid? If you've watched TV in the last ten years, you know there is always some husky, ugly bruiser who bounces the borrower for the bucks. Would an enforcer come to church? Were there rules for this kind of thing? I felt that puking feeling come to my throat.

How long had Bob been squandering church funds? How much had he spent? Lordy, if he could steal from his own church, the church he's sworn to shepherd and care for, then detail how he was going to murder me in cold blood, what else was he capable of? I had no answers, and my head throbbed. My nose was again stuffed up. I longed run to home to Mama, except I didn't have a mama who cared, and my house was filled to the brim with humans and a barking machine in fur.

I sat down right where I'd stood, resting my butt against the door marked Philemon Society of America. I closed my eyes. Could I, an underling preacher, one breath away from being ousted for my buttinski-ness, call the District Council and expose Bob? Why would they even believe me? The whole enchilada was so far-fetched, even I didn't want to believe I could believe it.

Pastor Bob Normal was a leader in the Las Vegas community. He'd taken Desert Hills Community Church, as I was so often informed with waving arms by Bob himself, from a tiny family church of under thirty souls into a mega church of over six thousand congregants each Sunday. He'd raised money for the building, negotiated with the builders, and cut corners to have everything a mega church should have so that he and the flock could reach out and help the helpless of Sin City. I'd heard this five to fifty times in the weeks since coming to the desert. I turned the IOU in my fingers. "Why?"

"Why what? Jane? You okay?" There was Tom, all six feet of him, standing in front of me.

I tried to scramble to my feet, lost my balance, and managed to fling myself straight into his chest. Even in the tangle of arms, and with only the slightest idea that I could easily reach up and plant my lips straight on his, I shoved the promissory note into the pocket of my Capris. Why? The police—which was definitely Tom, although he was dressed in a blue Hawaiian shirt and khaki slacks—didn't need to know about Pastor Bob's dirty deeds. "Fancy meeting you here."

The giggle sounded hysterical. "Am I on the most wanted list or something? How did you find me?"

"Actually, I called the church and Vera told me you were headed over to PSA. We need to talk, Jane." He took my arm, just above the elbow as he might do with a felon, and we headed to yet another McDonald's across the parking lot.

We sat in a booth. We sipped iced tea. We stared at each other. "Jane, there is something I need to tell you," he said, twisting the straw between his fingers and smiling. The guy not only was cute, he had perfect white teeth.

"What?" I snapped.

"Hey, turn that frown upside down." He took his fingers and demonstrated on his face. I know I was supposed to laugh, but I was royally ticked. He didn't give up. "Didn't your mother ever tell you that if you make faces they'll stick like that?"

I forced my lips to turn up. "It's been a tough few days, Tom." I took a long pull on the icy liquid. There were no right answers about Bob Normal except to do the right thing, which was to call the District Council. Did they need proof? I felt my pocket. The paper was here. Was that good or bad? And what of Bob's career? Headed for the toilet as far as I could tell, but then again, I wasn't privy to information held by the District Council. "So why are you here?" I asked.

"It's like this. Un-involve yourself with this PSA stuff. Just get out of it, Jane."

"I'm concerned, Tom, concerned for the children out there like little Mikel."

"Yeah, I know, well, just back away."

"Because you're saying so?"

"There's trouble in River City—or Vegas, actually—and—" He waved a hand toward PSA. "—it's all about what goes on in that building. I didn't know until I got this lousy promotion, a job with tricks up its sleeve. Seems like conspiracy material for *60 Minutes* or reported by that slick Anderson Cooper."

"Are you saying this is official business now? That's good, isn't it?" I watched his eyes. They didn't tell me anything except I wanted to spend a few years looking into them, and that of course wouldn't help any baby in the clutches of PSA. I turned toward the window.

"Look, Jane, look at me. I'm taking off my badge." He unclipped it from his belt, placing it on the table.

"Really, Tom, I'm not as much of a bumbling idiot as I look and didn't just now fall off the turnip truck. Just because you aren't wearing a badge, it's foolishness to think you're still not a sworn officer of the law." I shoved the badge back toward him and took a sip of the acidic tea. The taste had changed as my mood soured. I would not be told what I could and should not do. Especially by Tom Morales.

"You're right. This is personal with you and me, and I wanted to let you know I'm doing this for your own good."

"My own good? I am not a child, in case you've missed that. I make mistakes. I take chances. I do my job, which happens to be saving souls and helping sinners. I don't know exactly what God has in mind for me right this second, but I do have His word that it's for the greater good." I looked out the window, at the kids running around the restaurant, at the weary workers behind the counter. I refused to look at Tom, and when I did, our eyes locked. We both scowled. "What's really up with all this?"

"I'm not at liberty to say. Jane, you're a smart woman, and I understand more about you now that I've done a thorough investigation of who you are." Then he huffed, as if that last revelation shouldn't have come out.

I barked, "Before or after you told me your life story and led me to believe we could actually go on a date?" I was steamed. "You used police databases to check on me? Am I good enough to date a big strong police officer?" I jumped from the vinyl booth like my panties were on fire. "I hope you found out enough to realize a smart woman like me wouldn't put up with this baloney, Captain Morales. I don't like your style of getting to know a woman and now getting rid of a woman. What happened? Did the sound of my dateless situation for the last five years scare you off?" All of which came from my mouth as I bounced up so quickly from the booth that the iced tea flew from my hand, down my blouse and on to puddle on the floor. Or did I scream this as Tom stretched out and caught me in midslip as I slipped on the puddle, only half of me sprawled on the floor, only to rip the shoulder of my shirt? Or did the manager swoop over and plead that no lawyers needed to be called?

All of the above? Mighty smart of you. I scrambled to my soggy feet, sopped the tea off my shirt with a fistful of paper napkins, slobbered an apology to everyone in a four-block radius, and skipped the joint, while a shred of pride was still left in place.

Then? I made it out the doors and behind the wheel of the SUV. The tires hit the same squealing notes as Delta Cheney's Mercedes had when she peeled out of the parking lot minutes before.

Chapter 12

I didn't make it to the first signal before my phone rang. My cheeks were scalding, and I felt as graceful as Bridget Jones. I snapped back the cover and snapped. "Jane here."

"It's Vera. Better come back to church," she whispered, and since I didn't know she even could use an "indoor voice," that frightened me.

"Wait, I'm in traffic. Okay, I'm pulling over, Vera. What's happened? It's not one of the kids?"

"Jane, trouble's brewing. Jane? The District Council is here, well, one person, and she's asking for you, not old Bob. I haven't seen him in hours, since he rushed in here about eight this morning, dug through his desk like a whacko, screamed orders at me to have you take care of the church business, and split the scene like greased lightning." I could hear Vera inhale, and the next words came in a whistle. "And he was swearing like a teenager who just learned those four-letter words. Ah, it gets better, or worse, depending on your view of the mighty minister. You want to hear now or later?"

"I'm on Las Vegas Boulevard, and I'm about twenty minutes from church."

"Wait, I'll read her card. It says 'Louisa May Stephenson,' and with our church's denomination listed below. The woman's a prune, Jane. Looks likes she needs to add more fiber to her diet or has bad PMS or maybe ate lunch at the café across the street. Hurry, will you? She's scaring me."

"You can count on me," I said into the cell then ended the call at the same time I screamed to myself. Someone from the District Council wasn't supposed to arrive until next Monday. Crud. It's

Friday. Had stinking Pastor Bob Normal called them to come get me early when he couldn't dump my body in the desert?

Traffic crept along, and twenty minutes turned into thirty. I was sweating bullets and tripled that production when I saw Bob's Lexus parked in his shaded spot. He'd done it. He trumped up charges against me, and the DC was there to personally take away my ministry credentials. The jerk was blackballing me. I'd been in tight scrapes before, sure, but ministering was my life, my calling. The idiot wouldn't get away with this. I squared my shoulders and stormed into the church and down to Vera's office to more than likely to face a firing squad.

Vera yanked me back into the foyer. "I've been around, Jane, and never once has the District Council rep looked so angry. They just don't do this," she whispered with her booming voice. "She's only the size of a toadstool, but the meanest eyes I've ever seen except on that crack dealer who hangs out on the Strip."

Vera kept an iron grip on my arm. What could the woman have said to make Vera a basket case? It had to be Bob's doing that the DC lurked beyond.

"Now this woman from headquarters has come to—" But the words stopped as Bob's office door opened and musty, powdery-smelling perfume only some elderly aunt would wear preceded Mrs. Louisa Stephenson out into Vera's office. Vera looked at me and then to Mrs. Stephenson before she grabbed her purse and waved. "Quitting time," she cackled. If I hadn't moved, she would have flattened me with the speed of her exit.

I was alone with a woman who looked like Einstein in drag. As short as she was round, Mrs. Stephenson stood in the threshold of Pastor's Bob office and said, "Thank you for coming so quickly, Pastor Angieski."

Quick or slow, my goose was cooked, and from the scowl on her face, she was going to enjoy watching me squirm as she told me to take a permanent hike from being a pastor.

I didn't remember walking into Bob's office but I must have because I was standing in the middle wondering if she'd listen to my somewhat logical explanation. But then she said, "Sit down and call me Louisa, won't you?" She leaned forward. "We have a situation here." She swept her hand around Bob's office, and at least to me, it looked like post-Katrina hurricane damage with Hurricane Andrew thrown in. "Are you aware of it?"

Why was she being gracious when I was going to get the ax? Why ask me to use her first name if she was there to do the dirty work? Of course, this didn't make sense, but my world never did as you have come to realize. I looked at the brown iced tea stain down the front of my blouse and then to her. "More than I care to."

"We at headquarters are concerned." Louisa cleaned her glasses on a hanky. "This is a matter of grave importance."

I stared. I hadn't seen a handkerchief ever used before except maybe in a high school play. If she was this old fashioned, that swan song and the cooked goose would be roasting together. I gulped. "I'm sure Pastor Bob will clarify everything and tell you about my work here." I grasped the edge of Bob's desk, since there were papers on every single chair in the office.

Starting with the first visitor's chair, Louisa Stephenson scooped the litter to the floor with her pint-sized hand. She cleared the other in the same way, then scooted her butt on it. Her feet didn't reach the carpet. "I am sure you're aware that many pastors are leaving the ministry."

That's how it's handled? I "leave" the ministry? They don't yank my credentials? Less messy. Looks better on some stupid, blinkin' statistic someplace that some clerk tabulated for each denomination. Well, not this little gal who happens to be a minister, I'll have you know. The toad would have to ask me outright, I vowed. But she was saying something else. I stopped to listen.

"Situations like this," Louisa began, "always make us very sad, as you can imagine."

"Just cut to the chase and get it over. I have chocolate to eat, pounds and pounds of it. Wait, first, is there anything I can say before you complete your reports?" I dug into my purse for medicinal M&Ms, but they'd been gobbled on the drive over.

"We thought you'd be upset." Louisa's little forehead wrinkled more, making her look even more like Kermit the Frog.

I sighed. Without coffee or chocolate, apparently my bravado was zilch. "Are there specific situations you'd like to hear about, or shall I recount it all?"

"I want to hear everything," said Louisa, leaning back in her chair, crossing her baby-sized feet at the ankles.

The woman got an earful about sex slaves, the black-market baby trade and child abandonment. I told her about Pastor Bob Normal. Told it all. "Everything I've done has been with a pure heart, although some people—" I meant Bob the Gambler. "—may have told you otherwise."

"Yes," Louisa said, and nodded.

"When do you take away my job, take back my credentials?" The words squeaked from my throat.

"My dear, why don't you just tell me when you first suspected Pastor Bob of ministry violations?"

I was staring at her feet as she crossed her ankles in the other direction. For a woman as round and short as she was, her feet were delicate, even though her shoe choices, orthopedic-esque, made me queasy. I was looking at her shoes when *wham*, it hit me. "What? This is about Bob?"

She nodded.

I jumped up and down like a forgiven sinner at a tent revival. "You're not here to reprimand me, but Pastor Bob." I'm embarrassed to say I remember my moves were reminiscent of a running back making it to the end zone, swinging my booty, waving my arms. I finished this sight for sore eyes with, "You're from Dallas to discipline him, oh, thank you, Jesus," then ordered my mouth to clamp shut. For once, it listened to instructions.

"Now, Pastor Jane, calm down, please." She leaned forward. "We know you well, perhaps not personally, but from talking to others, we realize your methods are unconventional. That said, you are a fine pastor."

Yes, those were her words, at least as I remembered them because I was going to have them placed in needlepoint and framed for a picture. Bliss hit. I felt like Sally Fields when she accepted her Oscar. . .yes, they liked me. "I, um, well, could you be specific?"

"Back to business." She cleared her throat. "Information about Pastor Bob's behavior came to our attention a month ago. The tithes skyrocketed, a holy thing, but attendance went down. For summer in Las Vegas, that surely is not usual. When the associate pastor resigned and the youth pastor asked for a leave, we wanted to know more."

"But the youth pastor is having a baby," I said.

"Yes, that's true. I just came from her home. She was concerned about the stress of working with the pastor in her very early pregnancy since she'd been in fear of having another miscarriage. The council is aware of your skills in handling touchy situations. Hence, my visit."

She studied the lines on the tablet resting in her lap, or maybe she was waiting for me to say something. But what? Bob's debts? Bob stealing the church funds? Bob's attempt at murder? I didn't know I had so much to say, and without coffee, either. We talked till my bum was numb.

"Still, you did not contact the District Council, Pastor?" asked Louisa. This time I swear there was a sparkle in her navy blue eyes.

Phew. I spilled that, too. "I was afraid all this was somehow my fault. Like before. . ."

"Yours?" Louisa smiled, displaying a ring of tiny teeth, like a child's. "I do not know what happened to you when you were a pastor before, my dear, but historically our senior pastors, unlike Bob Normal, do not gamble away funds and threaten God only knows what when the staff doesn't cooperate with rants or depraved requests."

I sighed and rested my head against the chair's back. But then she said something that nearly gave me whiplash as I snapped to attention. "You'll help us, dear?"

"Me? Help? Headquarters? Before you say anything, please know I'm sorry for any negative publicity I gave the church. I have never, ever meant to hurt anyone with anything I've done, and I'm really glad I only talked with CNN a few times." I sounded like a kid in the principal's office or Beaver Cleaver talking to Ward, but that's how I felt. "I'm sorry."

"Tut, tut, child," said Louisa, and while I doubted she was ten years older than me, I lapped it up like a puppy. It was sick, but I'd been the ugly, sinister minister so long this was glorious. "Don't tell anyone else, but I have kicked some butt in my day." She tut-tutted again.

I believed her. She might be as round as she was tall, but the woman had moxie. I wondered if she was Polish.

"I am here today not to speak with Pastor Bob, but to you," Louisa added. "For your help. But first, I must know you'll be discreet."

"Anything," I said.

"We, the members of the District Council, would like you to find out Pastor Bob's connection with PSA. Just to clarify, Ms. Delta Cheney attends the church, but she's not a member, is that correct?"

I nodded yes.

"Good. Can you find out how deeply Pastor Bob is entangled in the PSA schemes?"

"You want to know if he's getting a kickback for the babies?"

"Unfortunately, yes," Louisa said. "We know your pastor is connected with Ms. Cheney. For goodness' sake, his face is on their web site. He counsels couples before and after adoptions, especially those that don't work out." She added a note to the folder she'd extracted from her baby-sized briefcase. "It could be that wire fraud is involved." She looked at a previous page of notes and said, "We'd like to know before others do. You understand. We know about the gambling, but until you explained about those debts, headquarters had no idea how much money was involved. Where is it coming from? Where is it going?"

It seemed a trifle strange that she didn't ask about the building funds or to see the accounts, but the District Council works in mysterious ways. Besides, she wasn't in the office to chew me out, but rather to ask little old yours truly for help. Amen and hallelujah, and I said, "What can I do? I'll do anything."

"You have helped already, dear. You're on our side now. I'll be in touch. Just be yourself, your curious self. I'll call you soon." She checked her watch and heaved her backside forward until her tiny tootsies, clad in tan Oxfords with laces, touched the floor. "Oh, of course, you could record conversations, take notes, snap pictures, little things like that."

And she was gone, without a final prayer. I fingered her card. There was no doubt that she was from the District Council. She had even given me her private phone number to call day or night. As for finding me? The church directory had me listed under 1-800-buttinski. I rubbed my hands together. The feelings of revenge might not be pretty, but they felt like a million bucks. Now that I had a license to snoop, it was pushing a billion.

*

I flitted and floated through the day repeating, "They like me," until I got a call making me regret I'd inhaled three dark chocolate Mars bars. In celebration for not getting canned, mind you.

It was late in the afternoon when a call from one of the moms whose daughter was a best friend of a kid that someone knew who had overheard Harmony talking about a problem when some girl thought it was Harmony talking in the girls' bathroom. You won't be tested on that.

Since Harmony grunted in response to all of my questions, we hadn't bonded in any old way. I punched Gramps' number into the phone. From the music, he was doing the two-step at the rec center. "Hold the phone, Jane. Okay, I'm walking outside." The music quieted. "Okay, let her rip, baby. What's up?"

"I heard a rumor, and you don't have tell me not to listen to gossip."

"You've already found the problem," he replied.

"At least you admit it, but big fat good that is going to do. Besides, as a pastor, I know some gossip is based on truth. What have you to tell me?"

Gramps yelled something to someone then came back on the phone. "I wasn't going to tell you anything. Didn't think you'd hear so fast."

"What. You knew about this all the time, and just when were you going to bother to tell me? I cannot believe this of you, you of all people." Steam surged from my ears. "You are a bona fide lunatic." I turned off my laptop, grabbed my purse, tucked the phone under my chin, and walked from the church building. I had to get home. The SUV was blistering, but I slipped in, turned on the engine and fired up the A/C as Gramps said, "Jane, get a grip, and for God's sake switch to decaf. Why should you get your britches in a bunch about this?"

"Oh, that is rich, Grandfather. Why in heaven's name would you think I wouldn't want to know? I'm way too young for hot flashes, but I am flaming, white-hot mad."

"Didn't think you'd care, being all busy and that stuff."

I counted to fifty before I could squeak, "Care? Care."

"Jane, they're kids. They do this."

"Yes, they've been doing 'this' since Adam and Eve, but it's still dangerous, and the consequences are plots used for movies on the Hallmark channel." I huffed and puffed. The man was deranged; that was the only answer.

"The kids deserve a chance at this, don't you think? Besides, they could be good. Hey, stop that heavy breathing, Jane, they're all kids, college kids, and renting here like you are. I can get them some gigs and maybe play with them. Why are you so steamed?"

I barely was able to squeak, forget speak. "Wait. What about Harmony? What of her future?"

"Hey, if that's all you want. We'll include Harmony if you like, but don't go ballistic, kid. It's just a band. She's a beginner, but I guess she could play."

"Hold that, mister. Whatever are you yammering about?" The A/C droned on, the engine purred, and I sat there in the parking lot. Stunned.

"Listen closely. Jane, take some breaths and think back about what I've been saying."

"Listen. I'm making breathing sounds. You'd better talk quickly. Why, if you knew for a long time that Harmony was pregnant, didn't you tell me?"

"Harmony and pregnant? What? Whatever are you talking about? No, this is about the young men who live in the house next door. I'm going to help them, with a condition. If I play with them and manage the band, they're going to have to stop singing smut and stay in school."

"A band?"

" You see, granddaughter, I've been watching you with all that's on your shoulders, with Harmony and the mooching pooch, the love you show without asking what you're doing or going to get from it, and I looked at how you've handled yourself with that nut-nick pastor. Yes, I've heard some gossip around. You've stepped up to the plate time and again, Janey. You're my role model, kiddo. Now, honey, *if* Harmony is pregnant and that's a supersized if, you need to click it down a notch. You come at her like this and the kid'll spook. Hear me on this?"

"Ah, jeepers. Okay, after I talk to Harmony, and if I can take some breaths and lower my voice, let's celebrate. What time is your class finished?"

"About six. Janey, one more thing. I've been thinking of my gal friend Gerry, too, and how wrong I've been to string her along. Do you think she might want to go steady with an old geezer like me?"

"Steady?" I shook my head. "Why are you asking me? And why now?"

"See you later? How about that big seafood buffet? It's at the MGM, I think, and then we can take the monorail and pretend we're at Disneyland. Check with Harmony, will you? She *was* looking a bit green today when I left."

"Gramps, wait," I screamed, but he was gone.

"Terrible things can happen when girls are on the street," I said out loud as I drove to the condo. I had been one thing to talking with teenagers about the consequences of sex, but this time, and with Harmony, I just prayed I was ready with the right words. A knock on the window, and ready or not, the decision was made. "Harmony." I unlocked the door, and she and Tuffy crawled in to settle in the passenger seat.

"Pastor, can we talk?" She looked straight ahead; we both did.

"Talk is good. I've been wanting to talk, but this has been a frenetic week." And then I gulped. "I'm sorry. It's me. I've been too busy to notice you needed to talk."

"Did you get into a fight at church?" she asked, and I looked down at my stained, ripped and sweaty blouse and would have guessed the same. Then she added, "I'm in trouble."

While Tuffy licked my face, smashed between us, we hugged. She was rail thin from the worry over the unplanned pregnancy. "Harmony, tell me what happened. Remember, I'm a good listener and no stranger to big problems. You know there are people who love you and will help you, don't you?"

"Yes," she said in a childlike voice because she was a child and now with child.

"The first thing we do is go to the doctor for a checkup."

"That's a good idea." She put her head against Tuffy's back and nuzzled the pooch. "Will that help?"

I took a breath. When I'd signed on to be a foster mom, I didn't expect to be a foster grandmother in the same week. "Why ask that?"

"Well, couldn't going to a nutritionist help?"

"Good eating is important for pregnant women," I responded.

"Who's pregnant?" She and Tuffy had the same questioning eyes, except Tuffy's were brown.

"You." I blinked.

"Pastor Jane, you've learned lots of stuff in seminary, but didn't they tell you a girl can't get pregnant unless she has sex? I haven't done that." Her face got the color of my favorite petal-pink blouse.

Mine had egg on it. The face, not the blouse, which was neck to belly with a tea stain. "Isn't that what we're talking about, about your period and not having it?"

"I'm anorexic. I think. The Internet has lots of stuff on it, and that's how I've come to figured it out. That's why I don't have periods. Maybe it's stress about Dad. I thought I'd be okay here, but I'm not. Help me, please. I'm afraid. Terrible things happen with this disease. I'm dying of not eating." Tears dripped on Tuffy's furry snout, and he cleaned her face like his life depended on it.

I grabbed her. "I owe you a bundle of big fat apologies, sweetheart. You're right. What did they teach me? Maybe it was how to be an expert on jumping to asinine conclusions."

"You'll help me?" She pulled back slightly, but didn't shrug from my embrace.

"Right now, I can. Let's go inside. I've got a list of counselors. One helps girls with eating disorders." I squeezed her hand. "I'm proud of you for talking with me. You're brave." I started to get out of the car, and she placed a hand on my shoulder.

"You might want to hear the rest," she said. "There's also a part about me being a total jerk. I didn't want to believe it, didn't want to think about it because he's going to go right back to prison for this. Stupid runs in my family."

"Your dad's gambling again?"

"You saw him, too? Me, too. I was at the shelter helping to serve lunch. Lots of ladies were there and they didn't need me, so I played with the kids. I saw my father drive a gray Lexus to the parking lot across from the shelter, and don't laugh now, but the other man looked almost like Pastor Bob. Does he have a twin? They walked inside that casino with the neon flamingos. That was a few days ago, and then today, they were there. I followed him."

"In a casino?"

Harmony nodded. "I watched them. For a long time."

"Did your father see you?"

"Not at first, then yes." She smoothed shaky fingers over Tuffy's rough-coated back and looked out the window.

What wasn't she telling me? "Did you talk with him? What did he say?"

"Nothing."

"Maybe didn't recognize you."

"Oh, he knew me."

For the millionth time in the last few days, my blood pressure went way beyond a healthful level. I gritted my teeth and said, "Harmony, trust me. I want you and Tuffy to go inside the condo. I want you to sit down and cool off. Take a shower or get something to drink, juice or bubbly water. I am going to find a nutritional counselor for you, and we'll handle your eating disorder."

I rolled down the window as Harmony and Tuffy got out of the SUV. "I'm going to pay a visit to your dad and find out what's really going on."

"Pastor Jane?" Her hand was at the door. "I ran after him, out the door. Dad pushed me aside, again like he didn't want to know me. He hates me." She rubbed her arm. "I slipped and fell against a slot machine, but he never even turned back to see if I was hurt."

"Maybe he doesn't know you, honey. Maybe he's so lost in gambling that he doesn't know what's right. No fretting. I'll find out. I'll tell you all the truth. Okay?"

"Okay," she said, barely audible above the whine of the car's A/C.

Back in ghastly gridlock, I drove like the devil was biting my butt. He'd lied to me. He'd thanked God and then lied to me. His own daughter saw him.

When I reached the house, circling the block three times to finally give up for a spot hiking distance from where Harmony's dad lived until he was officially out of the system, Albert Miller, now thought of as "that idiot," was sprawled in the living room.

He looked up and tossed aside the *Review Journal* as I stormed through the front door. He knew why I was there.

I didn't care if the other guys lounging heard. Maybe if they did, they'd knock some sense into the idiot. "Ignoring a child might not be abuse, but pushing one aside as you've done certainly won't make getting custody back any easier. Let's not even talk about the gambling issue. Yet. So what kind of a father are you, Albert?" I asked.

"A degenerate one, Pastor. Walk outside with me, will you? There's a covered patio out back. It'll be hot, but can we talk there." He shoved the tail of a worn golf shirt into his faded jeans and headed toward the cluttered kitchen then out the back door, walking without even seeing if I was in back of him.

I was. Close. "I am the one who will be listening, Albert. You need to tell me what's happened. I know the requirements of your parole, and just keep in that thick skull that I'm the current foster parent of your daughter."

I stood, hands on hips and eyes on the man who was hurting "my" child. I was burning up, and it had nothing to do with the bank sign I'd seen a few minutes before flashing the temperature. It was still over one hundred.

"You don't understand, Pastor," Albert said, pacing the ten-foot patio.

"Yeah, gambling means more to you than your own child?"

"You may not believe me, but I had to be there."

"Albert, this is murdering your chances of ever having a family, being a father, watching your daughter grow into a woman. What don't you get? She knows you'd rather gamble than be with her. Can you imagine how that slices into her heart?" Was that regret, anger, or what on his face?

He shrugged. "You don't have a clue about the battle I'm fighting, feels like everything evil and vile that you can name."

"There are ways to win, such as with honesty."

He paced. I watched. He paced. I longed for a Starbucks iced coffee. He paced. I would have even taken a McDonald's iced tea. Or a Coke. Or tap water. He paced.

He stopped and turned to me. "It's for her own good."

This time I could read the anger; it looked just like mine. "Her good? That's claptrap."

"Just take it that there are some vicious folks in this town, and they got me. I'm in their clutches. The only way to get loose is to play along." He began to pace.

Drugs? Alcohol? Pornography? Something more to do with gambling than the mess he was already in? "Hold that one second, my friend. Tell the truth, or I'm calling in reinforcements." The cops? Could I do it?

"Truth? But at what price? I'm locked in. Give up on me, Pastor, let me sink to the bottom of the filthy sewer, and I won't even make a whimper as the sludge drowns me."

"Have it your way, Albert. When you're ready to talk to someone—me or another pastor, but not good old gambling buddy Bob Normal, that's for sure—let me know." I handed him my card, pointing out the cell phone number. "Reach me any time. Why? Harmony loves you." I picked up my purse, dusted off my backside, and left without looking at the other men lounging in front of the television watching *Cops* or maybe the evening news blasting the details of another high-speed pursuit. I headed out through the desolate yard, past the gate that was swinging by one hinge.

My head pulsated. Sweat dripped and skidded down my back. I was furious, mostly at myself for letting Albert off the hook so easily. I stomped down the block, beating my sandaled feet into the pavement. The toe of my right foot caught in a crack. That's when I bumped smack dab into none other than Monica Wainwright-Dobson.

Chapter 13

Monica Wainwright-Dobson in that sordid section? I thought of pinching her, but why do it since I'd just bumped straight into her? She was flesh and hard muscle, even though she was a socialite. "Monica?"

"Oh, my goodness, this is a surprise." She patted her face.

Where was her limo? The driver in the swanky suit? Where were the Julio Somebody outfits and Jimmy Choos? She'd been transformed into a soccer mom with an *I Heart NY* T-shirt. The four-pound diamond earrings were gone, as was the Rolex.

"Did you come to visit someone in the house?" I gestured toward where Albert lived.

Her upper lip had droplets of sweat, but of course it was sweltering. Her voice came on all upper-crust when she said, "I often come to this neighborhood. There's the shelter, of course, too."

So, I'd been right when I thought I'd seen her dash into the shelter during my last visit. "But why?" Okay, it was probably because she was Mother Teresa. Monica was a saint. I'm slow. I cupped my hand around my mouth and whispered, "Is it because, like you told me, you weren't always dripping with money?"

"My reasons are purely selfish," she said, her ramrod posture indicating the end of this discussion.

She'd been gracious and caring before, especially arranging for Mr. Newton to be the surprise guest at the fundraiser, so why did all this seem odd? If it was the absence of jewels, I needed to get a grip. You don't wear that stuff in this part of town. I got all perky and happy since I'd just figured out why Monica was in Vegas' skid row and said, "Can I give you a lift? I'm on my way home." I nodded to my car. But she stepped back.

I saw her eyes cut to the side, across the street, and then beyond where we were standing. "Oh, no, I've forgotten something at the mission. I have to go back and get it." She backed up three steps, turned around and waved. Then added, "Come to the house tomorrow afternoon about three, and I'll tell you all about why I'm here. It's a long story and requires huge amounts of iced tea, I'm certain. Besides, Wayne will be there, too." With that she gave another cheery wave and jogged to the mission. In the heat.

Okay, a non-buttinski pastor would have gotten into her car, cranked the A/C, put on some music and driven home for a cold shower. A normal minister would have retreated to a quiet spot to pray for Monica, for Albert, for a corrupt senior pastor, and the mess with PSA. But oh, no, not me. I got into the SUV, turned on the A/C, and drove down the block, waiting and watching in my rearview mirror as Monica went into the shelter. When I didn't see her reappear after retrieving whatever there was to get, I did a U-turn in a driveway and pulled in back of a delivery van. From the reflection in the plate-glass window of a used furniture store, I could see the front door of the shelter. I waited. It was dusk by now, but still hot as the blazes of you-know-what.

Ten minutes crawled like a turtle on Prozac. I turned off the ignition, got out, locked the car, and tried to be inconspicuous. I'd been to the shelter dozens of times helping the church women serve meals, bringing supplies, and sorting the donated clothing, ministering to the visitors. This time, I hid in doorways, crept behind cars, peeked into windows. What was going on in the shelter? Why had Monica dashed in? Had she left out the back door? Why all this cloak and undercover stuff?

Lots of good people, lots of rich people, spend time and money on the less fortunate. She wouldn't be the first and, God willing, not the last. Okay, enough said, I crept to the storefront window, stuck out my neck to peek around a pillar, and Monica and Eddie, the knuckle-cracker herself, walked out and straight at me.

So this hadn't been one of my best days, but as luck would have it, it was about to get worse. There I was on the sidewalk, crouched down in a doorway, crammed between a pillar and a used sofa. Suddenly the two women came out swapping secrets like schoolgirls. The whispering stopped mid-whisper as they bounced off yours truly.

"Were you waiting for me?" Monica's voice was tight in her throat. Initially her eyes were larger, and then turned to slits.

Eddie jumped down my throat, hovering over me as I regained my balance and Eddie barked, "Or me?" The weightlifter's muscles twitched in an unbecoming way, except if one is competing in a Miss Olympic Muscle contest.

I blurted the first reasonable thought that came to mind, which was, "You don't seem to be the type to offer charity, except in a monetary form. Why are you really here?"

"Stuff it. You don't know anything," Eddie said, towering over yours truly. "Why don't you take your grungy, sniffling, snotty, Bible-belting nose out of this neighborhood? All that stuff you said about bringing Jesus to these kids, that was bundle of revolting lies. Wasn't it?" The second was definitely a rhetorical comment, not a real question. She puffed up her chest and shoved her double chin down, which collapsed her triple chin. She grinned at me, with a space between her teeth a small car could drive through.

This was not the time to comment on the miracles of today's restorative dental work, so I smiled. I turned slightly because one, I didn't want to look at The Intimidator, and two, I could always throw my body behind Monica, quickly, should Eddie attempt to give me the old heave-ho straight into the street.

I gulped. "Will you tell me why you are here, Monica? Even though it's none of my business," I added, because in all honesty it wasn't. I could have saved my breath. Should have, actually.

"Eddie and I have business together." She started to step aside and around me. I stepped in front of them. Stupid is as stupid does, and I stuck my arm out to make a point.

Eddie took my wrist like it was a twig and pushed it aside as Monica said, "It has nothing to do with you, Jane. I'm sure you don't share the details of your life with everyone, now, do you?" she asked.

That, also, was a rhetorical question, because I share more details of my life with strangers than strangers are comfortable knowing. "Are you okay here?" I covered my brazen stalking with concern.

"Excuse us, Jane. Eddie and I have an appointment. We're going to be late if you keep us anymore," Monica said. She smiled her billion-dollar, pure-white-teeth smile, and she and the Olympic bone crusher headed down the street.

My inability to speak probably saved them from dialing 911 to have me arrested for aggravated pestering. I watched as the two walked just a half block and got into a full-size Ford truck, so new it still had temporary plates, painted eggplant and with sunburst yellow and chartreuse racing stripes on the sides. Monica got behind the wheel. A few days ago, if you would have told me her perfectly padded posterior would ever grace the seat of a pickup, I would have laughed myself silly. Eddie provided a jaunty as she got in. They were laughing. At me.

Gramps would have said, "I'll be a monkey's uncle," making his voice sound like a character on the *Andy Griffith Show.* Monica shifted the monster-mobile into first and peeled out of the parking spot. I stood there mute, truly I did, with my mouth gaping wide enough to have a 747 zoom in and out.

What business could they have together? There were never two less-seemingly compatible people on the planet. Monica was rich, a high-fashion diva who owned purebred dogs. Eddie's neck was as big as Monica's waist, and I could see her cuddling a rattlesnake before I could see her snuggling a canine.

Lots of people never make snap decisions. I am not one of those. While my track record with quick and sensible decisions is less than stellar, this didn't enter into any thought process at all as I dashed to my car, jumped behind the wheel, did yet another illegal U-y in the middle of the intersection and took off after them. From watching police dramas on television, I stayed a cool quarter mile behind.

"What are those two doing?" I asked myself. No response came except an icky, sickly feeling as my curiosity shifted into overdrive. Okay it wasn't my business, but the whole affair was odd, and yes, that was my excuse.

When common sense asked, "What are *you* doing?" I had to override that. Every cell in my body had to know why they were together, and fortune for my snooping was with me as every single light was green. I had no trouble at all following the purplish truck with the extended cab straight onto I-15. As they increased speed, so did I. I even let a semi between us, yet stayed watchful that they didn't exit. Monica, and probably ninety-nine percent of Americans, would never consider that a pastor would be tailing them, and my SUV was invisible since there are so many gold ones. "Do they know I'm here and not care that I'm, well, stalking?" I said out loud, which was weirdness by itself. I chalked it up to the aforementioned nutty rationale and maybe that they had important things to talk about. Like what? I had no clue, nor did one appear as we drove in and out of evening traffic.

If Monica had hired Eddie for some work like lifting cement blocks and moving tractor-trailers at her home, she'd have turned off at the upscale parts of Las Vegas. But they continued north, out toward the desert. If we all kept going in this direction, we'd be in St. George, Utah, in a few hours. I kept a distance, but I could see them, and about an hour out of Las Vegas, they pulled off.

I slowed because the exit was deserted, except for us. I clicked off the headlights. Driving in the dark wasn't that bad because the night was clear.

Monica's brake lights flashed as they pulled into the graveled driveway of a small, stucco home with a few junk cars in the front yard. A single, industrial-strength security light illuminated the scruffy bungalow. The closest neighbors were blocks apart, and if Eddie had been driving, rather than Monica, I would have sworn the socialite was being kidnapped. But who would kidnap she of major muscles? Who could?

I inched along the rutted road, hoping no little critters were lounging on the dirt. Now it was past twilight, yet I could clearly see the house. The door opened and a troll-sized, very round silhouette stood aside as they walked in. Who were they meeting in the middle of the desert, after sunset, and down a deserted road?

Are you wondering whether I was planning to get out of the car, sneak up to the house, and peek through the windows, like a lunatic would attempt? Yes, I was. But I looked at my tea-stained shirt and saggy Capris and realized I didn't know what a girl wore for situations like this. I'm not experienced at this sort of thing, even if some people on the District Council might tell you otherwise.

My fingers gripped the door handle, and I was just sliding my butt across the seat when I it. Not possible. I hadn't heard a thing. But it was all too true. Red and blue lights flashed. The cops had arrived.

The cruiser silently inched to a stop behind my SUV, the car coming within inches of my back bumper.

I thought of it, I did. I could easily rev the engine and skid out of this pickle. It would take the officer about one minute to jump back in the patrol car, and by that time? The truth was, I would be driving down a dirt road in the middle of nowhere with the police in hot pursuit. I nixed the notion after about a half second of serious thought.

Like the law-abiding minister that I always am, I froze, bone still, breath held until there was a tap, tap, tap on my window. I rolled it down.

"Good evening, ma'am."

"Ah, hello, officer." Praise the Lord, it wasn't Tom.

"Are you okay, ma'am?" He shined a flashlight in my face, probably trying to smell my breath to see if this was a typical DUI.

"I'm not lost. I'm just out for a drive this lovely evening. Look at those stars. Isn't it breathtaking out here, this time of the night, when things are quiet and, of course, once the sun goes down and those stars come up, and it's still except for those crickets? Do they ever stop clicking?"

I blathered another few idiotic lines of that stuff-that-blubbers-from-the mouth sentence.

Then the cop said, "Would you be kind enough to step out of your car, please, ma'am?" He didn't look a day older than Harmony, but the badge on his breast pocket told me he was the real deal.

"Really, really, I wasn't speeding," I said. Heck, I wasn't even crawling down the lane.

"No, ma'am. Just keep your hands where I can see them. Please step out and leave the keys. You don't need them right now. They'll be safe right there."

I'd been sweating buckets when I got caught snooping on the sidewalk by the shelter, but that was nothing to this. "Are you arresting me?" I'd opened the SUV's door, but didn't leave the car. How did the police know I was tailing Monica?

"Ma'am, I don't want to ask you again, but I will because the captain tells us we should be nicer to our citizenry. And you look like a nice lady." His voice lowered a notch, and he added, "Now, will you please step out of the car."

I did and stood ramrod stiff. "Should I stick 'em up, or put my hands on the hood and spread 'em or something? You'll have to walk me through the procedures. What of my Miranda rights?"

"No, ma'am, it's not necessary to do any of those things. You just need to stand there. Someone wants to talk to you," he ordered as a second patrol car pulled up to my own personal crime scene.

I would have known Tom Morales' swagger a block away, even in the dusky evening.

"We've got to stop meeting like this." I chuckled, but it was flat as the last soufflé that came from my oven. "Isn't it against the law to follow me, Tom? To stalk me like this?" Yes, it was a dimwitted remark since I'd just followed Monica and Eddie through most of the city of Las Vegas and out into the desert.

"We need to talk." He reached out to touch me, and I stepped back as he said, "Come on, Jane, get into my car for a minute." When I didn't move toward him, he ground out, "Please." We locked eyes. He won. I walked back to an unmarked sedan, opened the passenger door in back, and climbed in. Tom touched the top of my head, just like in those police movies, and crawled in next to me.

Tom seemed to get bigger inside that car, or maybe because I could feel the heat from his body, which was suddenly too intimate and yes, intoxicating. But that all was nixed when he growled, "You don't belong out here, Jane. You shouldn't be doing whatever you're doing." Again out of his tan uniform, he looked like a guy in the big and tall section of Eddie Bauer. His badge, stuck on the waist of his slacks, reflected the moonlight.

"You're right. I'll just skedaddle home, but since you're the law around these parts, what little one did I break that caused me to be stopped during an evening drive into the countryside? The city must have more criminals to take care of than a pastor going for a drive to get some air," I said, trying to make my voice light, but I knew it came out as a challenge. That was about as goofy an excuse as possible, but then it hit me. I slapped my forehead. "You're mixed up with what's going on here, aren't you?"

He turned away, checked his watch, and said, "I can't answer that, Jane."

"It's true. I knew it." I slapped my forehead one more time.

Why I was so happy to be right when I was sitting in a police car in the boonies and being told to MYOB by a police captain who was about to arrest me for stalking was beyond even my own somewhat questionable rational thinking.

"Please get into your car and drive back home," Tom said—well, actually barked. "Notice, this is a request, not an order, and I said please, Jane."

"I will not." My back shot up and I puffed out my chest. Tom's big, and I'm no delicate violet, so the backseat was crammed to the gills with stubborn streaks. "I'm not budging until you tell me what's happening in that house over there. And what do Monica and Eddie have to do with official police business? You may as well cuff me right now if you're not going to tell me, because I'm not going anywhere."

Tom's jaw clenched. Then ice formed, he withdrew his hulk-like body from the car, and he turned to the young cop who'd tracked me down. "Officer, take her downtown. I'll meet you there. You don't have to frisk her; I doubt she's carrying a weapon." As he said this, his voice trailed off and he bent down to look inside the car. "Tell me you don't have a gun, Jane?"

"Would you expect me to carry one?" And in that second I sorely wished I could have had one, just to make him flinch again.

"Jane, for heaven's sake, stop being pigheaded. Answer me or I'll get a female officer out here to strip search you. Do you have a weapon?"

"No strip search will be necessary, Captain Morales. Other than a lethal mouth, I'm unarmed. I do not have a gun." I sank down in the seat. Whatever was happening in the house down that dark road, two more dark-colored cars had pulled up and driven past the police units and their newest prisoner without even stopping, apparently unperturbed that the law was apprehending a felon, which was me.

*

I didn't end up in the slammer for the night because there was no official arrest. I wasn't fingerprinted or grilled in a room with a single bare light bulb glaring in my face. Instead, when we reached headquarters, Tom was already there to greet me. He opened the patrol car's door and led me to the lounge where we'd talked about Mikel.

Tom slid two dollars into the vending machine and handed me a Pepsi, getting water for himself. He sat at a table, heavy with fatigue or so I imagined. His shoulders rounded, and he sighed. I figured I could stand there all day being a stubborn pastor without a cause, or sit down to find out what was going on. I chose comfort.

He finished the water in a single gulp. "I asked you not to get involved, Jane."

"I had a prickly thought, like poison oak." I tried to explain about woman's intuition. "It went on red alert when Monica and Eddie walked out of the shelter together. They're the most peculiar twosome I've ever met."

"So you spent an hour driving through traffic, and another out of the city in order to satisfy your intuition?" The question sputtered out of his mouth; even to my ears it sounded ludicrous.

"I guess my intuition went bonkers when I saw Monica near the shelter and then palling around with Eddie."

He sighed. "If you were anyone else but a minister, I'd think there was an ulterior motive. So you have no idea why they were there, at that house, on the deserted road?"

"Yes, I have no idea, but I honestly wanted to find out. I'd bet the farm you know why, Tom, so what were they doing?"

He got up, bought another bottle of water, drank that in two gulps, and popped the empties in the recycling container. "Your car is outside. We had it driven back. You're free to go."

"Without telling me the why or what or the how and the where?" I sipped the Pepsi. No information, just dragged into jail and released after being forced to drink a sugary soda. Okay, I wasn't forced.

"That's it, ma'am. Please leave so I can get some work done. There are crooks and thugs and rowdies all over the city just waiting to meet me, and you're taking valuable time." He huffed the words and left.

When I finished the soda, I walked to the front desk, retrieved my keys, and found my car, with my purse just where I left it. I'd been lucky, I decided. What if Monica and Eddie were into something dangerous, and I'd sneaked down the lane, stuck my head in the window, and seen something terrible? I won't elaborate, but you have a good imagination and can probably come up with the same things I was thinking. Yes, I got off easy, because at least Gramps didn't have to bail me out of this one.

It was near midnight when I pulled into my driveway, and I knew as soon as it was dawn I'd do the right thing. I'd go back and snoop in broad daylight. If there were no cars in the driveway, I'd take a few long, hard looks inside. Door open? I'd go in. But then my cell rang, and plans were changed.

"Jane, it's Gerry, and you'd better start some of that yogic breathing that calms you down and that you are always spoutin' on about."

"I'm not going to like this?"

Gramps' gal pal and California State Senator sounded more upset than when she lost in a battle for shoes at a Nordstrom's sale. "Damn straight you won't. Listen, kid, something big is coming down in Vegas. Just keep your nose at church, your butt out of stuff, preach a pretty sermon, and don't do anything suspicious."

"Then you don't want to know what just happened?"

"Spare me. I'd rather not, if I know you," she said. "This is serious. Could rock the country."

"Aliens have landed in Las Vegas and the Feds are covering it up, like what happened near Roswell, New Mexico, in 1947?"

"What *are* you rambling about? Listen, I just got wind of this, and since I'm not supposed to know, you can't know, either.

Besides, your grandfather and I are an item again." Her voice was mushy and then got tough. "I want your word that you'll stay away from anything suspicious and no driving around on dusty desert roads, either. Now butt out."

"My whole world is suspicious, Gerry, my work is with sinners. There's job security in it, especially since this is Sin City."

"I'll accept that jab as your word." She was gone before I could demand to know how she knew about the twilight drive of Jane Angieski, and I was left with a dead phone against my ear. What's beyond red alert? Double red-red? Flashing fire engine red? Whatever, that's where I was, and I had a drowning feeling that the Feds were protecting PSA and Cheney. How did Monica, Eddie, and Tom fit into this? Had Tom been told to butt out, too? Had he been ordered to? Or was he part of whatever was coming down, as they always say in *Law & Order* or the other cop shows on TV?

I walked into the condo just to pace, eat, and pace. There was still leftover pizza, and I washed that down with some Ben & Jerry's Cherry Garcia followed by a few low-fat wheat crackers. A girl has to watch her calories. I finally got to bed. My head was swirling, and my jaw was tight from keeping my tongue between my teeth. I wanted to scream.

I wanted to blame my sleeplessness on the whole wheat. You cannot mingle fat and sugar with healthy stuff and not have repercussions, right? When would I learn that?

At two I threw back the covers and trotted from my room for some medicinal cookie therapy. The light must have disturbed Tuffy. Shredding the Charmin had become his favorite indoor sport, and since I wanted to do the same with Tom, Monica, Eddie, and Pastor Bob, I could understand. I popped in a new roll and then realized the precocious mutt had stopped shredding to tag at my heels. "We're alike, my friend," I told him, sharing a bit of sugar cookie. "So smart and clever and cute, but most of the time, we have no clue what's going on, do we? Wait, don't answer that." We plopped on the sofa. Tuffy stuck his fuzzy little nose into my hand, which I'd learned meant he wanted his ears scratched. "So what is up with Pastor Bob? What should I tell the District Council member when she comes for a report? Should I trail Bob like I pursued Monica and Eddie tonight? Should I check myself into a psychiatric hospital and get my blooming head examined? What if I end up in jail, or worse, on the front page of the Las Vegas newspaper?"

Tuffy yawned. Yes, I'd been expecting advice from a dog who'd run away from his owner who had forced him to live in the lap of doggy luxury. 'Nuff said.

*

I woke groggy from yet another night of slugging it out with the sandman and couldn't shake it even though, to my utter amazement, Saturday went by without anything resembling World War III. It also dropped into the low 90s, unheard of for a Las Vegas July. My track record of dealing with addiction, black-market babies, a midlife crisis with the grandfather I'd always trusted, and a few minor details like a foster child with an eating disorder who was going with me to a great therapist come Monday, responsibility for a dance fundraiser, the police hanging on my every movement, as well as the misdeeds of my senior pastor, scrambled my brain like a Denny's omelet that's runny inside. But for once in my life, I took someone's smarter-than-me advice and didn't return to the desert.

Instead I headed to church, which was busy even for a weekend. Since Monday and Tuesday were her "weekend," Vera was at her desk, whispering on the phone each time I happened to walk past her office.

"Jane, can you sit here and catch the phones for a while?"

With the rest of the staff was MIA, I agreed and took over her chair as she rushed out the door. I had spotted discount coupons for the Fashion Show mall clipped on her desk and totally understand why she had to leave. Can't fault her when they have incredible sales. Like Jessica Fletcher or any TV sleuth, I tried to make a list of suspects, but I had none—didn't even have any real crimes, other than possible black-market adoption, and Pastor Bob Normal and Delta Cheney were the only names on that list. I pushed the paper aside just as Albert Miller staggered in with a man slung over his shoulders. I stifled the scream exploding in my throat, which wasn't hard since my power for speech was history.

Albert turned around to give me a frontal view. Bob's face looked like it had been attacked with a meat mallet. Fully tenderized with drops of blood, crusty and dried. Without saying anything, Albert turned again and stalked into the pastor's office, plopping his cargo on the visitor's sofa.

"Ohmygoodnessakesalive. What happened?" I dashed after them and slammed the pastor's door.

Albert snorted. "Old Bob insisted on going back to the One Horse Saloon. Ten minutes after he went in, he came out looking like this, staggering and walking in circles. He was talking about waiting for the Rapture. The only rap he got was a good one or many to his skull. Those welts are going to be tough to explain on Sunday, sure to turn puke purple in no time."

"Did you call the police?" I flinched and cringed. I don't do well with blood or even a raw steak, for that matter, preferring all prime cuts well done. "Or for the EMTs?" I'm a good Christian, but this same man with the meat-cleavered face had threatened to kill me less than forty-eight hours before. I stood back, conflicted over whether to come to his first aid or let him suffer more.

Albert sneered. "To have his ugly mug, bloodied up as it is, plastered on all the newspapers and CNN and Fox TV? While I personally wouldn't mind that—heck, I'd relish seeing the jerk squirm—I couldn't. I didn't call the cops because of you and my daughter. I'm no Samaritan. I just know what's right."

"So you brought him here?" I'd backed flat against the wall, but when Bob moaned, I scooted to Vera's desk for the water I knew she kept there. I handed a bottle to Albert as he went to kneel next to Bloody Bob and took an extra in case I needed it.

"Open your mouth, man, and drink," he ordered, and Bob complied. Then Albert looked my way. "You'd better sit down, ma'am. You look like you're going to throw up."

Nothing makes a girl feel lovelier than saying she looks like she's about to vomit, even when it's the truth. I plunked my butt in a visitor's chair and managed, "Does he need medical care?"

"Nah, the wounds are superficial. He's just scared to death." Bob nodded and put his head down, moaning. Albert went on, "I've seen worse. In the Marines when I was a medic in Afghanistan. When I got out, I took a job in Orange County as an EMT before. . .well, before."

"Before your wife died. Harmony didn't tell me, but I've heard." I took tissues from my pocketed, wetted a wad and handed them to Albert. But my feet wouldn't seem to move toward Bob. I had to turn my head as he blotted the dried blood from around Bob's mouth that had dripped down the pastor's chin.

"Pastor, the man I'm nursing here and who I've tried to help and talk with these last few days is one sick puppy, a lunatic for poker. Gambling is cocaine for him, like it was for me. I learned. Wised up, but it took years in prison to get through to me. But for good measure, I guess, I had to see the ruin up close and personal. One part of me enjoyed watching the result as Pastor Bob got the sh—, um, stuffing knocked out of him."

Bob sat up and put his hands in front of his mouth, and Albert shoved a trashcan in front of him. I looked back as Albert kneeled down, looked into Bob's eyes, cocked his head and slapped Bob's face. And then made him finish the bottle of water. "Thank God you're alive, man, just thank God for that. Now act like a man, get cleaned up by yourself or, as God is my witness, I'm going to do it for you, and I'm not going to be gentle," he snarled.

Bob obeyed, heading to the private restroom off his office.

"If you've been talking with Bob about how gambling is ruining his life, why did you start it again?" I said, sitting on the edge of the sofa, trying not to breath vomit smell and looking up at Albert.

"Who told you that barrel of manure?"

"You said as much when we talked, and Harmony told me how you pushed her out of the way when she followed you into the casino."

"I didn't mean to shove her. I didn't, Pastor. I was so upset. Your minister in there, who just puked his guts out, told me if I didn't gamble with him, because he wanted a minion to rave about his brilliance as he lost the farm, he'd turn me back in to the parole board. Told me he'd lie, and I'd go straight to the slammer. That would've been my third strike. He said he'd make sure my daughter didn't get into one of those nicer foster homes, but the kind that hurts the kids. He said all that and more. The only time I went into a casino with him was the time Harmony saw me. That's it."

"That really frosts my cookies. You have no morals, Bob Normal." I yelled and then looked at my watch. "Albert, I need a big favor. This is above and beyond what you're being paid to do, but I have an appointment for the youth center fundraiser. Can you stomach being here with him? Don't let him leave. . .or talk with anyone. I'll be back in an hour, two at the max."

"That's my job, isn't it, Pastor Jane? I baby-sit this." He pointed his index finger at Bob. The pulpified pastor had returned and held his head in his hands, sitting on the edge of the sofa. "This miserable excuse for a minister."

"There's more water in Vera's desk and in the kitchen. I just put on some coffee on. You know where the kitchen is, right? Call for pizza if you're hungry, will you?"

"You just get some money for that youth center. That's why Harmony came here and stayed, and because of you. Thank you, Pastor." He waved as I grabbed my purse, cell phone, and keys.I had Monica Wainwright-Dobson's address scribbled on a scrap of paper in my purse and drove to her mansion-glutted gated community in record time. Before we could possibly talk about the fundraiser and her other ideas, I needed to know why she and her muscle-bound buddy from the shelter had driven out to the country to that shack at the end of a dirt road. Depending on her response, I'd stay or leave. If I left, it was out to the desert, regardless of what anyone thought. I'd been in a few scrapes in my time, and I was bound and determined to get answers.

After about one second of ringing the bell, it was Monica who flung open the door. Somehow I'd expected a butler, especially after driving through the lush, golf course-style grounds and in front of a two-story house I swear I'd seen on *Lifestyles of the Filthy Rich*, or one of those HGTV programs. Monica looked more like her regular diamond-and-dazzle-encrusted self, in a subdued, rich and stuffy Talbotish way, with a gold-colored golf shirt and tan chinos that clung to her body like the peel on a peach.

She wasn't the hugging type, so I didn't expect that. Yet as I reached out to shake hands, she didn't respond, but motioned me into the foyer. "Thanks for coming," was all I got.

We walked through a marble entry that was as big as my entire condo. A fountain dribbled water into an indoor koi pond with fish the size of baguettes, but much prettier. I stopped and stared as the oversized goldfish swam in circles, and wondered if I had any crumbs in my purse from the VBS cookies I'd snatched at church. I looked up, glad I hadn't fished out cookies for the fishes because Monica was frowning. I mumbled, "I thought perhaps you wouldn't let me in after yesterday."

She nodded, revealing wrinkles I hadn't seen before. She took my elbow to move to what I supposed was the living room, and off we went. Everything sparkled, from the platinum frames on oil paintings by artists I should have known, because I'd probably seen them in the Guggenheim Hermitage Museum at the Venetian Hotel and Casino. My view from the living room looked out to a monstrous pool that dribbled to nothingness, rather than having an edge. After that was an unobstructed view of Mount Charleston, soaring nearly twelve thousand feet above Las Vegas.

"There was a slight emergency at church, sorry to be late for our appointment, but. . ." The sentence was forgotten as I screeched to a halt, leaving heel marks on the marble. We weren't alone.

Monica bumped into my backside, moved over, and nabbed my arm, propelling me forward. I didn't want to move. Why?

Guess again. It wasn't Wayne Newton sitting there waiting. Instead, looking much like Alice in Wonderland when everything got really big, sat a familiar, troll-like woman, the pint-sized member of the District Council, prim and polyestered as ever.

"Louisa? I don't understand." I garbled more, I'm certain, but when Eddie appeared in all her bulging muscleness and walked to the window, cracking her knuckles, it didn't seem to matter what I had in mind.

Eddie had changed—not her smirk, but her outfit. Gone were the sloppy jeans and stained T-shirt. Gone was the dirty hair, but the multicolored tattoo of a flag remained on her forearm.

My brain threw my body into reverse. It could've worked, but Monica was now behind me, closing the sliding pocket doors. So much for my lucky break for escape.

"You were bound and determined to crash the party last night, and now you want to leave. You are getting what you deserve," said Eddie, positioning her muscular self by the patio doors and blocking another route to my possible freedom.

"I don't know what is going on here, but if you don't tell me quickly, Monica and the rest of you, I'm yesterday's news. I'm out of here. You're frightening me." I backed up another step, but Eddie dashed the short distance. The woman was as quick as she was large.

"Sorry, Pastor Jane, you're not going anywhere anytime soon. That is, not without one of us," Monica said.

"You're awfully nice to her. She could have ruined everything," Eddie grumbled. I was close enough to smell Dial soap, and that was far too cozy for my taste.

"This is against the law." Like anyone who was breaking the law would care if anyone said that. And pigs would fly at midnight, too, I thought. "You can't just stop me, you know." I huffed and looked toward Louisa Stephenson, waiting for her to jump up, toad-sized individual that she was, and rush to my defense.

"Actually," Monica interrupted my blabbering threats. "We can." She reached in the pocket of her tailored jeans and pulled out a wallet. She flipped it open. A bright, shiny badge and an identification card glared at me. "You see, Eddie and I are with the FBI. You're under arrest."

"Do I have any rights? Can I make a phone call?" I could hear squeaky sounds coming from my mouth.

Monica shook her head. "You're going to stay in our sights for a few hours, possibly a bit longer, whatever time it takes for the operation to be completed. There's a sting going on, and we don't need you to get in the way and mess it up."

Eddie glowered at me. "It's our job to keep you entertained."

"You have no right," I snapped, but knew that federal agents had whatever rights they wanted. Then I bluffed, "If you really are federal agents, and why should I believe you? What are you up to? Why hold me here?"

Monica motioned me to the sofa. "Just relax, will you? You're safe here. You won't get hurt. Please. It's for your own good, Pastor."

Eddie watched me, and I knew what a field mouse felt like at a hawk convention. "We don't trust you."

"Trust? I trusted you, Eddie, if in fact that is your name. I trusted you when we talked at the shelter. I trusted you when you said you'd help bring a VBS to the mission downtown."

I tried to give Monica my meanest look, but she just snickered. She was Cruella DeVille after all, but her voice was softer than expected when she said, "Wait, Jane, I am what I am. I'm also an agent, undercover and here in the city. When you followed us last night when we were meeting with other agents, you could have ruined everything, instantly. You were so stupid and close to ruining all our work. Years of it."

"And what is that everything, and why are you holding my superior here, too?" I looked at the dwarf snuggled in the sofa, and she smiled. I freaked. "No. Not you, too, Louisa. You're an agent? Well, duh. Of course." A hysterical belch bubbled up in my chest as I realized why the imposter hadn't been all that critical of Bob's potential swindles. She didn't give a fig in a famine. Why wasn't I screaming bloody murder? The pressure was there, but the sound didn't come. That frightened me more.

Monica walked to the wet bar and pulled out four glasses. "Yes, Pastor. This has been an operation for a long time, then you came along and things started to get messy. We have undercover operatives in a lot of locations throughout the country, but with the PSA right here we needed to slowly be accepted into the community. It's complicated. You're here so you don't mess it up while we get the goods on PSA."

Eddie blocked the door. "Morales—you know him well, we heard. Anyhow, he said you're quick-witted and cute, but you could be a blabbermouth."

"He called me names?" That wounded me. My stomach flipped. When was I going to grow up? Women preachers never got their Prince Charming. Heck, they didn't even get frogs complete with warts. I plunked down in an overstuffed chair.

"You'll have to ask him about that yourself. He's working with us, but not for us. What he does on his own time is his business," Eddie said, flexing her fingers and cracking her knuckles one at a time. I watched, counting one through ten.

"You bet I'll talk with him." I bent down to grab my purse. Let them think I wanted to call Tom to chew him out, but I was about to get emergency assistance until Eddie snatched it as I screamed, "At least give me a tissue."

Monica turned around to a cabinet in back of her, which

happened to be a refrigerator. "How about some iced tea or lemonade, Pastor?" she asked.

"I guess then you really don't want to have Wayne Newton at the fundraiser? Or even to have a fundraiser?" I thought of the hopes I'd had to leave behind a legacy for that so-needed teen center when I moved on to another assignment. That she'd lied about the support hurt more than my current state of arrest.

Louisa waddled over to sit near me, and I knew I could take her. Squash her like the gnome she was. I could grab her and force the Muscled One and Monica to let me go. I'd use the pint-sized woman as a hostage. All this sounded good but was a big bunch of broccoli, because they'd probably sacrifice Louisa, if that was her name, for their sting.

"We had to get your help and knew you wouldn't tell any old stranger everything because of your pastoral confidentiality," Louisa said, scooting her backside on the sofa. I changed chairs to move away.

"Did I give you the information you needed when you lied to me yesterday? Did you laugh about how easily I fell for your official visit?"

She giggled like a six-year-old, shrill and screechy. "Your secretary was busy making mushy looks at a young man when I came in, and then when you arrived—well, it was a snap. You didn't even ask for verification. Although I did have papers that would have fooled even your own senior pastor if it had been necessary. I had planned to see you this coming Monday, but things got moved ahead when you started putting your nose into our business."

My comment? "Oh."

"Yes," she continued. "We had to find out what you knew, Pastor, and your involvement with your senior pastor. It's our job to investigate, and since it is common knowledge from local law enforcement that Bob Normal is in debt from gambling, we assumed he was ripe for blackmail. Thought perhaps you were, too. Or you were blackmailing him."

"Did one of your goons beat him silly today?" I watched their faces; they didn't blink. Was it outlandish to think that Feds could have done that to Bob? If I believed half of what the newspapers printed about the FBI, the answer would be yes.

"I didn't know," Monica said.

"Wish I could take credit," said Eddie. "The guy's too slick. Walks into that shelter and parades around like the homeless should fall to their knees and kiss his ring. He just comes to bless their poor, downtrodden, sweaty souls and then walks out without offering any help."

"Don't like him much, do you, Eddie?" I jabbed, and she snorted as Louisa shook her head and giggled again.

"Whatever happened to your pastor is not our doing. I know that," said the woman who'd pretended to be from my church's headquarters. "Although from what we've learned about him, he's going to have some 'splaining to do. Our findings aside, and only because I am a curious investigator, what happens to bad apple pastors, Pastor Jane?"

"If you were really from the District Council, you'd know," I huffed, but my huffs had worn thin. I slumped back against the chair and realized I was under house arrest in a mansion. Okay, it could have been worse. I accepted tea and what tasted like shortbread cookies homemade in heaven. "Unless he has physically harmed someone or broken a law, he'll be reprimanded by the honest-to-goodness District Council. He'll be called to our denomination's headquarters in Dallas and asked to justify his actions. The council then confers and decides whether he should be disciplined. I'm guessing he'll get his credentials revoked. But they could just discipline him. If they just reassign him to another church, I'll scream bloody murder. There's enough stink going on in traditional religious groups right now without adding to the stench with Pastor Bob Normal. The depravity and dishonesty that's infiltrated churches is causing pastors to go astray. Then they are just resigned. I don't know what Bob's motives were. I can't judge him."

Eddie laughed at this. "I can and would in a heartbeat if I had a chance."

Monica squinted at her watch and pointed at me. The gal should wear glasses or contacts; all the squinting was giving me a headache. "Time to get her out of here, Eddie. I've got that fundraiser in a half hour, and Wayne will be here on time. The man's always on time." She fluffed a few pillows and replaced the iced tea glasses on a tray and slipped them under the cabinet.

"Wayne Newton? Really. Oh, my gosh. Really? He's actually coming here?" I gulped down the rest of the iced tea.

"Yes, Wayne and the other stars and their managers. I may be leading a double life, but I'm influential. I'm going to launch a soirée to raise money for the youth of our community."

"Monica, thank you, and just for the record, where am I going? Not that little house out in the boonies where you and Eddie met last night?" I picked up my purse, waiting for someone to snatch it from me. Of course, the phone was gone, so no one even looked at my hand.

Eddie fiddled with a set of car keys. "Just finish your drink. It's a long drive."

Slipping the purse strap over my shoulder, I didn't move but slugged back the tea. I held the glass out and obedient Monica, the good hostess she was, poured one more. I swallowed that in two mouthfuls. What if I were still sipping when Wayne Newton showed up? He'd surely rescue me from Eddie's mad clutches. I've seen his pictures. He's a big guy and wouldn't let a pretty and plump chunk of femininity like me be in jeopardy.

"Stop procrastinating. Finish your tea and let's go," Eddie ordered. The boom of her voice echoed in the palatial room.

"I'll be missed. You can't do this. My grandfather is expecting me back at the condo for dinner. My foster kid, Harmony, will wonder where I am. There's Vera at the office, who'll get calls for me, and I have an appointment at the PSA offices." I rambled even more quickly than I normally ramble.

"Monica." Eddie turned to her partner-in-catching-criminals. "You want to explain to her?"

"I called your grandfather earlier, nice man, and explained that you and I going to have a lovely and deliciously relaxing afternoon after the fundraising meeting. Why, we might even go to a spa. He understood. Told you to have a nice time and not to worry about dinner. He'd fix it for himself and the girl, and then they'd go to his dance class. He started raving about Tuffy, but really, I didn't want to hear that part." Monica scowled.

I actually thought I saw a flicker of emotion for the little dog as she but refilled my iced tea.

"Spa? I'm being kidnapped by the FBI, and you're going to treat me to a spa? I've been dying for a facial and maybe an herbal wrap, one of those that does away with cellulite." I was patting my bum when visions of a massage and a pedicure vanished as Eddie laughed. "There's no spa visit, is there?" I downed another glass of tea. It was passion fruit flavored. The adrenaline and the caffeine pulsing through my kidnapped body buzzed inside me.

A guttural laugh exploded from Eddie. "Sure, Pastor, you will be relaxing, that's for sure. You won't be able to butt in any way, shape, or form. I'll see to that."

Louisa cleared her throat. "We've determined you're a dangerous footnote to this case. What is it they say? Oh, yes, you're a loose cannon, as far as the Bureau is concerned, my dear," Louisa said, sounding like someone's aunt. "Yes, we know about your previous 'exploits,' Pastor. We cannot take a chance on you blowing this."

"Blowing what? What is going to happen?" I finished the pitcher of tea, and Eddie grabbed my arm, woman-handling me out of the house.

The black Mercedes in the driveway had leather seats that felt softer than my bed. "Nice car," I said as she opened the passenger door for me. "Yours?"

She hovered over me. "Not yet, but Monica is selling it to me after all this comes down, when it's over."

"Eddie, you're not going to kill me or anything messy like that?" I was locked in her car, Eddie got in, started the ignition. "Where we were going?" There were plenty of deserted places around Las Vegas. A preacher could be dropped off anywhere and never be heard of again. Like Pastor Bob's threats the night before, was this what she had in mind? "Are you supposed to, ack, murder me?" I swallowed so hard it hurt.

"You are even more fruity than I thought, Pastor Jane. Where do you get these dramatic notions?" She laughed, and it actually sounded like there was a hint of compassion for a nut like me.

"But we're driving away from the house, and I'm not being told where we're going." I tried the door handle, but it didn't budge. Yes, I had planned to throw myself out of the car at the first traffic signal.

"Forget trying to get out. Monica had these nifty, special locks installed."

"Just to kidnap a minister?" I asked, again trying the door.

"You're a piece of work. Naw, it's because she's got grandkids, rug rats, never understood that stuff. The doors have a locking control, and I'm in control."

So much for jumping out of a speeding car. I tried to nix the fidgeting, especially after Eddie barked, "I said, get a blasted grip. Oh, brother and dear mother. I'd be happy as an FBI agent on some beach in Bermuda to drop you in the desert, but that's not the way the Agency does things, contrary to what you might have heard. Wait, you watch those crappy TV shows? Yeah, me too. Worry not, my pretty, you're in my tender loving hands for just a few hours."

"I'm not going to die?" I leaned back on the soft leather seats and scrambled in my purse for gum.

"Some minute part of me is royally sad, but no, you'll live to tell about this adventure," she said, looking straight ahead, but I swear she looked disappointed.

I chewed. Eddie drove. Then I opened the ashtray, and Eddie let out a blood-curdling yell. "Hey. Don't stick that gum in there."

I slipped it back in my mouth as she began talking to herself. "Oh, yes, Eddie, you've got the easy one. Just keep the minister contented for a while until we call. Keep her away from the church and PSA. Yeah, and now I'm keeping a slob on ice. Why don't they ever give me clean freaks, hand washers, neatniks? No, I get mouthy slobs."

"I'll put it in a tissue in my purse," I said—anything to keep my mind off the pressure in my bladder. Besides, the gum wasn't taking my mind off it.

I tried to get comfortable. I willed myself not to think of what might be happening at church or the PSA office as Eddie carefully maneuvered through traffic. That didn't work. What was happening to Bob? Albert had a kind heart, but anything could happen if old bungling Bob Normal decided to go ballistic again.

"Does a prisoner get one question? Since I don't get a phone call. Are we getting near there yet?" I asked.

Eddie grunted.

I continued, "Is it a long drive?" I felt that need that cannot be quieted. I should have visited the bathroom before I left Monica's home, but they'd hustled me out, even though I pleaded for a pit spot as a limo had pulled in. I swear Wayne Newton was inside, which almost made me forget that feeling for half a second.

"You know you really annoy me. Do you ever run out of perky chitchat? Do you ever act like an average person?"

I assumed these were rhetorical questions, as she didn't look my way. She grumbled as we headed into the city.

I tried, I really did. Except my bladder kept interrupting. After four glasses of tea, what else had I expected? Definitely not being driven to God-knew-where. Would I be allowed to use the toilet when we got to wherever we were headed? "Much farther?" I asked.

"In all my years with the Agency, I never saw someone so anxious to get anywhere, especially when the place is isolated. You got a problem?" she growled.

"I do." I squirmed. "I really, really have to go to the bathroom. Like now." I fiddled with the stuff in my purse, hoping to take my mind off my bladder. There were car keys, keys to the church, more gum, tissues, lipstick, that promissory note with Bob's signature on it, and a CD of the garage band that Gramps wanted me to listen to.

"Forget it. Think of something else," she ordered, which as everyone knows never helps.

"Can we listen to music?" I asked. She nodded. I opened the plain, bluish-colored jewel case just as Eddie nearly rear ended a limo, and pushed the CD into the player as if on automatic pilot. Nothing happened. "Does the player work?"

"How would I know? I told you, the car's Monica's." She grabbed the CD from my fingers. "Hey, stupid, turn the silly disk over. You put in it wrong." She swore at me or the CD, it didn't matter, but still nothing happened.

I pushed eject, placed it back in the case and in my purse. "Well, that was no help, and now I have to go even worse. Unless you want me to piddle a puddle of pee right here on the leather seats, we're going to have to stop, Eddie."

"Think again, lady." She continued to inch along in the stream of cars and taxis that clogged West Flamingo.

"Hey, Eddie, you're a woman." I pressed my knees together. "Just this favor. I'll be quiet for the rest of the trip. Look, there's an Outback Steak House in that next shopping center. You can go in with me and stand by the stall. I don't even have to close the stall door. If you don't care to see me squat, I don't care, either— of course if I had my druthers, and since we really aren't that chummy, nor do I ever want to become that chummy, although you're a really nice person down deep under those muscles, and I'm certain of it, because well, because. . ."

"Put a cork in it, will you?" The growl came from between her teeth, and the space in the middle made a whistling sound as she swore words I won't share.

"But, Eddie, I have to go now." Desperation increased. The bouncing and jiggling and crossing and uncrossing of legs must have penetrated her hide, or maybe it was the line about the piddle on the seat.

She sighed in a burst of breath, clicked the turn signal, and made a right turn into the restaurant's lot. She put the car into park. "Here's the deal, Pastor. I'm going to be right here." She poked the butter-soft seats with an index finger the size of my fist. "I do not care to watch you sit on the john or even listen to you use the bathroom. And look. From here I can see the front door and the back. Return in five minutes or I'll be coming in for you. It won't be fun."

I was futilely flipping the door release, but she wasn't about to let me out yet. "Thanks, Eddie. Thanks so much. If I'm not out in five minutes, I'll be sitting at a table ordering appetizers—those onion blossoms have four zillion calories and every single one is scrumptious. Shall I get one for you?"

"Cut the crap." She reached across my chest and held me in place. "If you call the police, lots and lots of innocent lives could be lost. Babies will probably die in the process. I don't have to tell you this, but here it is. The Agency has everything under control. Delta Cheney is assuredly going to get caught with her fingers in the criminal cookie jar. The ditz has no clue anyone has anything on her, so she'll just keep compiling records, grabbing money, and bilking unsuspecting Americans. Right now she's probably out peddling babies. Petra Stanislaw will be sent back to Poland lickity split or sent to the big house that Homeland Security handles. Doesn't matter to me. That bungling gambling pastor of yours will get his in the end." She laughed and continued. "Monica and Louisa will come out of it with promotions, and I'll be in Nassau, lounging on the beach, sipping a drink with a pretty umbrella as a pool boy brings me suntan lotion. Those are my long-overdue vacation plans, and you're not going to botch this. Blow it and you're history. So don't blow it. Understand? Okay? Remember the babies."

The pressure was on. Disaster pending. No time to waste. My bladder was going to burst. I would have agreed to anything. "Yes, yes, yes. Promise."

I'll pass on the details of what happened in the next five minutes. I am woman. I multitask. I used that time to pray for wisdom. Most normal, moral citizens would have quietly gone with the FBI, leaving matters in their beefy, legal hands. I would have, too, except I'm not typically a normal citizen. But something Eddie said came raging back as I flushed the toilet. She'd said, "The ditz has no clue anyone has anything on her, so she'll just keep compiling records and bilking unsuspecting Americans."

Au contraire. The ditz did have a clue. She'd been sweating like a stevedore when we bumped purses the day before. The ditz was probably packing for Brazil whilst I sat on the toilet. It didn't take a psychic to see that Delta knew the jig was up when she sprinted to her car. Would the Muscled Madam cracking knuckles in the Mercedes believe me? I couldn't go to Tom, because he certainly wouldn't buck rank with the FBI invading Vegas like ants at a picnic. I had to do something. And quick.

Well, duh. I had to get away. Or she'd be banging on the stall door and breaking through with one of her meaty shoulders. Walking out of the door marked "Women," I bumped right into an answered prayer in the form of newspaper reporter and lovesick boyfriend of Gramps' dance instructor. It was Carl Lipca. I grabbed the man by the collar.

He choked as I twisted the collar of his shirt and grabbed him around the shoulders. Then I gushed, "I am so glad to see you."

"Jane?" He attempted to wrestle out of my half nelson. "I know you must be lonely as a preacher and all, but hooking up in the toilet is kinky even for me."

Before I could scream, "Slime bucket," reality informed me that I didn't have time to put the jerk in his place. "Carl, I'm not making a pass at you. I need your help. Someone I want to desperately avoid is waiting outside. I've got to get to church. I have to get away." Albert would help me. He might have a prison record, but he was a good guy.

The plan was simple. I'd sneak out of Outback. . .um, somehow. get to church, and have Albert take me to the PSA. We'd break in . . . I'd gather all the files. I'd call Gerry, and she'd tell me what to do.

Carl gasped, which was reasonable considering I was currently twisting all the extra fabric from his collar, and I shoved the restroom door open wide enough to drag his body inside.

"You know what you're doing, Pastor Jane?"

"Don't be a dolt." I snorted. "You got a problem talking in here?"

A man and a boy were washing their hands. Another guy dashed from a stall, zipping his fly. A teenager looked up from finishing at the urinal. They all turned and stared. A fourth man bounded to the door, tripped on my foot, bounced against me, loosening my death grip on Carl, and blew the joint.

Whoa, apparently in my frenzied state the above restroom wasn't the one I had previously been in. I clamped my eyes shut, also clamping onto Carl's shirtsleeve. "It's the men's room?"

"Yes, Pastor."

I dropped my sumo hold on the journalist and cupped my hands around my eyes like blinders on a horse and scooted to the door. But not before I heard the kid say, "Look, Daddy, it's that lady minister from church, the one you're always telling Mommy that she looks like she's a hooker," while his ashen-faced dad hustled out.

In the corridor to the restrooms, I pleaded, "Carl, listen, I need to get to church. I don't want to call the police. Just get me away. If you care at all for Petra and what happens to her, you'll help me."

"Care for Petra? Oh, it was fun, but that's it. And can't we just trot outta here and get into my car?"

"No, I can't. I need help. Carl, there's someone out there in the parking lot I don't want to see me leave. Can you humor me? Maybe if we change clothes? As weird as it seem, we're about the same size." Sometimes I think I understand everything, and then I regain consciousness.

Desperate situations require desperate measures. There was no way on God's green earth I was going to return to the clutches of Eddie, if in fact she and Monica were real FBI agents, which was suspect since the FBI doesn't usually foot the bill for mansions such as the one where Monica lived.

"I don't think so, Pastor. I'd like to help, but I don't think my dressing in drag and you fielding questions about your gender orientation when you're meeting folks from your congregation in the men's room are going to improve your reputation."

I was about to scream, "Reputation be damned. Lives are at stake," And quickly realized I had.

Then he said, "Wait, maybe, sure, I've got an idea that could work. But you've gotta promise to give me an exclusive after this is all over."

"Yes, anything, the answer is yes." I gulped.

"Look, the reason I'm here is the reason you'll be able to leave." This time he grabbed my arm and marched me toward the dining area. There sat Vera, she of the church secretary role, who looked up at us just after pinching a male food server on the rump. "Vera, look who I found in the men's room."

She jumped up as if the server retaliated, and perhaps he did. "Jane, you don't look well," Vera said, popping a large red straw hat back on her head, twisting a boa around her throat, and wiggling her generous hips as she nudged me aside to snuggle-close to Carl.

Carl looked like he'd said "g'day" to too much Foster's beer at Outback. "Vera and I are, well, we're friends."

"Carl, baby cakes, tell her the truth. You love me. And ooh la la, you make me feel like a kid," Vera said flickering her false eyelashes and adjusting the cleavage in her low-cut and skin-tight tank top.

I would have gagged if I'd had time, but the seconds were clicking down to when my abductor would storm in and grab me away. "I don't care what's going on with you two. Right now I've got fish to battle into a frying pan. Get me out of here, please. Help me, you two, or I swear I'll tell the entire city, including your husband, Vera, all of this and more, now that I've put two and two and two and two together." There was no four, six or eight at the end of my two-and-two desperate outburst, but it worked.

"Okay, Jane," Carl said. "Vera, give the minister your hat, and that purple scarf thing. Now let's get thing going, ladies, and I use the term loosely. I've got a scoop to scoop."

Ignoring his dig, I tucked my hair underneath the hat, pulled the boa nearly over my ears, put my hand on Vera's, and we walked out the big wooden doors. I twisted my head away from Eddie's car and placed a napkin in front of my face, making sneezing sounds. "See that Mercedes? I don't want the woman driving it to see me."

Carl nodded. "I've got the blue one over there. Ready?"

I hunkered down and tilted my hat away from a black car. When I sneaked a peek up from the brim, I saw my goose was in the oven, and the timer was about to bing "done." Eddie recognized me.

"Hurry, Carl, open the door. Start the engine. Forget Vera. No, she doesn't need to come with us. Eddie is going to get me."

Carl opened the passenger side, but instead of helping me in, he shoved me out of the way. "She's the one who is after you? That woman punched me out when I was just asking some questions down at the shelter. In front of a bunch of ladies. I've got an ax to grind. Just get out of my way, Pastor." With lightning speed, he yanked a bowling ball from the back seat and slipped his fingers in the holes. Suddenly Vera was screaming, "But Carl, that's *my* bowling ball."

The ball sped across the twenty yards between cars. It looked like it was square on target, but it hit a curb. It missed the Muscled One, hit a light fixture and bounced and slammed straight into the Mercedes' windshield.

"Now get in," he yelled. "And they said my bowling skills would never amount to much. Call you later, Vera."

I would've jumped at the chance, but at that second a silver Lexus zoomed into the lot and screeched to a screaming halt. I jumped back as it nearly nicked Carl's car. It would have broadsided me if I hadn't inhaled, thought thin thoughts, and gritted my teeth. You can fool some of the people some of the time, but you can't fool all of the people, especially Albert Miller driving the formerly good Pastor Bob "the gambler" Normal, who was riding shotgun.

Bob was out of his car before I could untangle myself. "Jane, forgive me for my sins. I need your help right now. Get into the car. We can't spare a minute."

I didn't agree to anything, mind you, because he didn't give me a chance, opening the back door and giving me the old heave-ho. Eddie was about three feet from me, and I could feel the steam of her breath.

Once I tumbled into the seat, I slammed and locked the door. "What are you doing here? How did you know where to find me?" I clung to that seat for dear life. I didn't want to be tossed to the floor again as Albert gunned the engine and drove over the lawn, speeding away from Eddie, who was screaming, swearing, and making obscene gestures.

His words came in puffs. "A call came into the church a few minutes ago about you using the men's room at the Outback Steakhouse. . .a complaint about your behavior. Oh, but no, praise Jesus, it was a prayer answered." Gambling Bob Normal raised his hands to on High, but of course the ceiling of the car stopped that.

"But where are we going?" I yelled over the grinding of gears and Albert grunting something I chose not to hear about someone's parentage and ability to control a car. I tried unsuccessfully to find the seatbelt as Albert drove straight over the center median, flipped around the car around and in the opposite direction.

"The PSA offices. Delta called to warn me to leave town fast. The Feds, she said, were closing in, and she wanted to warn me. She's going to destroy all the adoption records. All the backgrounds of those babies will be lost forever. We must get there before she does it."

Chapter 14

You've heard how opera singers can shatter a glass with a certain octave. Bob's scream could have done it, too. "Jane, we have to stop her." He was beating his fists on the dashboard so hard, I was certain the airbag would deploy. "She'll do it. She's that cruel, possessed with evil."

I leaned forward, still with a death grip on the seat to keep my balance. I kept my voice to a low and quiet scream; talking to lunatics in that way works best, at least so I'd heard on Dr. Phil. "Bob, what exactly is your connection with PSA? What do you know about their dealings and the children they're bringing in for adoption? What about the orphanages in Poland? What of the women forced to become sex slaves? The human trafficking? Whatever were you thinking?"

He flinched.

I screamed, "Didn't you ever think of saying 'no'? Well, what do you have to say for yourself, you creep, and that's a euphemism for what I really mean, which is—"

"You don't understand, Jane," he interrupted.

"I am sick and tired of being told I don't understand. I do. If it's about the money, Bob, then what happens to the money that comes and goes through PSA?"

As he turned, Bob's eyes reminded me of the pink cotton candy they sell at the circus that gets mushy before you finish. The gooey blood was cleaned from his chin, but his cheeks were the color of tomatoes that rot on the vine after the first frost. His bottom lip was sliced in the middle, and should've had a stitch, but heck, I'm no doctor. Trust me, it looked nasty. Albert swerved to avoid a semi; I gulped, digging my fingers into the back of Bob's seat.

He gulped, too, and twisted my way. "I tried to stop it, Jane. I tried, at first. Then I couldn't. Delta is powerful. I gave up. I have sinned."

"Darn straight you have. You'll get no disagreement with me on that." A girl's gotta call 'em as she sees 'em. "Did you even think of the human rights violations? The welfare of innocent babies? The broken lives and hearts? Did you even think about the inhumanity of selling and reselling people—flesh and blood humans—as if they were a commodity?" I had plenty more to say, but we were all going to die in a car wreck at any minute, so I held my tongue. The speedometer was steady at eighty.

I concentrated on the scarlet welts that had turned a darker shade of burgundy mixed with molasses on Bob's face. Not a nice view, but the only one I had if I didn't want to look ahead at the road or at my white knuckles.

"I sinned because I didn't stop the cycle. I could have, but then money began increasing in the weekly offering, far more than the families who attend Desert Hills ever gave. The tithing was enormous, beyond anything I'd ever seen. We built the gourmet kitchen and the new sanctuary with the offices, the playground, the basketball courts, the preschools, and the possibility of having an elementary school on the campus. Without having to go into debt. We built it with cash."

Albert swore, slammed on the brakes, and skidded past a car that seemed to want to drive the speed limit. Then drove through a red light, *again*.

I gulped and spat out, "Paid for with dead babies, as far as I can see, Bob. Besides, how could you be sure it was PSA and Delta's doing?"

"I wasn't at first." He hiccupped, "But then when I began talking about buying that tract of land where the recreation center now stands, Delta came to me and offered to finance it if I'd counsel some parents who had 'somehow' found their adopted children were handicapped. All parents get counseling sessions before the child is returned to the orphanage for re-adoption. Again and again, these sweet little children came and went to yet more inappropriate homes, only to be eventually dumped someplace, to struggle, or worse, to die in a back alley."

"Where do the promissory notes come in?" I stammered, because reasonable conversation was impossible at that speed and because of the big ol' bloomin' fact that we'd just made yet another left turn on a red light with traffic heading straight at us.

"At first I counseled out of appreciation for Delta and her generous contributions. I felt certain it was God's hand placing so many disabled babies in our area, not specifically in our church family, but we do have a few, as you know."

"And the money, did you charge for the counseling?"

"No. I tried to stop, but suddenly large—" He turned to face front. "—no, not large, but incredibly large amounts of money were deposited into my checking account, the joint account with my wife. I couldn't explain them. How could I?"

"Your wife? What did she do?"

He cleared his throat and winced as he attempted to puff out his chest. "I'm the man of the family. I handle these things, or at least I did."

I swear Albert abruptly changed lanes just to stop Bob's posturing about how a big man handles the wifey's money. We knew how Bob handled it.

I dug at him anyhow, and the car slowed. "You're saying the little good Christian wife shouldn't be told about big old dirty money?"

"No—well, yes, we have a traditional family." He started to raise a hand, bumped his chin, and cursed. He whispered, "We did. Wrong on that count. I have been so wrong. At first it seemed the smart solution, just gamble it away and our church's headquarters would never see it," Then he stopped, blinked and I saw a flicker of the crazy guy who was going to dump me in the desert. In the next instant, the some-what normal, Bob Normal returned and said, "And gambling as I did seemed to deaden the pain in my heart about the babies and children who were dying. It worked for a few weeks, but the money poured back in. One day my wife, Prudence, opened the mail, something she never did, and saw there was nearly a million dollars in our personal account. I refused to tell her about it. She didn't need to know. A man must lead his wife." He took a breath and let it out in ragged lumps. "She left me, accusing me of having an affair with Delta, but that's not true, believe me. An affair could have been ended. I'd sold my soul by then. After my wife left, I gambled to ease the pain."

"Give me a break and let me guess, Bob—then the money stopped. But you didn't. What happened?"

"Delta demanded that I not only use Desert Hills Community Church in PSA's advertisements, but insisted that our denomination provide endorsements. Suddenly my picture was plastered on PSA's materials."

"I've seen them, Bob. The photos make you look like the village idiot," I said, which wasn't exactly true—he looked like an Elvis impersonator doing the village idiot.

Albert grunted again, speeding through the intersection and dodging a car that just happened to think a green light signaled its right to cross.

Bob continued, "There was a reporter from the local newspaper snooping at her office—think it was the same guy I just saw you with—and then a British couple pretending to want to adopt a disabled child, demanding one because it was God's will, came into my office."

"So much money," I sighed, knowing each dollar cost a child or a woman part of their heart.

"The PSA has franchises, like a pyramid scheme, all over the country. Delta gets a lion's share of it all. It's Satan's work, and I was caught in his claws. I could have gone to the District Council when it first happened, but I thought maybe it was God's plan to build our little church in the desert. Yet the money just kept pouring in. I gambled for the buzz. Forgive me, Jane, forgive me and help me. Please?" He tried to grab the hand I was unsuccessfully using to keep myself upright.

I flicked his fingers it away like a big horse fly, but then he said something that made me flop back against the seat. He coughed and said, "There's more. Something I've hidden all my life. I'm not Bob."

"What? What are you saying?" I screamed not because anything the potentially criminally insane buffoon had to reveal, but because we were taking another corner, on a red light, at eighty miles an hour.

Bob sobbed. "It's worse. I'm not Bob. Bob's a name I took for myself. My birth name is Absalom."

"Absalom? That power-hungry guy from the Old Testament? You really are Ab Normal?" I started laughing and it even sounded hysterical to my ears.

"Yes, yes, it's been my curse my entire life, no matter how hard I tried to cover it up. Now I've lived up to the name." He screamed like a girl as Albert cut off a mail truck.

We veered right and then left. "Don't we all, Ab?" My fingers were numb from the death grip on the seat, and I decided that next time I choose a career, I'll get one where I can ask, "You want fries with that?" Even with teeth ground together, I managed, "I hate you, Bob Normal. Just in case you needed to know that. However, since I've been plotting to destroy the PSA for days, I'll help."

We fishtailed to a skidding stop in front of the office building that housed PSA. Delta's cream-colored car was in the lot. I looked both ways. No police sirens could be heard, and Eddie's car was not in sight. I didn't see any FBI agents in riot gear, nor had the SWAT teams arrived. Life was good.

So far.

Albert hadn't put the car in park before Bob's girly scream demanded, "Hurry, there's no telling what she'll do." Bob pulled the scarf, and I came with it. Luckily, a desert gust of hot air snatched the hat, because it wasn't my look anyway. We ran to the office marked Philemon Society of America. I turned to see Albert still in the car. This wasn't his fight.

Bob threw back the walnut doors and dashed into the conference room. Delta was there. She sneered and turned back to the shredder. She was madly shoving reams of files. "They'll never trace any of this to me." She exploded with diabolical laughter, honestly, that could have come straight out of a black-and-white horror movie. Putrid, plastic-smelling smoke belched as she tossed another CD into the blaze that came from a metal trash can near her side.

Delta's eyes darted to the files, to Bob, and then drilled into me. I screamed, "Don't do it, Delta. Don't destroy the records."

"How will the babies get back to their real parents if you do this?" Bob pleaded. He was crying, on his knees pleading with her.

The sickly smile on her face and the glassy eyes confirmed the woman was two donuts short of a dozen.

"Delta," I said slowly, and she looked my way. "Look at me. Bob's right. Please don't destroy the records."

"Burned what I couldn't shred. Just this one main file with all the locations of the orphans." She dumped her purse upside down on the table, and the contents spilled over the conference table. "Where is that stupid file. One more and I'm done. No jury can prosecute me if they have no evidence."

I thought of arguing, but at that second Delta was caressing a CD case.

"It was a first-class con while it lasted," she said, her voice raspy husky from the billowing smoke. She tossed the case from hand to hand, like playing with a ball. She flipped open the case and looked at the silver plastic disk, stuck a finger in the center and twirled it. As if she were about to toss a Frisbee, Delta pulled back her wrist.

Common sense is a good thing. But you can't beat spontaneity. In the second that it took Delta to move her elbow and wrist, I leaped across that walnut conference table. I screamed bloody murder because she would not murder any more if I had a breath left in me.

Papers flew, and Delta and I butted heads as I put a death grip on her wrist. Some unkindly things were said about me, and I'll spare you. Delta's chair flipped backward; I was on her waist straddling her and fighting for that silver CD. The trashcan was knocked on its side, and the papers that were strewn everywhere kindled a blaze.

Flipping me over like I was a rag mop, Delta was on me. What I lacked in strength, I apparently had in quickness, because we both wanted the same thing. I screamed, "Be reasonable, Delta," but that's Looney Toon thinking as a mad woman was making mincemeat out of my middle. She was using her butt to bounce up and down on my tummy, attempting to pin back my arms as the fire sprinklers came to life. The disk slipped in my grip, but that slip made me get more serious. I'd become a human punching bag. Delta was strong, much stronger than she looked all dressed in linen and silk.

I vowed right then that, if I lived through the beating, I'd take up weightlifting or kickboxing and return to Weight Watchers. Sometimes my mind wanders; sometimes it totally leaves.

Delta punctuated her salty language with a punch to my face. I would like to tell you that I turned the other cheek, but my face didn't move fast enough. Her knuckles hit their target—my nose. I screamed. She cursed more. I wondered where Bob was in all this, and then I saw him. He should have been selling tickets to two chicks fighting. At least that would have been useful, but he was cowering in the corner, in a ball, crying.

The power shower from above must have finally gotten to Delta. She looked up at the sprinklers, and her fingers slipped. I got the CD and used it to shield my face with my left hand as I grabbed at her hair, attempting to inflict pain.

"Don't touch my hair." she yelled two inches from my nose.

So I grabbed even harder and the bleeping' thing came off in my hand. Her hair, not her head. She took a breath, and I looked at what I had. A full wig. The puppy was heavy, too. We stared, eye to eye. Delta Cheney was no lady. She was a guy. Being that close, I saw the stubble on his chin.

It all made sense in a retrospective way, but since I had a guy straddling my waist, punching and slapping me because I'd mussed her, um, his hair, I didn't take the time to ponder: transgendered or cross-dresser? Thank heavens Delta fought like a girl, or I'd have been out for the count.

As if the walls were exploding, fierce shouts erupted.

"Get away from her."

"Grab the maniac lady."

"You stop that this very second."

"Stop it right now."

I opened one eye, then the other. The Buscia Brigade had landed in full force. Pouncing redheads, gray heads, and a few blondes were inches from my face. They held Delta by the shoulders, but couldn't move him or her off me. The lunatic slapped, pinched, and screamed.

Suddenly more people piled on top of the heap-o-me. Manly voices echoed in the office filled with bodies, rancid smoke, sprinkling spring-like showers of fire sprinklers, and the wail of the fire alarm pulsating in the same rhythm as the welts on my face. All the time, Delta, or whatever his name was, continued punching me in the ribs.

"Stop. Federal agents. Everybody down. Get on the floor. Get down. All of you. You, too, little lady, hey, don't hit me. Wait, no,

I'm not married. I'm sure your daughter is a beauty, but you'll have to get on the floor. Get on the floor. On the floor. Right now."

I didn't have to move to the floor. I was on it and whimpering. I wanted to see the agents, wanted to thank the grandmothers, but I couldn't lift my head. Slowly, like after college linebackers sacked the other team's quarterback, bodies peeled back from mine. Then male arms circled me. I fought Delta, or whatever I should call him. Or was it Pastor Ab Normal? His help was more repulsive than ever. This might not have been the most Christian response, but if he was going to grab that one last file and conceal it from the Buscia Brigade, he'd have to fight me for it. If just one baby could be reunited with his biological parents or placed in a loving home, it was worth this beating and more.

Then I felt breath on my cheek and heard a lyrical whisper.

"Tom." I gasped for breath. "Are you an honest cop?"

He held the corner of the jewel case, but I didn't let it go. "Yes, Jane."

I released the CD as he pulled me into his arms, crooning, "*Esta bien.*"

"Tom, don't let Delta, um, him have this," I mumbled. My body throbbed, and my brain was about to explode. My nose gushed blood down the front of my formerly stain-free blouse that I had just bought, on sale, at Nordstrom's Plus Size section.

"It's okay, Jane." Tom's voice filtered through in a gentle wave, a sweet Spanish lilt on his lips like a ripple on a quiet pond.

I relaxed and sighed, just as I heard Monica Wainwright-Dobson ranting, "I knew she'd do this, I knew that silly bitch Pastor Jane Angieski would ruin it all. It's all your own fault, Captain Morales. Geez, get the local law in, and suddenly it's like Mayberry RFD. Where's Sheriff Andy? The case goes from bad to totally bungled. Step aside. We'll take over from here. Get back to walking the beat and let the Agency do its job."

*

Here's the point when I tell you, "When I woke up," and it's true. I woke up in a hospital bed, but trust me, I remembered it all, until everything became a swirl and I landed in a happy place. That is, I blacked out.

I recalled how stern and somber the men and women in bulletproof vests. FBI was emblazoned on their caps, and they crammed the conference room way past overflowing. I remembered the shouting as the guy formerly known as Delta pulled my hair, screamed yet another obscenity, and tried to kick as they pulled him away. I propped myself up on my elbows as Monica screamed and shook her fist at Tom. I was shocked that she knew the words she was using as she told Tom how his ditzy, lame-brained girlfriend ruined the entire operation.

Then I heard Tom giving it as good as he had gotten, hollering about how he was going to report it all. Not in those G-rated words, but you get the idea.

I heard how I was to blame in detail about me and my buttinski. The Feds had memorized my sordid past, and Monica squealed it out loud enough so I swear pig farmers in Kansas were wondering what was riling the sows. Then she turned the outrage on the Polish grandmothers, but they simply shoved her aside, let her know they didn't care, and trotted out.

As I woke up, this was what I remembered. Pleasant thoughts? Bad guy caught? End of adventure? In the movies you see the heroine—that would be me—waking up in a hospital. Her lipstick is straight from Maybelline and her hair is Rodeo Drive perfect. If it's a drama, there could be just enough peachy color on her cheeks to tell that, ohee, she'd been in a rumble.

I touched my face and needed to stifle the scream. My nose was bandaged, and my forehead felt fat, puffy to my touch. There was an IV in my arm, and I had trouble swallowing.

Gramps' head was resting on the side of my bed. It was dark outside. Just a beep of some machine and his snoring interrupted the silence. I lifted the hand not connected to the IV. "I'm awake," I said, and patted his shoulder.

He looked up, and tears spilled from his eyes. "You are so stupid, Jane. What did I tell you about fighting? Remember when you got in that fight in first grade? Remember that black eye? Well, you should see the shiners you have now." He wiped away the tears and laughed. He laughed so hard he nearly tumbled on the floor.

I couldn't because of the bandages strapped around my middle. I touched the gown and felt the pain of broken ribs through the flimsy fabric and the massive amounts of tape.

As he recovered, I had plenty of time to sip icy water from one of those glorious hospital flexi-straws.

"You might be doing God's work here, but next time you should make sure He has you wearing protective face and body armor," Gramps managed before being overtaken with a fit of laughter. Then the room was filled with all the faces I wanted to see. Harmony, Tom, and Albert were there and, along with three little redheaded buscias who were serving poppy seed cake and coffee. I swear it was weird, but it happened. Then Petra and more of the Buscia Brigade were crammed in my room.

I was alive, even with the splitting pain that went from ear to ear, straight through my skull and whatever brains I had left after the beating. Since there were no federal agents hovering bedside, apparently they'd wait to arrest me for obstructing justice and ruining the operation to catch Delta before she destroyed the documents until, when? After I left the hospital?

"Where is he? Where's Bob?" I asked in whisper.

"You just hush up, Jane, baby, and don't worry about him," Gramps said. "And don't worry about the Senate investigation that Gerry's cooking up. They'll just have to wait until you feel better for you to get to Washington. Interpol and the Feds need to duke it out for a while, playing the blame game."

I sighed all the way to my toes. Justice, at least for Delta, would be done. Bob wouldn't come out lily white, either, I fervently hoped.

With a bark, Tuffy hopped on the foot of my bed and snuggled down as if the mutt was a therapy dog. I had no clue how they smuggled the pooch in. I wouldn't have put it past them to wrap the mutt in a baby blanket, telling folks the little one looked just like his mother, Jane Angieski, crime stopper. The talk about federal hearings felt like licking the chocolate frosting off a spoon—that delicious—and I begged for details.

"Are you sure you're ready to hear it?" Tom asked, smoothing his rough fingers over my forehead. "We can wait, you know."

"You arrested Delta, or whatever his name is? Did you get that CD with the files? That one last file that could help some children find their roots?" I managed in a raspy whisper.

"Yes—well, no." Tom's lips made a flat line. "There was only music on it. After all that."

"Of course there's music on it," I screamed, and that hurt, but it just hit me. "Harmony? Did they bring my purse here? Go get it. Inside. Do you see a CD case?"

Harmony gave me the case and the sweetest hug on the face of the planet. We'd bonded, although this time I screamed internally from the pain inflicted by her embrace. Love hurts, they say, and in this instance, "they" were right. "I know you all think I've had ten too many blows to my brain, but Tom, try this. Really, listen, a few days ago the guy formerly known as Delta and I bumped purses, and stuff was scattered. I had the CD with the records all the time. I thought it was the music CD from your young garage band, Gramps. The jewel cases were the same color. See?"

"We'll make sure it gets in the right hands, Jane. I promise," Tom told me before kissing my forehead. I tried to crane my neck and position my face so my lips would be in his line of fire. Tom chuckled and changed positions. I got a peck on the cheek.

I put my head back as they told me the rest of what had happened.

Petra said, "That twelve-timer Carl is not worth the paper he's printed on." We all agreed.

My came were in a horsy series of grunts, but I managed, "What about VBS for this coming week?"

Gramps rubbed his chin and looked out the window to the night. "Heard Vera's teaching archery, belly dancing, and how to mix a good martini, stirred not shaken."

Forget the horsy grunting—this was a scream that, I swear, rattled the windows. "Noooo."

Gramps patted me. "Just kidding, honey. Vera's decided she should retire. And did. The board brought in a temp. Then the lunch ladies, the women who take food to the mission, stepped in. They're going to be handling VBS at the shelter, too. Hey, you heard about Greta and Drexel adopting little Mikel? Not the kid they were looking for, but they say it's the right thing to do." Gramps held my hand.

Voices turned into a melody, and drugged sleep snatched me away to a lovely ball where Scarlett O'Hara had chosen my outfit, including the jewels, and Tom was better looking than Rhett.

When a hand touched my shoulder, wanting to break into the waltz Rhett and I were doing, I shoved it away. I squeezed my eyes shut to keep out the daylight from my happy nap. "Not yet, Tom, come back," I pleaded.

"Jane, oh, Pastor Jane, please listen to me, please, I beg you." It was Gambling Bob Normal; he was kneeling at my bedside. I was certain our faces matched in the bruise and bashing department because he grimaced at me.

"If it isn't the minister—formerly, I hope—of Desert Hills Community Church."

"Don't talk—it must hurt. I want to ask for your forgiveness. I've talked to the police, and I've talked with our leaders in Dallas. I've resigned. There will be some legal action, but I won't bore you with this. For the next few months I'll be doing social service work in Texas. My wife is coming back, Jane, praise God for that. I've been asked to find out if you'd consider taking over the pulpit." He smiled.

I nodded demurely. Oh, yes, here it comes. "Thank you, Jesus," I thought. Oh, yes, finally my own pulpit. This was the promotion I'd longed for, and now it had happened. I would have jumped out of bed to do the happy dance if it were not for the IV, the broken ribs, the splitting headache, and the general nausea of being beaten to a bloody pulp by a mad woman, um, guy. I managed a smile and look pious at the same time, even with the pain.

He looked down to the tile floor and said, "Until they find a senior pastor."

"Well, joy of joys. Always the bridesmaid," I mumbled and closed my eyes. He didn't need to see the pathetic downer look in my eyes. It was time for him to get the heck out and let me wallow in my potential pity party. I didn't want to talk anymore. I'd forgiven him. The black market baby business had been stopped, and the FBI was working with Interpol and the government of Poland. Eddie had been right, however; Monica and Louisa did get a promotion, and for all I knew, the Muscled Madam was lounging in Nassau chatting it up with pool boys and sipping drinks with umbrellas. I knew in my heart that God had better plans that for me to stay in Nevada, but I just wish that disappointment happens He'd give a clue once in awhile, don't you?

Contrary to what the slogan says, "What happens in Vegas, stays in Vegas" wouldn't work with PSA, because according to what I'd read in that morning's paper, they'd learned that when criminals play games of the heart it gets deadly. Earlier in the day, I'd been served with a federal subpoena to spill my guts to the committee headed up by none other than Senator Geraldine English. When I get around to writing my bestselling memoir, I'll use the transcripts as they slam the book—or is that close the book—on Delta and the assorted scum who ran PSA. Maybe Bob, too.

What I heard next was heart-stopping delicious and I didn't open my eyes because I wanted to bathe in the sound of that protective rumble from, literally, the man of my dreams.

"Why *are you* here, Bob? Let go of her."

"Um, ah, Captain Morales—" Bob tossed my hand to the bed.

"Don't you have something to do? Like pouring Clorox on your reputation? Be decent for once, man, and let Jane rest," Tom growled. It was a growl I wanted to lust after, even when directed at me.

Then I sniffed the air, peeked just a slit. Tom had placed an unmistakable gold box of Godiva on the table near the bed. The man came bearing gifts. This was a good sign. A chair squeaked, pulled close. Tom's rough hand caressed my arm. His voice caught in his throat, all mushy and tender as he said, "*Eres mi heroína, Jane*," and crooned, "*Esta bien, esta bien.*"

What? I was Tom's hero? I twisted my pulsating noggin, allowing his crooning words that it would be okay to sink in. I also positioned my lips so we could smooch and we did. He was still hot; I'm still a woman.

Tom was right. Everything would be okay, that is until my do-gooding soul flipped into hyper mode and became a buttinski. Again. Hey, like they say in Vegas, "You can bet on that."

Acknowledgments

Always and always again with happily forever after, my first reader and my favorite fan, I must acknowledge and thank my life partner, my husband Joseph. He always tells me the truth, and that's hard to do when dealing with the sensitive feelings of a writer. I couldn't—wait—wouldn't be the writer I am without his love, opinions, common sense, and belief in me.

Thank you to Jennifer Lawler, my editor at Crimson Romance Books, who read the manuscript and wanted it. In April 2012, Jennifer emailed me saying, "The book is a delightful romp." Music to my ears. Now, months later, she continues to wow me with her encouragement and advice, plus the way she makes me think I'm the only novelist she's working with. Now, *that's* a gift.

Thank you to the devoted, intelligent, and capable staff at Crimson Romance, from my copy editor to the talented designers who created a cover that really speaks to the reader and to me. Thank you to the publicity staff and especially to the booksellers.

Thank you, too, to my Crimson Romance "sisters" who are inspirations. Your friendships have been a delightful perk since joining the CR "family."

To my online students—more than 50,000 of you "out there" now—thank you. Helping you to become the best writers possible, being your mentor, and nudging you all the way toward publication, you have helped me become a better writer and person in the process.

Thank you to my early readers: Paulette Stewart, Ellen Hobart, and Dr. C.J. Johnson. Your encouragement meant the world to me, especially in the early stages, when I told you I was writing a mystery/romance/comedy about black market adoption.

On a personal note, this book is dedicated to my mother-in-law, Stella Angieski Shaw. I am certain she's now in heaven serving up cakes, coffee, and laughter-filled conversation just like the buscias—the Polish grandmothers you have met in this book.

A Note From the Author

This book came about after reading an article in the *San Diego Union Tribune* about black market adoption schemes where profit-hungry companies sold "return" policies to adoptive parents. These unscrupulous companies were "selling" toddlers to prospective parents without disclosing their hidden and heartbreaking mental challenges to cash in on the exorbitant return option. I couldn't get it out of my head or my heart.

Then I learned about the squalor found in many eastern European orphanages and women kept as sex slaves to produce "made-to-order" babies sold to Americans. Sure I could have written an article about the crimes, but I wanted to show the faces and hearts involved. A novel with plenty of mystery and a quirky protagonist that could make you smile became the vehicle of choice.

I started writing as soon as I could hold a pencil. At eight, I wrote *The Teddy Bear Trilogy*. For a long time, especially when I was a shy, bookworm teenager, I only "wrote" novels in my mind, but boy what elaborate scenes. Because of an undiagnosed hearing loss and two strong-willed sisters as a middle child, I found comfort in reading. It was about this time, too, that I started talking with my characters and asking them what they wanted to tell in a story. Sounds a tad psychotic, but most writers do this and I continue to do it with each novel.

I think of you, the reader, with each word I write. I work to spin characters that you love or love to hate. For the main characters, I strive to build heroines and heroes that make you want to know them better and make you miss them as the last page is finished.

As a writer, I need the story to carry you along. I don't want to interrupt you from thinking, "Now what in the world did the writer have in mind?" I believe good fiction writers should be nonexistent. You don't want to know me. I'm boring. You want to know the people in my books. You want to be involved in what's making them laugh, angry, fall in love, or do something you've always wanted to attempt. That's what I want for you, too.

I keep on top of trends and try to foretell what readers will want in the next year or three or four years. From the time I get an idea to the time a book is published can be 3 months to 18 months, depending on the nature of the contract with the publisher. I struggle not to "date" the book with current events, a freakish blizzard or some movie star's latest rehab exploit, so that 18 months from now it'll seem fresh.

My online writing students, although they don't know it, have been most helpful to keep my writing clear and help me stay on top of trends. I teach six different online writing courses available at 2000 colleges and universities worldwide. How do these faceless and nameless (because of privacy, I know nothing about my students) writers help? They force me to write clearly and with the tightest writing possible. When they don't understand something about writing, whether it's fiction or an essay, they ask. I supply the answers. They want facts, not fluff. Teaching has taught me to write more succinctly and with purpose. I'm a better writer because of being a writing professor.

I love to write. Don't tell publishers, but I'd write for free if that were the only way. So sitting down at my computer in my cluttered and comfortable home office to write isn't a problem. Stopping is the problem, because I always have to stop before I'm ready.

I have an incredible, full life. I'm blessed with a wonderful husband Joseph who still makes my heart pitter patter after decades of being my partner in life, a playful Welsh terrier Miss Rosy, an incredible garden that's always begging for my attention, paintings to start and to finish, books to read, friends to hang out with and volunteer with activities in my community, church country. I'm a board member Days for Girls, an international organization that works to increase personal dignity and sanitary products to girls and women throughout developing nations. I run out of hours long before I run out of determination or creativity for each day.

As a seven-days-a-week writer (with Sunday morning off for church), I have a flexible schedule. Each morning, Joseph and I talk and solve world problems as we take Rosy for her six-mile daily walk. She doesn't know she's 13 and I'm not going to tell her. After lupper (a combo of lunch and supper that we eat, since we both work from home) we always have a cup of tea or coffee while we sit in the garden. As a breast cancer survivor, I've learned to be good to myself and cherish the small things, like spending time with those I love.

My best advice for any writer, of any age, is: Read in your genre. Study it like your life depends on it. Learn from those who write well. For instance if one is struggling writing dialogue, study the work of Debbie Macomber. If one is struggling with storytelling, check out the work of John Grisham or J. K. Rowling. Don't put off writing, if it's calling to your heart. There is never, ever a good time start except right now. Take a class, find a mentor, and ask for help from someone you admire.

I apply the Golden Rule to writing and to relationships. When I've helped someone to learn, to understand, to relax, or to better cope with something, I'm humbled. I'm happiest when I've given someone the keys to a door they've wanted to open and they've not only opened it, but rushed through and succeeded. I get this feeling in my online courses when writers start to love writing and get published. My greatest disappointment is that there are only 24 hours in the day, and I have to sleep about nine of them. I want more, I want more time to write, more time to read, more time to teach and share. I work to squeeze more time into every task and hence I've become a cracker-jack time manager.

I love meeting my readers and those who've read my books or taken my online classes. When a reader or one of the writers I've mentored in the online classes (more than 50,000 when I figured it recently) comes up to me at an event, I cannot contain myself. The connection is intimate and it's wonderful.

A few years ago, I was at the launch of *What to Do When a Loved One Dies: A practical and compassionate guide to dealing with death on life's terms.* This was at a national convention for death care providers and vendors who provide services for the industry. A woman stopped me and told me I'd saved her life. She explained, "On my only son's twenty-first birthday, he and colleges buddies went drinking. He swallowed twenty-one shots and died on the spot. I nearly died, too. All the well-meaning drivel that friends and family handed out just made it worse. Then someone gave me a copy of *What to Do*, and truly you saved my life with the solid information, the facts of what I was feeling in this horrific experience. I was this close," she squeezed her index finger to her thumb, "to taking my own life, until I read about physical and emotional grief." We cried together for a while, hugged, and I never saw her again.

I have been blessed with similar experiences with fiction and nonfiction time and again. When does one know a book is a success? If there is one smile, one "aha," and, like the woman at the convention, one life changed or one time to forget the troubles of the world because a novel is plain fun to read, that book is a bestseller to me.

I'm looking forward to meeting you, my reader, so please visit my site and meet me at that next workshop or conference.

Eva Shaw
Carlsbad, California
www.evashaw.com

In the mood for more Crimson Romance? Check out *One Hit Wonder* by Denyse Cohen at *CrimsonRomance.com*.

www.ingramcontent.com/pod-product-compliance
Lightning Source LLC
Chambersburg PA
CBHW010633100726
47900CB00011B/2817